THE Maiden

JEHANNE D'ARC · BOOK I

ALEXIA SAINT CLAIRE

First published in Australia by Aurora House
www.aurorahouse.com.au

This edition published 2024
Copyright © Alexia Saint Claire 2024

Cover design: Donika Mishineva (www.artofdonika.com)
Typesetting and e-book design: Amit Dey (amitdey2528@gmail.com)

ISBN number: 978-1-922913-97-5 (Paperback)

A catalogue record for this book is available from the National Library of Australia

Distributed by: Ingram Content: www.ingramcontent.com
Australia: phone +613 9765 4800 |
email lsiaustralia@ingramcontent.com
Milton Keynes UK: phone +44 (0)845 121 4567 |
email enquiries@ingramcontent.com
La Vergne, TN USA: phone +1 800 509 4156 |
email inquiry@lightningsource.com

DEDICATION

We dedicate this book to Sathya Sai Baba
for his guidance, direction and love.

ACKNOWLEDGMENTS

*F*irstly, I would like to dedicate this novel to my family. They, whose words often lifted me out of low moments and pushed me to achieve my dream of becoming an author. Without their support and encouragement, this novel would have remained a fanciful dream. Also, their courage to read the raw version of this novel was no easy task.

To my husband, for his understanding and unwavering support.

To my publisher, Linda, for giving me a chance to make this book a reality and for her patience with a new writer.

To my editor, Meredith, who edited the manuscript to a publishing level.

To my proofreader, Jieun, who worked with a meticulous and thorough eye to correct all spelling and names of all my beloved characters.

And last of all, thank you, Jehanne.

For your bravery. For your story.

CONTENTS

A BRIEF HISTORY OF FRANCE IN THE EARLY 15ᵀᴴ CENTURY

One of the longest wars in history is known as the Hundred Year War.

Since the early 14ᵗʰ century, France and England had been engulfed in war. It was one of the most significant conflicts of the Middle Ages, interrupted by several truces but continuing shortly after that through five generations of English kings who wanted to expand their rule to encompass the French kingdom.

In 1415, King Henry V of England launched the battle of Agincourt in France, which saw the French army routed. Seven thousand French soldiers were killed by five hundred English soldiers; one thousand five hundred French were taken prisoner.

In 1418, the English occupied Paris with the help of the Duke of Burgundy, who was known as John the Fearless, a Burgundian lord who allied with the English and battled a civil war against the French crown.

The current King of France, Charles VI, was mad. Illness made him ill-equipped to rule, so he handed the kingdom to various family members to regain power. Still, the rulers needed to show the capability to overthrow the English. France's rulers showed the worst possible selfishness, plunging France into a downward spiral. To worsen matters for the French crown, the three oldest sons of King Charles VI and Queen Isabella of Bavaria—the dauphins Charles (1), Louis, and Jean—died in succession between 1401 and 1417. The only remaining dauphin was their eleventh child, Charles (2), who was fourteen then.

In May 1420, the Treaty of Troyes was signed, officially declaring King Henry V of England as regent and next in line to the French throne. In this treaty, the King of England was to marry the daughter of King Charles VI of France, Catherine of Valois, and renounce Charles, the King of France's last legitimate heir's claim to the French throne.

In August 1422, King Henry V of England suddenly died at the pinnacle of his youth and victories. A few weeks later, in October, King Charles VI of France died at fifty-three. His remaining son Charles, determined to claim his right to the throne and remove the English from the French Kingdom, established his court with his last loyal supporters in Bourges and Poitiers, the south of France, the regions still controlled by the French aristocracy.

France was in peril. Struggling to reconcile with the Burgundians and continuously attacked by English forces occupying the northern region, it was a period of great desperation. Ravaged by wars and devastated by epidemics, France needed a miracle.

1

THE LADY

'A marvellous maid would come from the Bois Chesnu, the ancient wood, to save France.'

– Merlin, C. 540

Autumn, 1422
Domrémy, France

*T*he first time I saw the Lady was in the oak forest.

It was a thick, healthy forest full of long, dark trunks—like columns stretching high above, with extended branches that formed a dense, green canopy. The oak forest sat on a hill at the back of our stone and mud cottage. It wasn't eerie nor foreboding but a stage for my creative tales. I would skip over their intertwined network of roots, thinking they were holding hands like a mother and child because they looked so close, so connected, like a big extended green family where I was always welcome. It was my hidden place of joy and tranquillity.

The superstitious people of the village would say it's been there for centuries, haunted by gnomes and fairies. My mother would say the forest was there before the Great Duke landed in England—she would always use the Duke's landing as a reference of time. My mother wasn't superstitious like the other villagers and didn't mind me playing in the woods. To me, it was my escape and suited me perfectly, for nobody ventured through it.

Except me.

It was autumn, and the oak forest looked as if it were painted with thousands of tiny dots of orange, red, and brown that moved together like the scales of a swimming fish. I was ten, freckly, and very dirty after finishing my chores. I wrinkled my nose as the smell of the old hay lingered on my dark grey dress and shabby beige apron, which was patched with old, stubborn stains. Chickens pecked at the ground, and the damp earth squelched under my shoes. I could smell fresh hay, urine, and wet grass.

The freshly collected eggs lay in a rattan basket, and I sprinkled cereal flakes across spurts of grass that peeked through the damp earth here and there. The chickens swayed around me, lifting their stick-like legs high and moving in their alert fashion.

Finally finished! I thought to myself, satisfied. Brushing my hands on my tattered apron, I looked at the sky. The sun was past its zenith. *It must be early afternoon.*

Wind washed over the trees, and they bent and swayed like waves. I closed the gates of the chicken pens excitedly and unsecured my cap from under my chin. My fingers were stiff from cleaning the chicken's pens, washing the kitchen cloths, and carrying tools for my brothers to the fields all morning.

I could meet Isabel and the other girls from the village. They might want to play in the oak tree in the village, I mused to myself, the straps dangling below my ears. I stepped out, but a sharp wind whipped my cap off my head. I turned quickly and saw it dancing away in the wind. My face broke into a broad smile, and I ran after it.

My cap flipped, skipped over the chicken pens, and flew a little more until it finally descended with a thump on the foot of the orchard. The orchard stretched over the rising hill, kissing the edge of the forest. I ran, my two red braids swishing like a horse's tail as I breathlessly dived for the cap, catching it like a cat's prey.

I stood victorious, yet the wind swooped past me. Leaves hurtled and rolled through the orchard, and my eyes travelled to the distant line of orange and brown oak trees. As if dancing to a song, the branches moved in unison; the leaves were like a thousand shimmering stars, and I imagined the forest calling to me from its deepest entrails.

As I admired their dance, a melody began to play in my mind. Like a flower blossoming, the memory grew inch by inch in magnanimity. When I was little, we celebrated the village's summer harvest festival. It was one of my earliest memories, and I distinctly remembered the smell of smoked wood and grape juice on a fresh summer night. Music was played by a travelling troupe that usually visited in the summer months. I watched from my mama's lap as young and older couples danced, little boys ran around playing games, and little girls held hands and traipsed around the colossal oak tree in the village's centre.

I remember hearing this beautiful song and humming it for days. It was a song I so much liked. Reminiscing, I let my imagination run its course. *Princesses dancing in a crystal hall… fairies enchanting the music and flying, glowing like candles… knights riding beautiful black steeds…* My excitement grew; my chest felt like it would burst from excitement. My stories were alight with creativity, and the forest was to be my stage.

I ran home.

Home was a dark grey cottage with a sharp slanted roof, gardens surrounding the front, back, and sides. It was quiet, the only sound was the wind pounding on the stone walls. The front door was always closed, but mama always left the side door open. Beside the side door stood a few wooden barrels filled with fresh rainwater, and I hurriedly washed my hands and face in one of them. My skin shivered from the cool droplets going down to my neck and arms. Drying my hands on the underside of my apron, I went inside.

We called this the 'backroom'.

It was a cramped room with a steep staircase leading to mama and papa's room upstairs. Underneath the stairs was my mama's small spinning wheel with a basket of sheep fur. To the left was a chimney and two comfortable chairs under a small square window, with a rough rug between them. On the walls were stacks of extra chairs and large sacks of legumes, grains, and wool collected from the farm. It always smelt of oats, wool, and dust.

A large empty door frame led to the house's hearth. Tepidly, I walked through. The kitchen was a long room, and in its centre was the large hearth. As always, it had an inviting fire.

It was always darker here, but the heavy air smelt strongly of herbs and grains. Next to the hearth, a thick oak table sat with simple wooden bowls of varying sizes. In the far corner of the room was a wooden bucket containing soapy water, and beside it, a number of shelves filled with clay pots. A narrow, long wooden table sat where mama was hovering and working tirelessly.

Mama was short and plump, only a little taller than me. She always wore a grey scarf that held back her strawberry-blond hair, which hung down her shoulder in a braid. Her hands nimbly rolled the dough, roughly the size of a pumpkin, next to a bed of flour. She reached up and unhooked a bunch of dried herbs that hung above her, which is why she always carried the faint smell of lavender. That's when she caught sight of me.

My voice sounded like a choir of crickets in the busy silence of her kitchen. "Mama, I finished all my chores. Can I go play?" I reached the table, and mama peered at me, her slightly slanted eyes as bright and sweet as bluebells.

"Have you finished everything, Jehannette?" She liked calling me Jehannette. It was my pet name when I was young. "The chicken's hay needs to be changed."

She reached under the table and brought out a small wooden bowl filled with dried fruit; she sprinkled some of it over the dough. Her apron was dusted with flour, and her fingers were thick, yet her practised hands left the dough fluffy and smooth.

"Yes, I fed them too." I rocked on my heels, my fingers grasping the table, excited to go and play.

"Well, yes, of course you can go. Where are you going?" mama asked, returning her attention to the dough.

"I want to go to the forest," I replied, quickly turning to the door.

"Ah, Jehannette." Mama's voice broke my stride. Before you go, change the kitchen water. Oh, and don't forget to come home before dusk, dear."

I always obeyed mama. She taught me the discipline of obedience alongside the sweetness of a caring mother's love. She never raised her voice nor struck me like I'd seen other stern mothers do in the village.

I backtracked and dutifully walked to the soapy water, which now looked grey with flecks of floating food—scraps from breakfast. I carefully carried the water to the door, through the backroom, and spilled it over on the grass outside. I returned with a bucket of fresh water from a cleaner barrel.

"Good girl, now you can play," mama said, her snowy complexion becoming rosy pink as she smiled. I beamed broadly as a tendril of dark auburn hair came loose from my cap. "And don't come home so late, hm?" Mama said, pinning up my chin affectionately. I nodded eagerly.

The orchard and fields went grey as the sun hid behind a body of dense and puffy clouds. The wind pushed and twirled at my clothes and the rest of the world, but I didn't care. I ran as fast as I could, passing the long grass of the orchard and to the first line of trees of the forest.

Suddenly, the wind that battered my ears and hair was gone. I smelled wet moss and fresh dirt as I entered the cool shade of the woods. I was surrounded by a rainbow of orange, green, and brown leaves that clung to the trees. The trees' trunks sturdily emerged from the ground, and here, it was difficult to separate where the earth and the trees began. It all looked woven together.

I peered upwards, and the canopy was so thick that only a few rays of light beamed downwards. Breathing the forest's fresh musk, I marvelled at the simple beauty of the trees and the distant songs of birds. I skipped down the familiar narrow pathway to my favourite place, my feet briefly touching the compacted dark, moist leaves, avoiding the protruding and entwining roots. *Not long now to my secret hideaway, to the clearing.*

This little clearing sat in the middle of the forest and looked like it was made by a practised axehand. Only a smooth stump roughly the size of a wheel sat forlornly in its centre. A thick, bare trunk lay across the clearing on its edge. I slowed down, nearing my favourite hideaway spot.

Almost there...

I brushed against a branch, manoeuvring my way down the narrow path by memory. *Finally!* I could see the familiar shapes of the trees surrounding the clearing and the vast open space up ahead. *The fairies can have leaves for their wings... and I can make them a little stick house... I can even go to the stream and fetch some green moss...*

All of a sudden, a strange stillness descended on the forest.

I looked around, perplexed.

The birds had stopped their singing.

I slowed down and looked up.

The wind no longer whispered high in the canopies.

Strange.

The moment I entered the clearing, I froze.

I was not alone.

Erasing my imaginative stories in one stroke was a figure sitting on the trunk.

I retreated. A twig cracked.

The Lady was in pure white. She was young. *Maybe she is a princess.* Her gown shone brilliantly in the wooden and leafy backdrop of the forest. Her long, brown hair tumbled down her shoulders, and her hands nestled neatly in her lap.

It must be a princess! Her carriage must have broken, and she's lost. I peered at her carefully. Her dress looked very fine indeed—the finest clothes I had ever seen. It had a v-shaped neckline, and the sleeves were embroidered with gold trimmings.

The Lady gazed at me. Her features were elegant and pretty. She was sloe-eyed, with a long, elegantly shaped nose that rose at the tip, and wistful, sweet lips that lifted into a smile.

The pearlescent dress glimmered in the sun's rays as they filtered through the tree branches. The Lady gently gestured for me to approach.

But I stayed where I was.

"Hello," she said, the empty silence of the forest swallowing her melodic voice.

"Erm… hello," I responded slowly.

"Hello, Jehanne."

My eyes widened. I felt as if rocks had dropped in my stomach.

I stared at her and unconsciously cradled my hands on my chest.

"Come, Jehanne. Come closer, my dear," the Lady said.

I felt my tense legs shuffling cautiously closer to her. I could see her better now. Her face was serene, and her smile warmed her eyes. But I swallowed hard.

"Madam… How… how do you know my name?" My high voice was ridden with astonishment.

The Lady smiled more broadly now, showing all her teeth. White and straight. "God told me your name. God knows all names."

My mind began to wander. *God sitting on a throne…*

"Jehanne," the Lady interrupted my thoughts.

"Yes, Madam," I answered promptly.

"I bring a message from the King of Heaven," she said as if sharing a secret.

Looking at her closely, I could see her smooth brown hair framing her fair and clean complexion.

"From the… King of Heaven?" I repeated, astonished.

"Yes," said the Lady. "Jehanne, you are going to do something very important. You are going to help God. God will send you three guides you will have for the entire time you are here on earth."

I stared at the Lady. *She was surely not mad, but…*

I looked at my clothes and around me; the forest was still—not an insect moved. "Madam... Are you sure... me?" I choked out. "But-but... I'm just a peasant girl," I said, puzzled.

The Lady's tranquillity was not deterred. "It does not matter to God, dear Jehanne. Peasants or kings, all fulfill his wishes equally. There is no difference. They are all his children, and all of creation is his."

The Lady's eyes became serious but not unkind. "Listen carefully, Jehanne, you must pray to God every night."

My eyebrows rose high over my forehead. "Pray?" I blurted out. "But God is far away, up in some clouds. I don't think he will listen to me."

The Lady laughed lightly. "Jehanne, God is not far away. God is in the heart of every being. God is in your heart and in the heart of your mother and everyone you know. God is very close, closer than your most loved family or friend, and I'll tell you a secret." Her voice became soft, and her eyes shone with sincerity. "God is always listening."

Unconsciously, my hands slowly lay down at my sides.

"Praying is our communication with God." She paused and looked at me earnestly. "Jehanne, do you promise to pray?"

While her question hung in the still air, I thought of all the prayers that mama conferred to God daily; it was enough for the whole family! Prayer was of no importance to me. The silence between us grew.

The Lady repeated her request, "Do you promise to pray? This is very important. It is the basis, the beginning of your spiritual discipline."

"Yes," I answered finally. "I promise."

Nodding, she continued. "In two more years, you will receive visits from angels who will begin to prepare you. They will help you in your mission."

I don't understand... A mission? What mission? And who is she? I blinked several times and fidgeted, my forehead scrunched into a tight knot. *Is she an angel?*

Then I looked down at her white slippers. She moved her foot slightly and wiggled her toes in the slipper, creating a wave underneath the shoe. I looked up at her hands on her lap. I could see her fingers resting and the veins on her knuckles. I shuffled closer, and she smelt of the sweet flowers from mama's garden.

Maybe she was a nun? She brought me a message from God… But she's not dressed as a nun. No, she must be an angel. But her shape was not ethereal, and she had no wings. She looked utterly human.

I couldn't contain myself. "Madam, are you a princess?"

"No, I am not a princess," she said good-naturedly.

"Are you an angel?" I asked with wide eyes.

"I am a messenger of God, just a messenger," she repeated.

"But where do you come from, Madam?"

"Beyond the sky and the stars, from the Kingdom of Light." She tilted her gaze to the sky, looking meaningfully upwards and down at me again. I looked up to the canopies and down to her again.

She gently took hold of one of my hands and leaned forward. "Jehanne, Jehannette. I know this may seem strange, but you will understand. Don't be overwhelmed. You will be protected. You will be strong."

A bewildered giggle escaped my lips. *Protected? Strong? What is she talking about?*

"Yes, Jehanne, you will be successful," the Lady replied, cradling my own warm hands.

I still don't understand. Grownups say strange things sometimes.

I tilted my head and asked, genuinely curious, "What do I have to do, Madam?"

She smiled knowingly.

"Jehanne, you will be a messenger of God. In a few years, you will help God on a very important mission. You will be an instrument of God to show men correct conduct and an example to follow."

I was hypnotised by her words—not because I understood their meaning, but because the woman's words were coated with a peace I had never felt before. I felt like my mind was swimming in a lake of tranquillity.

She looks real, just how I see mama…

"Jehanne, pray every night to God. Close your eyes and pray. He listens in your heart. You must form this habit. It will be your shield and refuge in the future. Are you going to do it, Jehanne?"

"Yes," I said resolutely. "Every night before going to sleep, I will pray to God in my heart." I put my hands on my chest.

The Lady smiled and added, "Be obedient to your parents and help people in need."

"Yes, I will obey my parents and help," but I was unsure how. "But how can I help?" I asked.

"You can go with your mother. Watch, and you will learn."

"Yes, Madam," I answered.

"Good, the King of Heaven wishes so," she told me.

This is no ordinary lady. She says she comes from the Kingdom of Light.

She gently let go of my hands and looked towards the narrow pathway where I stood only minutes ago. *I don't want to leave, not yet.* Something about her felt so familiar, like a forgotten memory. She was as affectionate and patient as an aunt or mother; a deep sense of familiarity had developed in this short time. Our conversation was the most normal interaction.

She turned her gaze back to me. "Your brother is looking for you."

I turned my head, looking at the narrow path that wound into the woods. "I don't hear anything," I said.

"And your father will be home soon. Your brother is on his way."

I nodded and carefully bowed to her. She dipped her head, smiling with all her heart as I turned to leave.

But I whirled around, my curiosity still needing to be fully satiated. "Are you an angel?"

"A messenger, just that, a messenger of God. Goodbye, dear Jehanne," she said with unwavering patience.

"Goodbye, madam," I answered, bowing again, and turned. I felt the leaves crush underneath as I walked to the pathway. I heard the branches creak in the canopies as the wind surged. When I reached the forest's edge, I looked behind my shoulder and gasped.

The Lady was gone. Astonished, I gaped and looked around, alarmed. My eyes searched the forest for any trace of her, any glimpse. But the forest sat still and innocent, undisturbed from its deep slumber. The wind broke through the canopies and swooped the leaves over the forest floor.

I watched, momentarily mesmerised, but the forest's silence confirmed that the Lady was gone.

Father is coming. Suddenly alert, I reluctantly backtracked, pulled myself away from the clearing, and ran down the dirt pathway.

The wind flew past me, and a crescendo of sounds thrummed in my ears. The birds commenced their calls, and tiny insects hummed and became alive again. The wind flew above me as I ran through the forest, tumbling through the dense, leafy branches. Life pulsated in the woods again.

The forest resumed providing refuge to all creatures, great and small. If it could speak, it would divulge fascinating tales. Still, this one would be most memorable—for it would say a young farmer girl, with a grey cap tied under her chin, dark brown eyes, and hair like autumn leaves braided into two plaits, was foretold her journey by a Lady in White. This was only the beginning of her mission—and what an exceptional one it would be.

2

PAPA

'He was not a perfect man, that I freely admit, but for all his faults, he loved each of his sons fiercely... If he bears any faults... it is through inaction. I remember few occasions when we exchanged words and few still when he sought to speak with me—save one.'

– Kaikeyi by Vaishnavi Patel

Autumn, 1422
Domrémy, France

I sprinted through the woods.

Emerging from the shelter of the forest, I saw the dusk sky opening like a magnificent map before me, dewy with pinks and midnight blues that crept over the horizon. My legs ran over the long, thick grass; the air in the orchard was chilly now. Insects swarmed in the empty pink ether above the trees, the chirping of crickets blared across the orchard, and the lights of the nearby cottage—grey with a slanted roof—were beginning to glow faintly in the growing darkness of night.

Almost there, I thought as I ran home faster. Excitement brewed in my chest. *Mama will never believe me. I wonder what she will say when I tell her*

I met a princess today. I ran down the hill, reaching almost halfway when a shape emerged from the cottage.

In the dim lighting of dusk, the figure was lean and tall, with a head of wavy curls. I recognised my brother, Pierre, immediately. He ran to the garden's edge and shouted, his hands cupped around his mouth, "Jehanne, Mama is looking for you, hurry!"

I yelled back between breaths, "I'm coming!"

Pierre turned and ran past the house towards the village.

I reached the cottage; the side door was still open. Red-cheeked and out of breath, I felt the reverberations through my body as my footsteps lashed the stone floor. Mama was hastily arranging deepset bowls onto the table, wooden spoons to the side. The table was laid with freshly made bread and thick slabs of butter. Cheese cut into small cubes were accompanied by dried salted meats.

My stomach growled, but I ignored it. There were more important matters.

I started, "Mama, you'll never guess what—"

"Jehanne, dear," she interrupted, turning to me, the remaining bowls resting on her hips as she laid them on the table in front of each of our seats with her other hand. Her face was flustered. "Be good and see to the animals. The cows seem hungry, so make sure they have water and hay and bring me more eggs."

She quickly laid down the last two bowls and tended to the soup brewing over the fire. Looking at me with quick glances, not to distract her attention from the hot pan, she said briskly, "Hurry, your father is coming home soon."

She took out the large wooden spoon to turn the stew, blew on it, and took a quick sip. Her bright blue eyes were alert, a wavy reddish hair tendril stringing past her forehead. She nodded, satisfied.

I felt like I had been drenched with a bucket of cold water and plunged back into the reality of the world. But I didn't want to let Mama down. If things were not done on time, Papa's anger would be a storm. The Lady of the Forest said *I must obey my parents*, I thought to myself.

"Yes, Mama," I answered.

I took the ratan basket from the backroom and hurried out of the cottage to the paddock to see the cows and check on the chickens. When I finished tending the animals, only a tiny halo of sunlight could be seen over the landscape. I walked back slowly, carrying the few extra eggs in the basket, careful not to move them.

The side door was closed. My stomach clenched. *Papa must be home.*

I carefully nudged the side door open, entered the backroom, and closed it behind me quietly.

Through the walls, I could hear the faint rumbling of papa's voice. The air was warm, and only the clanking of wooden spoons and soft chewing could be heard. The scent of vegetable stew filled the air, and my stomach clawed itself with hunger.

Five figures sat hunched over the long wooden table, papa at the crown of the table, his back towards me as I entered. He was a tall man who loomed high above the table with broad shoulders and straight, shoulder-length hair tied low at the back of his neck.

My brothers, Pierre and Jean (whom Papa only conversed with), sat closest to him on the long sides of the table, listening intently to his instructions. Mama and I sat at the end, and Mama was always praying as she ate. She murmured her prayers and never lifted her eyes save to check on her children.

Like a ghost, I glided past them and rested the eggs gently on the counter.

The fire crackled as papa spoke. "Next season will be wet and cold. We will take the harvest and store as much as possible in the barn and the backroom. We will start tomorrow. Pierre, you take the east side of the orchard and fields. Jean, you take the west. I will take the north."

Pierre and Jean both nodded as they chewed, but I could see Pierre's playful eyes spotting me as I sat silently next to Jean. His eyes were mischievous; I bit down a smile of my own.

Papa continued, and Pierre's soberness returned in a flick. I set my eyes on the table. Our table was humble, yet we had everything we needed.

My bowl was filled with a soup of lentils and vegetables, with some bits of chicken. The loaf in the middle of the table had huge chunks missing. I reached over and wrenched a fistful. I dipped it in my soup, and it softened and soaked all the flavourful broth. I hungrily spooned it into my mouth. Bite after bite, the bread crumbled in my hand.

Everyone's faces were lit with an orange hue from the candles on the table and the hearth that shimmered gaily. Papa continued, "We will take the animals into the fields during the day when it is not too cold, but we must bring them back at night. I've spoken to our neighbour, Claude, to exchange more hay to keep the barn warmer during the winter months."

Papa had a voice that went well with his face. It was as though his features reflected his stern mind. He had a box-shaped head with a rigid brow and below were a pair of walnut-coloured eyes that were as sharp and stiff as the logs for the hearth. He was always clean-shaven, which showed his lined face around his eyes and forehead.

"Papa, when will Claude bring the new stacks of hay?" Jean asked from next to me, wincing as he massaged his shoulder. Jean was eighteen and took after mama. He had light reddish hair and sky-blue eyes. He was broader than Pierre, and his arms and chest were always bruised from sparring with the other boys from the village.

"He said he will have it ready the day after tomorrow. I will need you both tomorrow but especially you, Jean. I need you to go to Claude and give him two bags of barley in exchange for his hay. After we've collected the barley, we need to prepare the soil. These next few days, we will need to take out the old and ready the earth for the oncoming winter season." Papa swallowed a mouthful of clear broth.

Jean's gaze was fixed on the middle of the table, and he had a faraway look as if he were thinking very hard, but he simply nodded. "Yes, Papa," he said, obediently.

Mama, who had stopped murmuring her prayers, rested her eyes on her firstborn. Concern passed over her face, but papa continued as if he noticed nothing.

Because, well, he didn't.

Jean resumed his meal, papa's rumbling again filled the room, and Mama's subservient face turned to her soup.

"And Pierre, I need you to go to Lord Remy and ask whether he needs extra help. I want you to work in his manor to help him. You'll make good connections there," Papa ordered.

Pierre looked more like Papa, save for his head of curls. He was only sixteen, but Mama would always say that the woman who married Pierre would be blessed with a good man. And it was true, for he was of jovial and happy character. He had a playful smile and small and straight teeth. He had a long nose and brandy-brown, almond eyes.

"Yes, Papa," Pierre said. His intelligent eyes shone with duty.

"I think Lord Robert will be wanting wood and barley. We will go to the woods and prepare some logs. Cut them but not too short in case he needs to trade them to other lords who are running the war."

At that moment, my mind flipped like a coin. *The Lady in the Woods!* I gasped in excitement, but papa continued. "They will surely need all they can get. The war has moved up east—"

"—Mama, Papa!" my voice cried, interrupting Papa, shattering the still and sombre atmosphere. "Today in the forest, I saw a—"

I quickly fell silent.

My father's affronted eyes travelled to my small frame at the far end of the table. His eyes were like shards of glass, his lips thinned into a line.

I heard Mama gulp, and her hand quickly reached across the table to mine. She shook her head urgently; her eyes were wide with shock and maybe a bit of fear.

Not another word! Her eyes read.

My eyes flickered to my brothers. Jean and Pierre both stared at me in the excruciating silence. They gaped at me, disbelief and fear rendering them perfectly still. Jean had a 'you're in trouble' look, but from across the table, I thought I caught a glimmer of amusement passing over Pierre at his little sister's boldness.

I took a fleetingly quick peek at papa. His jaw was tight, and he grew bigger, like a frightening mountain. Mama's face was now showing fear. I looked at my plate. "Sorry," I mumbled.

The silence continued for a few moments more. I felt my face grow hot.

After what seemed like an eternity, papa's eyes lifted from me. His tense frame even diminished slowly.

"The war will leave many of the lords wanting. Their resources are running low." Slowly, the sound of soft wooden spoons scraped the bottom of the bowls, and Mama resumed her soft murmuring, which was overlaid by Papa's lecture for Jean and Pierre. "Our supply of seeds is stocked, but we will need to resupply after winter is over."

I felt crumpled like an injured flower.

The Lady's visit was just beautiful, I thought glumly. My eyes were glued to my bowl. My heart slowly sank into an ocean of sadness. *It was such a genuine encounter, something so incredible! The Lady… she wasn't just anyone. She had this peace I had never felt before. The forest and her were one. She was as serene and beautiful as the serenity of the woods. And they'll never know.*

They'll never know that a messenger of God visited me in the woods.

I slowly lifted a spoonful of stew. Mama's and even Pierre's eyes flickered at me as I automatically began eating, barely tasting the stew. Hunger had disappeared into a little corner of my mind.

Mama and I were silent as we finished our meal. Papa and, occasionally, my brothers spoke at the table. After supper, I helped Mama clear the table and clean the bowls and pots, and then I went to bed.

For it always was like this. It was as normal and routine as the sun rises and sets.

That night, in my room, I lay in my creaky bed. My room was small and simple. It was next to the kitchen, as was Pierre and Jean's room. I changed into a warm sleeping tunic and covered myself in thick cotton blankets. Beside me, a candle glowed on a small stand, and I watched the shadows flicker on the walls. An old crucifix hung on the wall opposite me.

Maybe I fell asleep in the woods and dreamt of the Lady, I thought soberly. I turned over and gazed at the flame of the candle. *I suppose I don't need to tell anyone about her. She might just be a figment of my imagination.*

But I knew she was real. She was as real as Mama or Pierre. At that moment, the candle flickered.

"Jehanne."

In the doorway, mama's small frame stood. She had removed her cap, and her long hair hung freely behind her. She held a small candle in her hand that lit her face with an angelic glow. She also wore her thick beige tunic for sleeping. I sat up, smiling. She swiftly sat down and embraced me, smelling distinctly of lavender and clean cotton.

"My little darling," she purred as she peered down at me, stroking my hair and looking at me tenderly. "You were courageous today." She gazed at me more carefully. I nodded but stayed silent. We were not allowed to speak at the table. It was always this way.

"I have something for you." She reached to the collar of her tunic and took out a necklace. "This is a rosary. You see, it has many beads. Remember how I taught you the Hail Mary?"

I nodded, looking at the necklace in her hands. Most of the beads were brown, but at four points, they were yellow, with a wooden crucifix at the end. "Well, this is something for you to count your Hail Marys. I will teach you the other prayers when you're a little older." She handed it to me. Half the necklace dangled down from my small hands.

"Why do you count the prayers?" My tiny fingers carefully traced the smooth surface of the beads.

"Well, it keeps you disciplined. It keeps you concentrated in your prayers."

The lady… the messenger… I promised her I would pray every night.

I smiled and hung the rosary around my head. It was so big that the cross reached my lap. She chuckled and stroked my hair gently.

"Goodnight, my love." Mama kissed my forehead and blew out my candle. I heard her light footsteps climb the stairs and slowly recede until the house was silent. I snuggled deeper into the rough but comforting blankets; my heart felt lighter as I held the necklace in my hands. Mama was always a comforting balm that soothed and lifted my little spirit.

So, in the stillness of night, I began to pray. I hadn't told anyone about the Lady in the woods. I prayed for the first time. I prayed as I promised.

3

PIERRE AND JEAN

Autumn, 1422
Domrémy, France

"*J*ehannette! Jehanneeeeette!"
His voice travelled through the stillness of the woods.

I could only hear my breath as I ran through the dense woods until I saw him. Pierre was standing on our well-trodden path, hands on his hips, while he surveyed the disappearing path that delved deeper into the woods. Treading carefully, I weaved my way through, hiding behind the large girth of the trunks.

The Sunday morning was cool, but in the forest, mist came out from Pierre's breath. He turned his head, and in that moment of distraction I broke from my hiding spot and sprinted towards him. Hearing my on-rushing footsteps, he abruptly turned to me.

"Aaah!" Colliding into him, Pierre only swayed, his leg stepping back, and caught me in a hug, both of us laughing.

"Not quite yet, Jehanne. You need to do more than that to scare me." He bent down, with one hand on his knee, and the other ruffling my hair. "Time to go home, little miss."

"Alright," I said, shrugging.

Jumping onto his back, I hugged his neck, and he held my legs at his sides. "What games were you up to in the woods?" Pierre asked.

"Well, I was imagining one of my stories! There was once a Princess Catherine and Lady Belle. They were kidnapped by goblins, and they had to escape by using magic! A fairy was able to help them remember that they were once sorceresses, and with the fairy's help they were able to escape."

Pierre peeked behind to look at me, and said with an amused side smile, "How do you come up with these stories, Jehannette?"

I thought for a moment. "I think the forest helps me. Sometimes I sit quietly and I can see ladies, and I can see their magic. One of them can speak to animals, the other can read the future in the stars. Oh, and other times, I can imagine I'm in a castle, and the branches in the tree are like the beautiful, gilded walls, and the rooms have chandeliers, twinkling with diamonds!"

"You are a strange girl," Pierre said, laughing.

"Why?" I asked.

"Because you're not afraid of the tales. You know what people believe, right?"

I nodded, unfazed. "Oh yes."

"The forest," Pierre carefully emphasised these words, "is inhabited by demons or ghosts." Pierre playfully growled and bared his teeth like a bear. I giggled and shrunk lower behind the back of his head. "Children, especially little girls, usually do not venture into these places alone." He looked to the other side trying to catch a glimpse of me, but I dove into his opposite shoulder, evading his mischievous teasing.

Pierre then changed his playful tone to a genuinely curious question, "How are you not afraid to play alone?"

"If God is the creator of all this, why should I fear the woods?" I said, looking up at the sunlight reflecting on the leaves.

He chuckled and shook his head. "Where do you get these ideas from?"

I giggled.

"You really are a strange girl," he said, mystified, but I thought I heard a tint of admiration.

As the forest was becoming less dense, the trees gave way to open fields. The orchard stretched in front of us, reaching the old barn and the vegetable garden behind our house. The morning sun was shining brightly, but the wind was biting cold. Pierre put me down and said, his face breaking into a playful grin, "I'll race you home."

I looked down to the house and took off my cap, beaming. "Ok, let's go."

"To the house, ok... Ready... Set... Go!" And we bolted. But Pierre was older, and his legs were longer and faster. Laughing, I tried to get the back of his shirt, but I could never get close enough to pull him back. We bolted past the orchard trees and skidded to slow down as we approached the barn, startling the chickens in their pen.

We got home laughing, red faced and out of breath.

"Almost, Jehanne," Pierre said between breaths. "You almost got me." My chest was heaving, and Pierre patted my head. But I quickly tried to grab him. He jerked out of the way, grinning. I advanced, laughing, and Pierre began to run. My footsteps tailed after him.

I cornered Pierre against the wall of the barn, but Pierre, being quicker, swiftly swerved out and vanished into barn, exiting our game with his mischievous smile.

I heaved the door open only to stop short.

"Jean?" Pierre said.

Jean, my oldest brother sighed in relief. "Oh, it's you two. I thought it was Papa. Come in." His hair was dishevelled, the skin on his forehead shiny from sweat.

Pierre and I looked at each other as a sign of truce, and Pierre approached first. I closed the barn door. The barn was usually stacked high with hay and smelt distinctly of wool and soil. Jean was holding a wooden stick that looked smooth as it was repeatedly lashed against something.

"What are you doing, Jean?" Pierre asked, eyeing the wooden stick.

"What does it look like? I'm training. The boys in the village are practising their swordsmanship. They're quite good too. You could do with some practice, Pierre, come and practise with me."

Pierre was eyeing the stick and grimaced.

"Come on, you never know when you might need it. And Jehannette can keep score. Jehannette, every time I get Pierre with my sword, or he gets me, we get a point, understood?"

I nodded eagerly, sitting down on the mountain of haystacks, and watched them like a show was about to start.

"But Papa and Uncle Marcel already trained us when we were younger," Pierre said, his voice edged with a 'Why is this important?' tone.

Jean pointed his wooden sword at Pierre, the tip of it resting on Pierre's chest. Jean's face turned solemn, and his voice went quiet.

"Pierre, need I remind you a war is going on, that we're surrounded by the English and Burgundians? If we ever need to, we need to defend ourselves. The lords will only take care of themselves, and I don't want to be unprepared if I hear English troops are on their way."

Pierre looked at his older brother for a moment, then sighed. "Where is the other sword?"

Jean looked pleased. "Good man." He turned and swiftly flung the extra wooden sword to Pierre who caught it with one hand.

"You're always with Leonard and Bertrand at the Lord's property, is that where you're practising?"

"Yes. Papa doesn't know and I want to keep it that way. Pierre, listen, I've been thinking these last couple of months." His voice became strained. "I've realised I don't want to be a farmer. I want to get out of here. I want to make a living, but…" He grimaced, "I'm not sure how just yet…"

"Where will you go?" Pierre asked; despite the surprise, he positioned himself ready to spar.

"Well, Uncle Durand lives in a village smaller than this. But Uncle Marcel… he lives in Neufchâteau, a larger city. He probably knows more about different jobs posted in the city."

If Pierre was disappointed, he did not show it. He merely regarded his brother coolly.

"Alright, ready, Jehannette?" Jean fixated on his stance.

"Ready," I said, holding my hands out to count their points.

Pierre and Jean were both crouched and watching each other. Their feet nimbly stepped over each other as they circled.

"You're going to have to attack sometime, Pierre."

"I'm biding my time, Jean."

In a flash Jean stepped forward, lunging, but Pierre stepped out of his blow. Jean was not discouraged; he lunged again, and in a flurry of movements was pressing on Pierre, but Pierre was parrying and dodging his attacks.

"Good. You remember!" Jean commended. They continued like this until Pierre began to attack, the lashing of the wooden swords clamouring in the barn. Pierre heaved and pushed Jean until the edge of the barn, Jean pirouetting away to get more space.

Hay began to lift from their footwork. They fought nimbly, their clothes breathing a second life as air passed through them from the way they jumped and manoeuvred quickly. They danced and danced, neither of them able to catch the other, but it was very close.

I watched, hypnotised, my eyes stuck to their every movement. They acted and reacted in sync. Pierre began to laugh, and so did Jean. So absorbed in their sparring, I didn't even notice Mama coming in.

The barn door croaked, spilling the morning light into the barn around Mama's plump frame. She was carrying two empty, well-used buckets. "There you all are!" Her eyes landed on the sparring pair, and her expression grew perplexed. "Boys!"

But Pierre and Jean did not seem to hear. They continued to spar; Pierre ducked just in time for Jean to swing his arm overhead.

"BOYS!" Her voice was barely higher than a gentle admonishment, but Jean and Pierre both stopped. Sweat was rolling down Pierre's temple, and Jean's hand was rising up and down slightly, as his whole body was pulsating with his breath.

"Mama, we are just practising," Pierre started.

"We needed to practise. The boys in town are holding tournaments," Jean said.

"Playtime is over. Your father will need you in the fields before we go to mass. Come on, come on." Jean and Pierre both lazily straightened up, gathering the wooden swords and packing them away.

"Come, Jehannette, we need to go to the well and wash some clothes before we go. You hold this one, I'll hold the other." The bucket squeakily swung from its hinges as I took it and cast the wooden swords a forlorn look.

Playtime is over.

⁂

"Jehannette, hurry! What is taking so long?" Mama called urgently from the kitchen.

I bent down and looked under my bed. *Not there.*

I swept through my bed covers, flustered. *Not here either.*

Sunday was Mama's favourite day. She considered it the most important day of the week. It was a sacred time for her, and she didn't like to be late. I glanced under my bedside table. *There!* I quickly snatched up the grey cap and shoved it over my head. I came running to Mama's side.

"Jehannette, you have your head in the clouds, my girl," she softly chided, looking at me while her fingers hurriedly tied my cap under my chin. The fire was out, and the kitchen looked dark and unwelcoming. "Come, your brothers and father will already be there."

Sundays were like any other working day, except we always went to church in the morning. This Sunday was no different. The air was still chilly, and the autumn leaves were strewn all over our herb garden as we crossed it. Mama wrapped her hand over her bodice while holding my hand.

The clouds were high in the sky and the sun's heat offered us some solace from the icy air. I yawned as we hurried. We followed a dirt path that was surrounded by a line of high trees. A few minutes later, we reached the village.

It was quite spacious, with small houses made from mud and stone, tightly packed hay on the roofs. I could smell the lingering aroma of fruit trees as we passed the homes.

"Mama," I said. As we briskly walked into the village, the road opened widely. The church sat in the town's centre, flanked by a huge, burbled oak tree.

"Yes?" she answered.

"Do you believe angels are real?"

"Of course, Jehannette."

"Can we see them?"

"Yes... I think those who are special and pray enough can see angels— when they want to be seen."

By now, we had arrived close enough to see the church, which was overfilled with villagers. The wooden arch doors were fully open, and we could hear the singing, the voices of the villagers, carrying outside. The building was large, with a triangular, wooden roof and high spire holding a tower with a bronze bell.

As we climbed up the stone steps, Mama made the cross signage. I copied her. We found ourselves behind a small crowd of villagers singing hymns. Rising to my tiptoes, I scanned the crowd for a couple of minutes, then I saw Jean and Pierre's cinnamon-brown, well-used coats. I swiftly took Mama's hand, and I guided her through the standing crowd to my brothers.

The church inside was ample and cold. The quarry stone walls stretched endlessly to the raised dais where the village priest sat in the corner of the podium. His voice echoed like waves to the lines of people, joining the singing with slightly off-key notes. The singing echoed above to the high point of the wooden roof. The people held no notebooks, but only their humble peasant clothes on their backs and their sincerity of their holy duty. In these times, work and God went hand in hand.

Mama and I reached Pierre and Jean. Pierre smiled and shuffled back to let us stand in front of him. He was growing tall, almost reaching Jean's height. Next to Jean, Papa stood with his hands stiffly holding his farmer's hat in front of him. Once the singing stopped, Father Guillaume stood up and moved to the centre of the podium, his deep and baritone voice reverberating from the front podium.

"And now the Pater Noster." The priest was a round, short, jovial man who wore a thick black robe, with a cross hanging from a necklace. He had a tonsure on the nape of his head and a short beard. Father Guillaume began to pray out loud, while the audience chanted with him.

Pater noster, qui es in cœlis, sanctificetur nomen tuum…

I automatically began to recite; both Pierre's and Jean mumbling thrummed next to me.

The lady did not speak the Roman language. I suddenly wondered.

Mama had taught me the Roman words to say the Pater Noster, and I knew what it meant, but I couldn't help but look upwards to the old wooden arches of the church. My eyes trailed over to the stone walls that hung the wooden boards, showing Christ's suffering, and on the other side, saints with halos and wings.

The lady in the forest didn't have a halo. She didn't have wings.

The clear ring of a bell jolted me from my reverie. Father Guillaume was now carrying the thurible, a small, oval-shaped ball with a chain that emitted holy smoke. It whistled out in delicate tendrils.

Father Guillaume slowly circled the altar on the podium, reciting the Gospel, "Quoniam quidem multi conati sunt ordinare…"

The lady was not like the priest—not a nun either.

I looked around me. Pierre and Jean stared blankly to the front, Mama had an ardent look in her eyes, and Papa's face was unsmiling. As always.

No, nothing like that. The serenity of the lady's face was nothing like us. But perhaps, perhaps, when Mama slept deeply, there was that serenity.

Yet, it wasn't the same.

Not even close.

The priest's recitation ended but concluded the mass in our tongue.

"Thank you, everyone. I will see you all in our next mass. God bless you and protect you." He made the cross signage, to which the audience all responded in their own time.

The audience stirred and began to shuffle and talk in low tones. I tugged Mama's sleeve, "Mama?"

"Yes, my dear?"

"Mama, I have a question."

"Wait, my dear, let us speak when we are outside." And so, we filed out into the town square, peasants heading home to continue their work. Papa, Jean, and Pierre walked ahead of us, tracing the same path through the dirt road lined with tall oak trees.

We were now definitely out of earshot from the other villagers and walked together. "Well, what is your question?"

"Why should God only be worshipped in churches?"

"Well." She took my hand. "Churches give us a special place to pray to God."

"Mama, I have another question. Why do we worship God in the Roman language?"

"That's the language of the Holy Bible, Jehanne. It's the language of Jesus' teachings. It's the language of God."

"Does God… still understand us, if we don't pray in the Roman language?" I asked hesitantly.

"Yes…" she answered slowly, "but the prayers that we say are in Roman because that is the word of God."

I simply nodded.

But the lady spoke to me in my tongue.

And she visited me in the forest, not a church.

I looked back at the church now. It looked so desolate without the crowds hovering around it. Mama looked down at me, squeezing my hand and swinging it. I smiled and looked up to the trees. Tiny birds fluttered from branch to branch, and butterflies floated over the long grass in front of our cottage.

I think I see God more outside of the church.

Mama bent down slightly. "Jehannette, let us get some fresh milk and collect some eggs for lunch. We can have bread and honey with cheese, your favourite."

I nodded excitedly. Her warm eyes emanated her love.

And I definitely see God in my mama.

4

ARCHANGEL

"For He will order his angels to protect you wherever you go."

— Psalm 91:11

1425, Early Autumn
Domrémy, France

I always remember the cold.

Hidden in the vegetable garden at the front of our cottage, I sat with my hands deep in garden soil. I glanced over at the freshly picked carrots. *Mama said she only needed a few.* It was a clear, autumn afternoon and a gentle but chill wind was in the air.

This eve will see a deeper cold.

"Hail Mary, full of grace the lord is with thee…" I hummed as I stood up and brushed off the excess dirt. I surveyed the garden. Since the year the Lady appeared, Mama taught me to care for our vegetable patch and her lessons served well. The garden was teeming with vegetables and herbs; it sprouted in wild and unpredictable forms. I bent down and jerked the green heads of fresh turnips and suedes.

Three years passing, the garden and my farm life completely absorbed me, pushing the memory of the Lady in the woods to a forgotten corner.

But one thing stayed with me, and that was prayer. The discipline of daily prayer had become part of my life, probably because of my mother's example by her own devotion.

"Hmmm, hmmm, hmmm," I hummed as I gathered the vegetables into the ratan basket.

I strolled to the grey house with the slanted roof, and as always it smelt of lavender and vegetable soup. Mama's short and plump figure worked tirelessly next to the fireplace.

"Mama, these are fresh." I laid the basket on the large dining table.

"Thank you, my girl. Oof! My, haven't you grown! I barely noticed until you walked through. I would have thought you were Pierre or Jean."

I grinned. "And have you noticed? My hair is not so red. Now it's darker." I toyed with one of my plaits.

"Oh yes, like red wine," Mama remarked, admiring the crown and plaits of hair that fell over my shoulders.

"Mama, the fire is almost out, might you need some kindle?"

"Yes, thank you dear. Your father chopped some wood near the forest yesterday. Go and bring some for tomorrow as well."

<hr />

The field at the edge of the forest was full of high grass and some late wildflowers with small boulders sparsely protruding over the field. Next to the forest, I saw a pile of wooden stacks. The wind was becoming stronger, and I shivered, collecting the kindling quickly. The wind swept past me, back and forth, swooping my hair and dress in every direction.

I gathered the kindling undeterred until a sudden gust of strong wind sent me reaching for my cap. I quickly caught one of the straps, but at that moment the wind stilled, and the sudden silence filled my ears.

I felt a presence, as if I wasn't alone. I swerved my head around and to my astonishment, a man dressed in a plain white robe was sitting on the large rock. I dropped the kindling. Shaken to speechlessness, I stared at the mysterious man who was only a short distance away.

His robe reached his ankles so his bare feet were showing under his robe, and his light brown hair, parted in the middle, reached his shoulders. He had a relaxed and lean face and sat with a straight back. He looked about thirty years old.

He looks like a monk with vows of poverty, but monks wear black robes and generally walk with their feet covered. But this man does not look like a homeless man. He is clean and strong.

The man regarded me cooly, yet he possessed an air of authority.

"Good afternoon," he said.

"Good afternoon," I answered automatically.

Silence filled the space between us. Quickly reverting to my mother's lessons about meeting with strangers, and regaining my composure, I readdressed him. I cleared my throat, "Ahem. Good afternoon, sir. Are you alright? Do you need anything? A piece of bread perhaps?" I said. My voice was steady, but my palms were sweating.

The man's face was not familiar, and I hadn't seen him in the village. *He's not from these parts.* His face broke into a genuine smile, and said, "Jehanne, thank you, but I don't need anything. I have come to see you."

I swallowed hard. "Me?" My voice high and alert. "If you want any-anything, sir, I'd better call my father." I stammered, ready to fetch Papa or Pierre. "My father. He's working in the fields. I'll tell him that you are here, sir."

But the man stayed where he was. "No, Jehanne." Immoveable as the rock he sat on, the man said firmly but not unkindly, "Jehanne. I don't want to speak to your father. I only bring a message to you. This message is for you, and for you only. I want you to listen carefully."

I fixed my eyes on him.

He must be a lord or a general, I thought, my heart beating quicker. *He must be mistaken. There must be a different Jehanne, and he has confused me for someone else.*

The man stayed sitting, but I felt a small wave of invisible energy emanate from him. Slowly, like waves of an ocean, the feeling of peace touched my heart, and I felt my nervousness melt like ice in summer.

I have felt this energy before. I remember this feeling.

My eyes were cast down. After a while, my heart resumed its steady beat, and my hands stopped fidgeting. I slowly looked up.

Where? Where? I've felt like this before but where? I asked myself urgently. I felt as if I had been blindfolded and was grappling in the dark for an explanation. Then, the memory flashed like lightning.

The lady in the woods! A lady wearing a white dress. A deep peace emanating from her. A stillness in the air…

The man only said, "I see you have remembered." Smiling, his eyes were pools of tranquillity.

I blinked and nodded.

The man continued with barely a pause. "Our Father is pleased with your prayers, Jehanne. Your prayers are heard. You have developed the basics for your spiritual discipline." Rooted to the ground in shock, I couldn't put two words together, let alone a sentence. I only listened.

Unperturbed, he continued. "We will see each other many times in the future. Me, Saint Marguerite, and Saint Catherine. You will always see us in these forms. It will be easier for you." He gave me a moment to take that in. "Saint Marguerite, Saint Catherine, and I are going to be your guides and protectors in the mission you will undertake in a few years."

"Mission?! What mission?" I blurted out.

The man smiled. "You have found your voice," he joked, ignoring the panic in my voice. "It is important that you do *not* tell anyone about these visits."

"But what about when I need to confess?"

"There is nothing wrong with these visits. These are just conversations. You confess your bad deeds, don't you?"

"Yes," I replied.

"This is nothing bad, just talks and advice."

"I suppose I understand." I surveyed his dress and his face more closely. *But who is he?*

"What name may I call you, sir?" *Is he a saint?*

"My name is Michael," he said slowly. "Archangel Michael."

I blinked several times, and I felt a dozen rocks fall to the pit of my stomach. "You're… You are…" I stammered, unable to continue. *No… he can't be.*

Doubt loomed in my mind like a shadow that I couldn't shake off.

He looks nothing like an angel!

He was as ordinary and human as the villagers in the town.

I scrunched my face in scrutiny, stretching my neck to look at his back. *No wings.* He had no halo or light around his frame. I stepped back. *Can someone who looks like an ordinary man be an angel?*

"But sir, you have no wings or a sword. How could you be the Archangel Michael?" I asked, genuinely puzzled.

The man raised his eyebrows as if amused. "Wings? That is how men in churches paint me because they cannot explain how an angel is here one moment and then is not.

"As for a sword," he inclined his head, "I don't need that. You see, Jehanne, in the land of light," his voice turned gentle, "there is only joy, peace, and love. God is love, only love. The things they write are only metaphorical representations to explain truths in a way that can be understood by humankind, but with the passage of time, the true meaning is lost and only the representations remain in the pictures you see in the churches."

Unconvinced, I remained silent, and he tilted his head with a curious smile. He asked, "Maybe it would be better if I present myself with a troop of angels?"

Before I could respond, he raised his left hand. Immediately, columns of long, white lights appeared around him. The light was as blinding as the sun but not painful; in fact, it was the most beautiful sight I had ever seen.

The lights evaporated into mist and revealed figures of men and women in white robes. These beings surrounded the man on the rock like a battalion, but their feet did not touch the earth. Instead, they hovered slightly above the ground and emanated a brilliant, pure white light.

I took another step back. My mouth hung open from pure shock, fear, and wonder. In a silent stupor, I gaped at the scene before me.

Archangel Michael remained sitting, and his voice sounded clear. "Now, do you believe me?"

My heart pounded in my ears. I couldn't speak. My breath came out in short tufts.

"Do not be afraid, Jehanne," Archangel Michael said gently.

I nodded, but my hands kept trembling. I looked up at the light again, and it was flowing through and around the angelic beings. I could now see their faces in more detail. They looked like any other human being, but they gazed at me with a deep tenderness and patience—like the Lady from the woods.

I could see an undisturbed tranquillity—not like in romantic songs, or the human love we know, but something much deeper. A divine love. Like the love a mother has for her child but magnified enormously. My knees sagged to the ground. I felt like an ant amongst giants.

"I-I-I'm sorry. I'm sorry... for doubting—"

And then from a distance, I heard the echo of Mama's voice carried by the wind, "Jehannette!"

Recovering myself, I got up quickly and looked down towards the house. I reeled back to face the angels again but found myself face to face with an empty field filled with small boulders. The wind returned, playing with my hair and skirt.

I gulped hard looking back at the rock, my heart beating quickly. With no time to lose, I recovered the strewn kindling and ran down the hill.

The archangel told me to not tell anyone, I thought to myself. *An angel... An archangel!*

✿

I arrived at the door, panting and out of breath. I paused before entering. My heart was racing, and I looked down to my hands holding the kindling; they were shaking.

I closed my eyes and breathed in deeply. Feeling ready, I pushed the door open to find Mama cutting vegetables for the soup with a rustic looking knife over the table. "Oh, there you are, dear!" she said without taking her eyes off the vegetables.

Wordlessly, I dropped the kindle in an iron basket next to the hearth.

"I thought you found yourself talking to Isabel," Mama continued, walking to the hearth and scraping the vegetables into the pot. The broth splashed a few drops, causing the fire to sizzle.

The fire swallowed and coughed as I placed fresh kindle inside, rearranging it with an iron rod.

"Jehannette, now be a dear and get me a pumpkin, the one with the best colour, not the biggest, and remember to tap it to see if it is ripe."

I simply nodded.

Relieved to be alone again, and covered by the dense foliage of the garden, I could think without worry of Mama or my brothers finding me. I set myself to work, *a ripe pumpkin… a ripe pumpkin…* I tapped a few and checked their ripeness by their hollow echo. While looking, details of the angels began to resurface.

The man on the rock.

The frightening troop of angels.

The light that surrounded them.

The peace. The tranquillity.

I remembered the lady in the forest, and my fear began to fade.

Michael. Archangel Michael! The real Archangel Michael! A small laugh escaped my mouth. I shook my head and continued scanning the garden bed.

But my relentless thoughts turned back to the man in the white robe. *How he seemed like any person of flesh and blood. Only when the troop of angels appeared did I realise he was really an angel.*

I spotted a medium-sized, amber pumpkin cut from the vein and I knocked on it. A hollow noise escaped from within.

Placing the pumpkin in my apron, I walked back to the house. I gently laid the pumpkin on the table with a soft thump. "Mama, I found this one."

Mama put a fresh mound of dough into a heavy iron pot and carried it with both hands, setting it over the fire. Returning to the table, she quickly cast a look towards the pumpkin. "Oh, yes, that one looks fine." She took the pumpkin with her thick hands and steadied it on the chopping board.

"Daughter, take care of the fire. Don't let it get too strong."

I obeyed promptly and knelt in front of the fire. Grabbing the metal poker, I arranged the short logs to keep the fire even but not too hot. I heard my mother splitting the pumpkin on the table with short, hard strikes.

I arranged the logs absently. I still felt the glimmers of nervousness in my body, but at least my hands were no longer shaking. Although the memory of the Lady of the Forest managed to calm me down, I was still in shock from the supernatural experience.

Here I sat with the small, warm fire licking the chimney wall and Mama like a busy bee behind me. Yet my mind was elsewhere.

The angel said such strange words.

No swords are needed… a world only of love… I thought to myself.

Mama's voice brought me back from my reverie. "Aren't you a little thoughtful today." She sounded surprised and amused.

I looked up, smiling embarrassedly. "Ah… no… no, only a little tired today, Mama."

My mama, blissfully unaware of my experience, took the opportunity to talk about women's things. "My dear, you are going to be thirteen very soon and your monthly bleeding will come. We must be prepared. We have to cut a few pieces of cloth, about twelve, that you are going to change every day. The fabric must be thick."

Mama kept speaking.

I nodded and probed the fire. The flames relaxed me, and even though I really didn't want to know about monthly bleeding, I felt grateful for this normal semblance of my life. *Finally, my life seems normal again.*

Mama got up and returned with a clean, thick cotton cloth and began cutting it into long strips.

"To be prepared, you will use these for your first monthly. Remember to change these cloths regularly on these days."

All girls, peasant or rich, have their periods. It was nature. Other girls in the village would probably have these talks with their mothers. But I wondered if the other girls were also told they must complete a mission.

I wondered if these girls had seen what I'd seen. Why me?

5

SAINT MARGUERITE

January, Middle of Winter, 1426
Domrémy, France

Small snowflakes gently fell and melted on the beast's short, smooth,
and sandy coat. "Steady, girl," I said.

I held the reins, my hands stiff from the cold. Sheets of white snow
fell around us. Pierre, garbed in his best coat, woollen cap, and scarf,
yelled, his voice coming out with long fumes of white vapour. "Keep going,
Jehannette! It's only a little snow!"

The fields behind our cottage were long ribbons of white, and the
only remnant of the greenery was from the solid crunch of grass beneath
our boots.

I breathed in but did not move. The animal beneath me stirred.

Pierre hopped over the fence, his feet sinking two inches deep in snow.

"Now, concentrate, Jehannette. The horse only follows directions. You
must guide it. It has to trust you."

His voice was low, so as to not aggravate or stir the horse. But it didn't
work on me. "Also, remember what I said about balance and keeping your
back straight." He adjusted my heel slightly. "And remember to keep your
feet right below your hips."

Pierre's curly hair peeked out from under his woollen beanie and matted against his shiny forehead, for although the days had seen snow, the wind was biting cold. Michaelmas had just passed. And horse riding, especially teaching horse riding, was no easy feat.

"I thought you said this would be easy!" I hissed.

"Calm yourself, Jehannette. If the beast senses you are uneasy it will react."

The horse whinnied, and Pierre stroked the horse's neck and hushed it. He looked up. His brown eyes, similar to mine, were intent. "Ready?"

Breathing in, I nodded.

He carefully withdrew.

The horse stirred at his distance and began to look around in earnest. Sensing its trepidation, I began to hum and stroke its neck, where Pierre's hands had been. The hooves steadied onto the ground, and its breathing slowed. I continued humming but clicked my heels like I had done many times that day.

The horse gently began to walk, and we circled the small paddock behind our cottage.

"Aye, there we go! Now, turn the beast around. Remember, use the rein gently, gently, I say!"

The horse whinnied as I jerked the rein quickly, but it nevertheless understood and turned sharply.

"By God, be careful! Walk around a few times. And try again, slowly and *gently*," Pierre said. He was standing atop the panels of the fence, his jaw set.

I stroked the neck of the horse again and hummed again my tune.

"Good, girl."

Let's try that again. I gently lifted the reins to switch directions, and the horse manoeuvred around easily.

"That's much better!" Pierre said from the fence.

"Now, try trotting! Click your heels, like I showed you!"

Gradually, I regained my balance as the rhythm of the horse's steps quickened. I could now feel the wind washing over me gently. My face broadened into a smile, and I pulled on the reins to bring the horse to a halt.

Pierre whistled. "Well, well, Jehannette."

I gave the horse a quick pat, and descended beaming with triumph.

Pierre pretended to clap, for he was not sure what to expect today, but his little sister had surprised him. "So, my young apprentice, you've shown your valour. I knew you would learn quickly, although maybe it's your birthday luck."

I elbowed him and he chuckled as he took the reins of the steed, and we walked together. "I am not so young. I'm now thirteen. I'm getting older, and I only need to practise more." I shrugged, looking back at the beast that followed us with more admiration than when I started.

"She is good to practise with, this one. Very tame, only a bit skittish, but you calmed her. That's the most important. Tomorrow, you can practise again, but the day after I must return her to the lords."

"Oh…but…" I trailed off.

"Oh, the lords usually have us take care of their horses, Jehannette. You can practise again in a few weeks, and it takes time to learn."

Pierre opened the fence. The snow was falling much thicker now. He squinted upwards, white flecks gathering on his eyelashes. "Yes, time we went inside. Now, let's give Lasette some apples and water. I think Mama and Jean have a surprise waiting for you."

In winter, our cottage was teeming with garlands of pine and oak, and although we dried herbs all year round, Mama's cooking always reminded us of her loving care to detail. The sweet aroma of herbs hung heavily in the air as we entered.

"Oh, you're all drenched!" Mama said, whose voice still sounded like sweet bell, despite her admonishing tone.

"Pierre, you said you would teach Jehanne to ride, not to catch pneumonia," Jean said from the table, supporting Mama's sentiments. Pierre looked around as he took off his jacket and draped it over a seat in front of the fire.

"Jehannette needs to be tough. She can't be running inside if a little snow falls," Pierre said, shrugging, making his way to the dining table. "Where is Papa?"

"He has a meeting with the other farmers and the council," Jean replied, seating himself too.

"Here, my dear. Take off all the wet clothes, and change to something warm," Mama murmured softly.

"Mama, I'm fine. Only the gloves and hat are a little wet."

Mama hung the clothes over her shoulder and then assembled them over a clothing line, but my eyes were drawn to the glowing assemblage on the table. Many small, brightly lit candles danced as Jean and Pierre helped themselves hungrily to the generous plates of rabbit stew, onion and cheese pastries, cabbage and leek pie, and baked wheat bread served with aged cheese that Mama had made herself. There was also a sweet nut loaf made from the pears and apples from our farm.

Mama's hands squeezed my shoulders. "Do you like it?"

"Well, this year, we are snowed in, so we will have a jolly supper and I think it looks wonderful."

Pierre wanted to say something, but with his mouth full of pie, his complaint came out as a stifled whine.

"Yes, that's true. He gave Jehannette her first riding lesson," Jean said, before his next mouthful of rabbit stew.

Mama's voice was barely above a whisper when she began to cut and serve a piece of pie, its filling still hot; steam rose into the air. "Only Pierre, next time come inside when it starts to snow. Come, Jehannette, you must be hungry. Happy birthday, dearie."

<hr/>

"Thank you, Mama. It's beautiful," I said softly, looking at the pristine cotton cap. My fingers traced over the embroidered leaves and flowers.

"Try it on," she said.

Smiling, I pulled back my hair and adjusted the cap. I pulled it down to sit above my brow, leaving the straps dangling below my ears. "It fits well," I said, shifting it back.

"Yes, it fits you well," Mama said while securing it under my chin. "I was not sure if I made it the right size, now that you have grown so much this last winter."

"You have?" Jean said with the least observing eye of the family.

I stood up in my new cap, and swished my dress.

"See how short it is?" The edge of my dress reached just below my knees.

Pierre stood up too with his chest in the air, and measured my height. His face was studious.

"Hmm, little miss, you're still quite little I dare say," Pierre teased.

"That's why you've been sewing so much," Jean said, leaning back into the chair, his arms resting on his legs with a resigned look.

Mama and I nodded. Over winter, my clothes had become two sizes small, and we spent many nights cutting, fitting, and sewing new dresses, aprons, and undergarments.

"I'm a head taller than Mama," I said proudly, with my nose in the air despite my head being in line with Pierre's torso.

Mama rested her elbow on the table with her chin in her hand and looked at her children with glazed over eyes. She enjoyed the company of her children, and on her lips a warm and grateful smile shone forth at their playful banter.

The front door suddenly opened. Papa emerged, his scarf and cap so capped with snow he almost looked like a snowman.

Mama shot up and began to fill a wooden bowl with stew, and a plate with pastries and a piece of pie. And like that, all semblance of merriment funnelled into the ether, and we sobered ourselves to quiet mouses as the bear took his seat at the head of the table.

The night grew still and serious, Papa's voice a low rumble as the boys listened attentively. Mama and I, with our sleeves rolled up to our elbows, scrubbed the plates and pots until our fingers emerged from the tepid water, wrinkled and stiff.

⚜

The snow fell outside, slow and constant. There was no rush.

"Darn it," I said under my breath.

Mama looked up at me, her voice coming out was a strained whisper. "Remember, my dear, the needle must go up and around."

My face scrunched up in concentration. I held the material closer to the fire. I could hear the sound of harsh brushing and smell shoe wax from the kitchen.

"Pierre and Jean will need some new shirts for the coming autumn." Mama's hands worked quickly, and in no time held out my new tunic in front of her.

"Stand up, Jehannette. Let me see it fits you."

I stood up, and put the tunic over my clothes, "Mm, perfect! Good, now I've marked the pockets and buttons, dearie. Sew them quickly, and when I've finished with your brothers' shirts, sew the buttons." And like that, Mama fanned out Pierre's new shirt on her lap and began to work.

"Yes, Mama." I yawned, appreciating these simple yet precious moments of our life.

I knew little of the next surprise that awaited me.

⚜

The end of winter was heralded by the melting snow and budding leaves; the winter months had seen a wet end. The soil beneath us squelched as we walked to the fields and rain drizzled overhead. It was time to clean the fields for the next crop season, and Papa needed all the help he could get.

The fields were divided by bushes of wildberries and manured by our flock of sheep and goats. Bushes lined the fields because of their fruits but also because of their practicality as fences. They were thorny, making them a formidable barrier for the farm animals. In the spring, my brothers and I collected the fruit, and their sweetness would make a lovely afternoon treat.

I walked behind my brothers until their voices slowly receded into the next paddock. The fields were filled with old wheat stems, broken branches and strewn rocks, and I began to dig out and clean the fields with a well-used spade. The trees of the orchard and the forest were bare, and the branches moved stiffly in the wind carrying the musky smell of rainfall. After the 10th hour of the day, I had cleaned one quarter of the field, leaving behind stacked piles that sparsely protruded over the flat field. My cheeks flushed from the exercise, and I wiped my dripping nose.

Spring will be coming soon, I thought to myself, smelling the faint aroma of florals.

A wind rippled through the stick-like branches of the trees, whipping my new cap up and sending it bounding and bouncing over the field. As I turned, I stopped short.

Not again.

A woman.

A woman in a white tunic stood in the field.

The cap stopped right at her feet.

Startled, I opened and closed my mouth several times, but no voice came out. I stared at her for a moment, then I looked down at her feet. The woman was barefoot.

I held the spade tightly in my right hand.

"Hello, Jehanne," the woman said.

"Hello."

Every semblance of life seemed to quieten. No wind, no singing birds. I examined her closer and saw that her white tunic was light linen as if for summer.

How can she bear the cold?

Then, the white tunic struck a strange and bizarre memory.

Archangel Michael said I will have three guides...

The woman's voice broke the silence. "Jehanne, what are you doing?" Her voice was serene and sweet. She looked at the spade in my hand.

What an odd question.

The woman smiled, and I gathered my words. "Cleaning the fields," I said, fidgeting with the spade. "I'm helping my father for the next crop season."

"You are doing well. Manual labour will help you become strong," the woman said. Her sentence made no sense to me, but she carried on. "But you won't do this for long. Your life's mission will take you to other places. The Heavenly Father wants to unite this land, this kingdom, under one ruler."

I stayed silent.

"The English," she said finally. "The English must go. The kingdom needs to be stabilised and united under one King. Our Heavenly Father is going to lead the French armies to victory. God has chosen you to carry out this mission."

I suddenly felt dizzy and dazed. I leaned on the spade for support.

This must be a madwoman. She can't be saying what I think she is saying.

My heart began to race.

I need to leave; she is talking madness.

But the woman was looking at me with such tenderness and care, as if she knew exactly what I was feeling. She looked like she would have approached and soothed me, but she stayed where she was.

My decorum held my feet to the ground, and I found my words but barely. "Bu–but I'm just a girl, I'm– I'm a peasant girl!"

The woman just observed me and let me continue.

"I–I don't know anything about armies or weapons!"

My voice rose higher now. "God is wrong. God has made a mistake. You must want one of my brothers," I said firmly with total conviction.

Here, the lady smiled. She said softly, "The King of Heaven does not make mistakes." Then her voice became stronger. "And yes, you are a *girl* and a *peasant* girl for that matter, but there is nothing that is impossible for God. Nothing that cannot be done. All his thoughts are action, and all action is executed without delay."

The woman's words were comforting, but my heart tumbled and contracted into a million shapes. My chest was heaving as if I had just raced through the orchid. My knees hit the hard soil, and I clasped my hands, looking up at the tender woman who was asking me for the impossible.

"Oh, but I don't want to do this! I don't know how. Find someone else, can you tell God to find someone else?!" I cried. Tears stung my eyes, and I closed them, hoping with my whole might she would take this heavy burden away.

I felt a hand on my shoulder, but I kept my eyes closed. The touch was warm, and I felt my distress soothed away like a gentle rain, unburdening me and spreading a calmness that wasn't there before.

After a few moments, I opened my eyes slowly. I felt the tears drying on my cheeks and I looked up to see the woman's honey-brown eyes looking down at me. Her demeanour was peaceful. Her voice came out gently. "God is never wrong. He is truth and love, Jehanne."

I only listened now; my mind opened like a clear sky to a better judgement of the woman's words.

She laid her hand at her side. "Do not be afraid. This may seem impossible, but let me assure you, you will be victorious."

I kept listening.

"You will have help and advice from Archangel Michael, and you will be surrounded by lords and ladies who will help you as well." The woman paused. "Jehanne, you were born to do this."

My eyes turned tentative.

Noticing my confusion, the woman answered. "Yes, this was written by the invisible hand of God before you were born, eons ago. Have confidence, my dear, God does not make mistakes."

I felt myself beginning to trust this woman. Her words were strange, but the love they expounded made my mind melt like honey. "I… believe you, madam," I said hesitantly. From that moment, I felt as if a great weight was lifted from my shoulders, as if accepting the words of the angel was the right thing to do. "I will follow God's command."

At this, the woman smiled approvingly and nodded.

"Now you must listen carefully."

I straightened up.

"You must prepare yourself. You must become strong. This is very important. Do not avoid heavy work. Lift heavy bags and sacks. As you attend errands, run. When you go to the village or the fields, run. Do you understand? This is vital for your training."

I remained still and listened closely.

Hard work was nothing new to us farmers.

The woman placed a hand on my shoulder. "Jehanne," she said with courage and faith in her eyes. She was only a head taller than I was, but her touch emanated a warmth and strength that made me cling to her every word. "God loves you and God will take care of you. Remember that the one who is omnipresent, omniscient, and all powerful has delivered this perfect plan and you are going to be his emissary."

Stepping back suddenly, she added, "You must finish your duties. Your brothers will call you when they are finished."

"Madam, may I know your name?" I asked.

The woman's dress rippled slightly as the gentle wind resumed. "Saint Marguerite." And like that, I was alone again and facing an empty field with piles of rocks and branches.

My cap jerked lazily in the wind as I picked it up. The forest was shrouded in low, grey clouds, and I could feel the sparing droplets of rain. In the distant fields, I could see my brothers' hats tracing the fields like ants.

Possessed by an invisible force, I worked in the field for the whole afternoon.

"A mission… physical labour… training?" I muttered.

Saint Marguerite's presence was beautiful and gave hope, but now that she was gone it was like the sun had gone and the coldness of the night was setting in.

"Me? Why *me?*" I said aloud. "I can't lead an army! I'm just– I'm just a girl!"

I'm not even allowed to speak in my own home. I can't speak in the presence of my father. Dejected, I began pulling out the heads of stubborn weeds.

I thought of my mother. She did not mind being excluded from conversations or decisions. She did all the housework and took care of us, all without question. Always with a prayer on her lips as was her custom.

This 'mission' is ludicrous. I believe that woman has no idea what she is saying. I'm just a girl. My role is different. My whole life I've seen this. My family and my town. I see the same everywhere, and God wants me to lead an army?

I looked up to the sky, to the invisible creator.

I cannot go to battle. What is the lady thinking?

The war between the English and the French had been happening for as long as everyone could remember.

Only the silence of the fields responded to my mental complaints. Dejected and alone, my heart trembled with a new thought. *Battle.* All I knew about battle was the conflict between the English and the French. I couldn't comprehend that I would need to enter their world of horror and savagery.

I felt like I was falling down a dark pit of my own fears. Tears came, but I kept working. The field work was our livelihood; it needed to be done. My mind couldn't rest. It tumbled and squirmed as my back ached and my fingernails were darkened with soil.

Calls from the field over eventually caught my attention. "Jehannette, time to go!"

Jean and Pierre carried their tools over their shoulders as they made their way to the barn.

"Jehannette, come!" I heard my brothers call.

I waved in response, and slowly walked through the fields. My brother's laughter reminded me of the present and soothed my troubled heart.

"No, that doesn't count because the rock was a different size!" Pierre protested.

"Yes, it does! Fair and square, Pierre. We can do it again, but I think you just don't want to try again." Jean playfully began to play fight with Pierre with his spade. Pierre dodged. They began to run, and Jean chased Pierre to the barn trying to catch him.

I smiled as I watched their figures recede into the distance.

Remembering Saint Marguerite's instructions, I welcomed the thrill of their chase as I reached the barn out of breath.

"Where were you, Jehannette?" Jean asked.

My face, red from the exercise, masked my turbulent emotions from Saint Marguerite's visit. "Oh, just behind you. I wanted to catch up," I said, going to the bucket of almost frozen water. I shivered as I splashed my hands and face. I immediately felt better as the cool water touched my skin.

"Are you alright, Jehannette? If the work is too much you can stay home tomorrow," Pierre said, his eyebrows knitted.

"Oh no, I just got a little tired, but I can go back to the fields. I like the work, you know."

"Are you sure?" asked Pierre.

"Yes, and the work was fine. I can do it," I said with my best smile and remembering the angel's instructions.

Jean piped in, "Well, tomorrow it's going to be our last day so after we can celebrate. What do you think? Maybe you can ride one of the horses and I can show you some tricks, Jehannette."

"That's a good idea." Pierre smiled at his brother. "As long as the work is done, Papa will not mind with what we do. And the horses are pretty good. They would benefit from a little trip around the paddock," Pierre said, playfully elbowing me and smirking.

Hope rose in my chest like a sun.

"This time, the weather," Pierre added, looking up to the sky, "will be on our side."

I laughed as I remembered the snow and Mama's gentlest reprimand.

Pierre chuckled, and we walked back to our cottage—and like that, my spirit lifted.

6

FEAR

"Don't give in to your fears... If you do, you won't be able to talk to your heart."

— The Alchemist by Paulo Coelho

End of Winter 1426
Domrémy, France

That night, I tossed and turned. I dreamt of strange, dark fields with red clouds. The horizon was a line of a thousand faceless soldiers. Were they friend or foe, I never knew. I ran and ran, but my legs felt like iron.

I ran into a dense wood.

The woods became a muggy, unwelcoming marshland.

My feet sunk inches deep into muddy waters, and I heaved my legs, but they grew even more heavy. I heard the galloping of horses and the sheathing of a sword.

A glint of a metal.

Lightning.

Screams.

I woke up.

My body was covered in cold sweat. Only the chatter and wooden cutlery scraping against the wooden bowls could be heard in the dining room next door. I waited several seconds to get my bearings and calm my racing heart.

With no time to waste, I quickly dressed and walked to the dining room. As usual, the fire was steadily going, and Mama had prepared breakfast for us to eat before we went to the fields. Since Papa left early, my brothers and Mama were talking, although Mama was always quiet so it was mostly my brothers.

I sat down in my usual spot. In the centre of the table was loaf of bread, and around it was a slab of butter in a wooden bowl, a pan of hot milk, and boiled eggs. In my spot was a steaming bowl of porridge. Pensive, I poured some hot milk over my porridge.

"Gustav and Jeod will be competing in the tournament, Jean. They have been taught by the Lord's swordsman," Pierre said as he tore off a chunk of bread, spooned some butter over it, and put it entirely in his mouth.

Jean rolled his eyes in response, but he paused on seeing his little sister eating her porridge slowly, eyes puffy and hair brushed yet dishevelled. The real reasons for this despondency would have shocked him.

It must be the field work, Jean thought to himself. He side-eyed Pierre and motioned towards Jehannette.

Pierre cleared his throat. "Mama, after we have finished in the fields, we're going to tend the horses."

Mama simply nodded and continued eating quietly.

"We may also get a rabbit or two for dinner," added Jean, accustomed to Mama's quiet manners.

"And some produce from Jehannette's little garden," Pierre said; his brown eyes shone with a bit of merriment even at that early hour.

I glanced up and half smiled.

"Come, Jehannette, let's ready ourselves. Later, I can show you the beautiful mare we have."

I smiled gratefully and gulped down the last bite of porridge.

I gently scrubbed my teeth with the corner of my apron. The water was ice cold but refreshing indeed.

When we were ready, Jean, Pierre, and I walked to the fields. The morning was crisp, and the dense grey clouds blurred the distant rolling hills in the horizon. The mist slowly lifted from the fields and forests, and other early risers, also getting ready for the day's work, were also making their way to their own fields.

My brothers walked and chatted enthusiastically and loudly ahead of me, carrying the tools on their shoulders. I was a few steps back, simply gazing at the distant fields.

At the start, my brothers and I worked together on the same field. The sun stayed hidden behind a thick layer of clouds, casting everything in wintry grey. Working in the field was nothing new and my brothers were merry.

Only, I kept recalling yesterday's dream.

I tried not to think about it.

We cleaned the fields. My brothers dealt with the animal carts, and I pulled out the long weeds from the soil, putting them on a pile.

As the morning turned to afternoon, my brothers and I fanned out and I found myself alone with my hands and mind racing.

I leant on my spade, as I gazed to the distant figures of my brothers. My brothers were strong and hardy, and as boys they took on the harder and heavier loads of labour on the farm. Years of repetitive, heavy work led them to become reliable workers, especially in my father's eyes.

Why can't they go and save the kingdom? I thought to myself.

My sole purpose for my being on this earth is to… lead an army?

I audibly scoffed.

Even Father Guillaume has said, 'the order placed by God on Earth'. The Bible, the holy word of God, showed this. Men reigned and women followed.

This was normal. I saw this every day in my home, in my family. If God has an order, then why does he want me to break that order?

I dug into the earth, the spade making harsh contact with a rock.

Isn't this a sin? Isn't this going against God's law on Earth? I had never heard of women in armies or as soldiers, less as generals. *Could this mission be correct, according to God's law?*

Then the dreadful thought came again, the thought that haunted me since Saint Marguerite's visit yesterday. *How was I going to lead an army?*

As if tumultuous clouds of storms descended over me, my mental anguish took hold of my body. I knelt down in the field and started to pray, to beg to the creator.

"Please, this is too much. I cannot do this. You must ask someone else, please. I am just a peasant girl, please, please…"

I clung onto the prayer, silent and focused. Time seemed to stand still until I opened my eyes again. I stood up, and in that moment it was like my surroundings were quiet, in stillness. I wheeled around and I was not alone. In the field, Archangel Michael stood. He wore his usual white tunic and stood barefoot. His usual sharp, dark eyes were sympathetic and his head was tilted as if concerned.

He raised his arms as he said, "Jehanne, you are in such anguish. Your mind has been occupied with many doubts."

Archangel Michael always exuded an aura of authority, yet it was mixed with a strong energy of peace. It was a combination that I was slowly getting used to.

I looked at him, perplexed.

How does he know my thoughts? I just nodded.

He looked around the fields and over to my brothers working in the far distance. "Jehanne, are you out here in the fields, working alongside your brothers?"

"Yes."

"Well, you are no different. You are capable of doing the same things, and you are as capable as them. Jehanne, God is in the heart of every being in the universe. God is the force that gives life to the whole of creation. Everything that happens and what is going to happen, he knows."

My brows furrowed. "I don't follow, sir."

Archangel Michael didn't show any impatience to my lack of understanding and calmly explained, "God is in every heart. God is the principle that gives life to your heart and the heart of every living being in this universe. Jehanne, if God is in the heart of every being, then nobody is above anybody."

I said nothing.

"There is no corner in this vast universe where God is not. So, what is there to fear?"

As a loving father acts as a confidant, Archangel Michael's words put my mind at ease. I stared at the ground, and he waited until I mustered my words slowly.

"The village priest—" I cleared my throat. "He says that God has put everything in an order, men and women."

I took a deep breath and looked up at Archangel Michael. "Women and men can't do the same things."

He was silent for a moment, but there was the hint of a smile at the corner of his mouth. "Jehanne, for God, there is no above or below, strong or weak, rich or poor, kings or vassals, women or men. None of that exists in God. The rule that men and women are different was put by men in the sacred books, not by God."

My eyes widened slightly.

His voice became firmer. "Do not believe, Jehanne, that because of your femininity you are subordinate. No one is subordinate to anyone. In God we are all equal."

I listened closely as he continued. "Those written words were made by men to give places and roles to their citizens. But people forget the first law that God has given them: *Love God and your neighbour.* That is the only law that matters.

"Nothing else has the same value or importance in this world. Don't worry about the laws of men, just follow God. Nothing, nothing else, has the same importance," he said, emphasising the last words.

His voice became soft. "The only thing that God values above anything else is a pure, compassionate heart where love can dwell. Like a mirror, God can reflect in each heart because God is love, Jehanne."

I was stunned and transfixed; it was like my heart opened and an ocean of peace cascaded into my soul. Yet another thought came to sting my revelation. "But if God is love, why is there so much suffering?"

"Jehanne, that happens when men turn away from God. Jesus gave a single commandment—*love your neighbour as I have loved you*—but men pursue the ephemeral, the temporal, their short-lived desires. In the end, it has no value and blinds the heart from the truth. Thinking this way, humanity bring suffering upon themselves through their bad actions."

His words felt true, and it was like I had been cast in a world of darkness and someone finally lit the light of truth.

"I understand."

I clasped my hands together and bowed my head.

"Thank you for showing me the truth, sir."

There was one more thing that was pressing my heart, like a thorn pressing into my side. I thought about my next words carefully, saying them slowly as if they weighed on my conscience. "I am afraid of war. I know nothing about battles or swords." I hesitated. "I–I don't know any-thing." My voice came out small and weak.

I kept my gaze fixed downward. I looked at my hands, holding a spade and stained with soil. Living a peasant life, I was used to labour, but I was in no way fit for combat.

Archangel Michael's features softened, and he dipped his head to meet my downcast eyes. His voice came out quiet, "Jehanne, you are right."

Relief erupted in me. I held my breath.

Archangel Michael continued, "You don't know anything, this is true… but your preparation has not started yet."

Shattered, I felt my tumultuous feelings crash over me like a tsunami. I sniffed and looked down again, hopeless.

"You will learn to use the sword, which will happen soon. And we will be your counsellors and guides. We will be by your side, always, when you command an army." Archangel Michael's voice sounded distant.

This is too much. You are asking too much of me. I'm just a peasant girl…

"Jehanne." As if a clear bell rung, I snapped my head up. Archangel Michael was looking at me, his gentle demeanour gone, and I felt like I was looking at the force of a mountain.

"Discard the doubts in your mind," he said firmly. "Do not let them take over. They will only cloud your judgement. Focus, focus, on what you have to do." His voice steadily became more magisterial, like the words of a general, giving me a clear path on my purpose.

"You will be an instrument of God and the will of God is not impossible. Everything will be fulfilled to perfection because God is perfect. Even if it seems impossible, never doubt. This is your destiny. You were born to do this. You'll have our counselling and our help, always."

His voice regained its softness, and his eyes became sympathetic again. "Jehanne, trust fully and without reservation that God's love is ever-present."

I listened with my entire being. His words filled my heart with inspiration and strength. They were accompanied by a deep conviction and energy that left no doubt in my mind.

"I will trust you. I will trust God… Thank you for dispelling my doubts."

The archangel just smiled.

"You are doing well, Jehanne. Keep doing the hard work. Run, if you can run. Lift the heavy bags, if you need to lift heavy bags. Don't be afraid of hard work. This will help you prepare your body. You have to be strong."

I heard the calls of my brothers in the distance. It brought me back to my world, to my chores, to my family. The fields were waiting for me.

"Finish your duties."

And with those words, I was alone again.

As I got up slowly, my knees ached with discomfort. I hadn't realised how long I was kneeling. I brushed off the remaining soil that was left on my dress.

Destiny... Angels... And farmwork?

I dug through the fields, wrenching out the stubborn old growths of plants. *You know, I think I am learning more and more about God.*

The rain drizzled overhead and pattered over the strewn leaves that dotted the fields.

7

THE VISIT TO NEUFCHÂTEAU

Early Spring, 1426
Domrémy, France

My lungs were burning. Sweat trickled down my forehead. I jumped over the fence and ran through the orchid. By spring, the air was fragrant with the floral sweetness of baby apples. The grass was long, and the sun was in its second hour of the afternoon.

I skidded to as stop as I approached the cottage and glanced back at the fields.

Everything has changed.

Since meeting Archangel Michael and Saint Marguerite, life seemed to become a parallel existence of farmwork, family, and the mission and angels.

I must make myself strong.

My chest heaved, and I lowered myself over a barrel of water, splashing water over my face and neck.

"Jehannette!"

I whipped my head up. Mama stood in the doorframe, a basket of wet sheets and clothes on her hip. Her face was shrouded in confusion, a question on her open lips.

"I just went to – check on the sheep – I let them out earlier today – and one is still – heavily – pregnant – I expect the babe – will come by the morrow," I said between breaths.

Mama's gentle blue eyes illuminated with understanding as she walked slowly to the other side of the cottage. "Dearie, go and get some a bag of flour for me. Oh, and on the morrow, we will go to see your uncle Jean-Marcel in Neufchâteau. Check on the vegetable garden for anything we can give him as a gift. As well, check on the sheep and ask your brothers to help get some wool."

"Yes, Mama," I said. She disappeared behind the wall, leaving me to regain my breath.

Domrémy was a small village, and we seldom travelled outside of it.

But a few times a year, we travelled to the southerly city of Neufchâteau. Neufchâteau was bigger and fortified with walls. It always exposed us to new accents, sights, and smells.

Often, we went to trade with Papa's younger brother Uncle Jean-Marcel, who owned a shop selling flour, oats, and legumes. He lived there with his two sons, Jean-Paul and Jean-Claude.

Remembering our cousins, I felt a flicker of apprehension as we packed our goods into our small cart, which would be pulled by the oxen.

"We have the salted meats, the cheese, the bread, the apples…" Mama said, counting with her fingers, her sweet, bright eyes alert despite the hour.

"I think that is everything," Jean said. He covered our goods over with a rough ratan blanket. "It is dawn, we should go." He lent his hand to help Mama up onto the cart. Mama and Jean sat at the front, Jean took the reins, and Pierre sat with me in the back.

At that early hour, our wagon bumped and trudged its way through the quiet streets of Domrémy, the houses still slumbering with few people out. The simple appearance concealed their warmth and the wealth that came from the land.

It was enough. We lived well.

Once we reached the outskirts of Domrémy, only the surrounding green-ery lay before us. Travellers on horseback and carts passed by wordlessly or exchanged small greetings. Safely out of sight of any wanderers and curious eyes, I wordlessly hopped out of the wagon and began to run alongside it.

Mama's eyes travelled down to me, and I could feel her concern and slight disapproval. But my brothers had a different view on the matter.

"Hey, Jehanne, are you training so you can escape the boys from town?" said Jean, smiling slyly as he chewed on a long piece of wheat grass.

"Oh, no, she is running to get to Neufchâteau faster than the other girls, perhaps to a sweetheart?" said Pierre, leaning over the cart. His shaggy brown hair ruffled from napping over the blanket of goods.

"Tell us which boy holds your heart, Jehanne," teased Jean, squint-ing as the sun steadily rose in the sky, which was lined with long, string-shaped clouds.

"I'm sure there are many...." said Pierre, rummaging through the cart and pulling out an apple.

I rolled my eyes. "It's nobody. I just like to run."

Mama said nothing, preoccupied.

Jean said, "Hey, Jehannette do you think you can outrun Pierre?"

"What do you think, Jehannette? Do you think you beat me now?" Pierre munched loudly on the apple.

"I don't care about that." But in my heart, I felt myself tinge with curiosity.

"Eh, Pierre, be careful!" Jean teased, not taking his eyes off the road.

I leapt onto the cart, out of breath and sweating.

"Water, O soldier?" Pierre lay on the cart with his eyes closed but holding a water skin up with an amused smile.

"Thanks."

"You have improved," Pierre said, adjusting himself to look at me with eyes half open.

"What do you mean?" I asked, after quenching my thirst.

"You used to get tired much easier, but now you can run longer," he said, as the wagon rocked side to side.

Mama looked behind to us, as Jean led the oxen.

Pierre motioned behind him to where mama was sitting and mouthed. *"She is worried."*

I looked up at Mama and nodded.

I rummaged through the supplies we brought. I tore off some bread and stripped off a morsel of cheese. Pierre shrugged, and closed his eyes as he dozed off.

Mama thinks I have too much energy for a girl. She does not approve. But since my period has not arrived yet, I must focus on running and getting stronger. My period will come later.

At least Pierre and Jean have noticed my getting better, even if they think it's amusing.

<hr />

"Not again, Jehannette!" Jean exclaimed.

I resumed my steady jog. My legs felt like lead, but I persisted.

Ok, until the tree. I felt myself getting tired much quicker. But I kept going.

Ok, until the end of the field. I kept going.

Ok, sprint as fast as I can up this hill and stop at the top. I pushed and pushed myself. The sun was beating down on me, my face was red hot, and my body was begging to stop.

I reached the top and stopped and stared.

There, over the hills and green fields, lay the city walls of Neufchâteau. *I did it.*

I turned back to the wagon, climbing slowly up the hill and called, "There! We have arrived!"

<hr />

Indeed, Neufchâteau had a fortified wall surrounding the houses with a large gate through which many people were traversing to and from the city. Guards stood on either side of the gate like silent statues. Our cart slowly clambered our way through the crowd as travellers on foot easily glided past our wagon.

Entering the gate, the small city opened into a wide cobblestone street lined with white stone two-storey houses. The street was bustling with city merchants and dwellers alike, haggling and complaining with the Neufchâteau and other provincial accents. A woman from a high window, her hair brusquely pushed back by a bandana over furrowed brow from a hard-day's work, emptied a bucket of water on the street, splashing the wheels of our cart.

Urine and waste wafted in the air.

"Careful, ye beggar woman!" the merchants exclaimed, throwing their hands up and glancing up. I suddenly craved the fresh country air.

"We're not far from Uncle's shop," Jean said, grimacing and urging the oxen on.

We turned into a smaller street with only mice scampering about, and Jean comfortably pulled the reins to halt the cart. Uncle's shop sat on the corner between the main and small street, and we saw at once that he was open for business.

And doing very well.

Despite the street being a quiet paradise for mice as they gallivanted to their pleasure, Uncle's shop was on the first floor, and customers flurried in and out like flies. The second floor, which was accessed through an open staircase on the side of the house, had a firmly closed door that was reserved for Uncle and our cousins' private lodgings.

Jean jumped off the wagon and dusted his hands. Mama heaved herself slowly over the cart and said, "Jean, greet your uncle. Tell him we are here with our products."

"Yes, Mama." Jean's tall frame disappeared inside the shop.

A few minutes later, Jean returned with Uncle Jean-Marcel. He was shorter than Jean, with a potbelly and jet black hair that had recently started to go grey on the sides, and walnut brown eyes that matched Papa's.

"Hello, my dear sister-in-law and nephews." He kissed Mama on both cheeks and repeated the ritual with every one of us.

He held me by my shoulders; his fingers were thick and rough, but he had a gentle, fatherly touch. He said, laughing, "What do you feed this girl, Isabel? She is almost my size." He gave me two kisses on each cheek.

"Oh, she has too much energy, this one."

"Oh, that's okay. She'll be a pretty and strong woman. The boys are going to chase this one," said Uncle while winking and nudging Jean's ribs with his elbow.

Pierre and Jean chuckled.

"How is my older brother, Jacques? How goes his crop?"

"Father is well. Last winter was only mild, and our crops grew quickly. We now supply for the lords of Domrémy, Pierre occasionally works with the horse master, and we take care of the horses and train them," Jean said.

All the while, Mama looked at her oldest son with beaming eyes.

"Ah Jean, you're becoming more of a man every time you visit!" Uncle patted his shoulder, and clapped his hands to discuss business. "Well, what have you brought me this time?"

Jean and Pierre went to the back of the cart and Jean lifted the ratan basket, exposing ten big round cheese blocks, multiple crates of apples from the orchid, and layers of precious salted meats that were delicately piled into a long cotton strip. Uncle's eyes were unblinking as he wordlessly picked up a round cheese block and brought it to his nose. "Oh Isabel, this smells exquisite! As always, you excel in your cheese making."

"Thank you, Jean-Marcel," said Mama with her sweet smile.

Jean exposed the salted meats of the sheep and goat legs and ribs.

"Oh, this looks well prepared. The meat looks in good condition," said Uncle while jerking off a small piece to taste.

"Mm, good and fresh flavours. So, you have brought more than I can give! Heh heh, now tell me, what do you need?" But before Mama or Jean said anything, Uncle continued. "I have beans and chickpeas from merchants in town. It is very good quality."

"Yes, we need legumes," said Mama.

"Yes, yes, ah, come, come inside the shop." Uncle ushered Mama gently to the door.

Uncle looked back to the boys expectedly. "Jean, Pierre, bring the goods inside, will you boys? And Jehanne, come, come inside dear."

⚜

Though the shop was dark my eyes adjusted quickly, and shapes began to form. It was an ample, open space with stone floors and white walls. On the right corner, there were many barrels and a bench, and sacks of flour and oats and other grains sat in the other corner.

Behind the bench, some charqui hung from hooks in the ceiling. To the left were a couple of hay bales and a big double door that opened to the patio.

"Yes, sir. We have barley, only let me check our bags," a voice said.

"Ah you remember my boy, Jean-Paul?" Uncle said.

Jean-Paul stood behind the counter; he had a handsome face with short black hair. He was 18 and good friends with Jean and Pierre. He side-smiled at my brothers as they came in and nodded before ducking out to check the barrels.

"The shop has been very busy this year. I had to ask the boys to stay and help me a few days a week," Uncle said.

Jean-Paul returned in a flurry to the bench, "Yes, but we need to help our Papa in any way we can. There ye go, sir." Having finished with the client, he sighed with a hand on his hip. "Hello, Aunt Isabel."

Mama bowed her head. "Hello, Jean-Paul, you look well."

"Aye, Papa reared healthy, meticulous sons. Working in the smith, Jean-Claude and I need to look after ourselves." His eyes landed on me, and I felt myself shrink under his gaze. "Well, well, if it isn't our little cousin!"

Oh God, don't start.

"Jean-Paul, I need your help to pack your aunt's supplies," Uncle said, wiping the bench with a damp cloth.

Jean-Paul threw me a sly smile, as if he knew what I was thinking.

"Ah, little cousin, until later."

I nodded, trying not to show my relief.

⧽⧽⧽⧽⧼

That afternoon, Uncle was the perfect host.

Every client to enter the shop was welcomed with his jovial and generous character, as Mama and I accommodated ourselves over the counter eating bread and cheese. Mama was able to converse and get her fill of the juiciest gossip of the city, while Jean, Pierre, and Jean-Paul went to the smithy to visit Jean-Claude.

By early afternoon, Uncle had carried the sacks of flour and oats, and two smaller sacks of chickpeas, beans, and peas to the wagon.

"You are well supplied now, Isabel. Don't forget me when you have more of those cheeses and salted meat ready," said Uncle, while kissing Mama goodbye. His smiled so much his face looked pinched, as if he sucked on a lemon.

"And Jehannette, goodbye dear girl, take care." He kissed me on both cheeks again.

I got in the wagon first and I helped Mama.

"Send my regards to Jacques," he said, stepping back.

"We will, Jean-Marcel, goodbye," Mama said.

"Goodbye, Uncle!" I waved as Mama whipped the reins once, and the oxen slowly started.

"We'd better hurry. I don't want to be on the road after dark," Mama said as she led us through the main street. The wide cobblestone street, which before was dense and crowded with people, smells, and noises, now appeared as a nearly empty canvas.

Children and dogs traipsed the street, playing with wooden toys and ribbons, the only remnants from the busy markets only hours before. A young girl and a smaller boy, their faces dirty, played a clapping game.

Above us, the sun was hidden behind a thin veil of clouds. At this time, Neufchâteau was a city of innocence and games after the cunning and crafty exchanges of merchants and villagers.

"I think I still prefer the country," I said to Mama quietly, as we passed the gate.

Mama breathed in, welcoming the fresh breeze of the open countryside. "As do I."

Slowly, we travelled to the forge on the outskirts of the town, where Jean and Pierre were helping our cousins, Jean-Claude and Jean-Paul.

"Is it true that our cousins work in the forge three times a week?"

"Yes, that is what your uncle said."

"Mm."

"What is it?"

"I wish I had cousins that were girls," I confessed.

Mama looked sideways to me. "Oh! Well, Jehannette, your brothers are good fun. And your cousins too."

"They are much older... I feel so shy, and I never know what to say..."

Mama only looked at me tenderly.

"In time, dear, you will know what to say. Let yourself grow and become comfortable in yourself."

I nodded and the sky was beginning to redden for sunset.

But I have known them all my life.

Although our visits with them were short, we always maintained contact. Jean-Paul and Jean-Claude were like twins, only a year apart, but they were very similar.

"Hey Aunt Isabel, and you, little cousin."

Jean-Claude was like a twin to his brother Jean-Paul, only he was a little taller as he was 19. He grinned broadly and waved. Straight teeth, slightly longer black hair, a mole on the side of his cheek, and blue eyes.

"Ah hello, Jean-Claude, have you gotten taller?" Mama exclaimed as she pulled the oxen to stop.

"Most likely but bending over in the forge doesn't help," Jean-Claude responded, looking over at me with curiosity and mischief. "Ah, and how is little cousin? Well, she is growing up fast!" he said with a slightly playful smile and listening attentively.

I peeped behind Mama's shoulder, smiling quickly and looking down.

"I'm good. I'm helping Mama," I said in a quiet voice.

Pierre and Jean both hopped into the cart at the back, and I mentally thanked them for their distraction.

"We need to leave before it gets dark." Jean said, wrapping himself in a cloak.

"Mama, do we have any apples?" Pierre said, rummaging through the bags.

"Alright, boys. We best be off to Domrémy. Farewell, thank you for everything," Mama said, giving a flick with the reins.

"Goodbye!"

"Goodbye cousins!"

I studied the endless fields as we returned home.

Herds of cows and sheep roamed the grasslands and lined borders of paddocks in the countryside. I glanced back, and once Neufchâteau was out of sight and travellers were scarce, I hopped down and began to jog.

"Oh Jehannette!" Mama said.

I could feel the momentary confused looks of my brothers, but too tired to tease, they nodded off. Mama relented; I suspect she was too exhausted to dissuade me also.

Ok, until the bridge with the creek.

I kept going.

Ok, over the hill and run as fast as you can down the descent.

Domrémy appeared in the hills, snuggled and hidden away with only the long ribbons of smoke rising and bending to the will of the wind, to announce the presence of our small village.

I ran back to the wagon and hopped onto the seat next to Mama, red faced and appreciating her silence.

The sun's last rays were fading, and the evening wind carried the familiar sweet scent of the beech trees. Unlike Neufchâteau, Domrémy was open; one could see the plain but sturdy houses spaciously spread out across the landscape.

The wagon slowed to a halt in front of our small cottage, and we clambered out. It was dark, and the shadows of the moonlight rays passed through the branches of the trees. The wind was cold, but I didn't feel it much; my body was warm after the exercise.

Mama and my brothers stretched their limbs and slowly began to unload the bags. Our breath came out like small clouds in the chilly air. Jean and Pierre carried all the heaviest sacks inside the house, while Mama directed them.

I came around to the front and detached the oxen from the wagon. As I patted them down, Pierre appeared next to me.

"I'll take this one," he said, motioning to the other ox. Silently, we both led them to the fields at the back of the house.

The fields at this time were filled with the white glow of the moon. Pierre opened the gate and we let the oxen pass through, freeing them into the fields. We watched as they fed on the grass and drank the water from a shallow wooden container.

The nights were always quiet in Domrémy. The full moon and stars kept us company as we both enjoyed the night air.

The silence was interrupted by Pierre, whose tired mood would never turn down an excuse to tease. "You must be hungry after all that running."

My eyes widened a little and I smiled, suppressing a chuckle.

"By the way, why do you do it?" he continued.

"Do what?"

"All this running?"

I shrugged. "I just like it."

"You like it?" he said, chuckling. "You're the strangest girl I've ever known." He messed up my hair and started walking back.

"You ask too many questions," I said, running after him back to the house.

Pierre and I raced into the back room and stopped short to find Jean sorting the grains into large barrels and Mama reheating a stew.

That evening, tired and spent from the laborious journey, we heartily warmed our hungry stomachs in silence. Mama's eyes were downcast with fatigue and she was having difficulty with her usual concentration in her prayers. Jean yawned loudly while Pierre slurped on his last bit of stew.

"And Papa?" Pierre inquired, as he leant back into the chair.

"He's gone for a meeting with Lord Robert," Jean said, elbow on the table and his fingers massaging his temple.

After washing the dishes and pots, the cottage was shrouded in darkness. The hearth was put out, and Pierre and Jean slumbered deeply, their feet hanging over their mattresses. Mama's gentle footsteps creaked as she went upstairs, her candle providing a halo of light that gently receded and left the downstairs ensconced in darkness.

I turned over in my bed, the beads of the rosary cool in my fingers. Intending to recite my usual prayers, I humbly fell into sleep's embrace.

8

ACCEPTANCE

"Be comforted, dear soul! There is always light behind the clouds."

– Little Women by Louisa May Alcott

Spring, 1426
Domrémy, France

A routine was established.

Night after night, I prayed.

Hail Mary full of grace… Dear God, please protect me and my family…

Our father, who is in heaven, blessed be thy name… Dear God, please bless the goat who gave birth to her babe today. Help the babe and mama…

Our father, who is in heaven… Dear God, help Pierre heal his arm. He injured it today… Please give me strength. Please give me courage to fulfil whatever you need to do.

But, one cool and quiet night, I sniffed and sat up.

But… why me? Leading an army? How am I meant to do this? Even after the Archangel Michael's words of trust and strength, my stomach turned and squirmed.

How can I face battle? How can I do this? A wave of dread made me shrink into a ball of fear, I felt my hands grow warm and my heartbeat begin to quicken.

After a few moments, I wiped my eyes with my sheets, looked up at the crucifix that hung on the opposite wall, at the foot of my bed.

A bizarre memory surfaced.

The Lady in the woods.

Angel Michael.

Their memory showered a precious silence to my mind that was in a tumultuous storm.

The birds quieted down… a deep bliss emanated in the air…

My heart began to slow down, and I could feel myself beginning to cool. I measured my breaths. Immersing myself in the quietness of my room, I stood up.

The wooden floor was cool against the soles of my feet. I made my way to the small window that peeked into the depths of the night sky. The stars hung like unmoving statues and were silent observers to this little world of ours. The moon was half full, but its pearlescent light shone tenderly on the young girl who huddled against the wall, looking up for some semblance of hope.

I heaved a sigh and felt the pull of sleep tugging my eyes downwards. I rubbed my foot from my pins and needles from standing in the cold. Then a thought came like a stroke of lightning.

Why am I so afraid?

Soldiers.

Battle.

An army.

I trudged back to my bed, my hands and feet welcoming the warmth of the covers. Curving into a foetal position, my mind lumbered between wakefulness and sleep until I heard the boots of papa overhead and the rooster crying at the break of day.

Dawn.

The cottage was spotless.

The floors were swept, the sacks of grains were moved to the barn, and everything was dusted and wiped to its rawest condition that it was almost as if the house was tumbled, scrubbed, washed and spat back out by the sea.

Mama was expecting visitors, and no one could say that Isabel d'Arc was a negligent hostess. In fact, mama's humble little kitchen looked decadent to our village eyes. A bouquet of flowers sat in the centre of the dining table as a ruler oversees their subjects, as underneath, many ceramic plates were filled with mama's lovely concoctions of recipes that she never flaunted but quietly offered as her gift of service. Fruit loaves decorated with freshly poached pears and apples, alongside bowls of cheeses and salted meats with freshly made bread.

A lot of bread. Yet the mother and daughter of the little grey cottage did not notice their hard work until the finale. For they spent the entire morning, alongside their usual chores to prepare for this day. But this was not a singular event, for the women of Domrémy would often meet with their daughters, and it was an entertaining afternoon of sewing, needlework and, most significantly, gossip.

The backroom was cleaned and swept to the dust mite. Several wooden chairs sparsely positioned around the small fireplace that was rarely lit.

"There," I said, satisfied, with my hands on my hips, looking at the whole scene. The previous night's sleep left my body unusually more tired, but the day began with many things to do that I quite lost myself in my chores.

"Jehannette, run to the barn and fetch some more chairs. I think we can leave some around the fire as well," Mama called from the dining room.

I sauntered through the cottage. "The backroom is ready," I said with a proud smile, picking up a slice of apple and chewing on it gaily.

"Excellent," Mama said, as she wiped her forehead with the back of her hand. Her cheeks were speckled with dots of sweat, and she turned away, continuing to wash the remaining dirty dishes from the busy morning. "The ladies will be here soon, Jehannette, don't tarry dear," she said, hunched over, her voice carrying through the cottage.

I dashed to the barn but stopped and quickly scrubbed my hands and face in the barrel of clean, rainwater. Invigorated, I shook my face to let the droplets of water fall, and I pushed the barn door open.

But it was already ajar. I froze mid-step, ignoring the water droplet falling over my cheek. Landing his hard brown eyes on me, Papa turned sharply with a flicker of irritation from the wall of tools across the barn.

I darted a quick look to my left where more chairs were stacked against the wall. Papa's eyes narrowed and his hostile glare made his brow wrinkle deeply into a T-shape. Tearing my eyes away, I snatched the chair from my left and scurried from the barn.

Thunder clapped overhead as I hurriedly made my way to the house, already hearing the melodious greetings of the guests. My lips trembled slightly, but I kept them firmly shut.

"Oh yes, I have so much news from my sister who lives in Neufchâteau!" a woman's voice said with a high melodious lark.

"Please, ladies sit, erm Jehannette?" mama's voice called.

I took a few deep breaths in the back room and quickly patted my cheek dry. *Mama needs me.* I mustered my best smile and appeared, awkwardly holding the chair. The ladies were all standing in front of our dining table, and all gushed when I approached.

"Ah, Jehannette!" said a short woman with a pixie face and a small turned up nose.

"Hello Angelique," I said meekly, placing the chair near the fireplace.

"Oh, my dear, you've grown so much!" said an elderly lady this time. She was a little hunched over, and her face was lined, and she had rather thin lips that formed into the sweetest u-shaped smile.

"Hello, Leura," I said, as she pinched my cheek affectionately, her wrinkled hands smooth and soft.

"Jehannette, why don't you show the girls where they can start their sewing," mama said, as she gathered more plates and placed them on the table.

The two young girls of the group looked at me expectedly. Isabel had long, windswept chestnut hair, with bright, inquisitive eyes. She always wore flowers in her hair, and her small fingers were always twiddling a small stem of leaves. Josephine on the other hand was a prim, proper young girl with velvet black hair, a snowlike complexion, and a freckled nose that she often wrinkled to her distaste.

"Let's go," I said, my merriment already dissolving my sadness into crumbs.

"Jehanne, do you know the game Jingling? The older girls were doing it last week and I want to try," Isabel said, as we sat down on the chairs, and they brought out their works. Isabel brought out pair of thick woollen socks and peered at them, biting her lip while Josephine flicked her long mane of black silk hair and proudly brought out a tunic with missing buttons.

"Isabel, I do think you're making it much more than it is," Josephine said, jutting her chin in the air.

"Maybe we can try," I chuckled. "What must we do?" I said, tugging on more strings of wool to start on my small beanie for Pierre.

Isabel's eyes were gently downcast as she explained. "Well, it's more of an outdoor game. You see, one person is blindfolded and must try to catch the other. I even saw the boys play something similar, and it does look like such fun."

Josephine peeked upwards at the mention of the boys. "And what were you doing looking at the boys?" she asked slyly as a fox.

Isabel blushed, "You needn't suggest anything Josy, my older brothers like to play and invite their friends along. That's all."

Josephine smugly smiled, hiding well her own curiosity.

Girls and boys... I thought to myself, remembering papa.

A pang of hurt resurfaced, "Well, I'm sure whatever game the boys were playing Pierre would know it too." I said in support of Isabel, who smiled at the response. I continued, "I see my brothers playing and the boys come to the barn and practise wrestling, sword fighting."

"Well, *my* sister, Claudette, and her friends, Charlotte and Marguerite, know all the lady-like games we can play. We can try your game, Isabel, of course, but Marguerite has a piece of die to play with, and I've seen it. It's jolly fun."

Josephine innocently turned back to her sewing as Isabel and I exchanged an exasperated smile.

More and more girls of Domrémy arrived with their mothers, and the role as the hostess' daughter bade me to adjust, fix and comfort the girls in many ways that I quite forgot my worries and papa's awkward encounter.

It was only after I realised my woollen ball of string was running low, that I ventured to the dining room full of mothers and grandmothers chatting animatedly while they tended their needlework. Only, I noticed a line of conversation that stopped me in my tracks, and I leant by the empty doorframe and peeked inside.

"—and the English army. Apparently they've hired a group of deadly mercenaries from the east, the Holy Roman Empire!" Angelique said, sitting across my mother who was having a private conversation. "Truly?" mama gasped.

"Indeed," Angelique said with solemnity.

"And the King's army. How will they be prepared for this?" my mother said, her linen tunic lay on her lap, quite forgotten.

Angelique brought her hand up to her forehead in exasperation "Oh the French, they are a *lost* cause!"

I leaned in closer, straining to hear more.

Angelique continued, "I hear, gamblers and prostitutes fill the ranks!"

Maman was shocked, she shook her head with disappointment, and she stopped short as she spotted me peeking through the open doorway.

In a hurried tone, she said, "Jehannette, my dear, go sit with your friends, darling."

Startled, I regained myself and wordlessly held up the small ball of wool.

Mama understood quickly and gave me another. Sitting with the young girls again, I heard their voices, but my mind was elsewhere.

The army… Papa never lets us travel if the army was camping nearby… Everybody I knew did not venture near the army… It was like looking for trouble… and I'm going to be among those men … lead those men…

I felt nauseous and dizzy.

"Jehanne?"

My head snapped up.

"Oh, I'm sorry, I get quite lost in my daydreams sometimes," I smiled, half-embarrassedly.

The group of girls blinked dumbly, "Has your mother talked to you about your period yet?" Isabel asked tentatively. She had a searching look in her eyes.

"Uh, oh yes, mine hasn't come yet. I think I'm a late bloomer." I shrugged, colour rising into my face and quickly looking down again to my work.

"Well, *my* sister has hers and *she* says the few days are painful, but mama made her a chamomile water, and she felt instantly better!" Josephine said with a little jiggle to her head.

The other young girls *ooh* and *ahhed* to Josephine's contentment, and Isabel looked over at me with an amused smile and a joking side-eye roll. I bit my lip to hide my smile, and the rest of the afternoon I was brought back to the happy and lively company of young girls their entertaining conversation.

Later that night, I kicked away my bedsheets in frustration.

Why can't my mind just go to sleep? I thought miserably. That night, my fears were wide awake, and again, my frustration was boiling over like a water pot.

I laid back down.

Commanding an army of… barbarians and gamblers?

I turned.

Me? In command of rough men?

I tossed.

What if they're just like papa? They won't see me as a general… They won't respect me… They won't listen me… This is just no use!

Papa's encounter that day added to my mountain of worries and hurts. Then unconsciously, I fumbled for the rosary on my bedside. I laid back down and my fingers traced over the small beads of the rosary. As I had done for many nights now, I just started to pray.

Dear God, please help me… Dear God, please give me the strength… But a small thought disturbed my rhythm. *But you heard what Angelique said… The French army is a lost cause… it is filled with mercenaries… all kinds of brutes…*

The girls helped me forget about my troubles and papa during the night, but overhearing Angelique and mama talk… I laid there reminiscing on their words.

They're right. The army's always been a warning of danger. The villagers never liked the army nearby, for robberies and fights would break out. And the brazen groups of women that followed… But this war, it's just not stopped… the army is necessary…

That night, sleep slipped its fingers under my troubled mind, and carried me, whirling me, into the unconscious depths of my soul.

The field was filled with beautiful white flowers. My hands brushed against their petals as I walked through the long stems. The sweet smell of summer lingered in the wind, and the sun was shining brightly, casting everything in a beautiful golden glow. Nearby I could hear the trickling of water from a creek.

All around me, the golden hue of the sunlight became brighter, stronger. But I wasn't afraid. I didn't flinch from its rising warmth; it felt like I was wrapped in a comforting, warm blanket. Everything around me glowed with a yellow brilliance. And then I heard a clear and pleasant voice. I looked up to the heavens.

"Don't be afraid. I'm always going to be with you. I'll always protect you."

As quick as the blink of an eye, everything became blurry, and I was surrounded by large and stocky silhouettes. They glinted as they walked past. Their armour was stained with mud and dirt.

In the gaps of the moving silhouettes, I saw amongst it all, a woman. Her auburn hair was cut short and tucked behind her ears. She spoke with a group of haggard-looking captains, their faces smeared with blood and mud. Yet there was grit in their eyes.

As the woman spoke, the men's eyes grew. Vivacity. Strength.

The woman held their focus, as they hung on to her every word. Her words, though I couldn't hear, fuelled their fervour. Their tenacity. Their jaws tense and nodding with passion. Their loyalty could not be denied but their strength was indomitable.

The woman's eyes were deep and mystical as stars, and her armour was white.

She glowed with majesty.

With divinity.

I suddenly woke up in my room in the early hours of the morning. Stunned and overcome by the vivid dream, a realisation arose within me like a flower.

I am not afraid anymore.

Life continued to be a stream of visits from angels and farm work.

Since the end of the harvest, my brothers helped my papa in the fields. I wouldn't see them until dinner time, and I resumed helping Mama, especially in the garden and with the farm animals.

My mama was the safeguard of seeds for our produce. She usually kept them in precious large sacks in the house or the barn. Ever since

I was little, she taught me how to sow the seeds, and plant and care for the garden to harvest vegetables. By thirteen, I managed the vegetable garden by myself behind our small home, and it was covered by bulbous bodies of pumpkins, cauliflowers, and cabbages peeking out of the rich green foliage.

The next day after my dream, I awoke to feel refreshed and spritely as a sunflower. "Mama will need some vegetables for today's supper," I muttered to myself as I dug into the earth with a small shovel. The dream had left me feeling rejuvenated and my faith had been restored.

But it left me pondering. I felt like my life was divided.

Like a coin, it was split into two faces that never met. The closest to my heart was my family. I had chores to help sustain our family; I worked the garden and cared for the animals. On the other side of this coin, my life was uprooted by the angels and their prophecies of what was to come and my duty.

Yet this divide felt like having a secret friend, a glimpse of the world that I would never have understood or imagined. And during this time, I kept this secret. I kept this silent call of destiny to myself.

"Jehannette!"

I snapped my head up, feeling snatched away from my reverie.

Pierre came panting from the fields. His curly hair bounced, and his footsteps heavily landed as he slowed.

"We are working in the fields today. Papa needs you to lead the sheep to the southerly part. Can you do that?'

"Yes, I can help," I said, standing up and bundling the load of ripe vegetables in my arms.

⚜

The sheep advanced but slowly up the hill with the boulders of rocks. I glanced up to the boulder where Archangel Michael appeared and smiled to myself. *Now, I don't even flinch when they appear,* I thought to myself amusedly.

Since Archangel Michael's visit, the angels visited frequently and not only did they give advice and instructions on how to prepare for my role, but it became a time when I could confide in them about anything. I always felt comfortable in their presence as it was filled with advice of all kinds, so I felt free to ask what was in my heart.

The conversations ranged from explanations of nature to ordinary daily life issues, and also how I should behave or what to say in certain situations. They were patient and reminiscent of a parent, explaining and instructing their child with the utmost attention and care.

Ever since our conversations became so frequent, and my questions received such openness, I felt my trust opening and I felt the inkling to share a wounded feeling that was surfacing that I had never openly addressed before.

Papa. I always felt a rejection from him, and I never understood why. Why did he dislike me so much?

For as long as I could remember, papa was always a stern and serious man. He always spoke in a serious, low voice, and his words carried a heavy weight. No one dared to interrupt him. With my brothers, he talked of the farm and the tasks of upholding a prosperous farmland like ours. He did not acknowledge my existence in any form. My brother's playfulness and my mother's affection always masked his distance from me, but I nevertheless felt his rejection.

Since that day in the barn, I convinced myself.

It's always been this way. Come on, toughen up.

But a part of my heart was hurt and rejected. It did not stay quiet, and my mind replayed the sharp censure and immediate dislike from the memory. It was like a wheel that endlessly circulated and repeated the scene before my mind's eye.

That afternoon was cool, and I wore a shawl over my bodice as I ushered the straggling sheep up the hill. Saint Marguerite stood at the peak of the hill; her white dress illuminated brightly from the deep shade of forest. In the midst of our conversation, the memory that pressed his rejection weighed unconsciously on my heart, and I found myself quiet and taciturn.

"Jehanne, you have some worries, do you want to share them?" Angel Margaret asked, her serenity was like a still lake.

My voice became small and mouse-like, "I... yes... I want to know... about my father... Why does my father dislike me so much?"

She sat down on a boulder and motioned me to sit next to her. Rarely did I see her serenity broken but instead her face turned resolute. We sat together, looking over the view of the fields, the trail of smoke from the cottages of the Domrémy, and the distant rolling hills that looked like giant green orbs all clustered together.

"Do not spare your worries on your father, Jehanne. He is a man of his time. This will not matter in the depth and longevity of your life."

After a moment, she added, "When the time comes for you to leave, it will be easier for you. This way you won't be so attached to him. You worry enough for your mother."

In the end, she was right. My relationship with my mother was the complete opposite to that of my father. My mother was very sweet, loving, and slow to anger. Very few times I saw her agitated or upset, and that was when she saw children who were uncared for. She was a kind, Christian lady, who set a good example of community service, always helping and teaching others. She would advise and assist the new mothers in the village, especially tending to their young children. The women in town respected her and they always came to ask her for advice; they knew she was a trustworthy woman who would not divulge their problems. I smiled thinking of her. She rarely spoke at home but did a lot of good deeds and loved and cared for her children deeply.

A silence between us ensued.

Saint Marguerite turned from the view and peered over to me with a knowing smile. "Do you remember when you let the chickens out of the penthouses?"

I stared at her dumbly for a moment, then trickle by trickle, inch by inch, the memories came flooding back to me. My mouth fell open and my back straightened up as if jolted by lightning. "I... oh yes! I was uh...

maybe 5 years old. Perhaps 6, and I accidently left the chicken penthouses open, and they were all scattered about the front garden..." I trailed, laughing lightly to think of such a thing happening now.

"Yes, and what did your father do, Jehanne?"

Birds cried in the distance as I recalled the event, "well... mama was so afraid... She was clinging onto Pierre because she didn't want..."

I looked up to Saint Marguerite.

"She didn't want?" Saint Marguerite said, looking at the view of Domrémy. Her eyes scanning the hills, waiting for my response.

"She didn't want me to be punished," I finished.

"Yes," she nodded.

"And... well, Pierre at that age was about 12 and he looked so worried, and... now that I remember he was taller than mama!" I lightly chuckled.

The scene kept unfolding "And papa got his belt... and he... I remember I held up my hands, my little hands, and he..." The field was silent with the sounds of sheep blaring in the background.

"He didn't do it," I finished.

Saint Marguerite turned to look at me, and nodded, "Yes, you see Jehanne, when he saw your little hands held up, something in him shifted. When you held up your hands so quietly and bravely, you helped him see sense. Yes, your father is distant, even antagonistic, but he is a good provider for his family. And you see, even if he doesn't show it, he has a good heart."

I nodded.

"And it is important for you to remember this for your future. Men in the army will respect you because of your bravery. Because of your fearlessness and mettle. Because of your strength."

<hr>

That night by the fire, mama and I sat on the corner of the dining table. Mama was an excellent needlewoman, and her skills captivated me enough that I practised with her every evening after supper, learning the different points of embroidery and mending clothes. She spoke softly, barely above a whisper softly, looking over my work, advising how I could improve here and there.

Pierre and Jean sat in the opposite corner working with leather, scraping the leather over and over, with repetitive and monotonous movements until it was smooth and soft. Papa was in the far corner of the room fixing a wooden tool.

Looking at this picture, I knew my mother and brothers would always love and care for me. And having the angels as my friends and guides, I felt like my life was complete and safe.

And as for my father, I remembered at that moment to accept him as he was.

Just a man of his time.

9

MARRIAGE AND THE MIDSUMMER FESTIVAL

Summer, 1426
Domrémy, France

*A*ngelique and her daughter, Isabel, were simple, hardworking folk who, like us, lived in Domrémy. Their home was small, made from wood and stone, and was beside a creek that was often visited by the locals for a swim in the summer. Isabel's father, Renaud, was a kind, gentle man who took care of his little family with his humble profession as a labourer for the Lord of Domrémy. They lived off the land and the small livestock that pastured their block of land. Their arrival to Domrémy was a stark reminder of the war that rumbled outside of our safe little sphere. Isabel was only 6 years old when her family from the north migrated to Domrémy. Their village received a warning that incoming English armies had been spotted nearby, and with naught but the clothes on their backs, they flew and never returned.

On the first day of their arrival, mama brought me along with her to visit the newcomers of the village, with a basket of some jam, strips of cold meat, bulbous vegetables, a few eggs and a loaf of bread.

We waited after mama knocked on their front door that was wide open. Angelique at that time had dark, long blond hair that that was braided over her shoulder and walked down the long dark corridor with a candle. It was dusk.

"Oh, good afternoon. I'm sorry we were not expecting visitors," Angelique said in her northern accent that was much stronger. Stepping out of the hallway, we could see the dark circles under her eyes.

"Oh, no, I've just come to give a gift of welcome. I'm a neighbour, my name is Isabel d'Arc, I live on the southern side of the village, and this is my daughter Jehanne. We know that you have just arrived, and I'd just like to offer a gift and my welcome." Mama held out the little basket, and Angelique looked quite stupefied.

A little cap then appeared at Angelique's elbow. The little girl had rounded blue eyes, and her mother's pixie nose. Angelique looked at mama's gift for a long moment, speechless for a moment.

"Thank you," she said. Her voice was hoarse as she wanted to keep it steady.

"And who is this?" Mama said pleasantly.

"Oh, this is my daughter Isabel. She's six," Angelique said, peering down affectionately at her daughter.

"Ah, my daughter Jehanne is also six. Maybe, once your settled Isabel, Jehanne can show you all the lovely places to play."

I nodded and smiled to the shy little cap with the big blue eyes.

"We know you must settle in, but please call on me if you need anything. I live in the house with the vertical roof, can't miss it." Mama smiled with all her goodwill and took my hand.

"Thank you, thank you very much," Angelique put her arm around her daughter as she held the basket with a sad, but grateful smile.

As we walked away, I turned back and waved.

A moment later, a small hand in the dark doorframe waved back.

Isabel's home had flourished quite beautifully as the years passed. The house had a lovely front garden with posies, lavenders and sunflowers that Isabel often made grew and picked to make garlands for her friends. The walls were covered in climbing wild roses and they jauntily frolicked in the breeze. On a particularly sunny afternoon, mama and I walked to this small cottage that had their door wide open.

It was the day of weaving and embroidery, and that afternoon, we were to meet Isabel's house.

"Jehanne!" Isabel appeared at the door with a bright smile, showing off her large bunny rabbit teeth.

She embraced me and embraced mama who offered a loaf of bread and some cheese.

"Aunt Isabel, thank you for coming. Mama will be happy to see you. Please come inside." Her dark brown hair that was in two plaits swished as she turned down the corridor. The house had a long, dark hallway with the first doorframe to the right opening to a large hearth, a table, and a kitchen. Chairs were formed into one group, and another smaller group.

That afternoon, the little house by the creek received mothers, daughters, and of course young babies and toddlers who had no one else to care for them. We younger girls sat on the floor by the fire as there were not enough chairs, adorned with our maroon caps and our needlework on our laps. The mothers sat at the dining table, talking of the latest news from other villages, some with their babies in their laps or their skilled hands fiercely embroidering sparc beanies and gloves for the colder months.

Isabel who was introverted by nature, sat next to me, and today we both enjoyed the banter of the older girls. However, on this particular afternoon, the conversation turned to matters of the heart—marriage.

Charlotte, who was a tall, gangly girl of sixteen who had curly red hair that peeked out from under her cap and a pronounced hook nose. As she embroidered a pair of thick cotton trousers, she grimaced and put the work down and massaged her hands. She was a cook's helper in Lord Robert's manor just outside of Domrémy, peeling and cutting vegetables all day did not agree with her.

"Oh, this will not do. I can't sew for my fingers get so cramped," she muttered and looked consolingly at her fingers.

"Never mind that, warm them by the fire and they'll be better. They just need some rest," Isabel said, in her soft-spoken tone.

Charlotte was touched by her sentiments and reached over and patted Isabel's knee affectionately.

"Oh, you sweet thing, I so wish I had a sister!" she proclaimed, rubbing her hands over the fire as if invigorating them.

"I have three younger brothers, and they can be such a menace," she said, pursing her lips and not taking her eyes away from the fire.

Maribelle and Magdalene who sat on either side of Charlotte were also sixteen.

"My mama says boys can be a source of heartbreak or happiness, and one must practise intuitive instinct to sift the good qualities for a husband," Anne said, an older girl with cropped short hair, whose fingernails were rimmed with earth, and whose complexion was darkened from the hours labouring in the sun.

Maribelle chortled.

Magdalene said, "I'm sorry Anne, but it is just too difficult! How can we young ladies sift through the bachelors if there aren't any to choose from?" she exclaimed in an exasperated whisper.

"You are too picky!" Anne said, extending her neck high and jutting her chin out.

"Girls."

All heads snapped in unison to Isabel's mama, Angelique, who suddenly appeared behind us.

Holding a jug of water, "Does anyone want some water or bread?"

As if breathing a sigh of relief, the girls softened and shook their heads, and gushed.

"No, thank you, Aunt Angelique," Anne said.

"Thank you, Aunt Angelique," Charlotte and Magdalene said.

Angelique passed back to the mothers.

"What do you think, girls?" Maribelle said, who also seemed to enjoy the banter between her friends.

Isabel and I looked at each other.

"Well, maybe some of the boys are not totally invested to find wives just yet... Maybe their attention is diverted elsewhere," Isabel shrugged as if sharing the most innocent suggestion but thinking with a wisdom well-beyond her years.

Their reactions were all particular to their characters, Magdalene's side cheek pinched upwards as she half-smiled and flipped her hair back with a swish of her hand. Anne raised one eyebrow and cooly regarded Isabel with silent approval. Maribelle shrugged as if the answer neither enlightened nor scandalised her.

Now, Charlotte's reaction was rather curious, for her eyes widened, and she looked sharply down as if many thoughts were racing their course.

The fire crackled in the silence that ensued, then... "I didn't see your brother today, Jehanne," Charlotte said, raising her quizzical, brown eyes on me briefly and continued massaging her hands by the fire.

I felt my cheeks redden as the older girls peered over at me but also because it was no secret that Charlotte's beau was non-other than my brother, Pierre. Who, to Charlotte's lack of luck, had no idea of her existence.

Now, as the cook's helper in the manor, Charlotte would often see Pierre deliver the salted meats and produce from our farm. Pierre, in turn, was blissfully unaware of Charlotte's less than subtle staring.

The girls went quiet and looked at Charlotte then at me.

"Oh, I think he was busy in the field," I said simply, shrugging my shoulders hoping to change the subject as quickly as possible.

"Will he be at the manor next week?" she said, looking up at me.

At this, I felt a pang of conflict. I didn't like revealing intimate things about Pierre or Jean. Maribelle and Magdalane smiled but kept their eyes on their embroidery.

"I'm not sure," I responded.

"But he does deliver them still to the Lord of Domrémy?"

"Yes, I believe so."

"And does he usually work by himself, or does your other brother help?"

"Erm, well both my brother Jean and Pierre work in the fields—" but before I could finish, Charlotte interrupted.

"—Well, I just… think he's such a good worker. And has *he* spoken of marriage? He's so strong and reliable. He would be a catch for any girl."

"I… I haven't heard him speak of it… no," I bit my lip, hoping her line of questioning would end.

Charlotte nodded, and went back to her embroidery, and feeling safe to do so I did as well.

"And are you *sure* he will come next week?"

"Charlotte," I started, my patience running short, "I think you should talk to Pierre and get to know him yourself. I am sure he'll want to talk to you. He is friendly enough."

At this, Charlotte looked as if she had just been slapped, and her cheeks turned almost the same colour as her hair.

"Oh, well, I–I believe I will– you know, it's only a matter of time, you see—"

"—You see, Charlotte, now you *have* to talk to him," Magdalene said, slyly.

"Time is going by Charlotte. The chase begins," Maribelle said.

The group erupted into giggles, but Charlotte just rolled her eyes, and began to ferociously sew as if to make up for her plans that were somehow thwarted.

But Anne chimed in, rather matter-of-factly, "Well, *I* think Phillip is the most handsome boy in town."

Like a ball thrown to divert a group of puppies, Maribelle, Magdalene, and Charlotte started a lively debate on who was the most handsome. Grateful that the attention was not on me, Isabel and I sewed and listened shrewdly to their conversation, entertained by chit chat of the older girls.

Then Magdalene turned to me and asked, "What about you, Jehanne, have you thought on marriage yet?" Magdalene was quite a pretty girl, and she knew it. She was blessed with smooth and shiny bronze hair that tumbled down her shoulders, and long eyelashes that she liked to flutter to her satisfaction.

Her question took me by surprise, "Oh, erm, me…? Erm…"

"Is your heart set on anyone?" she questioned, looking back down at her embroidery.

I shrugged. "No, not really, I think I'm still young."

"Young? You are fourteen now. My mother was married at fifteen. Listen closely, Jehanne." She looked up from her embroidery and leant forward to steady herself and not be overheard by the mother's table nearby.

"It is better that you start thinking of someone. Make some plans or you will end up alone, and you *don't* want that," her voice was laced with secrecy.

And to my surprise, Maribelle and Charlotte nodded in agreement. Anne said nothing.

"Well, what about devotion to God?" I asked.

The older girls all stopped their sewing and looked at each other as if they hadn't considered that thought.

Anne spoke, "You are quite right, Jehanne, and there are many ways to be of service to God. There is being a wife and taking care of one's children, but there is also devoting one's life to the Church and helping the community. Neither is better nor worse than the other," she added with a slight frown to Magdalene.

I didn't say anything, but I knew my life was going to be different.

"Oh, well yes, yes you're quite right Anne dear," Magdalene said, waving her hands in resignation. "The church is an option as well, because well, marriage is expensive! It takes years to build a sufficient dowry, *and*" she waved her index finger in the air, "you must find a good husband," Magdalene said with a dry smile.

"Magdalene, do you have a beau? Do you think you will get married soon?" I said, my voice piping up.

"Well, *I* want to," she said, putting her hand over her chest, "but my father's profit from the land is not enough, and he needs a few more years to build up a dowry. My brothers are still young, so it's up to me to help mama and papa." She finished and looked over to the fire. Silence followed as Charlotte and Maribelle both peered over to their friend, who quietly picked up her knitting needles and embroidered three small woollen scarves—shouldering her responsibility without complaint but with a price.

And that was the sad reality for us.

Our work on the land was the basis of our lives. Marriage was a costly matter, and always second to our work on the field. Magdalene was a fair young girl with three younger brothers, but she had to put aside her own wishes to help her family in the fields so they could produce goods and food to live. And by marrying, she also would need to have a dowry, which was usually livestock.

After a moment, Charlotte's voice chimed in softly. "Has anyone seen the lavenders coming through this season? They've been so lovely. I'm drying some to put in a sachet."

And like that, the conversation returned to more pleasant things— the flowers in bloom and festivities for the midsummer celebration these coming days.

As all the fields around Domrémy were full in full growth, harvest was coming underway and to celebrate the village organised a bonfire, feasts, and music to reap the reward of their labour.

Maribelle, a girl of fifteen years with wavy blond hair, and dark button eyes said, "Well, I'm looking forward to the midsummer festival as I don't need to help in the fields anymore. I stay indoors and help mama cook," she said reclining back, finishing her sewing with a satisfied smile.

"Maribelle, please do ask your mama to make her grape juice and cake. We so love them," Charlotte said, coiling up the extra string over her two fingers as the dusk was approaching, and the festivities were on everyone's mind—there was much to do.

Each family had their speciality, and we always shared our rewards with one another; it was tradition.

That week in June, our midsummer festival was on the lips of every Dom-rémy villager.

The days were warm and long. Papa and my brothers spent the days collecting the grains, and they returned home every night—haggard and dirty—ate their supper in silence and went to bed straightway.

The garden was also abounding with vegetables that mama and I were on our feet the entire day of midsummer-eve, preparing and cooking for our celebratory event. On midsummer morning, we awoke at dawn to a clear sky and a certain excitement in the air. The celebrations began after Sunday mass, and the villagers came together in the town square where there was a giant, gnarly oak tree. Its large branches stretched overhead, and there, we set up a few long tables and ensconced ourselves comfortably under its protection.

The fathers of each household brought a substantial amount of kindle, and we all helped set up the bonfire, the tables, and chairs. Soon enough, a small troupe of musicians arrived and began to play sweet and soft tunes as mamas from each household brought chairs, jugs of grape juice, and cakes to enjoy for the afternoon.

"Jehanne!" I voice called out. I turned from the tables and saw Isabel and Josephine running towards me.

"Jehanne, you must come. The girls are making garlands made from flowers and they're dancing around the tree!" Isabel said, the excitement of the day brightening her bright blue eyes.

"Come, Jehanne, they are having *such* fun," Josephine said, reaching over and tucking a flower behind my ear. I looked at mama questioningly who sat with other mothers of the village, and mama nodded.

"Ok, let's go!" I said and we raced together to the tree that had a group of girls holding hands and circling around the wide girth of the trunk—their laughter echoing high up over the canopies. Nearby, Charlotte, Anne, Margaret, Maribelle, and some other older girls were sitting surrounded with an abundance of flowers, making crowns and bracelets.

Usually after twilight, the lively notes of music filled the night air, and young children frolicked and traipsed around the large oak tree, playing over it, creating whatever fantastical adventures they imagined, while the villagers cleared a space for dancing.

At this hour, mama had gone home to reheat many of our dishes, and I went with her to help. We made multiple trips from our cottage to the town centre, carrying them with thick woollen gloves and covering them to preserve their heat. Mama made her infamous roasted duck and vegetables, her chickpea and lentil stew, and pumpkin and cheese pies. She even found time to make sweet pastries and dried fruit loaves with poached fruits—for they were delectable delights that young children enjoyed immensely, and mama couldn't deny them.

The tables were gradually overfilled with other platters of vegetables and meats, breads, cheeses and fruits. By dusk, the men of the village had created a fire at least the height of a doorframe, and the tables were filled with the food we worked from the land, and at that moment, we did not feel the limits of poverty. In fact, we felt rich in our abundance.

The older girls, Margaret, Maribelle and Charlotte, were adorned with flower garlands, and sang and danced beautifully. It was no wonder that they blushed as deep as the pink flowers in their hair when Jean's group of friends, Leonard and Bertrand, approached to dance. And it seemed that the musicians supported their motives, for the tune was lively and eventually enticed the whole village to participate. I even saw Pierre slowly dancing with mama, both reddened from laughing, but their merriment could not be denied. Then the villagers formed a circle, and like fluttering butterflies, we held hands and sang local songs that the stars overhead would have thoroughly enjoyed. The elderly held the babies in their arms and sat on the rim of the square, talking quietly, and enjoying this scene of life with contemplative contentment. It was only when our feet were sore and our throats were parched that we all sat down and enjoyed our meal, laughing and enjoying the sweetness that life had to offer.

These nights help me remember the joy of simplicity. That happiness was what we gave and shared in our cocooned village. We celebrated, we laughed, and we were happy—but little did we know that everything was about to change.

10

THE ENGLISH

"Beauty, youth, good fortune, even love itself, cannot keep pain, loss and sorrow, from the most blessed. For into each life, some rain must fall, some days must be dark..."

– Little Women by Louisa May Alcott

Winter, 1426
Domrémy, France

*M*ichaelmas came and passed, the days saw the snow slowly melting, and spring was beginning to unfurl its greenery and flowers.

The families of each Domrémy home all had very active ears that sought everything and anything that was happening outside the village, and it was one afternoon that mama and I returned from visiting a local elder, Leura, that we first heard of the most disconcerting news that was to change our lives.

"The English army are nearby?" Mama said, her voice high with incredulity.

Leura was a spirited, old lady, who despite her slow movements did not diminish her vivacity. Her husband had died, but her son, Oliver, had married and carried on the farm with his wife, Caroline, and their baby.

"Yes," she said firmly, "Oliver met with a traveller the day before yesterday. The traveller reported that other towns have needed to evacuate, and we should do the same." Mama and I looked at each other.

"Can you be sure to trust this stranger?" Mama said, her eyes were furrowed with worry.

"Isabel, I feel it in my bones. Something is coming and it ain't good. I *always*, trust m'feelings, Isabel. Oliver is talking about staying, but psh! I'll take Caroline and the babe even if I request it from the Lord of Domrémy hisself!" Leura said, her hand firmly closing around her walking stick, showing the white knuckles of her veins.

"And Isabel, make sure your boys don't be getting no ideas. Them boys from town can be so reckless!" she said, squinting one eye and pursing her lips.

"Jacques is a good father. He will not let the boys make such reckless decisions," mama said, trying to comfort the old lady, but it seemed that she herself needed to be comforted.

When we left, I took hold of mama's hand and squeezed it, looking into her eyes, both knowing what we were both thinking.

Our home.

The same unsettling rumours continued.

A day after our visit to Leura, Jean came back from the fields at dusk. It was supper time, and papa had not arrived yet.

"Come dear, supper is served," Mama said, serving Jean with a generous ladle of vegetable and legume stew as Pierre sat in front of the hearth, vigorously cleaning his boots with swift movements.

Jean's face was hard as he silently sat down. Mama began to serve the other plates, and I was passing them along the table.

"I've just heard from Leonard that his father just came back from Vaucouleurs and they've raised the alarm. The English have been spotted. They're laying siege on the villages in the region."

Mama and I stopped and turned to look at him. Pierre paused scrubbing his boots.

"I think we need to speak with papa. We need to do something," he finished.

"I also heard the same thing from the manor," Pierre said, shaking his head. "Everyone is worried. We haven't heard anything from Lord Robert, though," Pierre said with a grimace.

"Leonard and Bertrand… they want to stay. They want to stay and fight," Jean said, looking up at Pierre, mama, and me. "And if they stay, so will I."

Mama's face fell, and my mouth dropped open.

"Papa will not allow it," Pierre spoke first, straightening up.

"I know, but we can't just let the English come and raid our land, our belongings!" Jean said, exasperated.

"I agree, and I'll stay with you bu—" but Pierre's words were drowned out by the door suddenly bursting open and papa's heavy boots stepped into the house like thunder. Jean did not say anything but turned back around to the table and ate his supper soberly. My brothers knew much better than to confront papa, but it was only a matter of time before urgency could overpower their filial respect. Yet I knew it would not be long until papa would act. He would have heard these rumours as they were spreading faster than a flea on a horse. Papa and Jean were both very pragmatic in these matters, but papa was more stoic.

That night we supped, we cleaned, and we acted as if nothing was amiss. But on everyone's mind was the English army, and what we were to do.

It was only the next day that papa came home. His hard log-brown eyes addressed Pierre and Jean.

"Boys, I've been told of a town meeting this eve. The Lord of Domrémy, Lord Robert de Bautremont, has heralded a council. As you've heard, the English have been seen and we will make the decision to leave or to stay. Jean, Pierre, you will wait for me when I come back."

"Yes, papa."

"Yes, papa."

Papa nodded and left straightway, shutting the door and resigning us to fate's awful call to wait.

And just like that, we found ourselves face to face with the war on our very doorstep.

The next day, a sombre atmosphere fell like a black cloud onto our small village. For it turns out that the town meeting did not reach a unanimous decision, and this in turn sparked a panic and discontentment to grow very quickly in Domrémy. Neighbours were frequently stopping by the house, and the talk of the English was on everyone's lips, and it felt that we were swayed and pulled constantly to the whim of each visitor's own fantastical tale.

The king has abandoned the kingdom, and we are all doomed...

The French lords are secretly in a pact with the Burgundians...

We have spies in the village, and they've poisoned the wells...

The English plan to capture and enslave us...

Neighbourhoods organised a watch group for the next few days and nights, and we to farm and continue our lives as best we could, not knowing when we would hear the bell and the screams.

Time was passing.

And we were not doing any better for it.

On the second night of the meeting, papa returned tired, frustrated, and one thing I rarely saw—fearful.

Jean and Pierre stayed up until papa arrived from his meetings, and I listened from my room.

"—the Lord of Domrémy, he's put in a difficult position. None of the higher lords of the land can help. They've told him we are alone."

"Alone? How can we be alone, papa?" I heard Pierre say.

"There are no soldiers to send to our region. The nobles have spent a lot of their money on other sieges, and they keep losing. And they leave us with one grim decision, to sacrifice our homes, our land, our livelihood or to stay and fight."

Silence ensued.

"I voted to leave," papa stated, "but there are some in the village, especially young farmers, like that Oliver, to stay and fight." I feel like I could see papa massage the rim of his nose with his fingers.

Jean's voice was low as he spoke, "But papa... we can't just run away."

"You think it cowardly to run away, Jean?" Papa said sharply.

"No, papa. I just think—"

"No, Jean, we are all dead if we stay. Do not get caught in this frenzy to prove yourself. Protect your family, yes, but if we can leave, we leave."

"Yes, papa," Jean said.

"When is the next meeting?" Pierre asked.

"It is tomorrow eve. Tomorrow, all family members are to attend to vote. To stay or to leave. God willing, we leave."

We all felt the strain of this decision. No one wanted to leave, but did we have a choice? At that time, no one knew what to do with this war that seemed to go on forever.

Finally, the time came for the decision to be made. At dusk, the local village church was filled with peasant families standing before the podium where the Lord of Domrémy stood, waiting for the villagers to settle down and begin.

The crowd softly murmured, and I craned my neck and looked around. I recognised a few familiar faces. My close friend Isabel, and her mother and father. Leura, and her son, Oliver, with his wife Caroline holding their baby. Our neighbour, Claude, and his wife and sons and daughters. Even some of Jean's friends, Leonard and Bertrand, with their families.

The Lord of Domrémy cleared his throat, clearly signalling the time to begin. The Lord Robert de Baurtemont had an egg-shaped head with a double chin and was dressed in fine velvet tunic and hoses. His shoulder-length white hair fell limply under a black chaperon, and although he hadn't addressed the audience, he was sweating profusely and wetted his lips multiple times. The lord would often carry a handkerchief with which he used often for his coughing fits.

"Well, he doesn't look like the picture of inspiration," Pierre muttered to me as we stood with the entire community cramped in the crowd.

The audience all of a sudden became subdued and the lord began to speak. "Villagers of Domrémy, we have gathered you all today for a grave matter. It is confirmed that the English are in our region, and they were spotted nearby. Our Duke and King cannot help us now in our moment of need. The sad reality is there is no help from anyone." Lord Robert of Domrémy lifted a handkerchief to cover his mouth while a coughing fit passed.

The lord cleared his throat. "I implore you all to consider your families, your wives, sons and daughters that need you. The best option is to flee. I know there are some who wish to stay but be warned you will be alone." His tone relayed defeat.

A voice from the crowd called out, "It would be suicidal to stay and protect the town from the English. We'd be slaughtered like cattle!" It was Claude, and he nodded to everyone looking for support.

Papa nodded openly, and other villagers murmured in agreement.

Leonard and Bertrand were also in the crowd, and they held their faces up inscrutably. I looked up to my brother, Jean, who watched impassively the whole scene. His jaw was set, and his shoulders were stiffened when the next man Oliver spoke. Oliver had bright blond cropped hair with a short beard, and in attitude he thought himself aware and intelligent, but in years and in reality, he was nothing more than three and twenty years with an inherited title from his father, and little to no experience compared to the hardened farmers like papa.

"But our homes! Our land! We can't just give this up. The English will destroy everything!" Oliver's cheeks that were ridden with acne flushed when he finished and I could see Leura, Oliver's elderly mother, shaking her head and looking at her son with scrutiny.

A few young men called out in agreement. This time Jean's friend, Leonard, called out, "Eh, what about our stock, our produce? We will come back to nothing!" Leonard had a handsome face with thick, brown locks and sharp, obsidian-coloured eyes. And as they say that the eyes are the window to the soul, this rang true for Leonard as his verve was too strong. His will too robust.

Papa's nostrils flared as he stared with a deadpan expression to Lord of Domrémy, who raised his hands to assuage their calls.

He cleared his voice, "There are not enough weapons or men who can cope with a contingent of the English army," the lord continued. "I must implore you all, for the safety of our families, to spare your sons, spare your lives. We just do not have the manpower."

The young men in the crowd shuffled uncomfortably and looked around for support. Out of the corner of my eye, I saw mama's hand gently grasp Jean's forearm, and she looked up to him with such tenderness that in that instant I could see Jean's hardened resolve melt.

Leonard and Oliver both looked at their families, and in the presence of their little children, their mothers, and their siblings, it seemed that a shift occurred, and they realised what was more important.

Family.

Papa nodded solemnly and looked to all of us. We were all in silent conviction to flee. Jean bowed his head to his father and Pierre did as well in silent agreement of their vote.

The lord, noticing the weakening force of the young men, looked more comfortable and he leant forward, raised his arm in the air, and said slowly, "Those who wish to leave Domrémy, repeat aye."

His words hung in the air for a moment, suspended like a hanging mannequin that was awaiting the response of the crowd. But the lord's words were met with many affirming ayes including papa, Jean, and Pierre's, and even Leonard's and Oliver's. Some men even hollered in agreement.

And finally, we decided. Finally, we were to leave Domrémy. We were to leave our home.

After the meeting, the next day, we saw to it that our little home would receive a proper farewell as we packed our belongings to leave.

Time was of the essence, and we were to leave before dawn the following day. Two of the measures discussed in the meeting were to not leave any food, and anything as big as furniture that could not be carried in the wagons must be left behind.

As I was helping with taking bags of clothes and sheets to the wagon, it felt surreal to be leaving our home.

Is this really happening?

Even entire villages were at the whim of the powerful forces of the English. We were so helpless.

The entire morning and afternoon, Mama and I packed and prepared food, personal belongings, clothes, and kitchen items, and packed them into the wagon. Erstwhile, Pierre, Jean, and Papa were out in the fields organising the transportation of our animals. As I entered through the backdoor, I found mama in the kitchen, flushed and in a flurry. Loud clanging and shuffling of pots resounded in the house, as she turned to me, "Jehanne, I need you to round up the chickens. On the side of the house by the vegetable garden, there are some small compartments made from raspberry canes. You are to put the chickens into them and carry them to the wagon, then come back and help me with all of this," she motioned to the rising pile of plates and cauldrons.

I hurriedly ran and found the small compartments, but as I was walking, I glimpsed a large pumpkin growing in the garden. I etched closer for a better look and saw its plump body and yellowy-green skin growing underneath the array of green leaves.

At that precise moment, the sun broke through the overcast sky and its brilliant rays shone on the vast greenery surrounding our home. My heart sank,

I don't want to abandon our home, but there is no other choice.

We had established a life here and I was not ready to part with it. I looked around at the small house, worry and grief passing through me as my mind lingered on the thought of armies passing through our peaceful and happy fields. Shaken from the thought, I regained myself and looked down at the compartments.

"It is far better to be alive," I muttered, carrying the compartments to the chicken's pen.

11

NEUFCHÂTEAU

Winter, 1427
Domrémy, France

*T*hat night, the wind howled against the house.
I drifted in and out of sleep like the receding and pushing waves of an ocean. Until I woke up, restless and startled.

Dawn.

A feeling had blanketed the house and latched onto us. For the first time, the home we so dearly loved and worked to upkeep felt vulnerable and small. We felt small against the wind. We felt pushed. We felt we could break at any moment.

I lay awake and heard the first remnants of movement in the house. I got out of bed and started to get ready. I shivered as I felt the sting of cold air, but I changed into my tunic dress quickly and wrapped my shawl over my bodice. By the time my mother silently came into my room, I was already dressed and putting on my cap.

"Oh, good, you're awake. Make sure you don't leave anything behind, and hurry."

There was no sign of fatigue in her voice or face; her eyes were wide and alert. I nodded. *It doesn't seem anyone slept much.*

I got up and collected all my blankets. The room was bare now. Nothing remained but the naked furniture and my mattress. I glanced around sadly and closed the door. The house was dark except for a few lit candles on the long wooden table. As I walked outside, the chilly air greeted me and the night sky was black; the moon shone brightly, and the stars twinkled as if they had a secret.

The wagon was outside, densely packed with all our kitchen utensils, clothes, and food. I squeezed my blankets into a small corner and went back inside the house to gather the remaining blankets and possessions from each room. Downstairs, I joined Mama as she was packing the last of our belongings hurriedly.

Mama and I worked quickly, barely speaking, as we were in charge of clearing the house. The urgency made time drag slowly, but in reality, we worked like busy little bees. Papa and my brothers were loading the chickens and ducks and getting Mama's favourite cows to come with us. The rest of the animals were guided away from the house and into the open fields.

I was looking around the kitchen one last time, hoping we hadn't forgotten anything that we would need, when I heard Mama's voice behind me with a trickle of panic, "Jehanne, we must leave before dawn arrives. Come, girl!"

"Yes, Mama. Just checking we didn't forget something." I turned and closed the door behind me. The sky was still painted black with the moon and stars hanging over us. I looked back at the house. Its slanted roof and dark windows seemed foreign and empty.

With a heavy heart, I walked to the fully packed wagon. Mama's three favourite cows trailed in a line behind the wagon. My brothers were sitting at the rear of the wagon, their legs hanging over the edge. I saw my father with the reins, his eyebrows furrowed and a frown cast on his face. Mama was sitting beside Papa making herself more comfortable and shuffling her dress, but he was looking to the forest, as if he could already hear the English coming.

I made my way to the back of the wagon to sit with my brothers. A tense quietness settled over us. We all waited to leave, expecting to start our journey, but Papa stayed rock still. We waited but he was deep in thought, still looking over to the horizon. Finally, he stepped down off the wagon and walked to the house.

With a push, he opened the front door widely, then he returned to the wagon, taking back the reins. We all stared confused. Papa glanced at us and Mama, and with a deep huff, he said as mist plumed from his mouth like an elegant feather, "So those bastards don't break it."

As Papa urged on the oxen, we trudged and wobbled through the early hours in Domrémy. Our other neighbours were also making their way with their wagons, packed and ready to travel.

As we travelled, my gaze wandered up to the sky and I admired the dark, solar canvas. Although the town traversed in silence and we felt uprooted and helpless, the heavens looked down upon us sweetly and the chill air stayed with us like a loyal companion.

I felt a knot of emptiness form in the pit of my stomach. It felt strange, almost surreal, leaving home. It was never our choice to leave and become refugees on our own land. These were difficult times, and as my dear mama often would tell us, "*All that is in your plate is for you. It was written by God. Take it with your best disposition and deal with it accordingly.*"

Alas, all we must do was face them.

As we passed the last street, a procession of silent carts left the town like a trail of ants. Only the sounds of the animals interrupted the heavy silence. I left with the knowledge that the fate of our town undoubtedly would involve looting and burning of the fields. Our source of livelihood and survival. This was a fact of our times, and we all knew this.

The streak of slowly marching caravans silently travelled to Neufchâteau, one family after another in a chain of wagons and animals.

By mid-morning, green countryside spanned all around us, and the pale sun barely warmed up our bones. Nevertheless, we trudged on, the stony and austere atmosphere broken only by the clicking noise of the wheels over the dirt road.

As the wagons crept through the hills, I walked among the other girls, the children talking quietly and light-heartedly. When I found myself alone, I gazed across the fresh green fields and asked the Heavens to spare the destruction of our small town and for our safety as we were travelling to outrun the English.

We took a little longer than expected. The wagons were heavy, and the animals trudged through, growing weary. It was past midday when, in the distance, we saw the silhouettes of the stone and mortar houses and the distinctive tall steeple of a church.

As we came closer, we were surprised to see an assemblage of tents, French soldiers, and horses next to Neufchâteau. We neared the gates of Neufchâteau, and the small battalion was clearer. A circle of soldiers in white tunics were sparring, another man brushing the coat of his horse and inspecting its hooves.

In the centre of the camp, a large iron pan hung over a burning fire pit, with a man sitting beside it, hunched over, polishing some worn but sturdy shoes. The air smelled of burnt wood and dirt, but the camp seemed untroubled. We passed on, stoic.

When we finally arrived, the large wooden gates were closed and a group of people stood in front, awaiting us. From the distance of our wagon, they looked finely dressed; however, they stood grounded and apathetic. It looked like they were the Lords and priests, the authorities of Neufchâteau.

We stopped moving, as did all the wagons in our company, and Papa set off to meet the Lord and priests with the other men. The priest of Domrémy was the first to approach the gates of Neufchâteau, closely followed by the Lord Robert de Bautremont and the lesser lords of Domrémy.

We all looked on to observe the exchange. I squinted against the sunlight at the Lord of Neufchataeu. He was a tall man with shoulder-length hair and maintained a stony expression; few words passed through his thin and unmoving lips.

Frustrated, I quickly looked at Mama and my brothers. Their eyebrows furrowed and concern was in their eyes. An idea suddenly occurred to me. I quickly ducked and wedged my way through the crowds of Domrémy villagers to the front of the procession. Carefully hidden behind the first wagon, so Papa wouldn't see me, I crept closer and listened closely.

The Lord of Domrémy, Lord Robert was talking. "With the English so close, we had no—"

"We know the English are close," the mayor of Neufchâteau interrupted, his eyes hard underneath his bushy white eyebrows. The authorities of Neufchâteau were old and middle-aged men, dressed in fine tunics.

"Err, yes," said Lord Robert, a bit uncomfortable at the interruption. "Domrémy does not have the power to hold off an army of the English. I want to save as many French lives as I can. I ask, as a neighbour, for residence and safety in your city. We… we don't have anywhere to go." The Lord barely kept the desperation out of his voice in his last plea.

The Lord of Neufchâteau straightened up and sighed. He calculatingly stared at the Lord Robert for a moment. He shifted his head to look at the trail of wagons behind Lord Robert, and finally said, "How many of you?"

"Twenty wagons, around thirty families," answered the priest of Domrémy.

"You may enter and occupy the place in the town square."

Lord Robert relaxed, and he bowed his head in gratitude.

Unexpectedly, the Lord of Neufchâteau turned to the families and the long line of wagons, and raised his voice. "People of Domrémy, you may take refuge in the town square. Any of you who have family in the town, take refuge with them!"

It was as if a heavy weight was lifted off our shoulders. The people of Domrémy were relieved beyond measure. We were a quiet company, but our grateful smiles and silent pleas of thanks immediately lightened the air. And soon, we were all sent into a flurry to prepare the animals and wagons to start moving. Noticing my cue to return to my family, I quickly ran back and slid next to my brothers while they were preparing the wagon and cows.

I watched from a distance again as the authorities of Neufchâteau moved aside and signalled the gatekeepers. The gates opened and the procession of wagons entered Neufchâteau.

We began to move slowly, and soon Papa came back to our wagon and commented to my brothers, "They will let us lodge in the town square. Perhaps Uncle Jean will help us safekeep our belongings. I do not want to overburden him to lodge us all, in case he doesn't have the space."

Jean and Pierre solemnly nodded in agreement.

We entered the town slowly. We immediately felt the familiar cramped streets of Neufchâteau close in on us. Papa manoeuvred the wagon through the narrow streets as the townspeople walked by the sides. We trotted through the length of the main street until we reached the stalls and markets. The stalls were full of sellers and buyers, and at the end of the street of markets the steeple of the church rose high into the sky.

It was even more crowded in the marketplace. We moved slowly and consciously. Vendors looked at us curiously, but their attention was quickly diverted to matters of their own business. Then a man selling small trinkets called over to Papa. "Hey, where are you coming from?"

"Domrémy," answered Papa.

"How is the situation in Domrémy?" In the next stall selling fruits, another man piped up.

"The English were coming. We had to leave."

"The bloody English!" The man scowled and spat at the dirt.

Before we could reach the church, we followed the line of wagons into a large empty area next to the markets, turning left into a clearing of grass and some sparse trees. Some twenty wagons were already stationed.

"This must be where we're staying," I overheard Jean mutter to Pierre. We all filed in; the space snugly fit all the families and their wagons and animals.

We entered slowly, Papa guiding the wagon carefully and stationing us in a snug space next to other villagers from Domrémy. When we came to a stop, my brothers descended from the wagon, but Papa came around and said curtly, "Do not unload to unpack, just guide the animals with the others and wait. I'm going to your Uncle Jean's."

More wagons entered, and the space became louder and busier. Every family settled in the space they could find, and although we did not unpack, we did our best to help our neighbours.

As I was sitting on our wagon, Mama reached into the nearest sack and grasped some rustic-looking apples. She handed one to me, Pierre, and Jean and we ate in silence as people around flurried like flies.

The clearing was filled with the smell of animals, dirt, and burning wood. Although the villagers were tired, they never ceased to stand still. I could hear the crunching of apple flesh as we sat, fatigued, listening to the quiet conversations that flitted around us.

I strained to hear two low voices in particular, talking quietly and hushed. I looked over and saw two women sitting, preparing a fire. I recognised them to be Margarete and Oliver's wife, Caroline. "I heard the English are moving fast and burning what they find in their path," Margarete said.

Caroline pursed her lips, her eyes heavy with silent anguish.

Margarete continued, "I heard the people from other towns had to leave with what they were wearing. They did not have time to take their belongings."

Caroline sighed. "We are abandoned, Margarete. With invaders running amuck, the kingdom is lost. All we can do is pray. God help us."

At that moment, I heard laughter and hurried steps from behind me. I turned, and right then, a small group of young girls ran past, closely followed by Isabel and Josephine, and the other Domrémy girls. Isabel's braided hair was a little dishevelled, and she turned back to look at me. "Come on, Jehanne, I'll race you!"

I hopped off the wagon and ran after her. We winded our way through the wagons, through the tall grass, and onto the edge of the market, and veered right, towards the steps of the Neufchâteau church.

About four young girls sat on the wide stairs of the church—they were the Neufchâteau girls. One of them piped up, "We saw you coming, where are you from?" Her face was dotted with freckles and her long brown hair was braided into a long plait.

The Domrémy girls stood in front, their eyes rimmed with curiosity and playfulness.

"From Domrémy," Isabel responded.

"My name is Angelie. Do you know how to play tag?" We all smiled cheekily, and I felt the sweetness of new friendships blossom. Soon our troubles were forgotten. That short afternoon, in front of the Neufchâteau church, we played tag and once we were breathless and red-cheeked, we shared our different clapping and dancing games.

As we sat on the stairs of the church, playing a clapping game, my mother's figure approached us. The girls shrank and peered upwards towards my mother, expecting her to stop us playing and request we go back to the wagons, but she smiled sweetly and her gentle eyes met mine as I looked up.

"Hello, girls. I need to speak with Jehanne. Jehanne, come for a moment."

I stood up quickly.

"Jehanne, I am going with Jean into town. Pierre is at the wagon, so stay here with the girls and don't leave the church. We will be back very soon, alright?"

I nodded. "Okay, Mama."

She smiled quickly and said, "Okay, go on then," and motioned with her head towards the girls playing behind me. I smiled and ran back gleefully.

While the afternoon sun shrank behind the Neufchâteau buildings, the cold air began to set in and the market street began to empty. The stalls that held the produce and goods were gone, and the vibrant chat and activity was replaced by the current of wind whistling through the cracks of doors and beating against the stony walls of the houses.

One by one, the girls left to go home or, in our case, back to the wagons and tents that were set up and ready. I wondered if Pierre would need help building our tent, or if Jean and Mama had already set it up before they left.

As twilight crept over, Mama and Jean both returned to the clearing. By that time, only Isabel and I remained playing in front of the church, and as I saw Mama, we returned to the clearing together.

"Bye, Jehanne," Isabel slowed and turned to walk to the opposite side of the clearing.

"Bye!" I turned back and made my way to the wagon, where Pierre and Jean sat. The air was thick with the smell of smoke from the campfires, and their orange glow began to radiate warmth. Jean was talking in a low voice to Pierre as I approached. "Papa should be coming soon. When he arrives, we should be ready to leave."

They both looked at me as I appeared next to them. At that moment, my stomach grumbled loudly and a sudden fatigue ached at my limbs and arms, causing a pulsating ache in the side of my head. I swallowed, and my face fell with the sudden loss of energy.

"Where is Mama, Pierre?" I asked.

Pierre turned his head and nodded toward a group of women standing in the middle of the clearing.

"Jehanne, come and sit if you are tired," Jean said, while looking in that direction.

I looked over to Mama too, and she was talking to the other ladies of the town in low and hushed tones. Midnight blue was beginning to cover the sky like a blanket, slowly erasing the light of day, and the first stars were descending and hanging like decorations.

Around us, families were beginning to prepare supper, and the smell of stew began to waft in the cold night air as if to remind us of our hunger. We sat and looked forlornly to the campsites nearby, and their hot bread and tasty stews filled with vegetables and game.

Jean stood in front of the wagon and glanced every minute or so to the entrance for Papa. At last, when a lone figure entered the clearing, he stretched up his neck for a better look. He nodded and bent down to pick up his hat. "Papa is back. Jehanne, go and tell Mama."

I nodded and hopped off the wagon. By this point, the clearing was lit by many campfires, and families supped comfortably. As I approached, I saw that the group of women had reduced to two: Mama and Leura, the elderly woman from the village. I tugged on Mama's arm.

So involved in her conversation, Mama was jolted by my touch. She shifted her attention to me. "Yes, what is it, dear?"

"Papa has arrived," I said quietly.

"Oh, alright. Leura, I must go now, take care of yourself."

"I will, Isabel. Didn't I say my feelings ain't never led me wrong. Well, goodbye and take care. If you need anything, just ask!"

Mama smiled sweetly and waved, turning to walk back to the wagon. As we walked, she brushed a tendril of hair behind my ear, and put her hand on my shoulder. "How are you, my darling?"

I smiled wearily up to her and said, after a pause, "Hungry."

She chuckled and I smiled. "Come on, let us go."

We approached the wagon. Papa was standing in front of Pierre and Jean, who stood listening intently to Papa's instructions. His voice became clearer, as we got closer. "We will organise our sleeping arrangements when we get there. Right now, we will pack up everything and go." To Mama he said, "We are staying at Jean's house. Jean, Pierre, help your mother."

"What about the animals?" asked Mama as she began to pack.

"We are going to leave them here. I'll come later to see to them and secure them. Make sure they don't escape," he responded in his usual low and curt tone.

"And the chickens and ducks?" Mama called out as she busily organised our belongings in the wagon.

Papa paused to think, and responded slowly, "We take them."

Mama looked over and nodded to me.

Jean and Pierre made sure to secure the cows and goats in the clearing. I brought all of our chickens and ducks in their pens, and we all helped to make room for them on the wagon.

As twilight descended over the streets of Neufchâteau, we ambled through the quiet cobblestone streets. They were markedly quieter. Papa guided the ox forward and we wobbled silently on the wagon until we were within view of the street where Uncle lived. It wasn't until a little later, when we got closer, that we saw two heads poking out of the side door, on the second-floor landing.

My cousins' light-hearted and mirthful smiles greeted us as we turned into the smaller side street and stationed the wagon in the little street in front of Uncle's house. The front double doors were shut. I looked up towards the second floor at the two windows; an orange glow emanated from inside.

We soon began to unpack the load. Mama was busy allocating Jean and Pierre blankets, pots, plates, cups, and baskets of fruit and vegetables. Once my cousins arrived, they began to help with the load.

Mama directed me, "Jehanne, take the chickens and the ducks, and put them in your uncle's courtyard."

The courtyard was to the left side of the house, and it was surrounded by a tall wooden fence. Two double doors acted as the gate. I walked to the double doors and put my hand through the small empty square in their surface that looked inside the courtyard. It was eye level and behind the square was a thin rope. I pulled the rope downwards, lifting the lock, and I pushed the gate open.

Twilight covered the courtyard in shadows, but I remembered it was long and slightly narrow. To the left of the gate was a small, wooden wagon and at the furthest corner of the courtyard were piles of stacked wood. To the right, there was a faint outline of a door to the shop, but it was closed.

The same cobbled stone of the street covered the floor, making the air chilly. I shivered, and leaving the gate open, I fetched the chicken and duck pens, carrying them one in each hand. I left them next to the stacked wood. When I finished, I closed the gate behind me and made my way to help my brothers and cousins.

There were only a few bags and things left from the wagon, so when the last of us made our way to the house, that was our last trip. I climbed up the stairs, carrying a bag of flour, and turned inside to the second floor. It opened to a long, comfortable-sized room with a long, wooden table in the centre with equally long benches for seating. A small kitchen lay on its fringe, and to the right were two separate, smaller rooms.

There I saw Uncle Jean directing my brothers and cousins. "Come, come, difficult times, difficult times," Uncle Jean said. He spotted me and said, "Ah, Jehanne. You can put the flour in the corner of the kitchen," pointing at the far end of the room.

"Yes, Uncle," I responded. I looked towards the kitchen. A steady fire was glowing in the hearth, giving the room a warm glow. In the kitchen, I felt the warmth of the fire, and I heard the voice of Uncle Jean.

"Isabel, I know you have angel's hands, and I'll be honoured to try your cooking. It goes without saying you have quite a talent."

Mama's soft voice replied, "Thank you, Jean, so you don't mind if I cook dinner?"

I turned to watch the exchange.

"Oh, not at all. By all means, take over the kitchen. What is mine is yours," he said, bringing his hand to rest over his chest. My uncle was always a pleasant man, but tonight I saw that he was genuinely sincere in his words. His smile was grateful, and he nodded to her with such solemnity and respect. I could tell he was honoured to try my mother's cooking.

My intuition was confirmed when my cousin's tall frames appeared next to Uncle Jean, their excitement written over their faces. *They must be keen to have a break from Uncle's cooking*, I thought.

Mama spared no moment, and she quickly made her way to the kitchen. Seeing me there, she said, "Jehanne, dear, take some of the pots out of the baskets and make some bread, while I prepare the stew."

My brothers had carried up all the utensils for cooking and piled them in one corner. I took out some of the pots from the wicker baskets, one to prepare the bread and the other for the stew. I also was able to find some wooden spoons and some knives.

I heard my mother gather the vegetables and place them on the bench. She took a knife and was straight to work, peeling and preparing the vegetables and cutting some chunks of cold meat we brought from home.

For the bread, I held the sack of flour carefully, so as to not spill its whispery, powder-like contents on my uncle's floor, and began to scoop cupfuls into a big bowl. I gradually added some water, and kneaded it to make a rough, round dough. Finding a pot, I placed the dough inside and hung it over the fireplace.

Once I was next to Mama again, she was almost finished putting the chunks of meat into a large, worn pot. When she spoke, she kept her eyes on the vegetables. "The hotel lady needs a young person to help her twice a week. It would be good to go in tomorrow and talk to her, see if she agrees to have you."

"Oh." My eyes widened, and I looked over the bench as I slowly began to assemble the tools to help her with the stew.

She looked up, concern in her eyes, watching my reaction carefully.

"That's… that's good news. I'll go tomorrow." I began to peel some carrots and slice them into smaller pieces.

"Jehanne, is this something you want to do?" She glanced up again momentarily.

"Yes, I was only surprised. Besides, what am I going to do all day? I am happy to do something while we are here," I said, smiling up at her for a brief moment. I knew that these were difficult times, and the predicament of our home lay in unclear waters.

As the fire licked the underbelly of the pots, the food steadily cooked and the fire's warmth radiated all around the room. While we cooked, Papa and Uncle Jean were sitting beside each other facing the long table, talking quietly.

My brothers' and cousins' voices echoed from the smaller bedroom as they set up the floor with blankets and pillows. Their lively conversation reverberated through the kitchen and the house.

The meal preparation was quickly finished, and the smell of the stew and fresh bread brought everyone to the long, wooden table. I took the bread out of the pot and put it out to cool on a large plate at the centre of the table, alongside butter and fresh, soft cheese.

My brothers and cousins continued their lively banter on farm-work and forging, debating which one was more arduous, and seating themselves on either side of the long table. I occasionally saw their hands reach over for the hot bread, while they jovially talked. Papa and Uncle Jean took no notice of the boys and kept their tones low and reserved.

Mama, using a dry, thick cloth to protect her hands, picked up the pot of stew from the round handle and placed it over a piece of flattened wood on the table. At this, Uncle Jean and Papa's talk suddenly took a halt, like a burst bubble, and they took note of the food on the table.

Uncle Jean moved and sat at the head of the long table, and Papa sat to his right. I brought over a pile of rounded bowls, and spoons, and Mama began to serve and hand out the bowls, first to Uncle Jean and Papa.

I sat down next to my cousin, who nudged me playfully. I looked up at him, slightly taken aback. Their playfulness always caught me off guard, but especially now since we were eating together as a family.

My uncle waited patiently, until we were all served, and once Mama finally served herself with a bowl, he closed his eyes and said for everyone to hear, "Thank you, Lord, for this food. Amen." He opened his eyes, and like waking from a pleasant dream, he smiled gratefully and lifted the spoon to his lips.

Soon all conversation died down, and for a while, only the sounds of slurping, chewing, and scraping wooden spoons could be heard. After the initial bites of hunger subsided, the conversation lifted, and as usual I only listened and supped quietly. Mama sat next to me and as was her habit, she gently recited her prayers. Her soft mumbling was heard quietly under the colourful background of my family's conversations.

As we retreated for the night, Uncle Jean gave us one of the bedrooms for our stay. The room was rectangular and minimally furnished, with only a large trunk, a small table, and two chairs. The floor was covered in blankets. It was pitch black other than the small candles on the table. A small window facing the main street showed the empty and moonless night, plunging the Neufchâteau street into a deep darkness.

Jean, Pierre, Mama, and I all shared the one room, while Papa slept in the kitchen with a few blankets.

Having taken off my boots, cap, and vest dress, I laid down next to my mother. We all stayed dressed in our clothes. My brothers slept closer to the door, but Mama and I slept beside the window. The air inside the house turned cold as the fire was put out, so I pulled the blankets higher over me and Mama. Her quiet murmurings of the rosary filled the silence of the room. While looking at the ceiling, Jean blew out the candles and the room became black. Feeling the warmth of the blankets, my eyes drifted closed as the litany of prayers transported me to a deep slumber.

That night, I dreamt I was in a meadow. The grass reached to my knees and in the flat distance, I saw a figure on a white horse. I squinted to see them more clearly, and they began to gallop towards me.

As they came closer, I saw it was a man with shoulder-length brown hair, dressed in fine clothes. He approached me with purpose, as if he had an important message. He stopped short in front of me and drew a sword. I watched and looked up to him.

He leant forward and held the sword out to me. Taking hold of the leather-covered black pommel, I lifted it upright to examine its long, silver blade. The rider was silent as I carefully looked over it. I adjusted my grip on the black pommel and turned my wrist, observing its weight. It felt extraordinarily light.

The rider's voice broke the silence. "That's your sword. Keep it until it's time to use it." Then he turned and left.

I looked down again. Tightening my grip, I lunged forward, slashing at the air diagonally. Once, then twice. Then I twirled and holding the sword with both hands over my head, brought the sword downwards to the ground, landing on my left knee.

Impressed and excited, I let my palm hug the pommel, and my fingers comfortably curled and rested over the grip. The sword gave no resistance as I practised. I felt alive. An energy pulsed through me, lifting me and giving me the skill to practise more complicated manoeuvres.

At that moment, a voice from the sky said, "It's my will."

12

MADAM MARGERIE

Mid-winter, 1427
Neufchâteau, France

*A*fter staying at Neufchâteau for more than a month, I began to work at the l'ostal de Margerie. Madam Margerie was a tall, big-bosomed lady with generous hips and an abundance of reddish blond, long voluminous hair, which was often tied into a bun at the back of her head and always had tendrils of hair escaping, framing her face like a reddish halo. She was a hardy, active woman in her late forties, and her years of owning an inn gave her a thorough knowledge of business and horses.

"Treat the horses with care. They're very important to our clients," she would say. Her tough personality always rendered her to expertly manage and direct me as her assistant. The inn was on the eastern side of Neufchâteau, and it was visited by travellers and merchants on the road. It was a simple, two-storey stone and wood building, and beside it was a large, wooden stable where the horses were tended.

"Feed them, clean them, so they are rested when they return to the road," she said, while taking the old, damp hay to the corner and replacing it with fresh hay.

"I want you to bring fresh hay to the horses every day. When travellers arrive, their horses need to be given water as well. They are to be brushed, and their hooves cleaned." She brought a bucket of water and let its content spill into a large, rectangular basin.

"Also, a word of advice. Never," she said and then paused. "Never, stand behind a horse. I've had nasty experiences with stableboys getting kicked, and I don't fancy you wanting to share their same fate."

I gulped.

"Now horses, they're big animals, and they like to know people. You have to talk to them so they get to know you. Talk to them gently and pat them, so they know you are friendly. Come."

Her thick fingers edged me forward to the large, brown steed with white hooves in a stable cell. "This stallion has just arrived today. Now here's the brush, I'm going to…" As Madam Margerie continued to show me how to clean their fur and hooves, I watched carefully, memorising every movement and every instruction.

The horses were precious to her business, and although she was tough, she was happy to have the extra help. Having worked with animals all my life, the work at the inn was not complicated nor arduous.

Usually, I worked one hour after light, until late afternoon and I would arrive home just after supper time. I was paid with meals in the morning and afternoon, but every now and then, if I did extra work, she would give me a few coins. Inside the inn, I kept the dining room clean, cleared the table of plates and cups, and wiped the floors of spilt drinks.

Life at Neufchâteau became easier with my uncles and cousins. Even though I worked throughout the day, our families quickly became comfortable and worked seamlessly together.

Yet rumours of the English still circulated like flies in the air. Stories that were once heightened, deflated into small tales that passed and disappeared in everyday conversation. The most consistent rumour was that the English presence in our province was not a proper army but a small unit advancing through the region. Although the rumour inspired hope, the truth of the matter was no one knew for sure. We couldn't hope yet.

When Papa heard the news, he kept a reserved opinion. He didn't join Uncle Jean in his exuberant happiness and wishful thinking that the English didn't have the manpower to be a destructive force. He was quiet. He didn't want to create false hope in case the news was inaccurate.

Yet in our stay at Neufchâteau, I noticed Papa's personality adapt and change. His usually stern features became relaxed, and I knew the main reason was because of Uncle Jean. Ever since we arrived, they had been working together and spending a lot of time in each other's company, and Uncle's happy mood and manners had brushed some happiness into my papa's stern personality.

Even papa's austerity was not immune to uncle's infectious good moods, I remembered thinking to myself.

Uncle was about five years younger than my father, and I had never witnessed such different characters in one family. My father was taciturn and strict. He always valued good work and wasn't much for socialising or talking in general. My uncle was high-spirited and good natured, and it was easy for him to embark on a conversation with anybody; he knew everyone's life and had many friends. Although their personalities were like fire and snow, their joint upbringing always reflected their value of integrity and prudence.

Before my Uncle Jean's wife died, people would ask him, "Jean, why only two children?" and he would reply, "In these times you can't have so many children. These are tough times."

Papa's philosophy echoed the same principle. "Only have children you can feed."

My cousins inherited the same jovial character of my uncle, and they got along very well with my brothers, but especially with Pierre. They even shared a resemblance; they were like three brothers.

My oldest brother, Jean, took after my mother in his looks. But as he was becoming a man, his personality matched my father's the most. Although Jean still had his life ahead of him, a life in farming, it seemed that fate had other plans for him. And it was after the first few weeks of staying with my cousins that I noticed him being more taciturn and pensive than usual.

As the usual routine in Neufchâteau, breakfast was at first light, and everyone was awake and getting ready for the day. However, on this particular day, as I left the small room I was staying in, I pulled my shawl around my shoulders and gathered my boots and cap. The men of the family sat at the table, slowly eating, and still waking up for the morning ahead. The stone floor made the air cold in the bedroom, but as I entered the kitchen, the warmth of the low fire and smell of porridge invited me to sit down.

Perhaps it was just me, but Jean seemed more taciturn than usual. Mama was serving breakfast, and the rest of the family were eating at the table. I sat down on the long bench, my brothers and cousins across from me in their usual positions. I strapped on my boots quickly. The fire was warm, but my fingers were still cold. The windows were always foggy, and our tired faces made conversation light and scarce.

Mama came around and put some warm bread on the table. "Jehanne, do you want breakfast?" she said to me in a quiet voice.

"Yes. Today, Madam Margerie said I can come in a little later. They're not busy today," I replied, busily fumbling with the laces on my boots.

I heard someone clear their throat, and Jean's croaky voice rang in the silence of the morning. "I would like to say something…"

The boys, papa, and uncle stirred and looked over to Jean. Mama and I shared a look of perplexity.

"Being here in Neufchâteau with Uncle Jean has given me time to think. I want to help support my family and live comfortably." He paused and looked up to Papa. "I think I'd like to stay and take an apprentice job at the forge."

A silence ensued. No one spoke. I felt my own mouth open and my eyebrows rise. My mother's hand hung in mid-air as she held the ladle full of porridge over an empty bowl; her eyes were wide, and she was completely still. Yet something in her eyes softened, and gave birth to a light of pride.

She placed the ladle back in the pot and lowered the bowl, glancing over to Papa's figure at the table. Papa and Uncle's eyes never left Jean. Their expressions were masked, both difficult to ascertain. Then Papa's voice, like leather, unyielding and tough, spoke very slowly. "Make sure you pay attention, Jean." He paused. "To keep all your fingers."

Jean's face relaxed, a small smile creeping at the corner of his mouth, and he nodded solemnly. Papa dipped his head deeply. Uncle's face erupted into a broad, brimmed smile. "Well done, Jean. Look at you becoming a man before my very eyes! Well, you are welcome to stay here at my house. No need to find an inn," Uncle enthusiastically told Jean.

"Thank you, Uncle," said Jean, smiling.

My cousins also smiled from ear to ear; they congratulated Jean by slapping him on the arm and speaking words of encouragement. Yet beside me, Pierre was quiet. He didn't join in with my cousins. Instead, his eyes were pensive and his jaw was set. He looked at Jean with the dawning realisation his brother was changing without him. Lifting a spoonful of porridge and chewing somberly, he kept quiet as the conversation continued. Mama came and sat next to me at the table, with a hot bowl of breakfast, intently listening.

"Well, we will take you to meet Bastien, and see what he can propose for you," slurred Jean-Claude with his mouth full of breakfast. "An apprenticeship would be likely. It will probably take around a few years." Jean-Claude finished his piece of bread.

"What is Bastien like?" Jean asked, his eyes unwavering and focused. His shoulders were stiff and strong. I could see he was ready to prove himself.

"Bastien likes to see good work done. He values honesty and hard work, and once you show that, you will work well together," Jean Paul said.

Talking after his brother, Jean-Claude said, "We better go now to get there early. Bastien would want to see an early riser in you, Jean." Jean-Claude swallowed his last spoon in one gulp and cleaned the corner of his mouth with his sleeve. Then he got up, and that stirred Jean-Paul and Jean to also shuffle and prepare to leave.

As they were putting on their coats at the door and chatting more about the forge, I got up and started gathering their plates quietly. Pierre had finished his bowl, and also got up to collect his warm garments. "Mama, I am going to see the animals, if they need anything, and then I'll come back to help in the shop."

"Good, Pierre. Yes, and don't forget your scarf," Mama said quietly like a whisper as Pierre was within earshot. She turned and handed him the thick, woollen scarf that was draped over her chair. Pierre smiled and took it, wrapping it around his neck. His expression had relaxed, and his amiable self had returned.

Once the trio at the door were all clad in their warm vestments, they headed out the door, welcoming in the cold, dry morning air of Neufchâteau. Various goodbyes were heard as they walked out, Pierre closely following behind.

"Bye everyone," Pierre quickly said, closing the door behind him.

Well, I was wrong, I thought to myself. *Jean wants to stay and learn to be a forge master. It seems the cousins didn't deter his choice at all.*

My attention went back to my family conversing at the table. Papa and Uncle continued their conversation while Mama got up and began to put all the dirty bowls in a large barrel of cold water. I started helping her, but I couldn't stay long as I needed to leave to go to the inn.

And like that, our lives were in a motion of change. My heart sank at the thought that Jean wanted to leave, like a piece of our small family was being taken away and would never be complete again.

I wonder what other changes will come on our stay, I thought as I walked to the inn in the chilled air.

At that early hour, the sun still hid behind the east lines of packed houses and buildings in Neufchâteau, basking the streets in shade that made the air cold and damp. I walked through the streets that were once unknown to me. They seemed like an untraceable maze when I first arrived, but little by little, this city had become my second home.

Being in Neufchâteau, we had settled the best we could with Uncle. Everyone was very content with Mama's food. She loved to cook and never seemed to tire from it. Papa and Pierre also worked in the shop with Uncle, and for special occasions Papa contributed fresh meat from the livestock we brought with us.

As a gift to Uncle and his hospitality, Papa gifted duck meat to Uncle, which we ate and also sold in Uncle's shop. Although I missed our house and the greenery of our garden and the countryside, we were all grateful to be with Uncle. With them, things didn't feel so bad.

The day passed with little trouble, and soon enough dusk was falling. I shivered as I washed my hands in the cold basin, cleaning off the strong smell of hay. I removed my apron and hung it on the coat hanger as I left the stables of the inn.

The wind danced through the street, ruffling my long sleeves and the hair under my cap as I hurried towards home. I hugged my shawl closer to my body to keep warm. From outside the city walls, I heard the high call of birds echoing through the air, their last call for the night.

Red cheeked and panting, I ran up the main street, seeing my uncle's home in view. When I arrived, the shop was dark and the front door shut. I climbed up the stairs as quickly as I could and unlatched the door. The warm heat of the second floor enveloped my face and body, and I squinted slightly as my eyes adjusted to the candles on the table and fire-place burning.

The smell of bread lingered in the air; the remnants of crumbed pieces lay on a wooden plate. Papa and Uncle sat at the table, Papa making hand gestures and demonstrating the size and length of a particular object, and Uncle listening intently, his chin leaning on his knuckles and his eyes focused despite the circles underneath them.

I could see Mama sitting comfortably near the fire, and the boys all sat around her, two on the edge of the long benches and the other two on the chairs. Their voices floated in the air. Jean's animated tone resonated in the room.

As I secured the latch of the door, Jean turned to look over. His eyes brightened, and he smiled, beaming over to me. "Ah, Jehanne!"

"Hello, everyone," I said as I took off my cap and hung up my woollen shawl. Their animated conversation continued, and I brought the empty chair closer to Mama and Jean.

"How was your day at the inn?" Jean asked.

"It was fine," I said simply. "What about you? How did your talk with Bastien go?" I asked eagerly, taking my scarf off and leaving it on my lap.

"Well, you are now talking to a forge apprentice, Jehanne." He grinned proudly.

"Oh my, I'm so excited for you, Jean!" I said, while side hugging him. Immediately, Jean-Claude joined us.

"Yes, and now he's going to stay with us! And he impressed Bastien with all of his answers." Jean-Claude made a side smile. He was always glad to add to the conversation.

"Yes, we gave him little hints here and there to help our cousin, didn't we?" added Jean-Paul, playfully elbowing Jean-Claude.

Jean-Claude retaliated and playfully elbowed his brother back. Then he looked over at me, his eyes playful. "If you want us to give a good word to your lady boss, Jehanne, we would gladly oblige to it," offered Jean-Claude, giving an old-fashioned flamboyant hand gesture.

I smiled and chuckled. I was not so shy with them anymore. Time spent working at the inn with Madam Margerie had given me confidence to interact with many different people. I feigned an ignorant tone. "So, you want me to stay, mm?" and tilted my head, looking at him with a raised eyebrow.

"It would be our pleasure if our little cousin would stay on our premises," Jean-Claude responded in a high voice and affected manner, imitating a high-class voice.

"Aha," I laughed again. "I think you want me to stay, so I cook for the whole family."

Their faces fell, sheep faced and chuckling.

I continued my streak of teasing, "Honestly, you two have no shame!" I said in a mocking, scolding tone.

Jean Paul, still chuckling, said, "You have outdone yourself, cousin."

"I know your games. I have you both in my sights," I returned, pointing two fingers at them.

"Ah, we can't tease you anymore. You are becoming too clever," Jean-Claude said softly, laughing with a red face.

When the laughter subsided, Mama leaned over to me, and said in her gentle tone, "Do you want anything to eat?" My mother always asked me the same question whenever I was back from work, and yet I always replied with the same response.

"No thank you, Mama. I already ate at the inn," I reassured her with a smile.

She just nodded and leant back into her chair, continuing to mend some of Papa's shirts. While my brother and cousins resumed talking among themselves, and their voices filled the background, Mama continued to talk gently. "Jehanne, tomorrow, since you don't go to the inn, we can go after mass and visit Missy. What do you think?"

Missy was the name of Mama's favourite cow. "Oh yes, of course," I replied in a placid tone while moving slightly forward and putting my hands close to the fire.

"Earlier today, I gave Missy some water with herbs to stimulate her appetite, so she'll be hungry tomorrow."

"Oh yes, that's good. I have been wanting to go to the fields," I said smiling, remembering Domrémy. I looked around and saw Jean's eyes stayed on the fire; he was likely excited to see what chapter of his life was about to open. Jean-Claude and Jean Paul finally seemed relaxed; their eyes stared into the empty space before them.

Pierre was quiet as he finished polishing a pair of shoes, and, finally happy with the result, he began packing the oils and dirty cloth away.

I could feel my eyes growing heavy, and my limbs aching for sleep. "I'm going to sleep. Good night, everyone."

I brought along a small candle, placing it on a small bench, and closed the door. I quickly changed out of my apron dress. I changed my socks and put on a grey linen frock. The warmth of the blankets ensconced my tired body, and I fell into deep slumber.

As the early wagons and the dwellers of Neufchâteau began to stir in the street, we promptly got ready to go to mass. Mama wouldn't have missed it for an entire coffin of gold. I donned my best cap that Mama had made for my last birthday.

My brothers were simply clad and eating hungrily when I arrived at the table. The only sounds were their slurping and the clangs of their spoons in their bowls. Mama placed a bowl of porridge on the table in front of me, which felt warm in my hands, and I started to eat.

Soon, my brothers shuffled out of the seats and joined my cousins, Papa, and Uncle Jean, who were waiting outside. They went ahead, and once I had finished eating, Mama and I left the bowls in the water basin and went together to mass.

I pulled my woollen shawl closer around my shoulders and shivered as the cold air bit my cheeks. We exited uncle's home and followed the group of families to the centre of the city, to the church. Other passersby walked in groups of twos and threes, heading the same direction, chatting reservedly.

The morning was fresh, and overhead the sky was clear, but looming in the distance were bulbous, dark clouds.

It might rain, I thought to myself.

As we arrived at the heavy stone steps of the church's entrance, I paused and instantly recognised the style of the Church—the wooden panels covering the interior walls, the images of the angels, and the high arched ceiling—it was reminiscent of our church in Domrémy, only it was much larger and lit with a simple brass chandelier overhead.

The dense crowd shuffled as we squeezed past, making our way to the middle of the church, settling in on the far right. I was on my tiptoes looking around for my friends when my eyes spotted Isabel with her family to the left, and then I spotted the red hair of Charlotte a few heads in front of us. My attention was diverted to the altar as the priest began, reciting the Pater Noster. During mass, I noticed that many people looked lighter; they sang with joy and energy.

Perhaps, it's the recent rumours of the English that has everyone relieved and happy… If it's only a small segment of an army, they can't do much pillaging… Even I noticed myself joining in the hymns with vivacity, singing high as a lark.

Once mass was over, as we had planned, we prepared to take Missy to graze in the fields around the town. The clouds were much closer and high in the sky, the deep rumble of thunder resonating in the distance.

Mama and I were walking down the main street with Missy when I heard Isabel's soft voice. Turning, I waved at her. She was running towards us, with other girls from town, I recognised Margarete, Anne and Charlotte close behind.

We waited for them to catch up with us.

"Jehanne! Jehanne, where are you going?"

I looked at Mama and then at Isabel. "We are taking Missy to the fields," I said, patting the big cow next to me.

"You want to come? I mean, all you girls?" I asked.

The girls looked at each other and nodded eagerly. Anne responded, "Yes, we love a stroll outside the town."

I gave Missy's string to Mama so I did not have the big cow in the way and I could talk to the girls freely. We chatted animatedly, passing Uncle's home and the gate of the town.

"Ay!" a voice called from behind us, and from the church Jean and Pierre sauntered towards us, their eyebrows knitting together questioningly.

"We are going to walk Missy. Come if you want," I said.

They turned and spoke to our cousins, and they nodded and followed us down the main road to the gate. Going beyond the gate, the air was fresh, and the wind skipped and danced over our clothes.

I scanned the countryside. The light and dark shades of green grass were like waves as the wind brushed over the fields. Mounds of forests dotted the landscape in the distance.

No sign of any English, no smoke, nothing out of the ordinary, I thought. I couldn't help but wonder what was happening to the English unit. Were they gone? Or were they still plundering our meagre possessions?

Mama, the girls, and I kept pace, and a fair distance from the entrance of the gate, the wide dirt road split into two strips of road, each going separate ways. We took the right road to the eastern flank of Neufchâteau, and there, fenced fields cut up the land and farm animals grazed the fields.

Some other young people were also tending their animals, and we could hear their amusing conversations as they enjoyed the midmorning day. Jean-Claude and Jean-Paul both gravitated towards the group, greeting them as if they were old acquaintances and introducing Jean and Pierre.

Mama, the girls, and I stayed a little further away, when eventually Pierre came and joined us as we watched Missy. Missy wandered over at Mama's special calling: "Missy! Missy!" Mama cooed quietly as she patted and comforted her.

Charlotte, who never missed an opportunity to look at Pierre, stared longingly at him with admiration filling her face, but she quickly hid it if Pierre happened to turn and gaze her way.

We conversed over the fence about the cows and goats in the field, for a long while. At first, I actively spoke with the girls, but later I was content to just listen as they carried on. My eyes caressed the beauty of the open fields. I missed the sweet smell of the wildflowers and fruit trees.

While I rested my chin on my arms, which lay on the wooden fence, I quietly longed to be home again. I drank in the expansion of the fields.

By the time Mama suggested we should be going back, the clouds were above us—beautiful, impressive cumulus clouds that held the promise of rain.

The girls engaged in a lively chat with Jean-Claude, Jean, Pierre, and Jean-Paul as they all walked ahead. I spoke with Mama at first, but soon I slowed my pace and followed quietly behind; I wanted to see the soldier's camp that I had seen before, when we left town.

As we trudged back onto the road up towards the gate, in the camp, the soldiers stood stationed on the western flank. I slowed to a stop and stared intently. There were many small white tents set up in rows with fire pits at the end. Although we were still in Neufchâteau, I had never forgotten the angel's prophecy, and I knew that I would one day be amongst the soldiers in their camps.

I stood rooted to the spot and watched them come and go. I could hear their muffled voices in the distance. In what I supposed was their daily routine, they were tending to the horses, sharpening their knives and swords, and training with fake swords. Harnesses laid about and ropes were strung across the tents, with clothes drying over them.

While looking attentively at them, I thought. *These men have chosen to fight as a profession; they are not lawless people.* The men looked rough, but they hadn't caused any trouble in town; there hadn't been any fights or riots.

Sometimes people like to talk and make things bigger than they really are, I thought to myself while looking at the soldiers training, totally immersed in the scene before my eyes.

Suddenly, I heard my name. "Jehanne, daughter, what are you doing?"

I turned, looking at my mama down the dirt road, who beckoned me to follow. I hurried to reach Mama.

"Why were you looking at the soldiers?" she asked me when I came closer. I could hear the reproach in her voice.

"They don't seem so lawless to me," I said.

"Daughter, you don't know how they are. You're still young."

"All right," I said, but I was not convinced. Even though I was young, I could see they resembled working people, doing their daily training and causing no trouble.

I continued walking in silence, an edge of guilt creeping into my consciousness. *Can I trust my mother and tell her everything that is happening? The angels, their prophecy… what can I do?*

I felt Mama's arm encircle mine as we walked. We walked arm in arm, and we walked silently.

Mama took my pensive silence to mean I was somehow annoyed and approached me gently. "Is everything okay, my girl?" She caressed my left long braid. My mother was always gentle and judicious; she would have made an excellent nun because of her sense of calm.

"It's okay to be curious," she told me in a soft, friendly tone.

I smiled. Her sincerity touched my heart. I took her hand. "I was only thinking about our town and our house. Will it still be standing?"

"Well, if it isn't, we will rebuild it," my mother told me, smiling but with a strong conviction, like water splashing solid stone.

"We are still waiting for news. Not all is lost," she added.

"Mama… don't you get tired? Don-don't you wish things were different?" I suddenly heard my own doubt.

"What do you mean?" her brows furrowed slightly, and she tilted her head, waiting for me to explain.

"Well… I mean with everything. No war, no destruction, no English…" I trailed off.

"To want different things is to deny our Lord Jesus Christ," she answered promptly and with certainty. "Jesus did not want anything to be different. He accepted the will of God without reservation, and we have to follow his example, so life becomes easier and simpler than wanting something different from what God has given you."

"Okay," I said nodding, deep in thought. *So I must accept,* I thought to myself. "Yes, Mama. Thank you, I will," I repeated, smiling, while in the corner of my eye I quickly glanced at the soldiers' camp.

As we walked up together, arm in arm, we entered the Neufchâteau gates just in time for a bolt of thunder to cross the sky and drops of water to fall sparsely. We could hear more thunder and rain coming, so we hurried home.

I wonder if the angels will let me tell Mama about my life's mission.

Feeling like a part of me was hidden, I wanted to share with her, my dear mama, my big secret.

13

HOME

Midwinter, 1425
Neufchâteau, France

*T*he bells rang in Neufchâteau like a deafening drum. They thundered and thrummed like a war song through the city.

Ding, dong.

Ding, dong.

Ding, dong.

In my uncle's parlour, the hearth was flickering quietly, yet the coldness from the night still seeped into the wooden home. Everyone was clad in woollen coats, cupping bowls of porridge for warmth, in the early hour of the morning.

The sun's yellow glow was growing in the sky, but it had not reached over the angled roofs of the Neufchâteau homes. It cast the city in a cold dampness and made the ring of the bells even harsher as they woke up the town and sent everyone into a height of alertness and danger.

We all stopped instinctively and for a few spans no one moved. Only seconds before, we were occupied and busy, yet now as I looked around, I saw still and dismayed faces. Unspoken fear was clear on all our faces. The ringing kept billowing.

Uncle Jean's voice, uncharacteristically low and sombre, said slowly, "The bells... the English... the English... they might be here."

Dread settled over us as we sat ate the rest of our breakfast. As if time had slowed, every moment hung on the constant rings of the bells.

Ding, dong.

Ding, dong.

Papa quickly looked at Uncle and stood up from the table at once, his jaw tense and his eyes alert. "Let us see what is happening."

Uncle nodded, standing up. We watched as they took their worn woollen coats and hurried out of the house. My brothers and cousins quickly jumped into action and followed them.

Mama and I ran to the window facing over the street, opening the shutters quickly to let the morning light and cold air pour in. The street was filled with people briskly walking towards the church. The children were abnormally quiet and closely held by their mothers; men wore steely expressions of their fears becoming a reality.

"We better go and see what is happening."

I heard the concern in Mama's voice, low but calm.

Then turning, she went to get her shawl.

Taking a deep breath, I closed the shutters. "Okay, let's go," I said, quickly unhinging the shawl from the hanging rack and joining Mama who was waiting on the landing. As I closed the door, I wrapped my hands under my arms to keep them warm.

Quickly descending the stairs, we merged into the small crowds of people hurriedly making their way to the town square. Short bursts of fog appeared as we breathed out heavily. It was obvious everyone felt the cold bite of the morning—the people around us were garbed in woollen shawls, hats, and coats.

Despite the cold, the yellow rays of sun were starting to paint the city of Neufchâteau in gold. Just looking at the uneven cobblestone of the road, I felt strangely calm. A lightness descended on me, but I remained silent.

I looked up when the sounds of the bells became stronger. We had arrived in front of the church, in the town square. Almost the whole town was gathered in front of the church. A heaviness hung in the air, and the ringing bells permeated like vibrations. The townspeople were agitated. Everyone was talking, hands fidgeting, the cheeks and noses of young children pinched red, and older women with their hands, swollen from the cold, clasped in front of their chest.

I spotted Papa and the rest of the family ahead of us, talking with some other men in the middle of the crowd. Then the bells stopped and the chatter of the people filled the square, one billowing sound after another.

The crowd's chatter emanated like a swarm of bees, until a priest appeared through the opened door of the church. He was garbed in a long black robe, with a necklace of the cross hanging on top of his bulbous belly. Underneath his bushy eyebrows, his eyes were small but serious.

Next to him were the noblemen of Neufchâteau, silent and watching the anxious crowd. The atmosphere was heavy with worry, with anticipation of what was to come.

The priest held one arm up to the crowd, until the people quieted, then he began to speak. "Citizens of Neufchâteau and other towns..."

In the crowd, someone coughed.

"We have received news that the English have left Lorraine. Our towns are safe again!"

A great ovation erupted. The air filled with joyful cries and victorious yells, like a heavy burden had tumbled from our souls. Immense exhilaration filled me from head to toe. All around us, people embraced each other, crying and smiling, talking and hugging. Mama and I embraced, laughing and rosy-eyed.

"Oh Mama, we can go home! The Lord has heard our prayers!" I cried.

"Oh yes, the Lord has blessed us, my darling girl!" Mama said, her voice thick with emotion. She hugged me tight and left my cheeks wet from her tears of joy.

"Come, let us find the others," she said, taking my arm.

Through the commotion of celebrations, we made our way through the crowd until I saw Pierre. Having seen us, Pierre ran over, his eyes bright and beaming. He wrapped his arms around us both and landed a kiss on Mama's head. Jean came right after, enveloping us in one big bear hug.

"This is wonderful, what wonderful news!" Jean said. Clasping my hands, he began dancing with me. I laughed and twirled about with him. Around us, the people were all as one, sharing their joy and relief.

After the initial exuberant happiness had worn off, Papa came over to us. Pierre's arm was over Mama's shoulder, and Jean and I were still dancing. Papa's eyes brimmed with contentment; his mouth was a thin line, the hint of a smile in the corner.

"Jean, we are going home tomorrow. Help Mama pack our belongings."

Jean straightened up, his face red from dancing. "Yes, Papa," he said, still bubbling with enthusiasm.

Papa looked at him, a dry smile on his face as they shared their relief and felicity. Then he turned and his brown eyes rested on me. "Tell Madam Margerie we are going home."

I nodded, "Yes, Papa." I smiled at my brothers and straightway left for the inn. I ran as fast as my legs could carry me. Around me people were celebrating, their moments of joy echoing through town. When I was nearing the inn, I saw a tall woman standing in the middle of its opened double doors. She had long blonde hair that was tied back and I immediately knew it was Madam Margerie.

I slowed to a brisk walk, and as I approached, Madam Margerie questioned me loudly, "What were the bells ringing for? What is all this commotion?" Her eyebrows furrowed in a frown, and both hands on her ample hips showed her concern.

"There's news of the English, Madam. They've left the Lorraine district. They are no longer here. We are safe." I stopped in front of her, smiling again.

On hearing this, Madam Margerie smiled broadly, showing her straight teeth. "It was about time. I hoped one of the Grand Lords got off their asses and did something about this mess." She turned and moved inside the inn.

I followed her. "Madam, I am going home."

Hearing this she turned, her eyebrows raised. "Are you? Well, yes, of course you are."

"Yes, tomorrow we leave for Domrémy."

"Well," she said pensively, looking at the floor, as if calculating what to do next. "I'll need to get someone else soon. I can't do all the work by myself." Looking up with a smile and luminous eyes, she added, "The English are gone and that's all that matters now. I'll find someone tomorrow."

A bigger and broader smile adorned her face as she walked towards me. "Jehanne, it was very nice to meet you. Good luck, my darling, and if you need anything in the future, come. I'll be glad to help you. You are a good worker," she praised my work.

"Thank you… thank you for having me." Touched by her words, I was reticent. "Thank you." After a few moments of hesitating, I jumped up and hugged her.

"Oh! Haha, well there you are, my darling. Have a safe trip," she said, a bit surprised by my gesture. When I released her, her eyes were moist and glazy.

"Off you go, and make the best of your life," she said, trying to hide her emotions as she fixed her hair.

"I will. Thank you, Madam." I ran home, and all the way I could see people in groups talking animatedly, children playing, and the sun unfolding its golden light.

When I arrived at Uncle's home, the front doors of the shop were wide open and everyone was flurrying to and fro, carrying, loading, cleaning, or directing. The wagon was stationed outside the shop, and while it was almost fully packed with belongings, it still looked like there was more to do.

As I climbed the stairs, my happiness deflated like a balloon. Ever since we arrived to Neufchâteau, I remembered the reports that some houses were ransacked in towns near the east.

Now, although the English had gone, there was no guarantee that they hadn't ransacked our town and destroyed our fields too. All we could do was pray that the fields could be sown before winter arrived, or else we would have no crops for the next season. I wrestled with these anxieties, unable to stand the dark possibilities.

Today, we know that the English are no longer here and we can return home, I told myself.

Then I was upstairs and was once again swept up in the flurry of activity. Seeing Uncle's parlour being cleaned and our belongings getting packed, my mind began to buzz with excitement to go back home and my anxieties were laid to rest in the back of my mind for the moment.

This is the time of packing and going home… finally!

By late afternoon we had loaded everything onto the wagon, except the pens of the chickens and ducks. The next morning, before dawn, Jean helped me load them onto the wagon, fitting them closely to everything else. The wagon was overloaded, and our belongings piled up to shape a small hill.

"You might need to walk," Jean said absentmindedly.

Pierre had gone earlier to fetch the oxen from the fields outside the city and arrived promptly with the two beasts.

"I will wait for you outside the village," Jean said. "I'll be ready with the cows, then you will be on your way."

Uncle Jean-Marcel and the cousins were also up and adding last-minute items to the wagon, although it was full.

"I think that should be enough. More and the wagon will break," Papa said.

When it was time to go, we all hugged and said our goodbyes. As Mama and Papa mounted the wagon, Uncle Jean said, "Good luck with everything." He waved goodbye, along with our cousins, the three of them standing in front of the big wooden doors of the shop.

Papa edged on the oxen, and I kept waving goodbye as we moved off. I would never forget my uncle and cousins with affection. They were always in good humour, and Uncle was a generous man, always sharing his love for life.

The city was still sleeping when the wagon slowly made its way down the main street and towards the main gates of Neufchâteau. Pierre and I walked silently beside the wagon. The houses slumbered as we went past, the only noises in the stillness of the early hours the occasional bleep of the oxen and the wooden wheels turning over the uneven stones.

Other wagons followed us out of the city, and by the time we passed through the gates, the road to Domrémy was dotted with wagons.

"They must be people from Domrémy also travelling back," Pierre said to me in the quietness of the dawn. Above us, the velvety sky was welcoming the first rays of the sun. In the distance, I heard the early cries of the birds.

We met Jean in the fields outside the city. He was perched on the fence, waiting, the cows grazing nearby. When we stopped in front of him, I hugged him. He smelt of hay. My head reached his chin, and he stroked my hair.

"Good luck at the forge," I said when I released him, a pit of sadness in my stomach.

"Thank you, little one," he said smiling, his bright blue eyes sad but grateful. His gaze shifted to Pierre, who was walking over.

Pierre hugged Jean briefly and clapped Jean's right shoulder twice. "Good luck."

Jean nodded. "Thanks."

Pierre nodded too, an understanding brewing between them.

"Don't forget to send news," said Mama from where she was sitting in the wagon. Papa and Mama had already given Jean a farewell hug at Uncle's house.

After our farewell, Jean climbed the hill and went back to the city. He strode with confidence through the open gates and eventually disappeared through the town's narrow streets.

The sound of the wagon brought me back, and I turned as I felt a light touch on my shoulder. Pierre was watching me. "Come, Jehanne, it's a long way back home."

I looked back to the empty gate of Neufchâteau and sighed. Our family felt torn. I silently nodded to Pierre. I was going to miss my big brother, and the solemn gaze in Pierre's eyes told me he felt the same. Turning, I gave a slight nod and began to walk on the dirt road, behind our wagon.

The journey back to Domrémy was quiet, but I entertained myself by looking at the familiar views of the countryside. We walked gaily, enjoying being out of the city. When the sun was high in the sky, Pierre suddenly called out and pointed, "Look, it's the Domrémy church, Jehanne. I'll race you to the town!"

Without sparing any second, Pierre raced ahead. Not to be outdone, I chased after him. Pierre, being taller, slowly widened the gap between us, but as I was used to running everywhere, I pushed my legs harder and managed to keep up with him until we entered the village.

Our playing came to an abrupt stop when we entered Domrémy. Pierre and I both stood there and stared. "My God…" Pierre's voice trailed off.

The town was completely empty, yet an eeriness hung in the air. The town, which had once been bustling and filled with life, looked broken and lifeless. The houses were all untouched, yet the dirt streets were filled with discarded and broken furniture.

Chickens pecked and roamed freely, and everywhere we saw broken doors, tables, and chairs. Pierre and I walked through the ghost town, silently grieving, in horror of the destruction our village was dealt.

From the outside, our small house seemed mostly untouched, save for the empty door frame and the broken wooden furniture strewn at the front. We hurriedly entered and gaped. To our dismay, in the main room, everything was thrown everywhere. The table had a broken leg and the benches were broken. I was sure I had seen some parts of the benches out in the street.

Yet our distress subsided when we went to see the two bedrooms on the first floor. The rooms were untouched, the furniture intact. Everything was as we had left it. The mattresses were empty, and the bedside tables and chairs intact, with the trunks against the walls.

The small room next to the kitchen was also untouched. Our hopes were high as we went up to Mama and Papa's room on the second floor. Their room was unaltered. Pleased, we looked at each other.

Pierre said, with a shoulder shrug and a small smile, "That's not so bad." He went to look around the back rooms more closely and added, "Looks like they only had time to destroy the first room. They must have been in a hurry. The bedrooms are intact. The beds and all the cabinets are unblemished."

Then we heard voices and the sound of a wagon stopping outside. We hurried downstairs to hear Papa's raised exclamation bounding through the walls of the house. "Bloody hell, those bastards! Those sons of pigs!" He let out a string of curses.

Meeting him on the ground floor we saw him looking, unimpressed and with a scowl on his face, at the destruction in the first room. Mama's small frame was behind him, her hands clutched at her chest, and her eyes doleful at the sight of the havoc.

After a few minutes, Papa calmed down and said, "I can fix everything, starting with the front door." He looked towards my brother. "What about the bedrooms?"

"They are untouched. Nothing is broken," Pierre said.

Papa calmed down. "Jehanne, get the animals and see if there is anything in the vegetable garden."

"Yes, Papa." Promptly, I ran through the side door outside. In the distance I heard the voices of other villagers who were arriving. The town was slowly coming to life again.

At the wagon, I detached the pens of the chickens and ducks. The barn caught my eye then, so I left the pens on the ground and moved over to the barn. When I pushed at the barn door it creaked open and, as if opened for the first time in a lifetime, dust mites fell over me and spiderwebs dotted the ceiling and fell like decorations.

I gave a sigh of relief. *It's as if no one was here*, I thought to myself.

Luckily, everything was intact, and I went back to the wagon to retrieve the chickens and ducks. I took them to the back of the house. The grass was long; the greenery around our house looked overgrown and wild.

The cows and goats that remained in Domrémy were roaming freely across the fields next to the forest. I gathered them next and took them to a fenced paddock closer to the house.

When I went back inside, Papa had already taken out the front door and was fixing it with Pierre. I left them to it, and helped Mama clean the floor before we began to unpack. We took everything that was broken to the front of the house, and then cleaned the kitchen. That took us much of the day. When everything was clean, we unpacked the wagon and Papa, with Pierre's help, and took the wagon to the back of the house.

"I will get firewood to prepare the fire and start making bread," I told Mama.

She nodded absentmindedly as she took out some pots to make supper.

The town was slowly beginning to show remnants of life, as I walked out. Dusk was quickly sweeping over the sky, and villagers were ducking in and out of the houses like crazed ants, rebuilding their homes.

A surge of gratification welled up within me. "Thank you, Lord, for the English did not plunder and destroy our town so dreadfully." I remember Mama told me the last time the English were in Domrémy, the church was set on fire and many houses too, but I was little when that happened, so I didn't remember it.

I turned the corner of the house, to the back wall where we usually piled the wood for the fire. To my surprise, an immense pile of wood leaned against the wall. Astonished at the quantity, I began to heap some into my arms.

It seems as if the English were just here in passing. They had no time to pillage or really do anything. The English had no time at all, I thought to myself, still stunned.

The vegetable garden was across from the wall of the piled firewood. When we were home, we maintained it and pruned it, yet these past few months of our absence left it lush and bulbous. The plants grew over and under each other, and inside the small jungle of greenery was a collection of ripe and overripe vegetables.

"My God, how extraordinary!" I exclaimed, my mouth gaping and eyes wide. The entire garden was untouched, full of grown, green vegetables. I walked between the islands, looking at the abundance of vegetation, like a poor man casting his eyes on trunks of treasure and gold. "This is… Thank you, thank you," I said aloud.

As night approached—the sun setting behind the hills, and a chill breeze starting to blow—I returned to the barn and fetched a bucket to get some fresh milk. Kneeling on the grass by one of the cows, I reached under, felt the full udder, and began to squeeze out the milk. I couldn't believe our surplus of food. We had only been gone for a few weeks, and we had come back to such a gift.

I gathered everything to go back to the house. My arms were full as I approached the hunched over figures of Papa and Pierre in the front yard; they were fixing the benches and kitchen table. They looked over and their eyes widened at me—one arm holding a few planks of wood, the other holding a bulging basket of large, ripe vegetables. I smiled knowingly and went inside, the door already reattached.

The room was scant of furniture, as most of it was still outside waiting to be mended by Papa. Yet it was still peculiar to see Mama sitting cross-legged on the floor, with a large bowl in front of her. A sack of flour lay open next to her, and she was laboriously kneading the dough. Face flushed and knuckles bulging from the hard work, she looked up as I walked in.

I walked stiffly over to the fireplace, trying to not sway the bucket of milk. As I placed the bucket gently down and lowered the basket and wooden planks, Mama got up awkwardly and went to the wall of the kitchen. There, at a single stone in the wall, she seemed to be praying.

I watched as her fingers, so gentle and precise, moved across the wall until they stopped and pulled out a small loose stone that revealed an empty hole in the wall. Reaching her hand in, she took out something small and bundled in cloth. She motioned for me to come closer, and her mouth turned upwards to a cheeky smile as if sharing a secret.

"I left this cheese here, because this one needs to ripen a little longer. Oh, I didn't know if we would come back. And look, it's just perfect! Oh! And you brought milk, we'll have this for supper."

"Mama, also the garden… Look, I found all these vegetables!" I turned and pointed to the basket near the fireplace.

"Yes, dear. The garden can tend itself, and look at what treasures it can grow!" Mama beamed at the collection of fresh produce. "We can use them tomorrow. Tonight, we will have bread, cheese, and warm milk."

"I'll set the fire then," I said, smiling back at her, sauntering to the fireplace.

With the door up and closed, and the fire lit, the house began to warm up. Night had fallen and Papa and Pierre had finished their work. We all sat on the floor and ate our simple supper of bread, cheese, and hot milk.

Only the sounds of chewing and slurping could be heard in the silent night, we were too exhausted to talk. I felt my bones starting to warm up once my belly was full. My eyelids slowly drooping downwards, I longed for sleep.

My parents' faces were haggard, and their eyes were empty as they stared into the fire. Pierre was lying face-up on the hard ground, his hands clasped over his eyes. There we were, the firelight and our own company.

The fire was slowly becoming smaller, and the house began to darken. Papa was the first to stir. He shuffled to his feet and said gruffly, "Tomorrow will be a busy day. Everyone should get some sleep. Good night." This was followed by the deep thump of his footsteps, slowly receding as he climbed up the stairs.

Pierre slowly got up and murmured his goodnight, retreating to his room. The clanking of bowls made me look up at Mama; she was collecting everyone's dishes and placing the pots in a large water basin. She rolled up her long sleeves and began to scrub them clean.

I got up, wearily, and began to dry the pots and bowls. Before splashing water over the fire, I lit a small candle to carry to my bedroom.

A week had passed since we had returned to Domrémy, and life eventually crept back into the small village. We began to feel at home again as we resumed our chores and daily routine. Papa and Pierre were out in the fields, and I helped Mama with the chores at home.

Each day we followed a similar routine: getting up and quickly dressing, eating breakfast, then tending to the animals, cutting and gathering the firewood, and gathering vegetables and fruit from the garden and the orchard.

One bright and sunny day, about mid-afternoon, I was in the orchard. Domrémy looked more beautiful than ever. The rows of trees were never-ending, their branches dotted with apples. They were in season and the orchard was filled with their sweet perfume.

At the bottom of one of the tallest trees, which had wide and open spaces between its branches, lay a basket that I'd half-filled with fresh apples. I climbed up to get the best apples and picked the best-looking ones, throwing them down to the basket. The basket filled gradually, some apples with brown and green spots, others oddly shaped and resembling pears.

Happy with my lot, I was about to return home when I spotted something peculiar in the high branches. There, high in the canopy of the tree, was a large, perfectly rounded vermillion apple. Dangling with perfect grace, it had somehow managed not to fall despite its weight.

Approaching the trunk, I climbed and climbed higher, until I grasped a sturdy branch overhead and slowly traversed over a wide branch. Getting closer, I slowly reached out my hand, my fingers etching closer to the forbidden fruit.

Suddenly, a gust of wind blew the apple out of my grasp and pushed me off balance. My hands on the branch overhead kept me steady, but my foot slipped and I shuffled awkwardly to regain my balance. The wind continued to sway the branches and leaves of the tree in a whirlwind of movement. Disappointed, I retreated and climbed down.

Once I jumped onto the ground, the wind whisked my hair back and the fringes of my dress bounded past my legs. A feeling snuck up on me and I stilled. There was something familiar. Someone. A presence. I looked around, then turned behind me.

There, between the endless rows of trees, a lady clad in white stood in the grass. The wind was gone. It was silent, and almost everything was still. The lady began to speak, her voice silvery and soft. "Hello, Jehanne."

I blinked, and I studied her, but her face was unfamiliar.

"My name is Saint Catherine of Alexandria." The woman was fair with long, light brown hair, and bright and clear honey-coloured eyes. She was pretty. She would have been quite the lady in any court in the land.

I clasped my hands together and bowed my head. "My lady."

Saint Catherine smiled with tenderness. "Jehanne, I have come to tell you that it is time you start practising with the sword. It is time you learn to defend yourself."

I looked at her. *So soon?* I swallowed. "A sword? But... how? I don't know how to use a tool like that."

"Jehanne, our Heavenly Father has already arranged your teacher."

After hearing those words, relief washed through me. Then a memory resurfaced in my mind of a field, a noble on a horse, and a sword. *The dream in Neufchâteau...*

I broke away from my thoughts. "Who will teach me? Who has God chosen?"

Catherine inclined her head and said, "Your brother, Pierre. He will be your teacher and he will also accompany you in all your campaigns. He will always be by your side. You will not be alone."

Shock rooted me to the ground, and then I hung my head back and laughed.

"My brother, Pierre?!" I smiled at the obviousness, "Of course it's meant to be Pierre, of course... I-I don't have the words right now... only thank you. I just..." My voice became small. "I don't... I don't want to be alone. I didn't want to leave my family. Thank you for allowing my brother to be alongside me in this mission, thank you."

Catherine continued, "God will speak to him in dreams. Wait for him to mention his dreams to you first. Be patient and answer his questions, Jehanne. Later, Jean will also join you."

"So, both of my brothers... will be with me?" I repeated slowly and carefully.

Saint Catherine nodded.

"Oh, thank you! This is such a relief. My brothers, they'll be with me!" I exclaimed, the double notion of Pierre and Jean coming with me almost brought tears to my eyes. But my escalation of happiness suddenly dropped, and I looked up to Catherine with panic.

"But... but my brothers... they will be in war... they will be fighting... Will they be alright? Will they be safe?" The questions poured from me before I could stop myself.

But Saint Catherine was as stoic as ever. "No harm will come to them."

And like that, she disappeared. Like all the other guides, she delivered her message and left without alarm.

I picked up the basket of apples and began to make my way home. I felt light and as if everything was perfect in the world. At that moment, I heard a soft thump behind me. I turned and saw the perfect vermillion apple cradled in the long grass.

Yes, everything is perfect, I thought to myself, running back to pick up the smooth, red-skinned fruit and smelling it as I walked home.

14

A PERSONAL MATTER

Spring, 1427
Domrémy, France

Spring came late that year. The war had tumbled into another province
of the kingdom, but in Domrémy we immersed ourselves in our lives
as if nothing happened.

Days went by and I ruminated over Saint Catherine's instructions:
'learn the sword'. I remember feeling nervous and impatient. I wanted to
start my training, but Pierre betrayed nothing of importance. My impatience built and for a week I waited, every day looking at Pierre for any
clues, but he was his normal self.

One morning when Papa had gone early to the fields to see the herds,
we sat in the kitchen eating breakfast. Mama was quietly preparing some
dough, while Pierre and I sat across from each other. I was fidgety. Unable
to contain myself any longer, I looked up at him and asked casually,
"Pierre, how did you sleep? Did you dream of anything?"

He stared at me with confusion from across the table. His eyebrows
drawn together, his blinking eyes scrutinised me. "Why are you asking
such strange questions? I always sleep well." He smiled bemusedly and
his attention went back to his bowl of porridge, bringing a spoonful to
his mouth.

I just smiled and resumed a light air, shrugging my shoulders. "No reason, just asking." Resigned, I knew the best thing to do was to wait. Perhaps Pierre would come to me in his own time, and all I could do until then was be ready for when it happened—although I had to admit, patience was not one of my strongest qualities.

Mama paid no heed to my strange question at breakfast; instead, her sharp blue eyes were masked with worry. Later that afternoon, after I had finished all my chores, we were both in the kitchen. Mama took the opportunity while we were both alone to delve into some personal matters.

I was munching on an apple, sitting at the table, and Mama was cleaning some linen shirts for Papa and Pierre in a wooden bucket, placed on the floor between the table and the fire. "Jehanne, darling, have you bled this month?"

"Yes, I told you I got a few drops."

She looked over, her eyes wide and alert. "A few drops... again?" The water in the cleaning basin splashed and moved in a see-saw motion.

"Yes," I said absentmindedly.

She resumed submerging and rubbing the piece of clothing against a knobby wooden panel. "You have not bled more? This is not normal. You should have a flow for a couple of days."

"Well, the few drops stain."

She looked over at me, unimpressed.

I smiled, adopting a comforting tone. "Mama, I think it's fine. I am very healthy, I feel fine," I said, shrugging.

She stopped and turned to look at me. "You are already fourteen years old. A few drops is not normal, and you will not be able to have children. How will you marry?" Her tone betrayed her immense worry. Her hands, wrinkled from the water, rested on the bucket, and her eyes were deep in thought.

I looked at her sympathetically, trying to think of what to say.

Her voice broke my train of thought. "Let's go to the priest."

I could sense her determination. Her mouth was tight and her shoulders were rigid as she stood up from the floor.

I looked at her blankly. *The priest? What would the priest know about my period?!* Without showing my own reluctance, I said slowly, "Mama, I feel healthy. I feel good. I don't think the priest needs to know."

Mama gave me a reproaching look, the look of 'you don't know more than your mother'. Her mind was already made up. She took off her apron, drying her hands with it, then got up to get her shawl and cap.

I felt powerless as I watched her dash around me. I kept silent though. I knew from experience that my mother could be very stubborn, especially when she was worried. *She will not change her mind, unless...*

Looking at her walking to the door, a surge of rebellion passed through me. I was strongly against this.

I don't want to share this with anybody. Even if the angels told me to obey my parents, I feel that I should not submit to this. This is very personal and even if the priest had the total trust of my mother, it was my personal dilemma.

I was not going to be forced to share this when I didn't want to.

But I must argue with reason, to persuade her, to make her see my feelings.

Thinking quickly, I turned to face her. Mama was already at the door, tying her cap.

"Mama," I said. My throat was tight, but my voice came out firm.

She turned to look at me, her hand on the wooden handle and the front door slightly open.

I walked towards her slowly. "I know the town priest has proved on many occasions to be a sensible judge, and I share your opinion that he is a good person. I also find the priest to be a faithful servant of God, and his words reflect the love of God."

My mother listened, and her features softened slightly.

I walked a few steps towards her. "But Mama, this is *my* dilemma, and it is very, *very* personal, and I will not share it with anybody else. Only you know this because you are my mother. But *nobody else* needs to know. I don't want to be known as the town's barren and have people talking behind my back." I made sure to emphasise a few key words to help her understand.

"Please mother," I pleaded with her, but at the same time I was determined.

My mother searched my face, and I could feel her determination shrinking. After a moment of silence, not knowing if I had convinced her, she finally nodded. "Yes, yes... you are right, this is a very personal matter."

I took her hands and cupped them. "Trust, everything that happens is God's will. It's meant to be like this."

She looked at me with sad eyes. "Yes, I... I am worried, because, well, what if you can't have children, Jehanne? Who will marry you?" She approached the table. Sitting down, she took off her shawl and wrapped it in a bundle in her lap. Her features were screwed up into a ball of dismay.

Oddly, I felt like I was looking at an injured animal, licking their wounds.

I quietly sat next to her, taking her hand. "Well, it may not be my destiny to get married."

She looked up at me with tender surprise. Her eyebrows lifted. "Are you thinking of entering a convent?" I thought I saw a flicker of hope in the depths of her eyes.

I responded, "I don't know yet, but it would please me. I would like to serve God with all my heart."

At that, her eyes glowed with warmth, and she smiled contentedly. She took both of my hands and patted them affectionately. Softly, she said, "I've always wondered the meaning of the dream I had when I was pregnant with you."

"What dream, Mama?" I asked, genuinely interested.

She shook her head and waved her hand aside, gesturing as if it was unimportant or even crazy.

But I patted her hand again and insisted, "What dream? Please tell me, Mama."

"Oh okay, but don't repeat this to anyone," she told me.

"I promise, I will not say a word to anyone," I said, smiling with my right hand on my heart.

"Well," she began, her eyes hazy as she remembered from the distant pond of memories. "I was in a field full of flowers, like daisies, like the ones you see in a meadow. And oh, how it was full of beautiful flowers. I bent down to take one when I heard a voice asking me, 'Why do you want a flower from my garden?'"

"I looked up and ahead I saw a light in human form, and I answered, 'Oh Lord, they are so beautiful. I would like to take one home to decorate my table.'"

I listened eagerly, hanging off every word she said.

"And the light responded to me, 'You already have one inside your womb. I'm going to give her to you, to take care of until I call her to fulfil my prophecy.'"

My mouth lay agape, and as if a piece of the puzzle suddenly came into place, I felt complete. My journey was now making sense. It had even come to my mother when she was pregnant with me.

Overcome and touched by her story, I hugged her tightly. "Oh Mama!"

Her body shook as she chuckled lightly.

"I can't believe that! It's so beautiful!" I said, still enveloped in our embrace.

After I released, I looked up at her. Her bright blue eyes were full, and her voice was thick with emotion. "At that moment I knew you were going to be a girl, and I started to choose the most beautiful name I could find."

She wiped her eyes with her sleeve and smiled so adoringly at me.

"Mama, you chose the most beautiful one!" I said, full of love, hugging her again and kissing her on the forehead.

15

PIERRE AND SAINT MICHAEL

"The struggle for self-mastery that every human being must wage if he or she is to emerge from life victorious."

— Bhagavad Gita

Late Spring, 1427
Domrémy, France

Several days after my talk with Mama about her dream, I was in the barn sweeping the floor with a straw-fanned broom. Ever since, I felt a sense of comfort that everything was unfolding as it should be. Our talk gave me the comfort to not feel so alone on my upcoming journey and I understood that everything would happen in its own time. Even my preoccupation for Pierre withered, and I became more absorbed in the housework and helping Mama.

Dreams must be how God talks to us, I thought as I breathed in.

The air in the barn was musty, and the floor was littered with hay strands almost as thin as hair. The chooks cackled and peeped as I swept over the barn. I had managed to finish all of my chores and had just finished changing the animals hay when Pierre walked in. It was close to midday.

I was so engrossed in gathering the sparse hay in the corner, I didn't even notice him at first. I only heard the creak of the barn door as it opened widely, spilling sunlight inside, alighting the millions of floating dust mites of the barn.

I turned and he was sitting on one of the low benches against the wall at the entrance. I quickly resumed my sweeping, taking no notice. Perhaps he wanted something from the barn or wanted to rest.

He leaned over, so that his elbows rested on his knees. His mouth rested on the ridge of his fingers; his left hand covered his right, which was closed in a fist. Appearing deep in thought, his brow was like a straight line, and his eyes were distant and focussed on the ground in front of him.

I began to slowly push the pile of old hay, dust, and dirt that had accumulated from my sweeping towards the door.

Pierre released his arms, then began to draw something on the ground with his foot. "Jehanne," he said, his tone uncertain.

I looked up, but he said nothing more, as if he didn't know how to continue. He sat there struggling to find the right words, until he finally said, "I've been having some very strange dreams lately."

My heartbeat quickened and a hollow pit formed in my chest, making me breath faster and deeper. I tried hard to mask my reaction. I slowly concentrated on my breathing and forcing my voice to sound normal. "What do you mean, dreams? What kind of dreams?" I took the broom and began to sweep again. Fastidious though it was, the floor was spotless.

He slowly looked up. "There is a man in my dreams," he began, "who says that I have to help you because you have a mission to fulfil. The man in my dreams shows me a sword and tells me that I have to give it to you.

"At first, I ignored the dream. It made no sense. I simply attributed it to something ridiculous, you know," he said with a shrug. "Something I ate."

I glanced at him, stopped sweeping, and then gave him my full attention. My eyes were patient and curious, and Pierre took my silence as his
cue to continue.

"But in the last two dreams a strange… a strange light appeared to
me." Here, he chuckled dryly, as if he couldn't believe his own words. "It
told me that this is a command from God… that I must teach you how
to handle the sword."

Pierre stopped, as if remembering the words, then he continued.
"Otherwise…" He took a deep breath. "You are going to die."

A flash of distress crossed his eyes as he looked over at me. "And
then it showed me b-b-battles where you are fighting! You, Jehanne!" His
voice rose as if he couldn't believe what he was saying. His eyes fixed on
me. They were troubled and distraught. "You, i-in the middle of soldiers,
horses, and blood!" Pierre cried.

I stood there, impassive and silent. Taking in his distress, I waited for
a moment for him to continue. When he stayed silent, I left the broom
against the wall and walked towards him. I knelt next to him, taking his
hand. "Pierre, my dear brother, I know this is difficult. I know it must
seem… unbelievable!"

A small, dry laugh escaped my lips. "I knew that you were going to
have those dreams. The angels came to me and told me. They also told
me that this is my destiny. I-I have a mission… and… I-I don't know why
me, but God has given me this life for that. He says I was born to fulfil
his prophecy."

Breathing deeply, I continued talking. "I know this is difficult to see,
but this will make sense, I promise you that."

I heard Pierre sigh, his face screwed up. "That's what they told me in
my dreams. They said you are going to be the Maid of Lorraine!" His tone
was final. I opened my mouth to protest, but Pierre spoke first, "No, you
can't deny it. I have seen it in my dreams. I have seen you, Jehanne, God
has shown me," he told me seriously, no trace of doubt in his voice.

I just nodded.

"God has also shown me that I will accompany you in battles." He looked over at me, his eyes glazed with a determination I rarely saw. "If I am to go with you, I can protect you."

Before I could respond, he suddenly said, "I must get something. Wait here." He got up and left the barn, returning a few minutes later with a long bundle in his hand.

"Look here," he said, unwrapping the bundle and taking out two wooden swords. "So we can practise. I made them myself." He took one out and held it with two hands; he slashed and twirled the sword in the air.

Then he stopped and looked at me and said, "We are going to practise, and you are going to be as good as any man, I promise you, Jehanne. I will teach you everything I know because I know you can do it. You are strong and athletic, you run everywhere, and now I know why you are doing it." He raised one of his eyebrows and gave me a half smile, as if now revealing a secret.

His face turned serious. "I will teach you how to hold a sword." His hands clasped and moved around the imaginary pommel. "How to move with a sword." He stepped backwards and forwards. "And," he grimaced, "how to fight." He slashed an invisible enemy and carried out a flurry of movements in the empty space of the barn.

I watched him, admiring his skill.

He turned around and saw my face. "Jehanne?" he said inquiringly.

"I just… Pierre, have you told Mama or Papa?" I asked.

Pierre shook his head and formed his mouth into an o shape. "No, nothing. In my dream, the man said we must be very quiet about this. By the way, did I tell you that the man in the dreams said that his name was Michael?"

"Like Archangel Michael?" My eyes sparkled with amusement.

"Yes… wait, how do you know?" He inclined his head.

"If it is from God, it must be one of his angels. Also, Archangel Michael comes to me and imparts advice and messages." I shrugged.

"Well, if he comes to *me* in *my dreams*, then he must visit *you* in *real life*, little Jehanne," he said, ruffling my head.

I smiled and laughed quietly.

I breathed in and a deep sense of appreciation welled up in my chest. I felt unburdened, lighter, freer. The barn was quiet as Pierre swung his sword and practised, his feet shuffling over the floor. I simply watched in awe of his confident skill.

I knew if Pierre was with me, he would give me the strength I needed, and now that he knew about my mission, I no longer felt alone. He was going to be there.

He was going to help me save our kingdom.

From that day on, we started a new routine. In the afternoons after completing all of our chores on the farm and the house, we practised training. To avoid unwanted eyes, we went behind the house and orchid to the mouth of the forest. There, we would be undisturbed and train uninterrupted. Although my training sessions were important, I did miss meeting with my friends in the afternoon, but I knew this was more important.

We would leave the swords hidden under a pile of dry branches and leaves. Sometimes Pierre would take them with him, when the sacks of wheat had to be distributed to other towns close to home. Sometimes, I would accompany him, and when that happened, we practised in a safe and private place.

The sword was not heavy, but manoeuvring it with one arm was tiring, so I held it two-handed. The movements were repetitive and demanding, but Pierre would say, "Jehanne, you must learn them as if it were your second nature."

After completing the initial part of the training, which was learning defense and blocking movements, he began to teach me how to attack. He would often say, "Now comes the most entertaining part. Now try to touch me on the shoulder, arms, or my legs. Ready? Let's go." He put himself in a defensive position, holding the wooden sword two-handed in front of him.

Pierre did not hold back in our training. When I asked him for rest or to make it easier, he would stop and say loudly, "When you are in front of an English soldier, they will not stop *or* show you any mercy." He made an effort to emphasise his words.

I looked up at him, panting and fatigued. I nodded glumly.

"In battles, there is no waiting for your enemy. It is a fight for life or death." Blunt as he was, he tried to show what awaited us both, and his words rang with truth as I would later see.

"So, mademoiselle Jehannette, en guard!" he told me while raising his sword and getting into position to attack.

I had no choice but to continue practising. I gathered all my energy, and I held my sword high, blocking his flurry of attacks as best as I could.

For the first few weeks, I could barely hold my arms up. The day after every session, I woke up each morning with my entire body sore and tight. Pierre's wooden sword broke through my defences and left my sides, arms, and legs bruised and blue.

Yet as the weeks passed by, my muscles became stronger. Some days, we would spar for only an hour; other times, the whole afternoon. Beads of sweat would gather on my forehead, and my arms burned and begged for rest, but each time I knew I had to keep going. Gradually, the sessions became mine. I could keep up with Pierre, my arms were stronger, and I perfected his blocks and gradually held my own.

A week had passed since our last training. It was the afternoon after I had finished my chores in the garden and I was looking for Pierre, but I could not find him. I went to ask Mama, who was in the front garden. She was sitting on a chair with a bunch of herbs on her lap, binding the herbs with a piece of string, to later hang and dry in the kitchen. "Mama, have you seen Pierre?"

"I saw him leave towards the river with two small sacks in hand a while ago," she said with her gaze on her lap, busily tidying the herbs and leaving them on a plate on the floor, next to her.

I ran towards the river and found my brother on the shore filling the sacks with dirt. "What are you doing?"

"Wait and see," he replied laconically, tying the sacks with a linen cloth and lifting them over his shoulders.

We walked back home in silence. Pierre put the bags half-full of sand on the cart and left without saying another word. I watched his back disappear into the distance, wondering at his strange behaviour, but then shrugging it off, I went home. Mama was in the kitchen taking off her apron and putting her shawl around her shoulders. All the herbs hung next to the fire, ready when needed for cooking.

She looked at me and asked, "Are you coming?"

It took a moment for me to realise. "Oh, yes! It's embroidery day," I replied enthusiastically. "I'll get my things."

Quickly getting my cloth and box of needles, Mama and I walked together to town. We stopped at the front of Marianne's house, one of mama's friends. From inside, we could hear the mumble of voices and laughter. A short while after we knocked, Marianne opened the door. She was a little younger than Mama and was a woman with happy manners and a welcoming smile. Her long brown hair was tied up in a bun at the back of her head.

"Isabel, Jehannette, come, come inside," Marianne said, while stepping aside and closing the door behind us.

"Excuse us, we are a little late," said Mama.

"We just started. You haven't missed much." All the mothers were sitting by the fire in the kitchen and the younger girls sat in a circle, closer to the door.

"Jehannette, there is a stool for you," said Marianne, pointing at an empty stool in the circle of girls.

"Thank you," I said while sitting down.

Mama and Marianne chatted, all the while making their way to the group of mamas. The oldest girls were chatting lively when I sat down.

"Hello," I quietly said, trying not to disturb the conversation and taking my embroidery and placing it on my lap. Some of the girls smiled and nodded to me. Seeing Isabel sitting on the left of the circle, I gave her a quick smile.

Isabel was usually quiet and demure, and usually we younger girls would listen and follow the conversation of the older girls. Margarete, Marianne's niece, was seventeen. She smiled and nodded to me, and looked over at Charlotte and Magdalene with an amused eye roll.

Charlotte, with her fiery red curls and round brown eyes, and Margarete with long brown hair cascading down her shoulders, were busily sharing the latest.

Charlotte gasped. "I heard from my cousin that Philippe will be marrying a girl from Neufchâteau."

Margaret's eyes widened in surprise. "No! I thought he was promised to…"

Charlotte shook her head, while looking down at her embroidery. "I heard she was no longer fit to give her dowry. The crop season this year has been hard on everyone. And you know what the English did to their estate."

Magdalene frowned. "How unfortunate!" Her eyes looked troubled at the news. "I don't suppose anyone knows what will happen in these hard times."

Charlotte's gaze landed on me, and she asked, "And Jehanne, how do you fare? I hope you didn't lose much from the English?"

I responded, "No, most of the looting was fixable. We were very lucky."

"Oh good, and has your father found a suitable husband for you?"

I looked up and said, "No, no that I know of." I shrugged and continued, "I don't know anything about that."

"Well, you are growing fast and you are not bad looking. I mean, I would love to have your hair colour, like red wine. Mine is so ginger," she said while touching her hair.

I answered simply, "I have no intention of getting married. I want to dedicate my life to God."

All the girls nodded. Charlotte followed the conversation, her eyes becoming more and more mischievous. "Ah, well there is a boy who has been asking for you."

The other girls looked up in curiosity, but I kept my gaze on my embroidery and said, "I hope he is not deluded." I knew of the boy. Some news had reached Mama, and she told me he was Margarete's cousin from a neighbouring town.

I continued my embroidery, adding, "Whoever is asking is wasting his time, because I am not going to get married. I'm going to dedicate my life to God." I looked up, smiling.

The girls smiled at me and Magdalene responded, "Well, we need to pass the word around that Jehanne is not interested, so we all have one more man to choose from for a husband in the future." We all laughed, and I heard a murmur of approval among the girls.

Charlotte spoke again. "Pierre is handsome but very conceited, and he thinks he's better than us."

I remembered laughing and answering, "Stop bothering him and he will surely speak to you one day."

We all laughed and then Magdalene said to Charlotte, "You've got to give the boy some room!"

"What are all you girls talking about?" asked Marianne from the other corner of the room.

"Nothing, Aunt" responded Margarate, giggling. She then looked coyly down at her embroidery, humming a popular tune. Like water flowing from a jug, Charlotte's voice joined in and their voices created a beautiful symphony. Following their lead, we all began to sing. My cheeks were pinched from smiling and the rising of my voice.

16

A NEW UNDERSTANDING

Mid-Summer, 1427
Domrémy, France

*T*he sounds of our slow movements suffused the early morning. The stiff, wooden chairs felt hard, but the smell of hot bread and cooked warm milk comforted my groggy mind. Usually, while we sat breaking fast, Mama, Pierre, and I would sit in silence, but today I looked up as I felt a dull nudge on my rib. I looked over to Pierre questioningly, sleep and grogginess still clouding my mind like mist.

Tilting his head down, towards his chest, so only I could hear, he murmured, "When you finish your chores, meet me in the forest for training."

Mama was a safe distance away. Her back was turned as she tended the bread from the fire. Before I could answer, she turned, and Pierre resumed eating as if he had said nothing.

Acting aloof, I also turned my eyes back to my plate, but my sleepiness faded, and my curiosity was sparked like a kindle of fire.

Soon after, Pierre got up. "Alright, I'm off. I'll see you two later."

Mama absentmindedly responded, "Alright, darling," reaching over and collecting our plates to clean.

As the day wore on, I wondered what Pierre had planned for us. As we were training frequently, I grew more adept at the sword, quickly learning movements and techniques. Did he plan to teach me something new?

Finally, after finishing my chores, I washed my hands in the large bucket next to the door. I made my way to the forest, as I promised Pierre. It was still early afternoon, and by the time I saw Pierre in the distance, he was on the edge of the forest, leaning against a gnarled tree. I ran up through the long grass, pressing down a handful of stems with each step until I reached him.

"Hey, you finished early," Pierre commented. He sounded pleasantly surprised.

"Yeah, I didn't have much to do in the garden." I shrugged, slightly breathless.

"Good, more time for training. And just when I have a surprise for you," responded Pierre, with a sly smile.

My eyebrows rose with delight. "Really, what?"

"Come and see," said Pierre. He picked up the bundle with the swords from under some dry sticks. Smiling, he said, "Let's go."

He led us down the narrow path into the forest. The warmth of the afternoon sun was gone, replaced by the chill of the shade of the forest.

"Where are we going?" I asked, with a hint of amusement and bewilderment in my voice. "I have found a better place where we can continue our training," he said while walking fast and dodging some low branches. We went deep into the woods, walking until we reached a large opening.

I looked around and recognised it immediately; it was the clearing where I used to play as a child. I took in every detail. Everything was as I remembered. The clearing was still intact with the log lying on the ground, the stump in the middle, and the sun rays filtering through the canopies of the trees.

Pierre had placed himself at the edge of the clearing next to a sand-bag, the size of a large tray, hanging from a low, thick branch.

"Do you recognise this place?" he asked, glancing up at the dense branches covering the clearing below.

I nodded, smiling. A sensation of fond memories began to surface. "Yes, this is where I used to play when I was younger. It's the same." In my voice, I sensed I was far away, remembering my childhood stories and imagination.

The sound of the clack of wooden swords brought me back to the present. Pierre unwrapped them and handed one to me, pointing his sword at the sandbag hanging from the tree.

"This bag is for training purposes. I saw it when we were in the town of Neufchâteau, how the soldiers practised and hung bags like these for the recruits."

I nodded slowly, comprehending Pierre's plans. *Oh, this is going to be difficult.*

Pierre continued, "I was training the last two days. The bag is tough and helps you practise as if you've really sparred with another swords-man." He massaged his shoulder as he spoke.

"Well…" I said, pausing as I gulped. I was not looking forward to this new training regime. "Don't expect me to last as long as you do."

"Let's see," he said, while smiling, which did nothing to allay my trepidation.

"Okay, start doing the movements in the air first, left and right, then use the bag as your opponent, remembering what I've taught you," said Pierre while showing me the movements.

I approached the bag hesitantly, then performed the moves in the air, and slowly edged closer to the sandbag. When I first struck the bag, my arms and shoulders felt the impact. But as the bag moved, I shuffled around, maintaining a lightness of foot.

Fifteen minutes later, my clothes were soaked and I was out of breath. I bent over with my hands on my knees to keep myself from falling over.

Pierre's voice sounded far away as my heavy breathing filled my ears. "That's not bad for the first time."

When I had somewhat cooled down, Pierre and I started sparring. Recovering, I slowly picked up the wooden sword again and held my position to face him. As we sparred, I could feel sweat falling on my forehead, and my arms ached with pain. My entire body was tense and coiled, my hair was matted with sweat, and every inch of me was red. But when Pierre struck low to my side, I repositioned myself and brought my sword low to deflect it.

Attempting to lift my hands back up to continue, I felt my arms become stone. The heaviness of the sword weighed my arms down, and, overcome with weakness, I croaked, "Enough."

Pierre brought his sword down and nodded. I trudged to the closest tree and leaned against it. Craning my neck and resting my head on the oak, I closed my eyes and waited for my breathing to slow and my body to rest.

I slid down the trunk, and I could only hear the sound of our breathing interrupting the silence of the forest. Once I regained more strength, I looked around, taking in the stillness of the forest. Pierre was also silent and contemplative, and waited patiently until I felt ready to leave. When I got up wearily, he began wrapping the swords in the sack, and hid them under a tree.

"Ready?" he asked.

I nodded. "Let's go."

We walked back the way we came. When we emerged from the forest, the sun had lowered and, in effect, cast long shadows against the landscape. Even though we were training, I could still feel the chill of the wind as evening was approaching.

We walked in silence for a while, then Pierre's voice cut through the air. "Jehannette, you did very well today." I replied with a huff, but Pierre ignored my response. "No, really. Listen, I think you were meant for this type of training."

I cast him a look of surprise.

Pierre continued. "I'm teaching you ways to defend yourself, to know how to *win*. In battle." He gazed over the horizon as we walked, and from his pauses I suspected he was struggling to find the right words. "Men fight for glory or for adventure, but you, Jehanne, you have a *purpose*. You don't fight for greed or war-lust. I think you will fight for something higher. You will represent the hope this kingdom needs."

Pensive, I considered his words. His statement brought a new light to our training.

This is a bloody and brutal skill. I never wanted to be an instrument of violence, I thought to myself. I looked at Pierre and gave him a nod. "I understand."

Pierre gave me a small, reassuring smile and we continued the rest of the way in silence.

That night after dinner, as I lay awake in bed, I felt the soreness creep into my arms, shoulders, back muscles, and legs. I felt bruises swelling where Pierre struck me as we sparred. I massaged my shoulders and arms, careful to avoid the areas I knew would hurt most tomorrow.

I turned over, wincing at the new pains and aches. I reached over to the small drawer beside my bed and fumbled for my rosary. The thin cord of the necklace felt cool. I wrapped it around my fingers, counting the small beads as I prayed. I sank into the rosary; it was like a balm, flooding my entire mind and body.

The next sessions with Pierre followed similarly to our first practice. It was arduous and intense. Pierre was patient, but he liked to challenge me and also be creative in our sessions. At the beginning, the demands were intense, and I needed to stop and rest often. But as my body gradually became stronger and more resistant to the high intensity of the exercises, our sessions didn't leave me sore and bruised afterwards.

As for Pierre, he watched and scrutinised my every move, pausing our sessions to correct my movements and explain how to fight most effectively. He did not ask me any more of the mission, and I knew he was focused on getting me strong. He knew the weight on his shoulders, so he made sure we practised and practised.

In my heart, I knew that his duty would be the key to our success. Should I succeed and survive in battle, it would be thanks to Pierre.

Time passed quickly. Winter was quickly approaching, and our routines were set. We continued practising in the forest, and as we did my body changed. My shoulders and arms became toned, and my grip on the sword hilt became stronger; I could hold it upright for longer and longer.

Elated with my progress, I hadn't realised the prolonged absence of my guides until I received an unexpected visit one autumn morning. The sun was almost reaching its zenith as I turned and tilled the dark soil in the vegetable garden. Then quite suddenly, I felt a deep whoosh sound, a forceful push of wind that blew my cap off. Quickly catching it, I straightened up. Alarmed, I paused and looked around attentively.

The garden was waving and dancing, and my clothes and skirt pressed all around me. But the garden was empty. Not entirely convinced, I stayed still for a moment longer.

Then, a strong floral scent drifted into the garden. I looked toward the orchard, stretching over the fields. In the springtime, the orchard's sweet-smelling fragrance would linger in the air. Yet this close to winter, the branches of the orchard trees were bare and moved stiffly in the swing of the wind, so the scent was unexpected.

Confused, I almost turned away to find another source of the smell, until something on the horizon caught my eyes. There, hanging above the orchard was a large, warm yellow light. The light was circular, but its brightness shone like the sun, its rays spreading to touch everything in its vicinity. I stared, perplexed, my mouth hanging open.

The light seemed to flash and pulsate with power as if it was alive. Its brightness wasn't harsh on my eyes; in fact, I felt its warmth and its pull. It approached me, and I stood staring at it, until it was suspended at the height of my head, in front of me.

Unsure of what to do or what to say, I stayed still and marvelled at the beauty of the light, for it truly was a sight. Then, from the light, a voice emerged. Like from the deep depths of a lake, this voice commanded a powerful yet nurturing presence. It was not female or male, but a voice of love.

"Jehanne, you are going to start your mission soon, for this you were born to do." As the light spoke, the rays of yellow tendrils etched towards me and gently went through my body. At first, I felt its warmth, then the vastness of its incredible bliss. It was as if the light itself was compassion, love, peace, and bliss all together at once. I couldn't move; it was as if the energy had me pinned to the ground.

"You are going to be my instrument. You are going to be my soldier in the men's army. The princes, dukes, and captains will listen to you. You will lead the army to victories. I will give you those victories. The prophecy must be fulfilled. France will be liberated after a hundred years by a girl, a maiden, a soldier of God."

At this, the light rays were becoming stronger and enclosing me in their embrace, so much so that the garden and the house were slowly receding from my peripheral.

"You have been training well. Your brother will be with you throughout your campaign. You will only have one year for your mission. You will go to Chinon and you will speak to the Dauphin. You will initiate the campaign against the army in Orleans and from there, you will go up the valley, liberating every town, and in Rouen you will crown the King of France."

I stood, listening in awe. The words reverberated in my whole being, but at the same time wrapped me in peace. Then within me, from my heart, came these words. "King of Heaven, my life is your will," I said, my heart completely enveloped with this transcendental being.

The light expanded itself and enveloped my whole being. The garden and house disappeared within the light's powerful embrace. As if every cell of my being was immersed in the light, I lost the consciousness of my body and individuality. I didn't identify as my body, nor by my name, I was just wrapped in an ecstasy of divine love. I lost consciousness.

The next thing I remembered was the smell of the earth and my cheek pressed hard against the soil. Slowly returning to my body, I breathed in as my eyes began to twitch and slowly began to open. A deep joy emanated from inside my being. Brushing dirt from my cheek and clothes, I felt a strong sense of connection to nature. It emanated with a brilliance I had never comprehended before.

It was almost alive, and it was pulsating with energy that was the same energy that kept me alive. Above, the sun had moved past its peak, and I could tell it was already afternoon. I stood up, gingerly, and gazed over to the orchard.

The trees were bare and emanated an energy like love. Before, I saw them as beautiful instruments in the landscape. Yet with this newfound experience, my heart was glowing with a joy I had never experienced as I felt the immense connection to everything around me.

My eyes landed on the forest in the distance. It was as much a part of me as my own limbs. The forest was a reflection of my inner being: blissful and joyful. The incredible vast energy of love and peace in my mind was also running through the forest, through the entire world. I didn't feel separate from anything; in fact, everything was one.

"Incredible," I whispered to myself. I was connected with everything that surrounded me, an expansion of my inner being.

This knowledge does not come from reason, but from the heart, I reflected, enjoying the beauty of the light's love and bliss.

Then, as if another tide of water disturbed the stillness of a lake, another thought emerged. *If everything is created by God, there must be a connection underneath all of these different forms… There must be an inner unity that is not seen, like the air that surrounds everything… Underneath these facades, there is only one.*

As I looked around, with my mind completely silent and open, wherever my eyes rested I felt this connection of love. It was as if the world was no longer a place of struggle. Everything was as it should be. Everything was perfect. Everything was beautiful.

Without thinking, I began to walk. I didn't think where. I didn't think why. I just walked. Experiencing this omniscience in my being, I needed to be alone. In a place of silence. A place where I wouldn't be disturbed.

My heart felt more joy as I looked up to the giant trunks of oak trees, living statues of nature's beauty. I walked through the narrow pathway. I felt the vibrating energy of the forest. It was *alive*, just as I was. It was in tune with the love I could feel.

When I got to the clearing, I sat on the log, silent in thought. I brought my hands to my face, feeling my face. My cheeks were full, and I was smiling, my whole being still wrapped in total happiness, in union with everything.

I closed my eyes and stayed like this. Just feeling, rising above the constraint of time and worldly matters. When the sun was setting and the forest was cast in the shadows of dusk, I left and I knew I would never forget this day.

17

WINTER

Winter, 1427
Domrémy, France

The wind howled against the old but sturdy stone houses. From a distance, Domrémy resembled a collection of small black dots in the white landscape, as it was coated in a deep layer of snow.

After encountering the omniscient being of light, I had felt the connectedness and bliss receding like a campfire slowly dying out. When I left the forest, the dusk evening was painted in purples and pinks, and fringed with the approaching blue evening sky.

I could see smoke floating from the chimney of the house, and the glow of the fireplace and candles peeking through windows. I wasn't afraid. In fact, I was in a peace of mind that left me inescapably and inexplicably happy.

I joined Mama and Pierre in preparing for supper, and it was like joining a rehearsed routine. My mind was alert and present but full of love. Mama didn't notice anything abnormal. She and the others were all so preoccupied that they didn't comment or notice anything strange.

Mama, with her devoted, bright blue eyes on her plate, diligently repeated her prayers, and Pierre and Papa distractedly talked of the crops and the latest news. As the night wore on, I even helped Mama with the usual chores in the evening.

When I woke the next morning, the elevated state that charged through me like lightning had diminished. My consciousness was back to the flatness of reality, and it was as if I no longer had the lenses to perceive the interconnected relationship of everything around me. I saw everything as separate. I didn't feel connected to the world, and my stream of thoughts extended like an endless string. Slowly pushing myself up, I wondered, *was it a dream?*

I often wondered about these amazing experiences and why they happened to me. An interesting irony was that these memories always buried themselves in the attic of my mind, like a forgotten box. But it wouldn't be until much later that I would realise their importance.

Many weeks later we continued our training, and I felt my body become much more agile and stronger. When I started, I could barely finish the exercises on the sandbag. My muscles were sore, but after arduous training sessions, I could feel myself getting better and my body adjusting to the demands of the training.

Pierre, upon seeing the improvement in my physical condition, had begun to teach me self-defence. We started with unarmed defence, as he would say, "In a battle, Jehanne, it is quite common to lose your sword and you have to know how to survive without having a sword or knife in hand."

Training usually started with Pierre telling me important rules. His first rule in fight was to never let your opponent get you on your back because then you lost your ability to move and you made an easy target for someone with a weapon. He told me, "If you get pushed to the ground, roll away from your attacker and put distance between you and your adversary. Also lift yourself as quick as you can."

Then we started practising. My first exercise was trying to trip or otherwise throw my brother to the ground, in hand-to-hand combat. During these exercises, I tasted dirt far more than my brother did, but I was learning quickly and sometimes I managed to throw him to the ground by tripping him. Looking back, I think he made it a bit easy for me.

We trained when we could, alternating between the sandbag, sword, and sometimes hand to hand self-defence, but there was much to do around the house. Sometimes Pierre was busy in the fields with the animals, or he was sent by Papa to do some errands in other towns. When this happened, I usually went to the forest and practised by myself.

The rhythm of juggling our chores and training left me completely lost in terms of tracking the events in Domrémy, or of the English.

Yet, as we supped one evening, snow slowly fell outside, and our faces were hardened from the bitter, cold wind. Mama served Papa a hot plate of soup. His low voice resounded like a drum in the quiet and sombre ambience of dinner. "I heard from the men in town today. The English have retreated to the north and have stopped their pillaging."

Pierre looked up and listened carefully to Papa.

My anticipation rose but I kept my silence. The mention of the English always brought the memory of the day we left Domrémy for Neufchâteau. It carried a heavy weight of uncertainty and fear in our hearts and pinched our souls, like a sleeping giant awoken from its deep slumber.

When Papa finished, the table was silent.

"I do not trust this peace," Papa stated.

"Why? Have they not gone to the north?" asked Pierre.

"Because we are surrounded by the Burgundy soldiers, and they are allied with the English," he said, his eyes focused on the space in front of him. He appeared deep in thought. His hand rolled into a fist-like shape, and the outer edge of his index finger nudged the ridge between his nose and mouth.

I could see Mama's eyes masked with trepidation. She put down her spoon, clasped her fingers together, and began murmuring her prayers as a silent plea of help to the heavens. I looked at her, helplessly.

No… this can't be. Surely my guides would have told me if something was to occur, I thought to myself. *No, this can't go on. We cannot live the rest of our lives like frightened rabbits, always afraid of being driven from our land, and our homes being destroyed…*

This is wrong.

I reached across the table to Mama. She instinctively responded, and I gently held her hands. My resolve was stirred and held like a compact ball inside me. I knew my purpose, and I knew I was going to be strong.

I looked at her, in a way I had never looked at her before. I looked at her with a deep knowledge that everything was going to be alright. I looked at her and I remembered my guides. Their peace, their knowledge, their strength.

Even memories of the omniscient light, its happiness, its love, filled me with strength. It was like a cool touch to a sore burn, slowly diminishing my fears until it was a small speck of dust.

Mama's eyes softened, and I could see her shoulders drop and her eyes relax slightly. I gave her a wan smile and squeezed her hands. Her eyes were glassy, and she smiled and nodded, her lips curving inwards.

After supper, Mama and I sat quietly next to the fire as we mended clothes and sewed, while we discussed the demands of the season. As winter was upon us, Michaelmas preparations were usually underway, and all the stock of foods, fruits, and meats needed to be prepared. Mama and I usually arranged and organised for this ourselves as the boys took care of the fields and the harvest.

That season of winter, the snow was never-ending, and it continued to fall until there was a deep layer covering the land. The vegetable and the herb garden were coated in heaped piles of crunchy snow, and even our warmest clothes couldn't quite keep out the cold wind's bite.

For the ducks and the chickens, we assembled a temporary little house in the barn for them to sleep. "That way we can keep them warm and together," Mama would say as she plucked one from the group if we were making duck stew.

As we trudged around the farm and the house, running errands and completing our daily chores, the snow fell and fell, creating a thick white blanket on the earth and making our treks across the fields more arduous. We trudged across, the snow reaching our knees creating deep and narrow tracks. Domrémy did not usually receive so much snow, only in the high parts of hills far west.

In the harsh and strong winter, food had become more and more scarce. Papa and Pierre had been going to the forest to set traps for small animals, but our harvest of pumpkins, carrots, and other vegetables was able to feed us.

At the table that evening Mama sat across from me, and I observed her dedicated nature. Her prayers were never above a whisper, and her rhythm of recitation never faltered, instilling in me a deeper appreciation for her quiet and strong character.

Sometimes Mama shared food with needy families who had young children, though she could not help with their household finances. But she did it in a smart way, so Papa could not have noticed. Our stock of vegetables and preserves were always in good shape, and we had more than enough to share with others.

Five days after Papa brought news of the English, our usual routine of chores had begun to lessen as the snow kept falling. There was hardly anything to do in the fields, gardens, and orchards as everywhere was covered in a deep coat of snow.

The sky was grey and dark, and around midday I could hear Papa and Pierre clearing the snow from the entryway of the doors. It was then that I heard a new sound, a knock on the front door.

I walked quietly into the dining room, fixing my woollen cap on my head. The room was empty save for Mama sitting at the table, looking at a paper in her hand.

"Who was that?" My voice echoed through, and Mama got up quickly and waved her hand, unable to contain her excitement.

"It's a letter from your brother!" She showed me the folded, white parchment in her hands. "Jehannette, darling, why don't you come with me to see the priest?" Mama asked, as I began to look for my needle and pin to do some needlework by the fire. "The priest? Whatever for?" I asked a bit alarmed, unconsciously on guard.

"For the letter!" Mama waved the letter again. Her eyes were wide and urgent.

The realisation dawned on me. "Oh! Oh, yes, the letter." I breathed easier, slightly more relaxed.

Mama had been waiting anxiously on word from Jean. We had heard nothing from him, and Mama's apprehension had been growing.

"The priest will tell us what it says. He will read it to us." She gathered her thick shawl and cap excitedly.

"Yes, I'll come with you," I said while looking for my shawl and warm cap. "But let's not stay too long. No talking about all the souls that are in need of salvation with the priest, please? It's freezing out there."

"No, just the letter. I need to know what your brother says, that is all, and we'll come back right away."

"Okay, good."

When we left the house, the snowfall had somewhat lessened. It was like a white sheet covering the entire town. Wrapped in our wool bonnets, thick woollen shawls, and mittens, we trudged through the deep-set snow. Our calves and the bottom of our dresses were submerged in the snow's icy depths.

It took us double the usual time to get to the little house behind the church, where the priest resided. It was a humble small home, with a single oak door. From underneath the rim of the doorway, a yellow horizontal light shone.

Mama knocked on the door with her fist. Her glove muffled the sound, but we heard a raspy voice from inside. "Enter," it said.

We ushered ourselves in and immediately sighed in relief as the room was lit by a dancing fire. We submerged ourselves in the snug and toasty air of the room, rubbing our arms to gather more warmth.

The room was small, with a wooden bookshelf that towered against the wall on the left, a chimney on the right, and an armchair off to the side. A robust wooden desk was in front of us. The priest was sitting behind the desk and began to cough. He drank some hot liquid from a small cup.

He peered at his visitors with two clear ocean-blue eyes that sat beneath a set of thick, overgrown eyebrows. "What do you need?" he inquired. After drinking, his voice sounded clearer. He was in his early fifties, with a standard tonsure haircut, and a thick dark beard that came to his chest.

In the corner of the room, the fire glowed, and its fiery red and orange blades fluttered and licked upwards and downwards, almost keeping its tear-shaped form. The sound of the wind howling could still be heard, and the push of cold air rattled the windows of the priest's small abode. Safe to say, Mama and I were both relieved to be out of the cold.

When we crossed to approach him, Mama made a short bow. She handed him the folded paper and said, "It is a letter from my Jean. We need your assistance, Father."

The parish priest handed back the folded paperback to Mama and said, "Wait for me in the church. I'll come in a moment." Without another word, he got up.

Mama turned dutifully and made her way to the door. Reluctantly, I followed her and summed up the courage to face the elements again. Mama and I linked arms as we walked, and nearly trotted to the church. The large arch-shaped doors were firmly closed, so we both pushed, and with a heavy release, they opened to its huge interior.

Unlike the priest's small home, the air of the church was bitterly cold. The stone walls and floor were rough and magnified the coldness from outside. The high ceiling etched upwards, making us feel even colder and smaller at the same time. It was not a comfortable place to be in that afternoon.

There was only one thing that was mildly enjoyable and that was the light that entered the stained glass window. I personally considered this to be the only thing we could marvel and appreciate. It made the space more appealing; the rest was very plain.

I tightly tied my shawl across my chest, folding my hands underneath my armpits to keep them warm. I shivered and a white cloud whirled in front of my nose.

Mama, next to me, commented, "At least we are sheltered from the wind." As she talked, white wisps of steam gathered in front of her, and her nose was pinched red.

I just nodded, shivering.

At that moment we heard the hurried footsteps of the priest approaching, as he climbed the stone steps of the church. He entered the church wrapped in a thick woollen cape. He gave us his blessing and began complaining about the cold. Once he was at arm distance he abruptly asked, "Where is the letter?"

Mama took it out from her apron pocket and passed it to him. The priest unfolded the paper and began to murmur, while his eyes roamed the letter. Without his eyes leaving the parchment, he began to tell us about the contents of the letter.

"He says that he is doing very well, that he likes the job very much, that he is learning how to put the fire at the correct temperature in the ovens, and is also learning to recognise the different iron alloys. He is very happy living in the town and with his uncle, and adds he always helps his uncle with what he asks of him…"

The priest's eyes squinted at the parchment.

"… that he always prays for your health. The town is much larger, there is much more commerce, and he will not be able to come for this Christmas. He sends you his blessings… mm…" He paused. "That's all." The priest handed the letter back to Mama.

"Thank you. You're very kind, father," Mama said while putting the letter back in her apron pocket.

The priest sniffed and adjusted his stance. "Isabel, I'm actually glad you are here. You see, a young woman is heavily pregnant, and it's her first."

Mama's eyes were concerned and focused.

"I was wondering if you could help with her delivery when the time comes."

My mood plummeted. Who knew how long we'd be here in the cold. *They could talk about all the souls that need help and I'll be frozen half to death!*

"Yes, Father. I have already visited the lady, and everything is prepared. I also have help from other women who are experienced."

The priest said, "Well, I think all we must do is wait and pray that everything goes well." He smiled and added, "It seems to me that that last part corresponds to me. You are going to have your hands full!"

"That helps, Father. The prayers you confer are always welcome," said Mama.

"Very true, very true. Come on, it is very cold in here. Off we go," the priest said emphatically, as he began to approach big wooden doors.

The priest waited for us to exit first, then secured the wooden doors behind us. "Good night!" he called as he hurried off to his small shelter.

Mama and I waved and walked home briskly. The wind seemed to cut through our skin like needles, and the snow was every bit as tough, but the letter from Jean gave us renewed strength. We were almost smiling with glee as we travelled, and even more so when we took refuge in the comforting warmth our little house provided.

<hr/>

As we fell into spring, some snow remained, and the mornings were as chilly as ever. Grass was slowly emerging in the fields, but not enough to keep our cows strong and healthy. Mama, seeing how skinny they had become, began feeding them an oatmeal broth.

The fresh, cool air whipped past me as I carried it to the fields outside the orchards. The four cows, spread across the field, slowly walked over and took to their food with gusto. I patted them on their back, while talking to them. "I told you I would bring some food."

Their deep moos filled my ear, and I smiled. Above us, clouds gathered in the sky.

It may rain later, I thought to myself. Remembering that I still had chores to finish, I walked to gather some kindling for the fire. My arms were filled with wooden planks, and the edge of my dress was damp from the melting snow.

By this time, the woods were becoming second nature to me. I knew every way in and out, every path, and every hideaway. These woods were like my playground. Running through them, I felt safe in their familiarity. Hopping over a fallen branch, and carrying some kindling for the fire, I raced back home.

The next afternoon, Pierre came with me to the forest. He had returned from the fields early and offered to help. "Bring two sacks, so we can collect a good amount of kindling, at least for four days," he said, while getting his woollen beanie and jacket.

I responded enthusiastically, "That's a good idea. We can carry more and have a week of stock!"

"Yes, that's it," Pierre chuckled.

We were also going to take advantage of this trip to practise. We hadn't done any training for a long time; the days saw non-stop rain and were so cold that we were always shivering when we were outside.

My guides had not come all winter either, nor had I dreamt of them.

Pierre began talking. "Jean hasn't written lately, and Papa says he wants to go and visit him and see how things are over there, but he says he's going to wait for the snow to melt first before he travels."

"Ah, that's probably next week," I responded.

"Yep, probably next week will have warmer weather," confirmed Pierre.

In the forest, we moved carefully between the hidden roots, which were covered in snow. We walked in silence with our eyes on the ground, until we got to the clearing, then we looked for the sack hidden under the tree. Pierre, with his gloved hands, fumbled through the snow-covered branches until he discerned the rectangular brown sack.

Wiping off the snow, he withdrew our two wooden swords. He gave me a broad smile as he passed one over to me. My fingers curled over its rim. They felt stiff, but I adjusted my grip until I felt comfortable.

"Alright, ready?" Pierre said, looking over at me.

I nodded, and a white plume of air curled up in front of my face. Pierre's nose was red from the cold, and he nodded, as we took up our positions next to the sandbag. We took turns hitting, swerving, and practising our footing on the sandbag.

As we practised, I carried out a flurry of movements, side stepping and executing my hits with a practised precision and a controlled strength. Having practised non-stop with Pierre, these movements had been perfected, and I carried them out without pause or hesitation. I don't think I ever said it out loud, but remembering this I think I quite enjoyed training, and I had missed it.

After we were both warmed up, Pierre wasted no time. We delved straight into an intense sparring session, followed by a session where one of us focused on attacking and the other defended. By the time we were finished, we were both red faced and warm.

After an hour of training, we were both tired and we finished our session. I looked at the sack hanging about five feet from the damp ground and looked at the rubble of wooden branches fallen from the trees. Pointing to the ground with the wooden sword, I said, "We better start collecting wood for the fire, before it gets too late."

"Yes, you're right," said Pierre. He got up wearily, and started collecting the most suitable firewood, the pieces that weren't so wet.

I joined him, and while putting our best effort into doing this quickly, I asked Pierre, "Any news from town?"

"Not much, the usual people are complaining about the recent events that occurred in the past few months. You know, they complain we had the English raids, now this icy winter." He shrugged. "It's like one hard thing after another," he said with a note of sorrow.

I gazed at him for a moment, contemplating his despondency. "Yes, I've heard this too, from our neighbours, from everyone in town, really."

He smiled thinly and raised his brows as if uncertain. As if he, too, couldn't guarantee the safety of our lives, if we would ever be free.

I continued, "But I can't blame them, it's been hard lately. But you know… when I hear people, and their dismay and despair about what has been or what could be, I… I remember God."

Pierre turned slowly to me.

"I remember their strength, the strength of Angel Catherine and Archangel Michael, and their strength is really something incredible, Pierre." Inside my head I was reliving memories with the angels. "If only I could share them with you. You would see how wonderful they are."

I paused and rolled a thin branch between my fingers. Pierre silently contemplated my words, until I faintly smiled and began picking up some sparsely strewn leaves on the forest floor.

"Sometimes I just need to contemplate nature and I begin to feel this immense love. And from that feeling comes an internal knowing that everything is fine. Everything is as it should be. Although on the surface there is a whirlwind of things, underneath all this, I feel there is a great calm, something that sustains everything."

Pierre was listening attentively. He knew about the Light, as I had told him.

"That experience was amazing. Does it always come and visit you, or is it rare?"

"Oh, no, it only happened once, but I learnt that if I start praying then love fills my heart. I feel this inner connection, like an underground loving current, then everything is calm, everything is okay."

"I wish I could feel that way. I find myself wondering sometimes…" Pierre said, while looking around the forest for kindling. "…all this beauty we are surrounded with, you know, like this forest or the creek, the mountain, the seasons, well, nature in general. It's like a clock. Everything follows a pattern. There are rules. What you said makes sense… an underground current that sustains everything."

Pierre pointed out every peculiarity of nature around us, while we collected more kindling. Looking up through the high branches of the trees, Pierre said, "We better get home soon." The afternoon was fading.

Of the collection gathered in my arms, some of the kindling was dampened from the melting snow. "I don't know if this is going to be any help. Most of the kindling has been on the icy ground."

"Yes, it is wet to the touch, but we can leave it in the barn for a few days or line it against a sunny wall."

"Mm, the sunny wall sounds like a better idea," I replied, heaving the pile of wooden branches into an empty sack and carrying it over my shoulder. The musty smell of the forest left as we emerged into the edge of the forest. The ground was lined with trails of leftover snow, and we trudged over it, our steps heavy as we descended the hill. Dusk was settling over the town, casting in the shadows of the late afternoon.

Once we placed the kindling against the side wall, we went inside. The door was open, and unfamiliar voices trailed from inside.

"Wait, I think I have another cauldron," we heard Mama say. The chatter was quick, the voices were urgent. We peeped inside and saw two ladies around the same age as Mama. They were our neighbours, and both wore cotton aprons, as did Mama when she emerged.

"Ah children," Mama said as she greeted us. "Gabrielle has just had her baby, but we're in need of more water. Jehanne, go to the well and fill it." She turned to Pierre. "Pierre, your father will be home soon. Make sure the cows have been fed, dear."

Pierre and I nodded, and straightway he went to see the tasks were done. But before I left, I quietly asked, "Are they both in good health, Mama?"

Mama's eyes were wide and alert. "Both are in good health, mother and child," she replied, abated. I followed Mama as she fetched the cauldron. I was curious and wanted to ask a few questions, but Mama hurried me. "Jehanne, the water... I need it now."

"Oh, I'll go now." I left quickly, returning with a pitcher full of water. While filling the cauldron I asked Mama, "Did you deliver the baby mama?" I tried not to spill any water.

"Yes, me and two other ladies, we delivered the babe. She started before midmorning, and now she's resting. Many of the mothers are preparing clothes for the child now. Jehanne, after you have filled the cauldron, fetch the box upstairs. It's over the bed. We need to give the baby clothes from you and your brothers' infant years. We all help, we always do."

I nodded as I held the cauldron in both hands, adjusting to its weight. Mama glanced at the cauldron as I shifted it, then looked at me. Her face softened and she smiled sweetly, cupping my face with one hand. "Oh, the babe is beautiful, Jehanne, just a wee little thing."

My face broke into a smile, and I watched her hurry back as one of the women called for her attention from the other room.

"Isabel, come, we need your help," said Marie, standing in the door frame. Both ladies carried the cauldron to Gabrielle's house.

"Jehanne, put the veggies in the clay pot with water and let it simmer. I'll be back soon." She put her mantle over her shoulders and disappeared outside.

On the table, the vegetables were washed and some were peeled. I cupped them in my hands and put them inside the pot that was over the fire, and I covered it.

It was these kinds of memories that always swelled the admiration I had for my family and our little town. We all helped each other in those difficult times, and we would never see anyone fall behind.

The next morning, as I dug deeper into the black earth, I was thankful that the heavy rain over the past week had left the soil easy to turn. The shovel felt light in my hands, and in no time, I dug out a small hole. The strong smell of manure and wet soil lingered alongside the smell of rain.

My full attention was on the task at hand. I worked without a break for the whole morning. Then, when all the vegetable patch was done, I stretched my back and I walked towards the orchard, stretching my arms, my shoulders, and my legs. While doing my stretches, I enjoyed the wind blowing in the trees and the sound of the animals going by their daily routine. Around me, the orchard trees were bursting with new swollen buds, telling me about new leaves and flowers that were ready to emerge.

"Jehanne," I suddenly heard.

I whipped around to see Saint Catherine, radiant in her white tunic with her beautiful face and long hair.

She, in her sweet voice, told me, "When you turn 16, you will need to leave. That time is approaching."

I felt as if a stone had dropped in my belly.

"You have trained well." Her words hung in the air before she continued. "I know your efforts in your training sessions with Pierre have been difficult and painful. But all that work will be very well used when the time comes, Jehanne."

A feeling of contention arose in me, and when she finished, I felt compelled to say, "Saint Catherine, I want to know… why so much training? If God wants to win the battles, he will win them, regardless of whether I handle the sword well or not."

Deeply patient, she shook her head slightly and responded, "It doesn't work that way. If God wants to win a battle, the King of Heaven will not send someone who is not well trained. God never does things by halves, and if you are his soldier, you have to be the best soldier. This training has been absolutely necessary for your mission, Jehanne, and for your survival." Her face was austere.

I nodded solemnly, remembering the hardships of the training sessions. "I understand. Then I must practise until the day I leave," I said with conviction, ambition enclosing my doubts like a rolled fist of determination.

"Good." Her eyes sparkled. "You will see me again very soon, and I will tell you what you need to do."

She looked down and paused. "Your father is planning an engagement. Do not worry." Then, as quickly as I blinked, she was gone.

My eyebrows formed a V-shape and I stared into the now empty space. My mind raced. *An engagement?! What can she possibly mean?*

A week after Saint Catherine's prompt, Papa left for Neufchâteau. Papa sat upon the wagon and led the oxen through the village. The sounds of their trotting receded as he disappeared down the street and onto the distant road to Neufchâteau.

That afternoon, I sat outside, washing fresh herbs from the fields. The basin was large, and the once clear water had discoloured from the soil of the herbs. I sat and scrubbed the herbs with a cloth. My fingers were wrinkled already, and large spills of water splashed onto my face and apron. I heard footsteps approaching and I looked up to see Pierre.

He had arrived home earlier than usual and approached me excitedly as if bursting with a secret. "Jehanne, can you train today? Papa is gone, so this week is perfect for us to do as much training as we can. I did all of my chores in the morning."

Relieved that Pierre was as determined to train as I was, I kept my voice low as I responded, "Yes, I just need to wash these," motioning down to the herbs in the basin. "But don't come here. Wait for me in the clearing so we don't have to explain to Mama."

The thought hadn't occurred to him. He nodded. "Oh, good point, yes." Clapping his hands, Pierre said jokingly, "C'mon missy, let's go and train."

"Oh, c'mon, help me, I still need to finish," I said while scrubbing the herbs. The dirt was colouring the water into a murky brown.

"What do you want me to do?"

"Can you—" One by one, I took out a few large herbs. They were dripping but clean. "Put these on the table and tie them well. Mama wants to use them tonight."

"Okay, just like that?" said Pierre, showing me a bundle of herbs in his hand.

"Yes."

Pierre placed the bunch of herbs on the table in the kitchen and began the task of tying them up. With Pierre's help, we were able to quickly finish the rest of my chores, and we set off to the forest.

Training was arduous and intense, with few breaks to recover. Hours later, our hair and clothes were soaked with sweat, and Pierre leaned against a tree, resting. His voice arose in the midst of our heavy breathing. "Your techniques with the sword are very good. You are as good as any other young man in town."

"Thanks for training me so well," I responded, my chest heaving up and down as I sat against the tree with my knees bent up. I felt a glow of pride.

As Pierre leaned against a tree to rest, he said as an afterthought, "And I've been to many sword tournaments in town. It's an important skill to know how to fight, to know how to defend yourself."

I smiled, satisfied. My limbs and arms could definitely testify to my skill. They felt shaky and like jelly.

In our brief moment of respite, there was only one thing that left me insecure of my swordsmanship that I wanted to address. "Pierre, is an iron sword going to be heavier than a wooden sword?"

Pierre responded casually, "There is not much difference, only that iron swords are a little shorter, but I find that they are easier to handle than the wooden ones."

"Oh, so my arm will hold an iron sword with no difficulty."

He shook his head affirmatively. His eyes were red from training, and his face shone with perspiration. "That's right, you will have no problems with that."

I slouched back onto the tree and sighed with assurance.

We stayed silent for a while, enjoying the break and sounds of the forest washing over us. My mind went back to the house. *I hope Mama didn't notice our absence...*

Although my pride swelled with my skills with the sword, keeping these truths from her always stung me. Mama was my best friend, and yet I could not reveal to her the real purpose for my trips to the forest, or my incredible experiences with the angels and the light.

Saint Catherine's words rang in my head. *"You will leave in your 16th year."*

I didn't want to leave without telling her. Without telling her everything. She was my mama, after all. She wouldn't tell a soul.

When Pierre was busy, I resolved to train on my own. Usually, when I finished my chores early, I told Mama I was going to collect firewood and ran to the forest. But there were times I couldn't get away so easily. Sometimes the girls from the village invited me to their gatherings and I couldn't say no. The only times I could give excuses was if Mama was not present, but my friends were hard to convince.

18

PAPA'S PLANS

"If I am speaking for my rights, for the rights of the girls, I am not doing anything wrong. It's my duty to do so."

– I am Malala by Malala Yousafzai

Spring, 1428
Domrémy, France

It was midday when Papa arrived home from Neufchâteau. The oxen shuffled across the paddock to the field, and we all went outside to help Papa unpack. Though fatigued from his trip, he appeared in good spirits—in his own way. He said he would share his news later, once he had checked on the fields and the animals and had eaten something.

When supper was prepared early that afternoon, the four of us sat down, eager to hear news of Jean. Everyone's cheeks were red from the warmth of the hearth and the steaming bowls of supper on the table. Papa, elbows resting on the table, with a chunk of bread between his fingers, cleared his throat. "Jean is doing very well. He is no longer an apprentice, and he has certain responsibilities now.

"The master smith, Bastien, is a good sort of fellow. He's teaching Jean and he is learning quickly. Your Uncle Jean is quite happy with Jean staying with them. Your cousins are also enjoying Jean's company."

We all chewed silently and listened attentively to the news. Papa took a moment to eat while Mama resumed her prayers all the while radiating happiness from Jean's success.

"Jean will do very well," he said, satisfied, scooping the last remnants of his soup with the bread crust. As he finished, he looked in my direction, yet my eyes remained downcast on my bowl. He cleared his voice loudly. "There was a young man and his father in Neufchâteau on the last day. They approached me and the young man asked for your hand, Jehanne."

Pierre's head snapped up to Papa. Mama stopped praying. All movement ceased at the table. I blinked once. Twice. Then, I looked up. Papa's face was every inch as solemn as ever. The emptiness of dread filled my lungs. I couldn't speak. I looked at Papa, clueless as to how to respond. I tried swallowing my soup down, but my stomach was knotted.

Papa's voice grew distant, like a dream. "They are hard-working, responsible, and attend church regularly. They have good property. The young man is working, and he is very interested…"

I felt Mama's gaze scrutinising my reaction and saw Pierre turning to look at me and Papa.

This… this can't be. I don't understand.

Papa did not seem to notice my discomfort. He continued to speak for some time, but I didn't hear the words. I only noticed when his voice trailed off. My mind was haphazard, and I needed to organise my thoughts to show an impassive demeanour. Gathering what strength I had, I mustered up all of my concentration and prayed my voice would not falter.

Papa continued, "This will be a good union. Jean has also expressed his wish to marry once he finishes his traini—"

"Papa." My voice was clear and unwavering. He paused, and his eyes landed on me like a target. Apprehension began to rise quickly in the pit of my stomach, but I continued on quickly as to not give it time to entrap me. I looked Papa in the eye and spoke clearly, "I don't want to get married. I want to dedicate my life to God."

Papa's eyes were hard stones. He scrutinised me for only a moment, then stared resolutely ahead. "You feel this way now, but the union will not be until you turn eighteen. You will get used to the idea." His voice was like iron, no room for discussion.

I felt like a small tree blown incessantly by a whirling wind, unable to recover from its last push.

Papa's voice anchored on, "I have also enquired about this family, and everyone has said that they are good, God-fearing people. Your uncle knows them too, and says they are of good lineage. The young man is a friend of your cousins. He knows you, he saw you when we were in…" He took a deep breath when he saw my reaction. "It's what's best for you."

"Papa," I repeated, firmer now. "I am not going to get married. I am going to dedicate my life to God."

Papa's eyes narrowed and his jaw tightened. He looked at me squarely. In a voice that left no room for argument or interruptions, he told me, "I have given *my* word, and this is the best for you. A daughter will obey the word of her father. There is nothing more to discuss!"

By nature, Papa was a proud and stubborn man, and he was not going to listen to anyone, least of all me. According to his convictions, women were to only obey. I knew I was not going to change his mind.

Papa resumed his conversation with Pierre as if nothing had happened and took a letter and a gift from Jean to Mama, from his travel bag.

I silently retreated into my own thoughts, yet my heart was heavy. I went to bed that night with sorrow. *How was I going to get out of this?* I silently contemplated, as I lay in my bed and looked up to the ceiling.

Then a thought crossed my mind. If I had to go soon, God would give me a solution. The memory flickered of Saint Catherine's last visit; she had mentioned a planned engagement.

I began to pray as usual and gradually immersed myself in prayer; its usual lightness and comfort drifted me into the lull of sleep.

The next morning, I woke early. The house was dark, and I crept through the hallways like a ghost. While I fumbled in the stillness of dawn, I plead for help from the light, from Saint Catherine and Archangel Michael.

Although Saint Catherine mentioned the engagement, I still didn't know what to do about Papa. Papa was obstinate, and if I didn't do something soon, I grew nervous to think of my upcoming betrothal. "How am I going to get out of this engagement?" I asked myself while starting the fire in the kitchen.

While the fire flickered to life and steadily warmed the house, I shrugged on a woollen shawl and ventured out to the chicken house. The small chicken house was near the vegetable garden, and many of the hens were still resting. They gave startled cheeps when I woke them to peruse for eggs but didn't move.

Having collected enough eggs and gathered them in my apron, I exited, readying myself for the cold. That's when I felt the familiar stillness.

A voice broke the early daybreak. "Jehanne."

I turned quickly, and saw Archangel Michael, adorned in a white tunic, sitting on a pile of hay next to the hen house. He was a few steps away from me.

"Jehanne, what is it that worries you?" His voice was as detached as always.

I grimaced. "Papa wants me to marry a young man from Neufchâteau. He says that he has already given his word and he is not going to change his mind. You know how stubborn he is, what can I do? He will not listen to me," I said, resignedly.

Archangel Michael sat completely still, observing me with a placid expression.

"No," he said finally. "No, he will not listen to you, nor your mother or your brother."

I looked at him, hopelessness crushing down on me.

"What you must do is talk with the village priest. Explain your situation to him. Also, suggest that he summons the town council." I gaped at him, but Archangel Michael continued, "Because Jacques will only listen to those who have more power than him. You already know your father. This is not a problem, Jehanne. This is just training for you. It's a situation where you will learn to use your words."

"But what do I tell them?" I asked, exasperated, fidgeting with the edge of my apron, which was still holding the eggs. I was careful not to move quickly and damage the eggs.

"What you feel in your heart every time you pray," he said simply. "Tell them that you want to dedicate your life to God, that service to God is the greatest thing a human being can do in this life. Service to God is service to humanity." His voice lulled me into the serenity of his being. "Simply put into words what you feel in your heart."

I nodded slowly, understanding what he meant. "Yes," I agreed. "Thank you."

Archangel Michael bowed his head and faded into the air.

I shivered in the cold and hurried home, careful not to bump the eggs in my apron. As I clasped the side door closed, I heard shuffling sounds and pots being moved. Mama was in the kitchen preparing breakfast. I carefully put the eggs in a bowl.

She looked up and nodded to me as she kneaded some dough. As the last egg was carefully placed in the pile, I let my apron fall. I lowered my head as I began to walk, but I stopped and told Mama, "Mama."

Mama's head spun up.

"I am going to see the parish priest today."

Her blue eyes were bright and diligent. "I'll go with you, my daughter."

I half smiled, a seed of hope rising in me like a flower. Mama and I prepared breakfast together in the quietness of daybreak. The smell of bread and hot milk wafted in the air, accompanied by the sounds of movement behind the walls as Papa and Pierre were getting up.

Papa and Pierre sat silently when they entered the kitchen. We ate breakfast in silence. The fire flickered and we chewed sombrely, then Papa stirred and departed for the fields. Pierre lingered a little while longer, and he quietly approached me as I began to wash everyone's dishes.

Since my objection to Papa's plans the night before, I noticed Pierre observed me with a mixture of newfound awe and pride. No longer was I such a little sister, but I was growing up and strong enough to defy Papa.

"Jehanne," he said in a low voice. "Know that I'll support you with whatever you do."

Touched by his words and his conviction, I inclined my head gratefully. "Thank you, Pierre." He nodded and left hastily to the fields.

After waiting to see if Papa would come back, Mama and I wrapped ourselves in our shawls and caps. We ventured outside in the cold morning air. We traversed the soft path of stones and mud until we reached the church. One of the arch doors was slightly opened, and we entered quietly.

The only movement and sound came from the sacristy, which the priest was vigorously cleaning. Hearing the door open, he turned, greeting us. "Good morning! What can I do for you?" He resumed his cleaning.

I strode past the empty piers, Mama closely following behind. The priest, seeing me approach, left the cloth on the sacristy, and brushed both his hands together. "Father, I must speak with you."

The priest's countenance was gentle and welcoming. "What is bothering you, my daughter?"

I swallowed hard. Remembering Archangel Michael, I knew what I needed to say. "My father has promised me to a young man from Neufchâteau, but all I've ever wanted to do was serve God."

The priest nodded.

"Father, you know how my papa is. When I expressed my wishes to serve God, he said he could not go back on his word, and that it's for the best."

He touched a hand to his chin.

"I cannot convince him of my conviction, no matter how much I want to be with God," I said, shaking my head.

The priest walked slowly, looking at the stone floor and repositioned himself behind the sacristy. There, he leant his elbow on the shiny sacristy, as if deep in thought. "My daughter, are you sure you want to dedicate your life to God?" This time, he examined me closely.

"More than anything, Father. The only thing in my heart is the thought of serving God." He nodded, yet something in him remained fixed.

I remembered the feeling of peace when I prayed. "Every night, before I go to sleep, I pray to God. It helps me sleep. It's my own refuge. It soothes and calms my mind. I cannot explain it. It's like looking onto creation around us and admiring the splendour of the woods, the creek, the fields at sunset. Prayer is the greatest thing for me. Nothing compares to that feeling, and nothing else is greater."

The priest stared at me for a short while, then a smile crossed his lips. "It's the same when I pray." Lowering his head, thoughtful for a moment, then considering me again, he approached me and put a hand on my shoulder. "I understand you."

Then he turned and walked towards the image of the cross hanging on the back wall. He stood still for a moment, gazing at Jesus' image on the cross with his hands behind his back. The dusting cloth hung from his hands, and he stood there, as if contemplating what to do next.

After a moment he turned and looked at us. "How can we dissuade your father from this decision?" he asked us.

I let out a soft breath, not realising I was holding it. I composed myself quickly. "He will not listen to us. I'm afraid he will not listen to any of his family." I advanced closer to the sacristy, my mother shadowing my steps.

"Yes," he answered. "A stubborn but good man."

Anticipation rising within me, I said, "We can call the town council," echoing Archangel Michael's words from this morning.

He looked at me and his face brightened. "Yes, that could work. I can summon the council after mass this Sunday. The lords will hear this case and give their judgement accordingly."

My muscles relaxed in my face, as I half smiled at the priest, and Mama behind me.

Yet the priest did not seem finished. "Jehanne," he approached me. "It's very important that you tell the council exactly what you told me today. How prayer makes you feel, and why you want to join the church."

I nodded solemnly.

"When you are in front of the council, it will be the best way to reach the people," he said, touching his heart, "as you did today with me". He smiled warmly.

"Thank you, father." I bowed my head and leant down on one knee, and made the cross signage.

My mother did the same, and the parish priest also crossed himself. He said, "Go with God and we will see each other after mass on Sunday."

Usually, the council was called when an important matter needed to be resolved, or to communicate news that concerned the entire village. The most significant figure in this council was Lord Robert de Baurtemont, a local noble with white hair cut shrewdly to his shoulders, a bulging stomach that hung over a luxuriously made belt, and a pair of skinny stocking lined legs that carried his heavy frame.

We waited with anticipation for Sunday to arrive. The days approaching mass, my heart fluttered at the thought of speaking in front of the council, but I knew I was going to speak my truth. Nevertheless, I mentally prepared my words. I reflected long and hard on my experience with prayer, and the sense of peace that I always felt and wanted to share with the world.

That Sunday morning, I went to mass early. The church was empty, except for two elderly ladies praying the rosary on their knees. I joined them as I made my way to the front of the sacristy. I brought my hands together and bowed my head in concentration. And I began to pray.

I prayed for the courage to speak my truth, to find the correct words to answer the council's questions. As I prayed, I felt the usual silence, the usual serenity of my mind descending to the stillness of a calm lake.

Shortly after, the villagers began to arrive. I soon felt my mother's hand on my arm, and opening my eyes, I saw her standing over me. I stood up and hugged her. She squeezed me tightly, gave me a reassuring smile, and gently patted my arm.

More and more people began to accumulate inside. Among the crowd were Pierre and Papa. Pierre stood next to me, and Papa sat beside Pierre. Soon, a hush was ushered amongst the crowd, and the church fell silent and waited.

The priest appeared and made the cross signage as a way of greeting. He climbed onto the pew, and gazed upon the crowd, his eyes landing on me last. He then began his sermon, his voice echoed across the high ceilings of the church, reaching everyone's ears.

The sermon was of finding God in the hearts of men and women, and the most sublime thing was to dedicate one's life to God because service to God was service to humanity. I listened attentively, grateful to the parish priest, and thanking God for this reinforcement. Hearing the parish priest, I knew listening to his words would help me when I presented my case to the assembly of the lords.

As mass was slowly reaching its end, the priest made the signage of the cross and called the council members to assemble. My mother put her hand on mine, but I kept watching apprehensively as chairs were brought, and the lords of the village began to take their places at the front. I knew what I was going to say, but I could feel my palms becoming sweaty.

When the lords were all seated, the priest walked to the front, turned to the audience, and waved for me. My heart skipped a beat. I approached the priest gingerly, as did Mama and Pierre. We made our way out of the row of standing villagers.

My hands clasped in front, I cast my head down as I approached the council. Trying my hardest to stay composed, I focused on my breathing until I saw the hem of the priest's black robe and looked up.

He stood with his hands clasped together too, and he walked with me to present me. He turned to face the council, with me beside him. "This maid requires your attention, my Lords. Thank you." I could see Mama and Pierre flanking me, and I even saw Papa's tall frame slowly appear and stand next to Pierre.

I felt the hard gaze of the nobles on me. Somewhere, someone coughed. For a moment, only the wind howled outside, and the church was silent, until I began to speak. Readying myself, I said loudly so all the lords could hear.

"Good morning, my Lords. My name is Jehanne d'Arc. My parents are Jacques and Isabel d'Arc. I have requested your presence here today to plead my case. You see, I have become aware of a planned betrothal intended for my eighteenth year, and my father is insistent on keeping his promise, and going ahead with this plan.

"But my only desire in this life is to live for God. I know very well the duty of children towards parents, and I have been an obedient daughter towards my parents in everything they have asked of me. But this desire in my heart is greater than me, greater than the obedience of daughters towards their parents, because God is greater than everything."

I saw the Lord Robert de Bautremont raise his eyebrows and reshuffle in his seat.

"The desire to serve God is greater than my life. It is like the strength of the wind blowing with the force of a storm. I beg you to open your hearts to my humble plea, so I can undertake a life of service in the hands of God. So I can fulfill this desire in my heart and live a life of sacrifice and devotion to our dear Lord. I beg of you, my Lords, to consider my humble petition. Thank you, my Lords." I bowed my head.

The council was perfectly still. I felt a sense of trepidation. *Did they not hear me well? Should I repeat myself?*

A moment later, they began to deliberate amongst themselves. At first, their voices were low, but they became raised as they continued. The conversation then broke into smaller exchanges between the council members.

I waited there, my hands fidgeting. Then, one council member roped in the consensus. I could see their curious glances flickering to me, and the weight of their decisions in their minds. At last, Lord of Domrémy, Robert de Baurtemont, spoke, his voice gruff but not impolite.

"There is no question of your sincere desire to serve Our Lord, mademoiselle, which is highly commendable. It is one of the highest services in our society, there is no doubt about that. We have deliberated and together we have decided that no one can divert a maiden from the path of God. The people of Domrémy would be very proud to have a maiden like you, Jehanne, at the service of the church and of our Lord Jesus."

Scarcely believing my ears, my relief was boundless.

The lord continued, now looking at the man he supposed was Papa. "Jacques."

Papa stepped forward. "This council has decided your daughter is free to follow the desire of her heart and serve Our Lord Jesus Christ. This council also declares the marriage commitment invalid. The desire to serve God must come only from God, Jacques. It is a command of the Supreme, and we cannot turn a deaf ear to this desire that is born so strong in the heart of this maiden. She must obey her heart." The lord finished.

I peeked sideways at Papa. His jaw was locked, and his entire face was red. From humiliation or shame, I will never know, but he found his voice, responding to the council.

"My daughter will serve God, my Lords," Papa said, though he did not hide his dissatisfaction with their imposition.

The priest approached Papa, and murmured something, at which Papa nodded and followed the priest, and they walked out of the church.

Once outside of the building, the priest asked, "Jacques, what is the problem?"

Jacques was silent for a long moment as if he had a terrible internal struggle. "It is my pride, Father. I feel humiliated," answered Jacques truthfully.

"That can be a big stone in your chest. If you leave it there, it can crush you under its weight." The priest continued, "Jehanne has not humiliated you. She has fought for a desire greater than her. You heard her in the assembly, didn't you?"

Jacques sat on the steps of the church, forlorn and with his head in his hands. His gaze was fixed on the ground.

The parish priest asked him again, "Jacques, what is tormenting you so?"

Jacques responded without looking at the priest standing in front of him. "I had a dream when I was visiting my brother," he said, his gaze downcast.

"Go on, I'm listening," the priest said.

"I dreamed that Jehanne was in the ranks of an army. I saw Jehanne among the soldiers, Father. Do you know what that means?" His eyes were full of fear. Taking a few deep breaths, Jacques continued. "The only women who follow soldiers, well, you know who they are, Father. After the dream, I was worried, and I told my son Jean. I told him if you ever see your sister among soldiers that he must drown her."

The priest studied Jacques carefully. And what he saw shifted his understanding of Jacque d'Arc. In fact, seeing this deeper reason for arranging Jehanne's marriage allowed the priest to look at Jacques with compassion. He saw a concern for his family's reputation and livelihood.

"Ah, that's why you have looked for a husband for your daughter. You were afraid of that dream," affirmed the priest.

"Yes," confirmed Jacques.

"Jacques, have you ever had any doubts or suspicions about Jehanne in her moral behaviour?" asked the priest, as he sat down next to Jacques.

Jacques looked over at the priest, his eyes large with shock. "No, father! She has been brought up very well by Isabel. A devoted Catholic, very respectful and accommodating to her mother and I in the house."

"Well!" answered the priest, visibly relieved. "Then this is the work of the devil who poisons our dreams to make us doubt and lead us to other paths. We must see the situation, the person, their character, their behaviour, and if we still have doubts, pray to our Lord Jesus to enlighten us and guide our actions and our words."

Jacques nodded, allowing the words to wash away his troubles.

"Do not worry about your daughter, Jacques. Jehanne wants to follow God. She has said it publicly and she feels that great desire in her heart. No one can stop it because God has put it there. I tell you this because from my own experience, I felt the same way when I was young. Like Jehanne said, it is like the great wind of a storm that sweeps away everything, and no one can stop it. It is the love of God in our heart. It is the divine calling."

"I understand, Father. Now I understand," said Jacques, like a man relinquished—not of his pride, but his worries, his burden. He turned and looked the priest in the eye. "Jehanne is going to serve God, as her heart dictates. Rest assured, Father, I am a man of my word."

"Good, good man," said the priest smiling, as he patted Jacques on the back.

"Go with God."

19

MESSAGES

Spring, 1428
Domrémy, France

*A*fter the council meeting, Papa didn't show any kind of recrimination or anger towards me, but I steered clear of him to avoid any further conflict. Shortly after the council supported my decision to serve God, Papa and the priest left the church.

I knew not what was said between the two men, but I was grateful for the priest's support. For whatever advice he gave my father, it helped mitigate his disappointment and rejection, and promise my role to serve God.

Following the events of mass, life continued in its usual routine and no news of the English arose. It was as if everything was settled and in balance.

For now.

On one particular twilight evening, when darkness gradually consumed the beryl and white sky, a blustering wind howled through Domrémy. As I sat in front of the fire and stirred the pot, I listened to the wind.

Mama's voice broke my reverie. "Jehanne, fix some cloth under the door so the house stays warm from this wind."

I rested the wooden spoon back into the pot and stood up to find an old cloth. I walked over to the front door, and bent down to my knees, my hands tingled from the cold floor and the tendrils of wind that escaped under the door.

The winds of change…

A saying I would hear in the village.

At the end of winter, life in Domrémy followed its seasonal routine. The kitchen was lined with hanging fresh herbs, cheeses were wrapped in linen, and baskets were filled with vegetables and fruits. Garlands of flowers lay in bunches for the festivities, carrying the aroma of their sweet fragrance around the house.

I returned to the pot on the hearth. Once the meat from the rabbit was cooked and the vegetables soft, I adorned my hands in mittens and carried the pot to the rectangular wooden table.

When Papa and Pierre returned from the fields, their hair was matted with sweat and dirt. Their sleeves had been soaked when they washed their soil-ridden hands in the barrels outside. We sat down to eat as usual. Papa spoke to Pierre about tomorrow's work, and I sat silently listening to Mama's prayers.

The crickets sang loudly outside.

Although Mama and Pierre couldn't sense it, a change was approaching.

Bit by bit, I slowly ate my soup, contemplating the visit of Archangel Michael that day, and what it could mean.

That morning, the sun shone brilliantly but offered no solace from the wind, which travelled low and moved through the trees of the forest, hustling the mud and stone houses. Cleaning the barn, I was clad in a shrug. I was sweeping the old hay to the corner, when I felt the rush of the wind enter the barn and quickly pull out, slamming the barn door shut with a loud bang.

Startled, I looked up, and Archangel Michael sat, quite casually, on a pile of fresh hay. Unperturbed, I leant the rake against the wall and walked slowly to his seated figure.

When I stopped, about two arm lengths in distance, he said, "Jehanne, now is the time to prepare for your departure. You will need to travel to the city of Vaucouleurs, and when you arrive, you will request an audience with Lord Robert de Baudricourt."

I nodded. The moment I had been dreading but also anticipating at the same time—it was here.

It was finally time.

The angels had given me the direct order to leave home.

Lord Robert de Baudricourt, I repeated in my head to remember.

My second worry was Papa. *How will he react?*

"Should I tell my parents?" I asked, my voice betraying my uncertainty.

"If you want to tell Isabel, she will understand. She is very intuitive, and her heart is with God," said the Archangel, his voice certain and relaxed.

"As for your father, it will be complicated as he has many doubts in his head. He will not understand."

I nodded again. "I see. It is better not to say anything to Papa."

"That is right. It is better this way. Less complications, less worries."

Archangel Michael was silent for a moment more, waiting for another question. When he saw I had none, he continued. "Jehanne, you will need to tell your brother the details of this endeavour and the time of your departure. Your brothers will accompany you on your military campaigns. Do you have any questions?"

As I stood there, deep in thought, I simply shook my head.

Archangel Michael remained inscrutable as ever. Having outlined my duties, the mighty angel bid me farewell and disappeared.

The news that Pierre would accompany me assuaged my nerves and doubts about the situation. Knowing my brother would be there, I knew I wouldn't be alone, and it somewhat lifted the weight off my shoulders. Before I felt like I was balancing on a rope, but now it felt like I had the support of an arm to hold. Of course, I took refuge in the knowledge that my guides would provide guidance and support me too.

I just needed to pray and remember the love of the light, and the doubts would evaporate like mist in front of the morning sun. Feeling the power of the divine, I knew I would not be alone, even if sometimes I would feel it.

It was thrilling indeed, to embark on this extraordinary endeavour!

Papa's low voice brought me back to the table. Looking at my plate, I resumed eating the vegetable soup with calm and slow movements. I glanced up and watched Mama quietly eating, with the prayers on her lips, across the table. A sense of nostalgia gripped my heart, knowing that I would leave soon.

I made sure to memorise every detail in my memory: Papa's solitary voice swimming in the silence of supper, the dutiful service of Mama's cooking, making sure we were wellfed and strong.

In that moment, I silently savoured the tranquillity of my life. Mama's love and her ability to make everything beautiful was something she did so well, and I appreciated it. And Papa's protection. He had always been a good provider for his family. We had never lacked clothes or food on the table.

I looked at them, asking God to bless them. I knew in my heart I would miss Mama terribly, and even Papa. Despite his setbacks, I would miss the regularity and familiarity of this life and the role they both played in it.

That night I prayed. I prayed to God to enlighten my mind, to have the appropriate words to deal with highly ranked men, especially Lord Robert de Baudricourt. I wondered how it would be—a peasant girl speaking to the lords. I thought to myself, God must have a sense of humour to choose me as his messenger.

It was not something I ever wanted.

In fact, it went against the very strands of how things were in the kingdom. Like a brief breeze on a candle, the flame lay unextinguished, and my prayer continued. "Lord, please give me the intelligence to navigate the world of highborn politics," I said aloud in the quietness of the night.

Sleep weighed my eyes firmly closed, and I drifted into a restful sleep.

The chirping of birds awoke me. I lay in bed, listening to the world, and wanting to savour the precious, slow moments before the full day ahead.

Today at noon is the spring festival, I thought to myself.

By the time I dressed, braided my hair, and arrived in the kitchen, the sun was peeking over the hills, and smell of the dawn showers still hung in the forest. I tended the animals quickly, feeding them before mass and the festivities of the day. As I carried bundles of hay to the fields, a glimmer of white appeared in my peripheral, and a sudden blow of wind swept over my cap. A moment later, Saint Catherine's form was standing next to the gate near the orchard.

I kept walking but slowed down to lower the bundle, and I bowed, crossing myself quickly.

Her voice was like music, gentle and melodic. "Jehanne, when you go to Lord Baudricourt, remember to ask for an escort to accompany you to see the Dauphin. Tell the Lord you have an important message to convey to the Dauphin."

The angels kept telling me I should ask for an escort, but I could not see how a Lord would listen to a peasant girl. I just could not see it happen.

I voiced my concerns. "It will be very difficult for the lord to give me an escort, without a very credible explanation, especially from a peasant girl," I said slowly but with conviction, because I knew the huge social differences that divided our society.

With ease, Saint Catherine said, "Do not worry what the Lord might think or do, Jehanne. What God has arranged, it will be so. But I will give you the explanation you seek. You need to get in contact with Lord Robert and the people in his town. This will set the bases for your name to be known. Go, Jehanne, and be sure this first outing will set the wheels in motion to Chinon."

"First outing?" I asked.

"Yes. Lord Robert needs to know of you and the people in the town as well. Also, word will spread of you to Lorraine. The Duke of Lorraine will know about you. Be confident. This is the way things are going to develop."

I nodded, though I didn't feel entirely sure about the situation. At that moment, I could not think of anything else.

"Goodbye."

"Goodbye, my angel."

And with that, she left me alone in the field.

I hastily picked up the bundle and tumbled the fresh hay onto the dewy grass over the gate where the cows roamed. I ran back to the barn, ruminating over Saint Catherine's words.

Is God testing me? I wondered. *These are my insecurities getting the better of me again,* I thought glumly.

Taking off my farm apron and leaving it in the barn. I quickly made my way to the church for mass. Every harvest started with a mass, before the festivities in the town started. I covered more ground as I sped through the village, the grass tingling against my calves as I rushed past.

Yet what excuse will I give to Papa to go to Vaucouleaurs? How could I ever convince him to let me go to Vaucouleaurs? Well, there was Pierre, of course, and he would be there to help me...

I must speak with Pierre at once. He will have some ideas. He will know what to do. I can also tell him about Saint Catherine's request. Remembering this deflated my hopes for a thrilling adventure. *Will Lord Baudricourt really grant a peasant girl's request for an escort, or even my audience with the Dauphin?*

The demand seemed ludicrous in my mind.

Has Saint Catherine forgotten to tell me something? High noblemen would not believe a thing like that, even less so when it was coming from a peasant girl. This must be some sort of test.

All these questions culminated in my mind as the church slowly emerged in the distance. As I straightened my cap and slowed to a brisk walk, a pulse of excitement echoed through me. *This is actually going to happen!*

Like watching a miracle about to happen, I couldn't wait. The anticipation, the excitement, the angel's prophecy would soon become reality.

As I walked closer, I could hear the lonely voice of the priest echoing in the high walls of the church. The doors were wide open, yet the crowd of villagers spilled out of the building and flooded the entrance, only hearing the priest sermon with strained ears. I stood amongst the crowd, listening to the sermon until it ended.

Usually, the church was quiet and the villagers' faces were reserved and masked, but today, the crowd was jittery and the villagers walked gaily out of the church doors. As the crowd dissipated and journeyed towards the centre of town, I greeted Isabel and the other girls of the village with their mothers.

Eventually, I saw Papa, Mama, and Pierre emerge from the church. *Finally! Pierre can help me with this dilemma.* I walked over to them, and silently signalled Pierre to accompany me to the festival.

With my attention so focussed on Pierre, I didn't see Mama's short figure emerge in front of me, and she caught me by surprise. "Jehanne, I need you to bring the bread and cheese that are wrapped in a piece of cloth on the table at home."

I hesitated, my mouth agape, but Mama hurriedly tapped my arm. "Jehanne, I need them now, hurry!" She urged.

Swallowing my exasperation, I mumbled, "alright," and had no alternative but to run home. Running as fast as I could, with my chest heaving, I found a bundle of linen-wrapped cheese on the table and gently held it as I ran back to town. In the centre of town, there were many tables being set up in a u-shape, in the small square in front of the parish.

The tables were covered by white tablecloths and adorned with sprigs of rosemary and flowers, and on one side of the square was a large tree that we always decorated for these celebrations.

I saw Mama in the distance, and she looked over at me and pointed at the long table nearest to her. I nodded and put the bundle on the table, which was destined for the food. Already, the table held bowls of fruits, and bread.

The square was filled with people chatting. The air was sweet with the fragrance of the fruit. Under the tree, small groups of youths of varying ages chatted and socialised in their distinct groups. There, I saw Pierre chatting animatedly with some of his friends.

I began to make my way to him, but I stopped, suddenly unsure. I needed to speak with him, but I realised now, while he was surrounded by friends, was not the time.

"This will need to wait," I muttered to myself, resigned. I went back to where Mama was setting the table with her cheeses and salted meats, and helped her unpack the produce onto the tables.

As we unpacked, I saw some musicians entering the square and preparing their instruments. I watched them out of the corner of my eye. I placed the cheeses onto the wooden slabs, remembering their melodies from the past celebrations.

From the growing crowds, I saw the familiar braids of Isabel and her mama approach, alongside other ladies and their daughters. Isabel hugged me. "Jehanne, you were so brave when you faced your father in front of the council."

"Oh yes," Charlotte said. "Now everyone knows that you want to be a nun and that is why none of the young men of the town ask about you."

I laughed, and the girls all smiled.

"Now, in this town, there is one less girl to compete with." I shrugged, and the girls laughed in turn.

Mama cut the cheese into small pieces and served them on a slice of bread, offering them on a wooden slate to each of the girls. All was quiet as they enjoyed the treat, then the girls offered Mama many compliments of which she modestly and quite red-cheeked accepted. "Thank you, darlings."

From then, the party was ready to begin. The tables were set, the food was ready, and the musicians began to play a playful and happy tune. The people in the square began to pace around like ants into their positions to dance. Once the music started, it continued until nightfall only to stop for small breaks.

Both young and old danced in the square, and the townspeople switched regularly throughout the night to sit and enjoy the plentiful food and drink. A roast was cooking over a large fire pit, and the smell of burnt firewood permeated the air. Red-cheeked, I danced with my brother, knowing very well this would be my last of these events. I treasured every moment of it.

The light from the fire danced over their happy faces, and we skipped all through the square. In our happiness, Pierre rushed to Mama's side, and prompted her to join us. She did, rather reluctantly at first, but by the end her eyes and cheeks were pinched with the merriment of the dancing. When the song finished, I hugged her. We both fell onto the chairs with exhaustion. We were all very happy. The town's celebration lasted till evening.

The next morning, the sun rose lazily over the hills and the forest as we broke our fast with warm milk and oats. Pierre sat across from me, his face slightly haggard yet still alert.

Mama was sweeping the floor, gathering the fallen dots of flour that escaped during her morning baking. Papa was as stern as ever, and with a push of his chair and the groan of the table, he left for the fields, donning his hat and coat. Shortly after, Pierre followed, leaving me alone to finish my bowl of oats.

That morning, I completed my usual chores with the animals, changing their hay and water bowls. I didn't see Pierre until later when I was tending the vegetable garden. Having quickly examined the vegetable patch, I made my way to the barn to retrieve my tools.

The barn door was slightly ajar and, opening it fully, I saw Pierre sitting on a stack of hay, cleaning his boots. "Oh, I've been hoping to find you alone!"

Pierre answered me with a quizzical look.

"Well, never mind that now. I've got something to tell you."

He put down his boots, ready to listen.

"Archangel Michael and Saint Catherine have both told me that I must go to Vaucouleurs to ask an audience with Lord Baudricourt, and to request an audience with the Dauphin. They also said I must ask Lord Baudricourt for an escort."

Pierre continued to brush his boots. However, his expression was pensive, and I thought I could see the hint of a frown at his eyebrows and mouth. When he was silent, I continued, "Their instructions have always been clear, however this just seems… too far-fetched. If I just go like this, surely no one will believe me."

Pierre, having contemplated it for a moment, said, "Wait until everything is clearer and if another of your guides comes. Ask them for clarity and don't be afraid to express your doubts."

I nodded, but the core of my dilemma was not resolved. "There is one last thing…"

Pierre raised his eyebrows.

"Do you think we should tell Mama? About us leaving, about Vaucouleurs, and Lord Baudricourt?" I pursed my lips thinking of ways to tell her, but nothing came to mind.

"Jehanne, you have to decide that," Pierre said, pointing at me. His gaze softened as he saw the decision that weighed on my shoulders.

My shoulders slumped. It was not the response I wanted to hear. I wanted someone to show me the way. I wanted Pierre to make it easier for me, but I understood this was going to be my decision and mine only. "I'm going to pray that God clears my doubts."

20

ASSURANCE

Spring, 1428
Domrémy, France

*T*hree days later, the sun radiated through the oak forest, its beams shining through the trees and creating spots of golden light. This part of the forest rolled with bumps and a small ravine that entrenched the water passing through.

Below the oak trees, which had narrow trunks, water trickled over the smooth rocks. I followed the sound of the creek. The air smelt of moss and tingled my cheeks from its freshness.

It was early afternoon. I had finished all my chores and was trying to find Mama. Under the shade of the forest, I meandered through, enjoying the sunlight escaping through the leafy roof of branches.

Following the running water, I walked to our familiar washing spot and found her crouched by the creek, sleeves rolled up high, washing some clothes. A mixture of worry and excitement rang through me like a bell. I felt the time for my mission approaching and the growing apprehension to tell her the truth was growing stronger by the day.

Today is the day, I told myself, resolved. I strolled to her, ignoring the doubt pacing in the back of my mind like an incessant fly. *It's got to be today, for if I don't say something now I never will.* I was certain of it. *Now, Jehanne!*

I went down to the creek, carefully walking down the loose rocks.

Mama looked up as the shuffling of the pebbles startled her.

"Why are you coming that way? You know there is an easier path further down," Mama said while pointing to a dirt path that was a little distance downstream.

"I know, but this way was closer," I said, matter-of-factly.

Mama simply shook her head in amusement. "Help me with these," she said, pointing at a basket of washed clothes to her right.

"Are these ready?"

"Yes, ready to hang," said Mama.

I started hanging clothes on the lower branches of the trees near the creek bank. The sound of the rushing water from the creek filled the silence, as we tended the clothes. Being here, I suddenly realised I hadn't the slightest clue as to where to start. *How do I explain this story?*

It was the perfect time to tell her—we were alone and unlikely to be disturbed, and my conviction was unwavering—yet I was at a loss for words. Feeling desperate, I raised a silent prayer, asking God to give me the right words to explain the events to come. Soon, a memory flickered in my mind, and a sudden idea leaped through my mental block.

Once we had finished, Mama sat on a nearby boulder, resting for a moment. I sat next to her, carefully broaching the subject. "Mama," I started. "Do you remember the dream you had when you were expecting me?"

"Yes, I remember. What about it?" she replied, as she crouched again and wrung the water out of the small sheets with her thick, small hands.

I looked closely at her, really looked at her, and something in her serene and focused manner broke my conviction like glass. To tell her was to invite her worry and cause her pain. I realised the impact of my actions before I committed to them. I could see that telling her about my mission would have done more harm than good.

She would worry, question, and agonise over the possible outcomes. She would worry sick. At that moment, a strong feeling of protection arose in my heart. I wanted to save her from the torment of knowing her only daughter was going to battle, for at least a little while longer.

I swallowed hard and fidgeted with the hem of my apron, then the tail of my braided long hair. I studied a particular shimmer of light across the creek as the sun's glow and the water met and glimmered over the stationary rocks underneath.

Mama cast a quick glance my way, and said, as she continued wringing the sheets, "What's wrong, daughter? What about the dream?"

I rolled my lips, feigned a small smile, and looked at her again. "Nothing. I was just remembering it. It's a very nice dream," I replied quickly, smiling. I awkwardly lowered my gaze, and my fingers grazing over the moss-covered rock.

"What's in your head today missy? Come on, come'n help me with these clothes," she said, in a happy manner.

I joined her on the bank of the creek. I folded up my sleeves and began wringing out the water from the washed sheets. "Did Jean say anything new in his latest letter?"

"Oh yes, he said he's doing very well and that he will send gifts soon," Mama said, her face warming with cheer.

I nodded, unsure of how to continue, but Mama continued talking. "Jehanne, tomorrow we will cook some of the legumes that we have stored inside the clay pots in the barn." She shuffled over to the lowest branches of a tree that arched over the creek. There, she aired out the wet clothes and hung them over the branches.

"Alright, which one should I get, and I'll leave it in the kitchen when I get back?" I called to her.

Her back was facing me as she secured some drier clothes over her shoulder, ready to depart back to the house. She turned and said while folding some shirts, "Get the small black lentils, about a bowlful. I need to go to see Angelique this afternoon. She needs fresh linen and she's run out. Can you finish the rest, darling?"

"Yes, Mama. If Isabel is there, send her my love!" I called back to her, while wringing a shirt with both hands.

Mama walked past with an armful of dry clothes, and she gently rested her hand on my shoulder. "Of course, darling." She clambered up the path, her footsteps slowly receding behind the rushing water of the creek.

After the last of the clothes were hung up, I marvelled at my work. The oak tree was dressed in small garments that hung over the branches, resembling a quirkily dressed giant. I gathered the drier clothes in the basket, but the solitude of the forest pressed me to stay a little while longer.

I sat on the rock, bringing my knees to my chest, and watched the river dance down the stream. I observed deeply and found new details I hadn't perceived before. Ahead, on the opposite side of the creek, the creek-bed rose to a small hump where it was covered with thumb-sized pebbles. A thin layer of water trickled gently over it, whereas deeper ruts of the creek carried large bodies of water that meandered through the forest.

The rocks in the creek-bed nestled into one another, having not moved for eons, were like expressionless statues, buried behind the translucent torrent of water above. Drinking in its beauty and serenity, I felt lighter, my senses relaxing.

Immersed in my own reverie, I was stirred to alertness by a gust of wind. As if materialising from the forest's pure spirit, Saint Marguerite stood in front four paces in front of me, garbed in a beautiful white robe. Her rich brown hair cascaded down her shoulders, and her sweet and full lips formed the sweetest smile. She was close to the fringe of the creek, on a bed of dry pebbles I noted, as the water rushed behind her.

"Jehanne."

I stood up quickly and walked a few steps, kneeling in front of her. "My lady," I said.

"Jehanne, do not be concerned for your mother, she will be alright. God will give her peace in her heart."

Relief swept through me. I tried to speak but no sound came out. I breathed in, and said with a conscious effort, "Thank you," putting both of my hands over my heart. "Thank you so much for listening to me, thank you."

Knowing my mother would be comforted, that she will not suffer for the sake of my mission, was like a thorn removed from my heart.

"Jehanne, you must send a letter to your aunt Jehanne Lessoir in Burey-le-Petit, telling her that you would like to see her. Ask for her husband to come and get you. When you are with them, you will tell them about your mission."

My momentary bliss was cut short, and I felt like I just ran into a wall. I stared, unblinking, at Saint Marguerite. "T-tell them? Tell them... about my mission? And that I have to go see the Dauphin?" I said slowly, measuring the weight of each word.

Saint Marguerite eyes were like two hazel beads. She firmly nodded. "Precisely, Jehanne. You will tell them about your mission and also that you need to go to the town of Vaucouleaurs to see Sir Robert de Baudri-court so that he will give you an escort and a letter to see Charles Valois. Do not fear the reaction from your relatives. They will understand you and help you."

I was puzzled that Saint Marguerite did not mention Pierre. *Was he not coming?*

"And Pierre?" I asked, slightly apprehensive about the answer.

"So that your father does not suspect anything and does not object to you leaving, you must go without Pierre. You'll have to make this trip as an outing to see your aunt Jehanne as a family affair. Once you are with your aunt and uncle in their home, you will talk with them and from there go to Vaucouleurs."

"I understand," I said, but I felt disheartened knowing Pierre would not be coming and I would be by myself.

Another doubt rose in my mind. *Once in Vaucouleurs, how am I going to recognise Lord Robert de Baudricourt?*

Saint Marguerite answered my mental query as she continued speaking. "Jehanne, once you are in Vaucouleurs, I or Saint Catherine will accompany you. Not in our usual way as you see us now, but in a more subtle way. We will appear as a subtle light, on your shoulder, and you will hear our voices." Her head motioned to the side, and her eyes landed on my right shoulder.

Knowing that I would be accompanied by them, I felt somewhat reassured. I knew what I must do, even if Pierre wasn't with me. I would have help.

I bowed my head in reverence. "Thank you for your guidance, and for being by my side. Thank you." I looked at her with devotion and gratitude. "I will send word to my uncle and aunt as you have advised me. I will say that I wish to visit my aunt for a few days and request my uncle escorts me, so Papa will not suspect anything. In short, that is it?" My eyes darted downwards, in doubt. "Isn't it?" I asked diffidently.

"Yes, Jehanne," answered Saint Marguerite. Bowing her head, her form illuminated into a thousand small dots of light that withered and disappeared into the air. The noise of the creek and the humming of insects rushed to my ears, as I was alone again in the forest.

I slowly got up from kneeling on the pebbles and dusted off the moist dirt from my dress. Retracing my steps back to the rock on the precipitous edge of the creek, I began to mull over the plan.

Contacting my relatives in Burey-le-Petit will be the perfect excuse to request an audience with Lord Robert. Papa will not suspect anything is amiss, and Mama will not be sick with worry. It is the perfect plan. A glimmer of hope began to flutter in my heart, and I felt a wave of excitement.

I basked in the serenity of the forest a little while longer. "Am I ready for this?" I said, only for myself to hear. The wind tousled the leaves overhead, and I looked up to the thick powerful branches fanning the leaves out and dancing together in the wind. I felt the breeze arch downwards and embrace me, and ripple across the water and the branches curving over the creek.

I stayed like this, for how long I know not. But the chill air gradually ensconced me, and I knew it was time to go. The corners of the forest darkened slightly, making me look up again to the sky. *It must be mid-afternoon by now.*

Glancing over at the drooping clothes on the tree, I smiled slightly, humoured at its lumpy figure. *Who needs a scarecrow when you can dress the trees?* Walking over to fumble and check their dampness, I found the clothes were still moist and cold to touch. *I'll come back later*, I decided.

I headed for the path to the orchard and the fields. A small, hooded figure was coming through. When they took off their hood, their brown hair was tousled, and two long braids ran down the length of their bodice. "Isabel!" I cried out, laughing.

She waved to get my attention, smiling. I returned the wave. We sat on one of the bigger rocks near the creek, enjoying the beautiful afternoon and each other's company while we conversed animatedly. The time passed quickly.

The wind picked up again, but our conversation settled us in to stay and enjoy each other's company a little while longer. The hanging clothes were drying quickly too. Yet, after some time, we could no longer ignore the wind tugging at our clothes and hair, and the cold settling into the forest.

By late afternoon, the forest was coloured with greys and blues. The sun began to descend over the hills, casting the forest into shadow. We packed up our things, and Isabel helped me fetch the clothes from the tree.

Once we had everything, we ventured back home, carrying the clothes together. Mama offered some warm honeyed milk, and Isabel stayed with us. We chatted until supper was ready. When Isabel went home, the sky was swept over with greys and midnight blue as evening had come.

21

UNCLE DURAND

End of Spring, 1428
Domrémy, France

By the last few days of Spring, Domrémy resembled a little haven of greenery. The sun's warmth radiated through the fields and the plants, spurring their growth and an abundance of flowers and vegetables. The garden was thick and buzzing with life, with fruits growing fast and trees in the orchard full with new green shoots and an abundance of flowers.

Under the apple trees in the orchard, nothing but bird calls and colonies of insects and ants could disturb me. Some even came to climb over my dress as I knelt over the earth, covering the base of a tree in old hay. Its branches were late in bloom, and I looked up tenderly at its branches, which rose high into the blue screen of the sky.

Perhaps with a little more warmth, you'll bloom wonderfully like the others.

I knelt back and observed my work. Satisfied, I reached over to the bucket filled with water and poured a little over, flattening the hay immediately under the water's heavy force.

The garden was a little paradise for me, always astonishing me with its beautiful flowers and fruits. It remained a constant reminder of the

219

peace of the angels when they visited, and how their plan unfolded in the past ten days.

Not only is nature perfect, but everything in this world follows the will of God, I thought to myself, admiring the long grass, dotted with the tall stems of daisies. Since the last visit of Saint Marguerite, I was preoccupied with coming up with an excuse to write to my Aunt Jehanne in Burey-le-Petit. But as luck or divine consciousness would have it, we had received word from *them*, only a few days after Saint Marguerite's appearance.

Aunt Jehanne was unwell and asking after some herbs from Mama to help her recover. Elated and almost in shock of my luck, the spur of events was perfect! I offered to visit to take care of her until she recovered fully.

Mama approved of the idea and prepared her herbs for the illness. She packaged them into a small sack. Together, we sent back a response, with the help of Father Guillaume, telling them of my wish to care for her while she was ill, and if Uncle Durand would come and take me to Burey-le-Petit.

The events were in motion.

"Jehanne!" I heard a faint call from behind me. Mama was in the distance, walking towards the orchards.

"Over here!" I called as I got up quickly, wiping my dress of any excess dirt, and brushing the remnants of hay from my hands. Leaving the shade of the trees, I stepped over the long grass. I put my hand over my brow to shield my eyes from the bright rays of the sun. I waved and quickened my steps.

Spotting me, her face lit up with cheer. "There you are, I couldn't see you from the gate. Are you putting the hens' old hay under the tree?"

"Yes, it doesn't smell that bad. One of the trees is late in bloom." I motioned in the trees' direction. "Any news from Uncle Durand?"

Mama nodded. Her blue eyes shone with clarity. "A neighbour of your uncle came to deliver their message just now, saying Uncle Durand will arrive in a few days to escort you and retrieve the herbs."

Taken aback by his prompt arrival, I stammered, "Oh, so soon!"

Mama's glee paused for a moment as she searched my face, confused at my indecision. But I mustered up my smile. "Well, that's wonderful news!"

She joined in my felicity, for it was genuine. But in the corner of my heart, I knew I grew restless waiting on the sidelines, before departing for Petit-le-Burey and beginning the mission.

"Yes, it is dearest! I can't wait to hear about cousin Jehanne and the rest of the family." Mama's cheeks were pinkish as if pinched, and her smile never wavered. Her gaze wandered to the trees. I could see her admiring them; it was as if they mirrored the joy and happiness she felt.

"Well, I'd better get home and finish supper. Darling, don't forget to wash your hands, and I'll see you this afternoon." She squeezed my shoulders reassuringly and turned quickly, striding back to the house.

I gazed absently after her. It was all happening so fast. Time was advancing and it was up to me to keep up with it. I took a deep breath and plodded back to the tree. Picking up the bucket of water and a small shovel, I glanced upwards to the branches that spread out overhead like a thousand arms, their branches bare but for a small bud here and there.

Maybe you don't feel ready now, but you will bloom, lovelier and brighter than the others.

I bent over to tidy the heap of hay underneath the tree and gave it more water. At the time, I remember I was apprehensive for the changes to come, but I was ready. I knew I was. I had prepared myself, spread myself thin to achieve what the angels asked of me. I trained and practised with Pierre until I could no longer feel my limbs and we could no longer hold our arms up.

I felt ready to start this new journey. This was what I had been preparing myself for all these years.

True to his word, Uncle Durnad arrived by early Friday afternoon in small cart drawn by a sturdy oxen. Like many men who work the land, Uncle Durand had a wide frame with a pair of large, callused hands.

He was an inch shorter than Papa, and on his head was a mop of sandy brown hair with silver roots that hung thinly around his face. His face was lined with the faint lines of aging, and his nose was wide, with a rounded, large tip that sat comfortably above his mouth when he smiled.

After tending the garden and collecting the apples from the orchard trees, I entered the house with a basket full of apples, carrots, cauliflower, and cabbages. I found Mama and Uncle both sitting at the table next to the hearth. Uncle Durand sat with his hands cupping a small jug of hot chamomile water, leaving a trail of steam visible underneath the sun's glare.

"Jehanne!" He got up quickly, and I set down the produce baskets to embrace him. "Uncle! It's good to see you. How was your trip?"

"It went well. I'm just sharing all the news with your mama, Jehanne—"

I smiled knowingly and looked at Mama. I knew she was squeezing him for every last bit of news that had happened in Burey-le-Petit and had been interrogating him all afternoon.

His face turned serious "—your aunt is confined to her bed, so we must leave tomorrow, to get to her on time."

Mama added, "Jehanne, prepare your things so you can depart early tomorrow," and Uncle stepped aside to include her as she spoke.

"Yes, Mama." I turned to Uncle. "Don't worry, I will not take long to prepare and we can leave at the earliest hour."

He smiled and nodded, clasping his hands together. "Good girl."

That night, when Pierre and Papa arrived from the fields, we ate together as a family with Uncle Durand. Papa's usual sternness was softened with Uncle Durand's arrival, and that evening they talked of the land and the things happening in the villages.

As the night advanced, the bowls became emptied and only crumbs of bread remained on the wooden boards, yet the flicker of candles and lively conversation lingered. Pierre listened attentively as Papa and Uncle shared the events that had happened in the last few months with the English and Burgundians.

Uncle sighed audibly. He raised his hand to rub his temple. "We've been lucky. Our province has been the forgotten little land the English aren't too preoccupied with. Nevertheless, all is well in our village, and we haven't been disturbed much by the English or Burgundians."

At that, I could see Papa focus on a spot on the table in front of him, deep in thought.

Pierre piped up, "Do you plan to stay long, Uncle?"

Uncle's face loosened with a small smile. "I wish I could my boy, but poor Jehanne needs me to come home straightway."

"Then we will not intrude on your much needed rest. Let us finish so that Uncle can rest for the journey home tomorrow."

Papa stood up, his chair groaning loudly, and stirred us all into motion. Mama began collecting the bowls and bringing them to the basin in the kitchen. As we dispersed, Papa, Pierre, and Uncle retreated to their rooms, Uncle taking Jean's old bed.

The crescent moon hung in the sky, glowing ephemeral white as we drifted into the hazy dreams of deep slumber.

"Jehanne, do you have everything prepared?" Mama asked me as I approached the kitchen.

"Yes, I've packed everything, and I have prepared the garden and orchard," I said, carefully packing the small bag of herbs Mama gathered into my bag.

Dawn was shrouded in grey sheets of clouds, and the house was still dark. Mama and I awoke earliest, and Uncle appeared not long after. The corner of his eyes still filled with sleep, he noiselessly went outside to fetch the oxen from the fields.

Mama was in a flurry. "Good, you have the medicinal herbs. And I'll give you some cheese to take."

Her hands carefully wrapped a few small blocks of cheese in linen, embroidered in detail with intricate patterns. "I will feed the animals and get as much produce from the garden while you're gone." Wrapping the cheese securely, she packed it carefully inside the bag. She turned and smiled resignedly. "Tell your aunt I will send her my angel."

After eating a small breakfast, Uncle and I left for Burey-le-Petit. The sky brightened into light greys as the sun rose. Uncle guided the oxen as we travelled through the green hills, the countryside scenes changing as we crept along the wide dirt road.

The forests of Domrémy slowly grew into flat expanses of fields that travelled as far as the horizon would go. Dark clusters of tall trees dotted the blanket of distant greenery and waved in unison as the wind rolled over through the land.

It was quiet until Uncle said, "Jehanne, your aunt will be very happy to see you. She has spoken of nothing else since your message arrived."

I smiled. "It has been too long, and we mustn't let too much time pass by when we do not see each other."

He chuckled. "Aye, that is true. In these times, it's best to treasure one's family, God willing—" He glanced upwards, then back to the dirt road and continued, "—visit them every now and then."

Uncle and I talked intermittently, both of us enjoying the waves of silence and the changing countryside around us.

By noon we arrived in Burey-le-Petit. The village consisted of a narrow street, humble small houses with thatched roofs all packed snugly together on each side. As we rode through, Uncle slowed down and I could see small patches of grass growing in front of the houses. Some houses had carefully tended gardens with herbs and flowers spurting upwards and around the cottages. Uncle's was no different.

We slowed to a stop in front of a one-storey house, with one window and two doors on either side of each other. Above it was the downward slanted side of the roof. Encircling the house was a short stone fence, encasing the garden and the home inside.

Uncle descended from the wagon slowly, stretching his limbs as he walked around. A door creaked. I sharply turned and saw Aunt Jehanne's small frame in the open doorway of the house. An extra shawl covered her shoulders and frame, and her eyes and nose were red. She waved weakly, with a handkerchief dabbing at her nose.

"Aunt Jehanne!" I called out as I descended the cart. I could see Uncle fetching my things quickly. Walking past the miniature stone wall and through the little garden, I could see her clearly. My Aunt Jehanne was my mama's cousin, yet they resembled close siblings with their shared bright blue eyes and strawberry blond hair.

Aunt Jehanne was plumper and taller than Mama, with thin lips that upturned sharply into an endearing smile that revealed a line of off-yellow teeth. While she smiled, her blue eyes peered through small slits, as she held her hands open. I walked into her embrace.

"Aunty." I felt her chuckle.

"Oh, my dear." She released me and peered at me with a mischievous, intrigued smile.

"You should not be out of the house," Uncle Durand reproached her gently as he walked past with our belongings. His eyes were masked with worry.

"Oh, I am fine, it is just a mild flu," said Aunt, giving no importance to her condition. Setting eyes back on me, she held my hands and said, "Come, come, my girl, my you are tall! And that beautiful long, dark auburn hair. Some boy is going to snatch you up really soon!"

"Not a chance of that," I said, laughing.

Inside the house, we entered into a parlour. The roof was low and everything inside looked well-worn yet sturdy. We walked in and sat at a square, worn table with a large fireplace.

Aunt Jehanne was talkative and extroverted; her character was magnanimous. As we sat at the table, she said again, "My dear, you have grown so much! Tell me everything about your mama, and your brothers. Tell me what news there is from Domrémy."

As the afternoon passed, I updated her on everything there was to tell. I told her when we had to leave for Neufchâteau, and how we stayed in Uncle Jean's home. I told her about Jean's apprenticeship, and I told her I worked in a hotel where I took care of the horses. Her eyes keenly never left my face. Every so often, she gasped or grasped my hand in shock or amusement.

Remembering Mama's gift, I fetched my bag and took out the cheeses wrapped in linen.

"Oh my! Isabel is always so generous. Oh, the beautiful embroidery!" she said while looking at the white cloth in her hands. "Yes." She quirked an eyebrow at me. "Come, I will show you your room while you stay with us."

Aunt then led me to the far end of the parlour, where a door frame opened into a narrow hallway. On the side was an open doorway, the room beyond it lit. On the longer wall was a bed with a small nightstand beside it. A small window let the pearlescent light of grey skies from outside shine through. "This will be your room. Your uncle has cleaned and prepared this for you."

Aunt stayed glued to the doorframe, while I walked in and looked around. "You let me or your uncle know if you need anything."

I turned around, snapping my arms to my sides. "Well, that's what I'm here for, Aunt. To help you. Now Mama also has her herbs…"

During my stay, I helped Aunt Jehanne with the chores around the house and her garden. She had a garden like ours in the backyard, and a small grove of fruit trees that had wandering chickens and bleating goats underneath. Her health was slowly coming back to her, and she grew more and more vigorous each day.

A few days after my arrival, I knew it was time to fulfill my part of the angels' directions. I knew I had to tell my uncle and aunt about my mission. My stomach was in a knot. When I had arrived, I was distracted with the new environment and new place, yet now as things were becoming routine and settled, Saint Catherine's instructions were loud and clear: *Tell them of your mission.*

My stomach was lined with butterflies. I had no idea how I would approach the subject, nor how they would take it. Would they think I was mad? I felt like I was sharing a bit of myself that was too private—something I alone experienced that, if articulated, would seem crazy. But, for the life of me, I couldn't find any other excuse for an audience with Lord de Baudricourt.

A week after living in the slow village of Burey-le-Petit, we were sitting down for supper in the twilight evening. The angels hadn't arrived or appeared in any shape or form. They did not see a reason to come, and I was losing hope. Having prayed for the angels to give me the right words, I decided I couldn't delay the inevitable any longer. *Light up my mind, God. Please help them believe me...* I begged internally.

I heard my aunt and uncle's muffled voices, as if they were speaking from a great distance. I sat upright, swirling my bowl of stew with my spoon, and my other hand playing with my braid that laid over my shoulder.

"Jehanne?"

I looked up distractedly, and as if noticing them for the first time, I stammered, "O-oh, I am sorry aunty, did you ask me...?"

"Yes, darling, did you cut some wood?" she asked, her eyes concerned.

"Uh... Oh yes, yes, I did. I left it at the back of the house," I replied.

"Are you distracted, my dear? Are you worried about something?" Aunt Jehanne's face was healthy and radiant by now; all vestige of her flu had disappeared. Yet her usual merriment had gone, and her bright blue eyes were furrowed with worry.

I looked at them both, but before I could speak, Aunt Jehanne continued, "We have noticed you look preoccupied. Haven't we, Durand?"

"Yes, yes," responded Uncle Durand, looking at his wife then back at me.

This is it. If I don't do it now, I know I'll never do it. Putting down my spoon and leaning back into my chair, I stared downwards at the floor for a moment to gather my words. I looked back up and breathed out deeply.

"Actually, yes. There is something important I have to tell you."

"Do you, darling? What is it?" Prompting me further, Aunt Jehanne now sounded more curious than worried.

She sounds more entertained now. Well, hopefully she will like this story. Here it goes. There is no turning back.

My hands went to the opposite braid, fidgeting with it as the words fell from my lips, the first droplets of rain in a storm. "I have a mission from God. I don't know why, but God wants me to go and have an audience with the Dauphin. But first I need to go to Vaucoleaurs and speak to Lord de Baudricourt."

The table was completely silent. My gaze flickered to the stupefied looks on the faces of both Aunt and Uncle; they were still as statues. Then they both looked at each other, and Uncle broke the silence first. "Well, this is very unusual. How do you know that you have this mission?"

"I've been visited by angels, Saint Marguerite, Saint Catherine, and Archangel Michael, and they have told me about this mission. They have instructed me to go to Vaucoleaurs and talk to Lord Baudricourt. They told me to come to you first and ask for your help. I know this sounds crazy, but believe me it is real, and my brother Pierre also knows about this mission."

"Do your mama and papa know about this... mission?" Aunt asked tentatively.

"No, they do not, and I would prefer to keep it that way, so as to not cause them any pain."

"I see," she said, nodding as if understanding everything.

More silence.

I observed them quietly. Aunt and Uncle both seemed composed, and silent in contemplation. I looked at them even closer. My words hadn't affected them as much as I thought they would. I waited, wondering when the flood of questions would come, but instead I had a question of my own.

"Aunt, Uncle... you're handling this very well... I can't help but notice you don't seem surprised?"

"My dear Jehanne. It seems we also must confess something. When you asked for your uncle to pick you up, we both had a dream, didn't we?" said Aunt, looking at her husband.

Uncle Durand nodded at her, then looked at me and said, "Yes, we had a dream on two separate nights. Archangel Michael appeared to us and told us to help you in your mission."

My hands immediately landed on the table with a soft thump. "You knew?!"

"Well, yes, we know you have to go to the Dauphin and liberate France," said Uncle Durand with a smile. As if it was the most common thing in the world.

"We were waiting for you to tell us, dear," said Aunt, her face breaking into a generous smile and a playful gleam twinkling in her eyes.

I threw back my head, my hands covering my temples, and began to laugh. All this time, I was wracking my brain how to tell them, and they knew all along! Both my aunt and uncle joined in my laughter, and when we subsided our eyes were rimmed with water, and our cheeks reddened.

"Do you want me to tell you about how Archangel Michael and the saints Marguerite and Catherine came to me?"

They looked at each other again, their curiosity beaming from their eyes.

I eagerly told them how the first angel appeared as a princess when I was ten years old, and after when Michael appeared in the fields, and the following visits from Saint Catherine and Marguerite.

They were mesmerised. They took in every detail, and I recounted every moment, taking delicious delight in their impressed smiles and approving looks of my training with Pierre, and his involvement.

By the end, the stew grew cold, and darkness had enveloped the town, and only the firelight from the hearth could illuminate their eyes filled with wonder.

Uncle broke the silence when I finished recounting all the events leading up to my visit. "Your story, Jehanne… It is one for the ages. I have never heard anything like it. You are truly special, my dear."

My heart stirred. I smiled and I could feel my eyes watering. Knowing how painful it had been to keep this secret for so long, I was relieved it was a burden I no longer had to carry by myself. "Thank you, Uncle."

His eyes remained fixed on me, and he said in a voice like steel, "I will take you to Vaucouleaurs without delay, Jehanne. I have friends who can lend us shelter in the fortress."

Aunt Jehanne reached over and clasped my hands. Her voice was lightning. "We will help you, Jehanne. You are not alone."

22

VAUCOULEURS

Summer, 1428
Vaucouleurs, France

*T*he fortress of Vaucouleurs was an imposing sight. It stood on a large hill, with the roofs of the small village scattered at its feet. It was barricaded by high stone walls.

"That's it, isn't it?" I asked Uncle as we rode on the small cart, on the winding road leading to the gates of Vaucouleurs.

He cast a quick look my way and glanced at the fortress.

"Aye," he said as he lightly jerked the reins of the oxen. "Once inside we will find our friends. They should be expecting us soon."

I nodded, biting my lip.

We left Burey-le-Petit at dawn when the sky was pale blue, the earth was slowly coming alive, and darkness was slowly receding back to every crevice and corner. I knew of the opulent palaces and richness of the nobles, but it didn't fail to impress me. "It's like a different world," I muttered as the wheels wobbled over the dirt path, turning over loose rocks and twigs.

Approaching the gates, we saw soldiers stationed beside the entrance and patrolling the top of the walls. The gates were open and the guards were leisurely leaning against the walls, talking amongst themselves. We passed many travellers, coming in and out of the fortress, and we filed in seamlessly like marching ants.

Unlike Neufchâteau, Vaucouleurs' main street was wide, but it shrank into a narrow road the further you went, leading to the town square and the church at the end. Houses were stacked up next to each other along the pebbled street, some of them up to two to three levels high.

"Now, if I remember correctly," Uncle said, his eyes surveying the streets we passed, "Henri and Catherine de Royer live here." He turned into a quieter street and stopped in front of a two-storey house in the middle. "They are an older couple in their 50's. Henri used to be in trade, selling saddles and equipment for horse riding, but their children now provide for them as they've gone to Lorraine. They're honest and good people. We can trust them."

My uncle hopped off the cart, and I followed, stretching my limbs and neck, which were stiff from sitting for so long.

Uncle took off his hat and swept back the little strands of hair neatly, then bade me to follow him to the door. The house looked very comfortable and in good condition. He knocked, and we waited for a few moments. Once we heard voices and shuffling from inside, the door suddenly opened and revealed a beaming woman with a white cap and an apron.

"Durand! You are most welcome!" She embraced Uncle. Beside her appeared another face with an infectious smile

"Durand, my old friend. Good to see you!" The man was tall, with a wide frame and a friendly face.

"It is very good to see you both. I'm so grateful you could receive us on such short notice," Uncle Durand said, looking over at me. "This is my niece, Jehanne. She has been staying with us to help my wife get better."

The woman I presumed to be Catherine de Royer gazed over to me. She had bright curly blond and grey hair, waxen skin that stretched when she smiled and blue eyes that twinkled with merriment. "Of course, any family of yours is welcome. It's lovely to make your acquaintance, mademoiselle Jehanne."

I nodded, in response. "Thank you, Madam."

"In fact, we know your parents, Jacques and Isabel d'Arc. How are they faring?"

"They are well and healthy," I assured.

Catherine smiled, satisfied, but her countenance changed as if she remembered something. "Oh, please come in. You must be tired from your journey." She ushered us inside, and we followed her through a narrow, dark hall that opened into a small kitchen and dining room.

A small, wooden table with four seats was in the middle of the room, with a big and open fireplace that warmed the room pleasantly off to one side. Next to the fireplace was a long, narrow, wooden table with a window that hung above it.

A big basket with kindling sat next to the dining table. "We've baked some bread and cooked some soup if you're hungry?" Catherine went to the table and began to cut some warm bread. The Royers were as kind as they were simple.

The house was dark, but the fire was bright and sparkling. In the corner of the room was a door that opened to a steep wooden staircase, with a long, old piece of furniture occupying the whole wall next to the stairs. Their house was sturdy and solid. The interior had few lights and coal black coloured wooden panels.

"Come, come," said Catherine. She carried over some bread and warmed milk, and then motioned to the seats. "Please sit."

"Thank you," said Uncle, flipping the tail of his long coat back as he sat.

"Thank you," I said, sitting down.

"So, what brings you here, Durand? What business brings you to Vaucouleurs?" asked Henri, peering at him curiously and glancing over at me. Henri was more mellow compared to his wife, yet he had intelligent eyes that observed much more than his tongue spoke.

Uncle looked at me before he began. "My niece. She has an important message for Lord Robert de Baudricourt. It is very important that she speaks with him."

My eyes widened in alarm at his lack of subtlety. I fidgeted with my hands in my lap.

Filling some ceramic mugs with milk, Catherine replied, "You can find Lord Robert in the town square or at the entrance of the fortress when he arrives from his farmhouses, usually after midday. It's getting late today, so if I were you, I would be waiting to talk to Lord Robert tomorrow, my dear."

Her face scrunched into a question, and I could sense her next question forming in her mind, "Jehanne, what is the nature of your... *urgent* appointment with Lord Robert?" She peered over, brow gathered, as she filled the last mug.

Uncomfortable, I took a mug and sipped slowly. I glanced over at Uncle for encouragement. He gave a subtle nod, and I lowered the mug and took a deep breath. "I have a message for Lord Robert."

She put her hand on her hip. "A message for Lord Robert? From the Lord of Domrémy?"

"No, not from the Lord of Domrémy. This message... is from the King of Heaven," I stated, with all the confidence I could muster.

Catherine and Henri were completely still for a moment. Speechless. Catherine looked at her husband, and blinked multiple times, then back at me. "My goodness, are you... Are you saying you have a message from God?!"

I nodded. "Yes, precisely. Angels have revealed themselves to me many times and they've instructed me to come here and speak with Lord Robert."

Doubt was written plainly on Catherine and Henri's faces. They looked at each other. Then Uncle Durand intervened. "What Jehanne is telling you is the truth. We, my wife Jehanne and I, were visited by the Archangel Michael a week before our niece came to our house. The Archangel told us about Jehanne's mission. We knew about it before she told us."

"Goodness..." said Catherine. "So this is true. Angels have been talking to you?" Her eyes landed on me, pools of disbelief.

"Yes, since I was twelve."

"What exactly *is* your mission, young lady?" asked Henri. He repositioned himself, leaning over his hands.

I felt the room tip into insecurity. My mouth went dry. "I need to see Lord Baudricourt, so I can meet with the King."

"So, you are to help the King?!" Catherine said with both hands on her face in complete amazement.

"Yes," I replied.

"Henri, we need to help her. This is incredible, this is incredible!" She reached for her husband.

Henri was deep in thought, his face solemn as the truth began to sink in. "Yes, we should." He nodded, clasping his wife's hand.

"Jehanne, tell us about the angels," Catherine requested.

Uncle Durand offered a comforting smile, and I unclasped my hands and wiped them on the length of my legs. "Well… it all started in a forest with a princess…"

Both Catherine and Henri listened intently, their expressions inscrutable when I started but both grew in shock to the mention of angels, "Angel Michael?!" Catherine blurted out, her jaw hanging open.

I could feel Henri's resistance like a razor-sharp knife as he regarded me with scepticism from his seat, but I continued.

"Yes, there is more," I said, and further explained the experiences with the light and the feeling of divine love; I felt both Catherine and Henri melt like butter as their hard, inscrutable eyes softened, and my stories washed away any trace of disbelief.

Their questions drove our conversation to new highs, and I answered them as best I could until their curiosity was satiated. Each question allowed their solidarity to grow as I explained how the angels helped me and guided me. They became enthralled at how I manoeuvred out of Papa's planned marriage and trained with Pierre in secret. By the end of the night, they were convinced that my mission was true, and they would do everything in their power to help.

Once we ate our fill of soup and bread, Uncle and I retired to the extra rooms upstairs. Uncle patted my shoulder as he bade me goodnight. "Get some rest, dear. We have a big day tomorrow."

"Goodnight, Uncle." I carried a small candle that lit the dark, small room in its small yellow halo. The day's events had left me feeling satisfied yet fatigued. I felt like I had just finished a race and only now reached the finish line.

I put the candle down on a small table beside the long bed. To finally share my stories was as exhilarating as it was frightening. I often thought about how people would react. Would they always be so supportive and believe me?

The Royers were uncertain at first, but their affinity to the truth became apparent after I told them about the angels. My small glimmer of hope plummeted into deeper darkness as I remembered Robert of Baudricourt. Apprehension rose in my chest.

Whatever happens, I will have help, I thought to myself resignedly, as I changed into a warm old frock and wrapped myself in blankets. The wind howled against the house, making the wooden walls groan and creak. The house was a tomb.

The Royers had finished cleaning downstairs and must have gone to bed. I blew out the candle and began to pray in the silence of my room. "Hail Mary, full of Grace, the lord be with thee…"

I stirred. The room was brightened with the light of day. On the table, there was a ceramic bowl of water. Its translucent surface swayed, as if someone had just put the bowl down. I got up and filled my hands. Scrubbing my face and washing myself, I changed clothes quickly and braided my hair.

The sounds of cluttering pots and clanging metal rods from downstairs brought me to tiptoe down the creaking staircase to the kitchen. A small fire was slowly coming alive, and Catherine was bent over tending to it. "Good morning, Jehanne!" She heaved with both hands on her knees to get up.

"Good morning, Madame Royer."

Placing the rod back next to the fireplace, she began to change her stained apron for a shawl. "Oh my dear, we are well past madams. Why don't you call me Catherine?" When her shawl was secured over her shoulders, she smiled at me. "I'm off to matins this morning. Would you like to join me?"

Slightly taken aback, I contemplated it for a moment. I knew I would get bored staying here alone. "Oh, very much," I replied happily. I donned my shawl and cap, and we left the house, facing the rays of the early morning sun. We walked to mass, our breath swelling up into translucent miniature clouds.

By late morning, we had walked through the crowds of the church goers and were weaving our way through the streets, back to Catherine's home. "Here we are," Catherine commented, as we entered the house and walked through the dark hallway to the hearth room.

I felt my skin tingle as we passed by the cold air of the rooms, yet Catherine slipped off her cap and shawl. Uncle and Henri were sitting at the table, talking casually.

"Good morning!" Catherine announced, walking right by them.

Suddenly roused, Henri patted the table. "Oh, good morning to you both!" he said boisterously.

The warmth of the room pinched my cheeks, and I hastily slipped off my cap and shawl. "Hello." I looked at Henri and nodded to Uncle. Unsure of what to do, I looked over at Catherine, who was donning an apron, and collecting some pans and utensils from the benches.

"Catherine, may I help you?" I asked.

She poured a jug of milk into a bowl. "Actually, yes, Jehanne. Out back—" She motioned with her head to the backyard, "—we have our chicken pen. See if the chickens have laid some eggs and bring me a half dozen, dear."

The smell of cooked eggs and warm bread soon filled the room, and we all quietly sat together. The table was filled with baskets of bread, jams, and some cheeses, with warmed milk. I filled my plate sparingly, contemplating the day ahead.

"So, Jehanne, will you be meeting with Lord Baudricourt today?"

"Yes, I plan to."

Catherine began to allocate slices of bread to each of our plates and spread generously with butter. "Jehanne has an important task today, and we must support her, first by having a good breakfast."

Only once crumbs remained and glasses had small puddles of milk the size of buttons did Uncle go upstairs to fetch a shirt, while Henri went to sit in front of the fire with his pipe.

"Catherine, I was wondering if I could help you with your garden? I have one at home. Do you want me to help you with yours?"

Catherine perked up in surprise.

"…. It can distract me from other matters…" *I hope I don't sound too pushy*, I thought.

Catherine's elbows came to rest on the table, her chin resting on her knuckles. "Oh, Jehanne, the garden is yours to do with as you wish. Even better, if you can tend to it and put some love and care into it."

I smiled. "Thank you, Catherine."

She began to clean the table, and I went upstairs to fetch my top-frock.

The air was cold and brusque outside, as I took the small forks to the garden. The backyard was small and flat, with a miniature raised bed filled with overflowing herbs, growing in all sorts of directions. At the back of the yard were two mature fruit trees.

The chooks pecked and prodded around the garden, with their calls and occasional flapping disrupting the silence. *It's quieter here than in the street*, I thought to myself.

Fork in hand, I strutted to the herb garden and found my first call of duty. Beneath the profuse bushes of rosemary, green tarragon stems, and lavender were growths of spiked-rimmed weeds. Wasting no time, I began to clear the garden bed of them. Bushel after bushel, I worked through the morning, and it felt like coming home again.

The garden was my sacred haven, and it always nourished me, especially now, as it was time to take my first step into my mission, to face a lord.

My legs were starting to ache from squatting for so long, so I stood up to stretch them, and looked up. *The sun will soon be at its zenith.*

I wiped my brow with my sleeve and gathered the discarded weeds into a pile. I packed up the shovels and leant them beside the wall. The basin of rainwater was cold when I delved my hands and washed my arms and hands, and quickly splashed my face from sweat.

Here we go.

I stood up, and walked to the house, finding Uncle and Henri talking quietly. "I hear that the English have driven the King's forces so far they'll soon have all of France."

Uncle was leaning his elbow on the table, and he shook his head, massaging his temple in disappointment.

I cleared my throat, and they looked in my direction. Uncle's distress faded like smoke, and he leant backwards into the chair and smiled, attempting to mask the nature of their previous conversation.

"Excuse me, Uncle, it's almost noon. Would you like to accompany me to the plaza?" "Yes, of course," he said, standing up.

"Monsieur Royer, if you want to come..."

"Yes, of course, my dear! I was not going to stay here, while you two are going to have all the fun." He stood up with a spring.

"Very good." Feeling more comfortable, I added, "I'll just go and change."

I ran upstairs and quickly took off my dirty top-frock. I combed my hair and hastened downstairs, patting my hair back as I fastened the cap over my head. Uncle, Henri, and I left the house together, and we began to walk with purpose towards the square.

My hands were getting clammy. I felt my stomach flutter with a million bees. I looked up at the dark clouds hanging over our heads, making the day look much later than it was. *That looks like rain. I hope not now, please not now, Lord.*

Henri led us to the plaza in no time, but just before we arrived, three men on horseback arrived in the fortress from the front gates. They formed a triangle, the man at the head dressed in fine clothes. He was in his late forties with wide shoulders and brown short hair. He was riding slowly; his back was a little hunched as if he were tired.

The other two were young riders, following behind with rabbits and hares hanging on the sides of their saddles. While the riders passed slowly in front of me, I felt a presence above my shoulder, and Saint Catherine's voice was clear. "That is Robert de Baudricourt, the one who is at the front of the three riders."

Hearing this, I ran to catch up and get ahead of the horse.

"Sir Robert de Baudricourt!" I called, but he made no gesture to stop. His horse continued, and he stared ahead solidly. I kept pace with the horse, and called him again but with more confidence, "Lord Robert de Baudricourt!"

He stopped and glowered at the source of this address. "Who are you? What do you want, girl?!" he barked, everything about him scowling with intensity.

"Sir, my name is Jehanne d'Arc. I have come at the explicit command of the King of Heaven. I need to see the Dauphin of France. I have an important message for him."

Sir Robert stopped the horse and looked down at me again. Determined to be heard, I continued, mustering as much confidence as I could—even though I was terrified. "Sir, it is very important that I go to the king. The King needs me. France needs me! This is by command of God that I come to speak with you, Lord Baudricourt!"

I felt my adrenaline deplete, and with that my confidence. I became conscious of a small group surrounding us, but I couldn't break my attention away from the Lord on the horse. He continued to stare down at me with a deepening scowl and a fire growing in his eyes by the minute.

Then he looked down to my clothes, taking in my worn peasant shoes, my simple purple plain dress, and my shabby shawl. His eyebrows deepened and he scowled with disdain. The horse between us snickered, but he held it in place, fixating his vivid gaze on me.

Facing anger was familiar to me, and I held his gaze fearlessly, but his disdain for the peasantry was something I had never encountered before. I prayed to not falter in his eyes, but I couldn't help but feel ill at ease with his contempt.

When his eyes reached my face again, I looked back determined, but his face was as dark as the clouds above us, and his eyes were like thunder. His voice came out like a spark of fire, showing only a speck of the anger that was brewing inside. "Where is your father?"

"At home, my Lord," I answered, my body coiled and in a bunch of knots.

"And, are you alone?"

"No, my Lord. My uncle is with me," I replied quickly, turning to look at Uncle, although I was beginning to wonder where this line of questioning was headed.

"Where?" he asked, while studying the people around me.

"Here! Here I am, my Lord," replied my uncle, timidly raising his hand. "I am Durand Lassois of Burey le Petit, uncle of the maiden."

"Well, Durand Lassois." His gaze moved between us. "I should say this. Take this stupid girl home to her father, so that he will give her a good beating. Make sure he applies it with force, so it will discourage her from going around telling nonsense. Take her to her family and correct her!" he said fiercely, while spurring his horse to walk on, in no rush.

Numb with shock, I watched Lord Baudricourt trot away through the streets. He continued on his way at a slow pace, and the two men on horseback behind him passed by me slowly, staring closely. I felt their curious gazes on me, at the maiden who had made their lord angry with such a bold statement.

I felt my uncle's hand on my shoulder. "It seems that it won't be easy. Have courage, Jehanne."

"No, it seems not..." I breathed out deeply, and felt the tension being released from the heated encounter. Shaken, I looked again at the backs of the three men, riding slowly away through the stone-covered streets to the fortress.

I will not give up.

<hr />

Every day for a week, I waited for Lord Baudricourt at the entrance of the fortress. Uncle always accompanied me, as well as both Henri and Catherine Royer. The locals always gathered for a spectacle as entertaining as the first, but Lord Baudricourt completely ignored me. He rode by as if I was nothing but an ant and remained as responsive as a statue.

My dismay began to grow. First, it was as small as a grain of dust, but it developed into the thrashing waves of a storm. Slumped over the table, and deep in thought after a quiet supper, I could feel the glances of concern from the Royers.

Uncle helped maintain the hope, but I must admit I was depleted of all optimism. After I helped Catherine clean up, I excused myself to retire early.

The next morning, before dawn, I awoke startled. I had slept restlessly. I groggily got up and knelt in front of the crucifix, and I began to pray desperately. "Dear Lord, I have tried again and again. What am I doing wrong? I don't know what else you want me to do. Please show me the way. What can I do next?" I concentrated as hard as I could.

I felt an assuaging peace in my mind. I slowly opened my eyes, and the light of dawn was streaming through, illuminating Archangel Michael's face. "Jehanne."

I nodded.

"It's time for you to go back home now. Do not worry. You will come back in a few months. These first encounters were to prepare the groundwork for when you come next time. People will know about you, and you will open the minds of many people in town. And most importantly, the Lord of Lorraine. Go back, Jehanne. This experience is over for you now."

Those were his last words.

And as quickly as one falls asleep, he was gone.

That morning, the Royers' house was in a flurry after I shared Archangel Michael's words with everyone. Uncle and I prepared for our departure and left soon after breakfast. As we slowly traversed through the streets, we saw the approaching gates ahead.

Leading the oxen towards them, Uncle asked, "Jehanne, how are you faring?"

I paused for a moment before responding. "I do not feel accomplished. I was not able to convince Lord Baudricourt, but… there is always a reason for such things."

He nodded, deep in thought, and shrugged. "The Lord's work seems rather curious at first. All we must do is trust that it's part of the process."

I peered up and half-smiled, amused at the coincidence. "That is exactly what Archangel Michael said, Uncle. This was to prepare for what is to come. 'Prepare the groundwork,' he said."

Uncle smiled a toothy grin. I looked back, and felt the world stir.

The fortress of Vaucouleurs rose high in the distance, birds circling the pillars slowly. The walls, impenetrable and dense. But around us, the glances of the locals lingered, and they paused, watching us pass the gates, their expressions perplexed and curious.

The world is slowly waking up.

23

GOD KNOWS ALL OUR NEEDS

Mid-Summer, 1428
Domrémy, France

*B*y afternoon, Uncle and I were climbing over a small knoll when we saw the nestled village of Domrémy. The patches of forests on the outskirts were a myriad of emerald and lime leaves that shimmered like verdant gems.

As we rode through the village, nodding and greeting people, I sought out the familiar sharp roof edge of my home. Its washed out earthy-grey face slowly came into view.

When Uncle slowed the oxen to a stop in front of it, in the midst of getting out of the wagon, I heard a door open. I turned and Mama stood at the door, surprised and elated. She began laughing as I smiled and waved.

We hurried to each other and embraced tightly, my head resting over hers. We stayed there, hugging without saying any words. We didn't need words to express how much we missed each other.

We were ushered inside and sat down. Mama quickly went over to the table and hearth, and began carrying bowls and spoons. "How fortunate for you! I've just finished with supper, so you can have it fresh."

Uncle and I served ourselves generously, our stomachs growling and the skin on our hands dry and stiff from travelling. Uncle and I told Mama the latest news between mouthfuls, about how Aunt Jehanne recovered swiftly, of her garden, of the news of neighbours and locals of the war. We conversed animatedly, Uncle helping me with the details, all in the effort to conceal the true purpose of our travels.

Mama also didn't let any gossip from her side get curtailed. "Jehanne, dear. Your brother Pierre has been so busy. He's working as a helper for Lord Robert de Bautremont."

My eyes widened.

"Yes, he's been working on the Lord's estate, working on the fields," Mama said, glowing with pride. "And your Papa has taken up most of the work, so while Pierre is busy, Jehanne, can you take up some of his chores?"

"Yes, Mama." I nodded, a little relieved to be under the routine and safety of home. Although I knew it wouldn't be for long.

<hr/>

We stayed talking until evening arrived. Mama and I prepared Jean's old bed for Uncle. He didn't want us to go through too much effort and repeatedly insisted that he was fine sleeping in the kitchen, but Mama wouldn't hear of it, and Uncle ended up sleeping comfortably in Jean's bed.

Having cleaned up with Mama, I retired to my bedroom. After the month's events, I was glad to nestle in my own bed and be in the comfort of home. To sit at my parents' table again, and savour Mama's cooking and warmness.

Pierre arrived later in the evening after we had eaten, but even then, he and Papa did not miss their nightly conversations. Pierre smiled in greeting us. However, his face looked drawn, and after his conversation with father ended, he retired quietly to his room.

Life on the farm continued seamlessly. As Pierre was working for Lord Robert de Bautremont, I had to take over some of his work, especially the care of the animals. Wild flowers began growing in the fields. I brushed them as I walked by, smelling their sweet scent. They crunched with each step I took, and the wind often carried and flew them across the ground.

By the afternoon, usually after I had finished all of my chores, I made my way through the woods to the clearing where Pierre and I used to practise. Even though I was alone, I practised the moves, shifting my feet, swinging the sword, dodging imaginary strikes from an invisible opponent.

When my imagination had run its course, I practised hitting the patchy sandbag that hung on a low branch of a tree. My grunts and shuffling were the only sounds that filled the emptiness of the forest, and I stopped until my hair was matted with sweat, and my chest was heaving.

Pierre arrived later and more tired each evening, and though we were able to chat, our conversation could not go beyond the limits of the farm, family, and our chores. It was only a week later when we could talk privately and without guard on my trip to Vaucouleurs.

"Jehanne!"

Peering through the branches, I saw Pierre's figure approaching between the trees. The sun was shining brightly, but the wind carried a chill, and Pierre climbed up towards the orchard. As he walked up, his arms swung beside him. He seemed light and energised.

I picked up the basket of ripened apples and walked around the tree. My hand instinctively came up to cover my eyes from the sun. "Pierre, you're home early today!" I called out excitedly.

"Yeah, I managed to finish most of the work yesterday, so I could come home early today," he said, now standing in front of me. Looking around at the pruned trees, he asked me, "Are you done?"

"I could finish tomorrow. What do you have in mind?" I asked, picking up a forgotten fruit from the ground and checking its condition.

"We could go practise, what do you think?"

"Yes, let's go! Just let me finish this tree and get the things back to the barn."

"I'll help you."

Pierre, using a farm tool to shake the branches of their fruits in the higher zones, had the apples falling like rain. I gathered them up in the basket, and when the tree was mostly bare of its red fleshed apples, we returned the tools to the barn and laid the baskets of apples next to the other piles.

As we walked towards the forest, we began talking.

"So, what happened? Tell me, what did Lord de Baudricourt say?" Pierre's tone was curious.

I began to recount all that had occurred, from Aunt and Uncle and their support to go to Vaucouleurs with me, to meeting and convincing Catherine and Henri de Royer, and finally to the heated conversation with Lord Baudricourt.

Pierre was silent, listening intently as I told him everything.

His eyes furrowed slightly at the end, when I told him of Archangel Michaels' message and appearance at the end of my journey.

When I finished, there was a moment of silence. We were approaching the edge of the woods, and the sun shifted behind the tall pyres of woods. We were drenched in its cool shade. I looked over to the descending hills where our farm was ensconced. The grey stone roofs of the village houses peered over the feathery tops of trees, with the church's high pyre rising above, its cross floating above us as a strong emblem.

"I wonder, what are the plans? When am I going to go?" I said, without looking back at Pierre.

"You have no idea?" asked Pierre, perplexed, his arms crossed.

"No, I haven't had any conversations with the angels yet."

"Pray for clarification," Pierre suggested, deep in thought. He continued, "I am concerned. You have to leave without me again." His forehead was creased with worry.

I sighed. "Pierre, when I was in Vaucouleurs, God… God showed me something, Pierre. They made something very clear. Everything is… as it should be. Everything is carried out because they intend it that way. Lord de Baudricourt, even though he would not listen, God knew this, but this was not for Lord Baudricourt.

"No, this was for the others. Archangel Michael said my words would reach many people. Even the Duke of Lorraine. God arranges everything to be perfect. I know I will be protected. I promise you that as soon as I know anything from the angels, I will tell you."

Pierre ran his hand through his hair. "Jehanne, I know you're going to be fine. I just want to help you, protect you."

"And you will, brother," I told him. "You are going to be with me, I know it. I will need all the help I can get."

He smiled faintly and looked down.

"You know, Archangel Michael appeared to Aunt Jehanne and Uncle Durand?"

Pierre's face dropped. "No!"

I nodded, laughing. "Yep, God works in ways that we can't even imagine!"

He looked at me curiously, still laughing. "That must have been a surprise."

"It certainly made things easier. You see, Pierre, God prepares the road. All we have to do is follow it."

The change of topic seemed to lighten Pierre's mood and give him a little spark of hope. He nodded and pensively considered my words for a few more moments. "Come on." He nudged me and began to briskly jog into the forests. "I'll race you to the clearing!"

"That's not fair!" I yelled back, running behind him. We jumped and dodged our way through the dense forest, immediately feeling the coolness of the shade, and the scratches of the branches licking us as we sprinted past.

"Almost, Jehanne, almost," Pierre teased when we arrived in the clearing. His breathing remained normal, if not a little deeper, as he retrieved the smooth wooden swords from the sacks we hung on the tree. Pierre threw one of them over to me. "Now, let's see how much you remember." Pierre readied himself with his stance.

I positioned myself. "I'm ready."

After practising with Pierre, the days went by quickly. Life in Domrémy resumed its familiar rhythm. Sunlight and soil filled my day, as I spent my time in the gardens and tending the farm animals. Nightfall was filled with quiet and comforting suppers, with the crackling fire to help guide our sewing before we went to bed.

On a particularly bright summer day, Mama had gone to gather with the ladies of the town to sew clothes for a new baby. The air was crisp, and the smell of the rotting leaves left a sweet, dewy smell in the garden.

I ran through the inviting dusky brown fields towards the oak forest, the grass anklehigh and brushing against my frock. I ran quickly down the narrow dirt path that was fringed with small bushes with long bushy leaves. My steps slowed as I recognised the familiar clearing ahead.

While Mama's away, I can train a little, I thought as I picked up the sword, and quietly readied myself against the sandbag. I adjusted my stance and began to practise all the movements that I knew. I shuffled and swerved around the bag, keeping my breath steady, until my back and legs were covered in sweat.

Eventually, I walked slowly to a tree, my breath heaving, and sat down. My head leaned against the hard surface of the bark.

Perspiration coated my neck, but I didn't care, I just closed my eyes.

The sounds of the forest enveloped my ears. The buzz of the thousands of insects creeping, crawling, nesting, and flying. Their noise filled the forest, and yet the forest embraced this silent chorus of songs. In tune, they harmonised together effortlessly. I listened, knowing that every consciousness was one, that the earth was just another face of God. We only had to be quiet enough to listen.

My breathing began to slow down. I felt rested and light.

Listening to the forest is something magical.

I opened my eyes and noticed the sunlight streaming through the waving leaves, which were attached to their branches like families. Seeing this, a moment of déjà vu tickled my memory. *The day the light came to me.*

The light was magnanimous, and it expanded its incredible bliss and peace towards me so that no passing thoughts of judgement flickered through my consciousness.

What a wonderful sensation.

Remembering that, my eyes wandered around me. I felt connected to everything. The forest was perfectly still and beautiful in every way.

How can there be suffering in the world, but at the same time so much beauty? I closed my eyes again. My heart sank into sadness. Outside of my own bubble of paradise, the world was tearing itself apart.

The Kingdom is becoming overrun, and there are enemies on all sides. The land has seen war for over a hundred years, and there are battles every day, people dying… Why, God? Why do we insist on making a cruel world?

A voice interrupted my thoughts. "Jehanne."

I opened my eyes.

Standing in front of me, in the clearing, was Archangel Michael. He made a gesture with his hand for me to stand. I scrambled up quickly. His presence, as always, had an air of command.

"Jehanne, you will be the key to saving the kingdom. You will be the instrument to help France regain power. God, in all his compassion, listens to the French people's prayers to have peace. But sometimes, in order to obtain peace, you have to fight. Sometimes, for peace to be accessible, you have to take up the sword and win battles. But those battles are not for gold or lands but to restore balance."

But why me? I was not born a boy. I'm just a simple farmer's girl. Restoring the balance of the kingdom was not an innate part of my ambitions.

Archangel Michael's shoulder length, brown wavy hair glinted with brightness as the sun shone on him. He stood with an open posture, and smiled with his honey, deep set eyes. Small dimples creased his v-shaped cheekbones. "These battles have to be led by a person with a pure heart, an instrument of God. During the history of humanity, this has happened several times. God has used his instruments to restore balance on earth to continue God's plan. Have faith, Jehanne."

I nodded and looked down to the ground. Damp leaves densely coated the forest floor.

"Soon, you are going to set up your next trip to the fortress of Vaucouleurs. After Christmas. You are going to send a message to your uncle to come and get you again, but this time you will begin your journey to Chinon."

My eyes rose back to his standing figure. *Chinon? But Chinon…*

Archangel Michael continued, "Yes, to get to Chinon, you must cross English occupied territory. Now listen carefully, Jehanne. God knows this trek will be dangerous, so your instructions are to go to Vaucouleurs again. Don't be discouraged if Robert de Baudricourt doesn't listen to you, as it happened the last time you went.

"This time you will have important information that you will pass to Lord Robert, but there will also be two young lords. They will help you and accompany you in your journey to Chinon. You will also have an audience with the Duke of Lorraine. He has already heard of you from your first visit."

I strained to listen to every detail.

"Jehanne, once you are on your way to Chinon, we will guide you. You will hear Saint Catherine and Marguerite on your shoulder, and they will appear as small glowing lights. Just as it happened the last time you were in Vaucouleurs, they will guide you when you are among the people and soldiers. I will visit you when you need instructions or need to make important decisions."

"When do I have to go to Vaucouleaurs?" My hands, still holding the sword, became warm and clammy. I fidgeted with its handle. I wanted to be sure of the dates.

"After Christmas, Jehanne, everything is after Christmas. God had arranged it that way," answered Archangel Michael.

"It's late summer now. Will it be possible for Pierre to accompany me this time?"

"The best way to ensure that your father does not find out and does not cause problems is to keep the same arrangement as the previous time. That is to say, call your uncle so he comes to fetch you. You will need to alert your family that you are going to help your aunt. Your brothers Pierre and Jean will arrive later when you are in Chinon."

I slumped my shoulders slightly; he could sense my disappointment.

"They will accompany you when you start your campaign. Don't worry. As you cross Chinon, God will clear the road for you and there will be no danger."

I nodded slowly.

"God knows your needs very well," Archangel Michael said with a knowing smile.

"Thank you," I said.

"Do you understand everything, Jehanne?"

"Yes, I do. Thank you again. I'm grateful… grateful beyond words," I repeated, bringing a hand over to my heart and bowing.

"So be it," said Archangel Michael before quietly disappearing from the forest.

The forest was submerged in silence again. I brought the length of the wooden sword behind the nape of my neck and held it firmly down with my hands. I looked up at the gap from the branches to the blue sky above. I let out a sigh.

And here it starts again.

Archangel Michael's conversation left me with many things to consider. I knew my time to leave was approaching, and I knew many things needed to be done.

My gaze travelled to my surroundings again. A strange peace washed over me.

The forest lay serene and still.

How strange that a forest does not become irritated or moved. If I were to be anything, I would be a tree. They stand tall and strong, never faltering from the elements, nor from the animals that inhabit their arching branches.

I brought the wooden sword down and marvelled at this very moment, deeply observing my surroundings and enjoying the beauty of the trees. The sun's rays shone on the leaves. The bird called to one another. I took a deep breath, smelling the sweet wet earth.

Reflecting on the peace of the forest in my mind and heart, I uttered a small prayer.

"You are going to Chinon?" Pierre said, his eyebrows high and his eyes wide.

"Pierre, Archangel Michael said the path will be cleared. I will be protected," I explained.

He pursed his lips and sighed resignedly. "Jehanne, as soon as I know that you've left, I'm going too, because Papa won't be able to do anything anymore."

"Alone?" I asked him.

"No, that would not be wise." He laughed at the idea. He looked at the ground, thinking for a moment with his arms crossed over his chest. A moment later, his face lit up.

"I can tell Jean to join me!" he said effusively, looking back up at me. "Jean is never going to say no to an adventure, especially if it involves his little sister." He took my hands and starting dancing with me.

We danced around the barn, and I giggled. "Your idea is not bad. Besides, Archangel Michael said you and Jean are going to be with me throughout the campaign," I said happily.

"Then I will see to it that he and I are right behind you, Jehanne!" said Pierre, gliding and prancing with me as we danced.

24

RESTORATION

Late-autumn, 1428
Domrémy, France

*F*rom the dense clouds early snow fell around us, decorating the earth with falling snowflakes that later melted in your palms. We were slowly inching towards Christmas, and winter's hold was becoming stronger as the forest's branches slowly shed, baring their naked arms. The remnants of their orange and brown leaves gathered at the food of their trunks. Fields were unending white sheets that dipped and sloped with the curvature of the land.

The village itself was nestled quietly in the snow's midst. Chimney smoke climbed into the sky, and the ground was mixed with dark soil and snow, scraped and shifted by the constant movement of people and carts in and around the town.

Although the seasons came and arrived as expected, and the people of Domrémy went about their daily chores, gathering and preparing for Christmas, one would not have suspected the muted apprehension of the town.

Like a river, an undercurrent of unease began to grow. At first, it was subtle. Nobody commented on it; in fact, it was almost normal to feel this unease at this time. But whispers began to reach the villagers. Rumours of the English and their ruthless pillaging. Rumours of leaving villages desolate. Destroying, burning, and leaving ashes and dust.

It was one thing to avoid the destruction of a rushed enemy force that burned and destroyed out of sheer intent to mark their passing. However, it was quite another to avoid the blow of an enemy whose time was not contained, and their sacking was done with contemplation and intent.

Responding to our growing sense of uneasiness, on a bitterly cold and overcast morning, Domrémy was interrupted with the sounds of church bells, echoing through the town.

In the midst of gathering hay for the fields, working in the barn with my pitchfork in my hands, I glanced towards the sound of the bells tolling, to the church. I had a woollen shawl over my bodice, and a knitted cap with two plaits emerging underneath. My breath puffed and swirled as white steam in front of my face.

I walked slowly out of the barn. Flocks of grey birds flew from the town centre, towards the silent woods, behind the fields of our house. Dark grey and black clouds hung over the town's centre, and thunder rumbled in the distance. Gripped to the spot, I squinted into the distance. My fingers tingled.

A storm is brewing.

I jumped over the fence, and ran to the house, bursting through the door to almost run into Mama in her cap and shawl. "Here, Jehanne. Let's go to see what has happened."

I nodded and donned my shawl, and we briskly hurried into town.

A small crowd of villagers were gathered in front of the church. The atmosphere was quiet, save for some murmuring and whispers. We waited. Thunder rumbled and fell. Snow drifted and kissed the earth, blissfully unaware of our anxiety. Someone somewhere coughed. A slow creaking alerted us to a presence inside the church.

Guillaume, the village priest, who was clad in his heavy black robe with a wooden cross as a necklace, stepped outside with a solemn expression. Behind him, the lord of Domrémy emerged; his fur lined coat and feathered cap moved in the cold wind.

"People of Domrémy, I must alert you all that the English were seen near Vaucouleurs and are approaching Domrémy." Audible gasps from the villagers were heard. Mama tightly grasped my hand.

"We must evacuate the town immediately and travel to Neufchâteau. Gather your travelling clothes and go straight to Neufchâteau." Guillaume, the priest, emphasised his words loudly. "Tell everyone, and hurry, we cannot leave anyone behind, but we cannot falter. They are coming." Guillaume's face tilted downwards, made the cross signage. "God be with us all."

Mama and I turned to each other, lost in hopelessness for a brief moment. Her bright blue eyes then faltered, and she blinked several times. Recovering herself, she said, "We must hurry home and tell Papa and your brother."

Before we could, Papa cleared his throat. He was behind us, his face steely and solemn. His jaw was locked, and his eyes brimmed with austerity. His voice was low. "Let us get home quickly and prepare. Once Pierre is home we will leave."

The rest of the day unfolded in a blur. We hastily gathered some fruit, bread, and some cold meat for our trip. We did not know how long we would be gone for, nor if we would see our home again. But we had no time to hesitate.

We packed some warm clothes and blankets, and shortly after, Pierre appeared breathless and wide-eyed. Upon seeing him, Papa made his way to the side door. "Pierre, help me lead the animals into the forest. They will be safer out of sight."

Pierre nodded and motioned for me to come along. Miraculously, we led our animals quickly into the forest. In the distance, I could see Mama opening the chicken pens, and one by one the orange crescent tails of each hen hopped out, mama shooing them into the fields, and they flurried and flew until they were sparsely strewn in the greenery behind the house.

We walked down quickly and brought the wagon from the barn, keeping some oxen in the field for our trip. Loading our bags of essentials into the wagon, Papa began to attach the reins to the oxen, giving them apples and water before the journey. Once everything was loaded, Mama and I took one last longing look at our home.

Mama turned. "Come, Jehanne." Her voice was like a cool wind on a hot day, and her crystalline blue eyes held the strength of a tree, steady and grounded.

I helped her onto the wagon, sitting with Papa at the front. I wheeled around to the back, and Pierre helped me onto the wagon too. Papa set the oxen to go, and for the second time, we left our home. None of us spoke. We only looked forlornly at our home, slowly becoming smaller and smaller until it disappeared into the spangled net of other empty houses.

Uncle greeted us warmly. His crooked smile and happy manners soothed our fatigued spirits. Neufchâteau was coated in snow, and even colder than Domrémy as the stonecovered roads and walls exacerbated the chill. Yet his two-storey house was warm, and we arrived in Neufchâteau before dusk.

Jean helped us unload our bags, and we led the oxen to the fields, outside of the city. Even from there, we saw small parties of wagons and walking villagers like lines of ants, trailing across the countryside, filing over the hills and finding refuge in Neufchâteau or farms outside the town.

Staying with Uncle Jean, we easily accustomed ourselves to the familiar routine. Mama, Pierre, and I stayed in their extra room while our cousins and Uncle Jean slept in their normal rooms. Jean insisted Papa slept in his bed, and Papa refused vehemently, but in the end could not convince Jean otherwise.

The next morning, our cousins and Jean left early for their apprenticeship, as they all started working at dawn. When I woke from sleep, I tumbled and stirred from the bed, as if waking from a long dream.

Sitting at the long table at breakfast, Pierre and I listened to Uncle Jean's boisterous voice echoing through the walls of his shop downstairs where he was busy working. We ate bowls of porridge and bread. I looked outside through the foggy glass, and snow fell limply. It felt like nothing had changed yet everything had.

After two days, Pierre and Papa busied themselves with business in town during the day. Meanwhile, Mama and I helped Uncle Jean in the shop, and we cooked meals in the evenings and early mornings.

Mama and I made a habit of praying in the evening together before we went to sleep. On the second night, the candlelight flickered, and our eyelids were heavy, but we both brought out rosary beads.

"Ready, Jehanne?" Mama asked. She wore her long grey tunic.

Although the spare room was small, a cross hung next to the door-frame. We kneeled in front of it, and our murmuring filled the small room. Pierre did not stir from his position, and his slow and rhythmic breathing was not disturbed.

I lay there, in the night, wedged between Mama and Pierre.

The angels said after Christmas. Everything was to begin after Christmas...

Rain began to patter and patter on the rooftop.

Christmas is just around the corner.

After Christmas...

On the third morning, the sun shone through the windows that held clumps of snow in their corners. We awoke to raised chatter downstairs between Papa and another familiar voice. Their conversation rose and fell animatedly; Papa's voice was even straying from its monotone and austerity.

Mama was already dressed, and emerged into the room. "Jehannette and Pierre, get ready quickly. Pierre, your father is awake and talking with our Domrémy neighbours."

Pierre scrambled up, combed his hair flat, scrubbed his face clean, and quickly changed from his sleeping tunic to his working clothes. When his footsteps receded down the stairs, I changed my clothes, brushed my hair, and made a braid starting from the crown of my head.

By the time I got to the kitchen, Mama was busy kneading some bread and motioned for me to clean some of the bowls she used to prepare breakfast.

Footsteps ascended the stairs. Pierre's. "Mama! Jehanne, the English have left! The English have gone! People of Domrémy are going back today!"

Mama, mid-kneading, stopped. Her eyes were wide and her mouth agape. "What?! No! Is this true?"

Papa emerged behind Pierre. "That was our Domrémy neighbours. They have heard news from the officials that the English forces passed through Domrémy and were seen leaving in a westerly direction. They were told to tell everyone from Domrémy."

My mouth hung open, and Mama and I looked at each other. "What about the destruction? Do we have any news of if they burned down our homes?"

Pierre and Papa passed a look of worry between each other.

"Apparently, there is no news yet... but we will know once we arrive," Pierre said.

"My lucky nephew and niece!" Uncle Jean's voice boomed as he was climbing the stairs. "Looks like your stay won't be for long! The English are losing their touch, eh!" He came over between Pierre and I and embraced us, each with one arm. "You're getting good at missing them!"

Pierre and I laughed. Mama's eyes were wistful and her cheeks were flushed red; even Papa appeared lighter. We prepared a quick breakfast of oats and put the bread inside the pot over the fire; it would be ready later, for supper.

After hearing of the English's departure, we busied ourselves with returning home. The oxen were set and the wagon was prepared. Our bags were loaded, and we said our goodbyes to Jean, Uncle, and our cousins.

Other families were also on their way.

The air was crisp, and we rugged ourselves warmly against the wind, which tugged and pulled strongly. As Papa drove the wagon, Pierre and I played some games, and as we passed the wild forests and countryside, Pierre leaned up and peered over the wagon, to the front. "We should be able to see it soon, Jehanne. Go to the other side."

Careful, as the wagon was still moving, I got onto my knees and looked to the road. Two dark lines in the snow marked the road. The wind was bitterly cold, but that made the clouds high and the atmosphere clearer. As we rose over a small hill, there in the distance between the rolls of white hills was Domrémy. Pierre and I stretched our necks over the wagon to catch the first glimpse of our village.

"There!" Pierre said, his glee evident in his wide-toothed grin. He shook his fist with victory. But his joy was short-lived, for as we travelled closer, we saw the church spire loom closer.

Mama gasped and her hand went over to her lips. "God in heaven."

To our desolation, and especially to Mama's, the church spire was still upright and standing. However, it was darkened with spots of black scorch marks. My heart fell.

What if this is not the only destruction we find?

I could see the same thought echo on Pierre's face, and no doubt on Papa and Mama's as well. Our fear for our own home and the rest of the village was hanging by a thread. Would we find shambles and ashes?

I gripped the wagon tightly. We made our way into the village. To our relief, the townspeople were bringing it back to life. It was desolate, but there were voices inside houses with doors wide open, and flurries of villagers coming in and out, unloading bags, and taking care of their homes.

Our fear eased. None of the houses were burnt or destroyed. "It seems they just passed by the homes," I heard Pierre say, but we daren't say anymore.

We finally passed the church, which was surrounded by workers and Father Guillaume with his thick black tunic whipping around as he ran errands.

"Ah, what desolation!" Mama exclaimed. "It's the house of the Lord. How could they?" She looked up at the old church's face.

Pierre and Papa were silent, yet their eyes were pools of anger. I looked on, sorrow rising in my chest. It seemed that the stone foundation and spire had saved it from being completely burnt, but the wooden roof was burnt and had collapsed into the church. We did not want to think of any other damage the English wrought, but a voice disrupted our grieving.

"Ho there!" The voice was from one of our neighbours, Claude. Claude was a farmer like Papa. He approached the wagon, and Papa eased the oxen to halt. Claude was humbly dressed, but his clothes were dirty with soot and charcoal. Claude and Papa clasped each other's hands in greeting. "Jacques, my friend. 'Tis good to see you and your family well."

"Aye, good to see you, Claude. We have yet to see our home. We saw the church..."

"The church is the only damage the town received. I've heard from the other villagers and no one else has had their property damaged."

Papa's tone rose. "No one else?" He looked down to Claude's clothes.

"Yes, and the English seemed to have passed by the town quickly. They only really damaged the church. Our home was fine, as was yours and others around ours. We were the early ones and came to help the pastor before he received workers from the Lord of Domrémy."

"Oh," Papa said.

"Yes, what the bloody bastards did was terrible, trying to sack a church. Well, I heard that the church was to be restored by the funding of the local lords. Aren't we lucky, eh? We're lucky to be in winter too. The English can't burn our fields, covered in bloody frost—that's our land for ya!" said Claude.

"You were able to find your animals alright?"

"Oh yes, they didn't go too far, and they always go to that forest. It's their safe haven. That forest must be protecting them," said Claude with a smile.

I saw Pierre's eyes flicker to me, and we both shared a moment of realisation. "Claude, thank you. We were anxious when we saw the church."

Claude shook his head. "Jacques, you've helped me in more ways than one. I could only do so much. I saw from the outside of your home everything is intact, but just make sure—you never know with the bloody English."

"We will, thank you, Claude."

Claude stepped back and waved as he walked towards the town centre.

Mama and Papa looked at each other, this time their faces lit up with anticipation and hope. We set off again. By now, dense clouds began to cover the sky, setting Domrémy into its silvery glaze. The wagon wobbled and we waited patiently. If what Claude said was true, we had nothing to fear.

As we turned a corner, the familiar grey-faced home with the sharply angled roof appeared, thickly layered with snow. We heard an audible sigh of relief from Mama, and Papa leaned back and put his hand on his hip. His shoulders fell as he heaved a sigh.

The front herb garden was overlaid with frost and the snow on the ground lay undisturbed. There were no signs of a break-in nor of the recent footsteps of soldiers. We examined the entirety of the house, and Claude was true to his word, it was untouched.

As we began to offload our belongings and sort the house, small white dots of snow began to drop into our midst. Soon, Mama's cooking began to waft through the house, and with Papa and Pierre's combined efforts, they were able to gather the farm animals that had roamed in the forest into the paddocks.

I gathered the chickens and fed them inside the pen house, and later fed the goats and cows with fresh hay from the barn, which was also unsullied.

A month had passed after coming back from Neufchâteau with no further advice from the angels. Our lives were completely immersed in the restoration of the church, and upcoming Christmas festivities. Snowfall was never-ending, but like always we carried on in the midst of snow, storm, or hail.

The town was filled with labourers hired to rebuild the church's badly damaged roof before Christmas. Wooden beams were freshly cut and transported to the town centre. They worked tirelessly in the wintery conditions, and soon enough, three days before Christmas, the roof was repaired. The whole village was able to gather in its high echoing halls on Christmas morning and sing their hymns loudly and lovingly.

For us, Christmas was always the time of baking sweet bread with dried fruit and honey. The fireplace would crackle from morning to late evening, and Mama would skin and prepare freshly caught rabbits to roast or make her homemade rabbit soup.

After the excitement of the English earlier in the month, Christmas was a quiet affair. The townspeople relished in a temporary tranquillity while they still could as there was no news of the English or their whereabouts.

A few weeks later, Mama and I were entertaining the weekly gathering of spinning and sewing groups in the town, the younger girls in one room and the mothers in the other. Anne, one of the older girls, had gotten married while I was away, and now Magdalene was mentoring the younger girls on their sewing. Others, like Maribelle, were helping their parents uphold their farms. Younger girls were now joining in too, and we taught and corrected them on their spinning.

The conversation dipped and soared as we weaved and sewed. I sat next to Isabel. Her demure face was never creased with worry or anxiety. She was always gentle and completed everything slowly and with a quiet intent. We always enjoyed each other's quiet company.

"We are making goat cheese this winter. Our animals are giving us enough milk to produce cheese," said Charlotte, who's curly, cherry-red hair was tied at the back of her head with a ribbon.

"Goats are noble creatures. I like them," said Isabel, while collecting the yarn and putting it into balls.

"Just don't let them loose in the garden, Isabel. You do not want that—trust me." Charlotte smiled from behind her weaving. Small giggles escaped from the younger girls; Magdalene smiled knowingly.

"What are you going to make with the wool this time?" I asked Isabel.

"I need a new shawl and Mama needs new mittens. I think I'll make the mittens first," Isabel said with a smile. "They are easier to make," she added, wrinkling her nose.

I looked over at Charlotte. "What about you, Charlotte?"

"My younger brother needs new socks and I need new mittens", she said while showing us her worn mittens. Charlotte was sitting closest to the wood basket, and I noticed the basket was already half empty. I made a mental note to get more wood later.

"My, Jehanne, you must practise day and night from the way your weaving has turned out!" Magdalene sat opposite me, and she embraced the role as mentor quite well, for she taught the girls with patient words and an observant eye. Her luscious long brown hair was up in a net, on the nape of her neck.

Taken aback at the sudden attention, I said, "Oh, I think my mama has helped me a lot…" I looked again to observe my work, and it was a pretty pattern, floral, brown and white.

The small fireplace kept us cosy and comfortable, and the easy friendship ensured the conversation flow pleasantly. Mama came in and offered sweet bread and cheese with hot milk. Mama never failed to create a welcoming atmosphere, especially as the white winter's day whistled and howled outside. We kept spinning, knitting, and happily talking until early afternoon.

After the girls left, the afternoon became bitterly cold. I shivered under my cap and thick bodice, and my muscles complained with each move. I retrieved the axe from the barn and went behind the house, where we gathered collections of wood. The wind whipped and swirled with sharp tugs as I placed a piece of wood on an old stump.

The material of the mittens was thick and woolly, so I struggled to hold the axe securely. Resigned, I quickly took off my gloves, which plunged my fingers into the cold air, quickly numbing them and losing any feeling. Biting through the cold, I chopped a number of wooden pieces.

An icy sensation began to creep into my toes, and before I moved, I looked down to my feet. The coat on my shoes was damp from the melting snow. The bone-chilling wind nipped and pushed, exacerbating the coldness around my feet and hands. I groaned and sighed, hurriedly wishing I could finish this sooner to return inside.

The next moment, the wind had stopped, and I didn't feel so cold anymore. My hands were not as numb and began to recover their feeling, and my feet were not as chilled. It was as if the entire world was brought to standstill. I looked up, confused by the sudden change of sensations.

Before me was Saint Catherine, clad in her simple white tunic, touching the snow with bare feet. Her long chestnut hair was swaying slightly. With everything around me pacified, I realised this strange event was due to her presence. I lowered the axe to my side, and bowed my head in reverence, "Saint Catherine."

"Jehanne," she said, her voice clear but gentle. "It's time to call your uncle. Send him a message to retrieve you."

"Very well." I thought for a moment. "I will send my uncle and aunt a message by one of the neighbours that are leaving for Burey-le-Petit in a few days" I answered.

"That is right. Now, remember what I'm going to tell you. It's important. *You have to be by Charles Valois' side before Lent...*"

"Before Lent," I repeated.

"Good, before Lent," she repeated, giving me an assuring nod, then she faded into nothingness. Once she was gone, the cold and icy wind returned with a vengeance.

Assailed by the elements, I hurriedly picked up the bundle of logs, huffing as they turned out to be heavier than expected. I entered the house through the side door and refilled the basket next to the fireplace. After tidying the room from the girls' visit, I sat alone, and watched the fire dwindle and dance slowly, turning to embers.

Before Lent... Before Lent... Before Lent—my life is going to change forever.

25

DEPARTURE

"*Your fate awaits you. Accept it in body and spirit.*"

– The Twelfth Night by Shakespeare

Winter, 1429
Domrémy, Neufchâteau

*A*s Nativity passed, winter's snow remained constant. The days were dark and when the sun was out or behind a veil of fog, it didn't offer much warmth. The wintry days were filled with labour, which kept me busy, and I became engrossed in preparing everything I needed to do for my departure.

The anticipation to leave home grew, but the thought of never seeing Mama again became heavier and heavier—a burden that I did not want to contemplate. But the evenings always brought me face to face with this sorrow. It always brought a hint of melancholy as I knew I would miss my quiet life here with mama.

Usually, the nights were calm and quiet, and we would sit together and do our needle work with the comfort of a friendly fire while the winter wind whistled outside. Even here, I felt pressed to think of the tasks for the morrow, and the preparation needed for the future. But when I noticed Mama sitting next to me, sewing demurely with her gentle reflection outlined by the candle on the table, those were the moments that my heart felt pinched with sorrow.

But I could not give room for grief.

There were many things I needed to do first.

After Saint Marguerite's appearance on that cold, wintry day, my neighbours carried on my message to my uncle to escort me to Vaucouleurs again. He responded two days later with Claude who appeared at the front door, his craggy face heavily lined with years of working as a farmer in the sun that offered no solace in this icy season.

"Mademoiselle, your uncle in Burey-le-Petit says he will arrive in eight days to escort you to stay with them. He also says he will stay for the night and the next day travel back to Burey-le-Petit."

I nodded. "Thank you, Claude." He nodded and left, his coat flying with each stride as the biting wind blew outside.

As I closed the door, the house quietened, and I felt the warmth of the fire surrounding me again. It was late afternoon and supper was already cooking in the hearth. Mama was straightening and plumping up the cushions on the chairs in front of the fire behind me. "Poor cousin Jehanne's health is on the decline again. It seems like I'm sending them my only angel."

I turned and smiled wearily, bending my head down, as she leaned up on her tiptoes to kiss my forehead. I could smell sweet lavender on her clothes. She rubbed my arms comfortingly. "You will be back soon, my dear. Before you know it, you'll be picking this spring's orchard apples in no time."

"Oh yes," I replied absently, daring not to look up as my eyes betrayed my sadness.

"Come now, let's bake some bread for supper."

Avoiding eye contact, I headed spritely to the room next door, brushing my emotions aside. "I'll get some flour from the pantry."

When Uncle arrived, his wagon was packed with bags of gifts from aunt Jehanne and farmers from Burey-le-Petit. He landed from the wagon with a big thump. Mama and I helped him unpack all the gifts from his trip. We both wore shawls wrapped around our bodice, and when we arrived inside flecks of snow were caught in our hair.

The day was overcast, yet the clouds were spread out like a thin sheet, and the day was brighter than normal. The kitchen was arrayed with hanging dried herbs, and the aroma wafted over to the long table as he told us all the news from the family and the village.

Mama laid out her best cheeses and bread with honey, and the afternoon was spent with Uncle and Mama divulging the latest gossip and updates on family and the villages. Deep in their conversation, I made sure to slip away and clean my room, and I prepared my bag for our departure tomorrow for we were to leave early, and supper was yet to be made.

When Papa appeared in the late afternoon, his usual steady and stern mood instantly lifted when he saw Uncle seated at the long table. Uncle, with his animated and happy conversation, lightened the house, and dinner that evening was lively and amusing.

I excused myself early as my eyelids grew heavy. But I heard their voices muffled through the walls, and they spoke spiritedly until the candles were up to their last wick. I carefully opened my door, holding my candle holder—the light flickered and cast shadows across the walls.

My room suddenly looked very bare and strange. I had my bag at the foot of the bed. The bedside was almost empty, save my rosary, but everything else was packed or stored away.

This will be my last night in this room.

I looked around, examining every detail with a renewed value. The small window was a blank sheet of black, only broken by frost accumulating in the corners on the outside. The small cross that hung opposite the bed. The roof that was my canvas of sleepless nights when I was haunted by worries of the future.

Taking out my thick tunic from my bag, I quickly changed and covered myself with the thick cotton blankets, breathing in their familiar homey smell of oak. I rolled over and grasped the rosary next to the candle. I licked my lips and began to pray.

"Hail Mary, full of Grace, the Lord is with thee…"

My whispering voice filled the silence of my room. As the winds grew heavy outside, my father's and brother's voices emanated in the background like a melody. My eyelids grew heavy, and I sleepily rose to blow out the candle, plummeting me into darkness and into sleep's welcoming embrace.

The calling of the birds woke me. My eyes opened, and I turned over. The first thing I noticed was the candle wick, blackened and curled like a cane. I had fallen asleep quickly, although I tossed and turned restlessly.

I heard a small jingle and opened my hands. The rosary was scrunched up. Untangling them in the dreariness of waking, I leant up. The window outside was grey, and I could see the faint, blurred shapes of trees, and the snow, and the dirt ridden flatness of the fields, and the snow-coated fluffy vegetable garden.

The room was bone chillingly cold, but I had no time to lose. I shivered as my bare feet touched the stone floor. I dressed quickly and immediately began to fly around in preparation. I made my bed, packed my thick tunic in my bag, combed my hair, and braided it into two parts, the auburn plaits falling limply over my shoulders and reaching my navel. My stomach was jittery with excitement and apprehension. I could feel the build-up of nerves.

As I was heaving my bag over my shoulder, I heard muffled voices from outside. I peered out of the window and saw a hazy figure, the figure of a young boy who was approaching the house with a wheelbarrow full of fresh hay. Mama's melodic and friendly voice called to him, and they exchanged a little conversation at a distance apart. I squinted through the fogged up window and was pleased to see young George following Mama as she led him behind the house, to the barn.

"He's kept his promise. What a good lad."

A few days before, I made sure Mama would not be left at home with too many arduous chores, so I had stacked enough firewood to last for at least two weeks. But knowing that I would be away for longer, and other errands would need to be done, I sought out Charlotte's younger brother, George, and after a long session of bartering, we managed to come to an arrangement.

In exchange for chopping firewood and any other physical errands Mama would need, he would receive eggs or some freshly made bread. Mama would only have to ask him and he would cut more firewood or do any errand when necessary.

I carried my bag to the kitchen where Pierre and Uncle were eating hot porridge and some sweet bread. I had packed everything the day before, but I double and triple checked I had everything.

Mama came in from outside, holding the chicken eggs in her apron. She walked slowly into the kitchen and delicately placed the eggs in a small basket. Even she noticed my anxious movements. She gazed at me sympathetically. "You must have not slept well, dear. Get some rest when you arrive at Burey-le-Petit."

I nodded, trying to pack everything back into my bag again—for the third time.

"I'll be right back. I'm giving these to George." And off she went, her quick and short steps the only buzz of energy in the sleepy morning.

Once finished with their bowls, Pierre took Uncle's bag and Uncle took mine, which was bulging with Mama's gifts of cheese and salted meats. He made a funny face as he lifted his bag, feigning difficulty to heave it over his shoulder. I chuckled and Mama appeared in the doorway, taking my arm.

We walked behind Uncle, passing the herb garden, frost still clinging to each blade and tendril of herbs sprouting underneath winter's snowfall. I looked at it wistfully. It was the herb garden I first learned to care and tend for when I was little. I glanced back at the house, its slanted roof, and its small windows.

I have no idea what adventures still lay before me, but what I do know is that I shall be leaving everything behind.

Fog still hovered over the white fields behind the house, surrounding the forest in thin tendrils, making it look dark and mystical. The forest where all of this started. I looked at it, deeply breathing out.

My destiny.

As Uncle was getting his oxen ready, Pierre was checking everything was in order with the wagon. I turned and must not have noticed Mama quickly slipping inside again as she soon walked out of the doorway again holding a small sachet. Her small stature bobbed through the snow clipped garden, her little shoes wiggling in and out under the hem of the dress.

She took my hand and placed the sachet inside. "Here, have some leftover dried lavender to help you sleep, and give some to your Aunt Jehanne."

I swallowed hard, my feet suddenly feeling like lead. I looked at the little sachet and up to her. Her keen, bright blue eyes looked back at me, and in that moment the burden of my grief overcame me like a wave. I pretended to look down to the lavender sachet. I fixed my gaze to the floor. "Mama, this is so thoughtful."

Pierre, finishing up with the wagon, came and stood behind Mama. "You must be off now, mustn't dawdle," Mama said casually, hugging me farewell. I kissed her forehead, and we stayed like this for a precious moment.

I gazed at Pierre quickly. He was looking away—most likely giving us the privacy for our final goodbye. Because, well, it was.

"Goodbye, Mama. Take care," I said, holding her tight, savouring each moment. I felt a knot rising in my throat, and my eyes began to tingle with tears. I blinked hard.

No. She mustn't see you cry.

I tried to straighten my face.

"Goodbye, my darling girl. Don't forget the cheeses for your aunt." Her oblivious positivity stirred the painful emotions brewing in my heart even more.

"I have everything in my bag," I replied quickly, as we parted.

Pierre's eyes were grey and solemn. It was some comfort that he knew of my mission, and the real reason for my departure. We embraced each other without words. "Be safe, little one," he whispered, barely audible for me to hear.

I nodded furtively and went quickly to the wagon. Uncle was already waiting on the front seat. Witnessing our goodbyes sobered his cheeriness. The early hour of dawn was breaking.

After climbing up, I blinked hard several times and waved goodbye to Mama and Pierre. Uncle gave a small flip to the reins, and we slowly departed. The wagon tottered and crunched over the dirt and snow. I felt my chest tighten as we passed the familiar neighbouring houses.

At the end of the street, I turned to look back and saw Mama standing alone in front of the grey, roof-slanted house. Snow began to fall, and the wind gently moved her long dark red skirt. She waved again, and I waved back, but her figure was blurred by the tears filling my eyes.

Turning back, they rolled down my cheeks freely. I cleaned them quickly with my sleeves, but they kept coming. I couldn't hold them back. Uncle looked kind-heartedly at me and gently said, "It is never easy, lass. Let them flow, you'll feel better."

I just nodded, sobbing. Overcome with grief and sadness, Uncle and I travelled in silence for much of the journey.

As we approached Burey-le-Petit, I began to feel better as most of the sadness from the week had been released. I felt calmer, as if the storm had passed, and I was left with stillness, quietude. My heart felt lighter, and Uncle, seeing that I was much improved, decided to strike up a conversation. He filled the silence with stories of his childhood up in the north and his adventures as a young man, keeping the conversation light and easy, full of funny anecdotes.

After a long time talking, Uncle Durand, seeing that I was smiling again, decided to turn the conversation to more important matters at hand. "Are we going back to Vaucouleurs? Is this the real reason for your message?"

The sudden change of conversation topic brought me back to the road, to the journey of our endeavour. After all, it was the reason I left, but I wished that we could continue talking about his adventures as a young man instead. I had a mission, though, and I could not evade it.

So, looking at him, I replied, "Yes, we need to go back to Vaucouleurs and speak to Lord Robert. The guides said this time will be different. By Lent I will be next to the King Charles de Valois…"

"So this is it, isn't it?" Uncle said to himself, while looking at the road.

"Yes. From here, we go to Vaucouleurs and we request an audience with Lord Robert," I said while looking at the road. It curved and winded through the wild green countryside.

The path is here to follow. There was no turning back now. Today, we start the mission I was foretold all those years ago.

Determination filled me, vigorous and alive.

We arrived at the town of Burey-le-Petit around midday, and aunt Jehanne was waiting for us with a delicious snack. I gave her a warm hug and presented her with the sachet of dried lavender. Her face fell into a pure smile, admiring the gift.

She then looked up at my face and searched my eyes for a moment. Somewhere in my face she found the sorrow and sadness from my departure. "Oh, my dear." She hugged me tightly. "You are so strong."

I felt my sadness stir, and my eyes tinged with tears.

Once she released me, she cupped my face. "There, there, let us go in, you must be tired." She took my arm as we walked inside their small abode. As we entered, Aunt Jehanne led us into the kitchen where there was a heavy aroma of bread and vegetable stew. The table was set with humble wooden bowls and cups.

"Sit, sit! I baked some bread, and we have a vegetable stew if you're hungry. I went to the market to barter some of our eggs for apples and pears too." She went to the kitchen and began to prepare our meals.

Uncle and I washed the dust off our hands and faces from the road. As we sat down together, Uncle Durand began to tear off chunks of bread for all of us, as Aunt Jehanne served us bowls of the warm stew. I told her about Mama and Papa, and I also reached into one of the bags to give Aunt Jehanne Mama's homemade cheese along with a handful of jerky wrapped in a cotton cloth.

She was delighted to receive these gifts, especially the cheeses. "Your mama's cheeses are the creamiest and softest I have ever tasted," she said, while cutting some for all of us.

Uncle and I ate with gusto. We were hungry after the journey. After lunch, we rested as we chatted. My aunt was eager to know the plan.

"We have to go to Vaucouleurs, so I can speak with Lord Robert de Baudricourt again. I'm going to request an escort to Chinon for my audience with the King, and a letter from Lord Robert. That is how the guides have told me to do it."

Aunt Jehanne became thoughtful as she cut some pears; her eyebrows furrowed for a moment. "Jehanne… are you the girl from the prophecy?"

My uncle stopped chewing while he glanced at his wife, and back to me.

My face broke into an embarrassed smile, and I let out a light chuckle. I had never seen myself that way, but even then, I had no idea why I found that remark amusing.

I answered her truthfully. "I don't know anything about a prophecy. My guides haven't talked about it. They have only told me that I must unify France and put Charles de Valois on the throne. The King of Heaven has given me this mandate and I must fulfil it."

Uncle, who had been quietly listening for the whole time, excitedly announced, "And by God, we will help you, my dear girl! Be sure of that." His excitement showed in his bright blue eyes as he winked and smiled.

Aunty reached over and took my hands from across the table, and promised, "I'll help you with whatever you need."

I kept holding my aunt's hands and was silent for a moment. They looked at me expectedly. When I looked up, I said, "Please, take care of my mama."

Seeing my concern written in my face, Aunt Jehanne looked into my eyes. "I promise you, I'll take care of Isabel, my darling. Don't you worry."

"Thank you, Aunt Jehanne."

We continued to chat enthusiastically for the whole afternoon. By supper, we reheated some of the leftovers in the fireplace, and I organised my belongings in their extra room. When I entered the kitchen again, the candles were alight, and Aunt Jehanne and Uncle Durand were both settling into the comfort of their evening routine. Aunt was calmly knitting with a shawl around her shoulders, and Uncle was repairing a belt from the reins of the oxen. "Jehanne, supper is hot if you're still hungry, my dear."

"Thank you, Aunt." I bowed my head gratefully and ate a slice of bread with cheese and fruit. As it had been a long and emotional day, I wanted to be well-rested and with my appetite satiated.

When I finished, I went over to sit with Aunt Jehanne to knit some clothes I had been mending. As soon as I sat down, my limbs and arms melted into the chair from fatigue. My eyes began to droop, and before I knew it, I was drifting in and out of my waking state.

Shortly after, I gave in and said wearily, "I will retire early tonight. Thank you, Uncle, for escorting me today." Looking at Aunt Jehanne, I added, "Thank you, Aunt Jehanne, for the stew and bread. Thank you both so very much."

"It's our pleasure, isn't it, Jehanne?" Uncle said as he held his wife's hand.

"Oh yes! We are happy to help you. We too are following the command of God, through Archangel Michael's dream, darling," said Aunt Jehanne, her eyes happy though a little worn.

"Yes. Good night."

Aunt Jehanne passed me a candle to take to my room. "Good night, dear." Aunt Jehanne kissed my cheek.

"Goodnight," I said again. My voice was jaded, and I dragged my feet to the spare room. I placed the small candle on the side table next to the small mattress. I quickly changed to a thick tunic and tucked myself under the heavy woollen blankets.

Despite staying overnight in the house before, I couldn't help but feel a tinge of homesickness. The smell of the bed was different, and the room felt wrong. I felt displaced somehow. Yet the fatigue of the day descended over my bones and weighed over my shoulders. I rolled onto my side and huddled myself into the pillow.

I closed my eyes and was gracefully released from all of the emotions of the day and fell into a deep slumber.

26

JEAN DE METZ AND BERTRAND DE POULENGY

Midwinter, 1429
Burey-le-Petit, France

*T*he next morning, the wagon and oxen waited for us as Uncle Durand and I prepared for our trip to Vaucouleurs. I donned my maroon dress and apron, with a cap over my long red hair, and a wrapped woolly bodice to keep my chest warm.

Soon enough, we embarked on our journey to the town of Vaucouleurs, with Aunt Jehanne waving us goodbye in front of their small abode. Both Uncle and I were weary from the early start but eager to get started.

Another goodbye for another voyage, I thought as I turned back to the road ahead. The journey was slow but smooth, since this was safe territory and the chances of encountering any hostile English troops was negligible. Uncle seemed quite calm and even became talkative when he became more awake, pointing out areas of interest on the road.

The countryside was similar to that of Domrémy—flat pasture lands were grazed by cows, and every now and again rows of trees would line the roads, offering small spaces of shade in the long flat dirt road.

Just before midday, the Vaucouleurs' fortress appeared like a small monument in the distance. Slowly it grew, and the tall walls of the fortress became imposing to the eye. Inside, it was teeming with life. Specks of people fluttered in and out of the fortress, and the road that was quiet and solitary before, now became traversed by travellers on horse and on foot.

Dust and dirt flicked and floated around us, and as we approached the Vaucouleurs' gates, I saw the town was alive with merchants and carts full of items and produce coming and going.

Entering the commotion, we were surrounded by chatter and bartering. All the while, the air became dense with dust mixed with smoke from the campfires. A sudden realisation dawned on me, and I sharply looked up to see the sky. It was close to midday.

With only a moment to seize, I jumped down from the wobbling wagon. Uncle jerked the oxen to a stop. "Jehanne!" he exclaimed.

The oxen whined and halted, but I was way ahead. I ran to the entrance of the fortress. I got the attention of the guard on duty—a soldier with a bulging belly, an unkept beard, and pig beady eyes. "Excuse me, sir."

He turned and quickly, his face screwed up in disdain at my poor clothes. "What do you want, girl?" he said gruffly.

Ignoring his contempt, I asked, "Sir, has Lord Robert de Baudricourt been through these gates today?" I lifted my heels and tried looking past the guard's shoulder into the city. A sea of heads trailed inside the gates, but there was no sign of Lord Robert.

He shook his head and continued looking down the road, surveying the transit of people coming and going.

By then, Uncle had moved the wagon out of the way and was by my side. "Jehanne, has something happened?"

"Uncle, Lord Robert has still not come past the gate. Perhaps we could wait until—" I stopped, and my eyes landed on a small group on horseback, their figures emerging from the slope on the road and trotting towards the gates.

Uncle Durand glanced back, puzzled, as my eyes were glued on the figures behind him. Right then, we both recognised the stiff and unsympathetic scowl of Lord Robert, and his two younger companions as they came closer.

As Lord Robert approached, his eyes scanned the audience, and his eyes fell on me. His cold composure did not stir as he stared at me. Only, in his eyes. I could see them growing with recognition of me as his horse passed impassively through the gates, his gaze never leaving my face. Only after he passed me did he turn away.

I took a few steps forward. "Sir, you must listen to me. Sir!" I cried, but he continued undeterred. Lord Robert remained obstinate. Only his horse's hooves clicked on the pavement in response to my pleas. His two companions turned their heads at my voice, but they also continued without breaking a stride.

I stopped as they disappeared into the crowd. My shoulders slumped. Uncle caught up with me, putting a hand on my shoulder. "Don't worry, lass. Tomorrow we'll get him. He won't ignore you much longer."

I turned to Uncle Durand. My dedication to my mission was fuelling my determination. "He will listen to me, even if I have to throw myself in front of his horse." The figures of Lord Robert and his companions receded into the distance.

Uncle chuckled. "I hope we won't have to resort to extreme measures."

The crowd began to disperse, and chat normally, resuming its frenzied atmosphere. I heard Uncle's footsteps recede as he walked back, and I turned to follow. "Let us visit Catherine and Henri de Royer. They will be surprised to know of our presence, and we can eat something. The cheeses from your mother will be at the table for lunch today, I dare say," he said, climbing onto the wagon and taking the reins.

I half smiled, my disappointment receding in the back of my mind, and joined Uncle on the wagon.

The fortress was abuzz with villagers and farmers coming and going, and merchants selling almost anything I could imagine. Uncle drove the wagon carefully down the narrow streets of the town, taking a side street to the left. The street was empty except for a few stray cats, scattered and roaming on the road. We stopped about halfway down the side street, in front of the two-storey abode of the Royers.

We took a moment to descend, and patted down and straightened our clothes from the trip. Uncle walked readily to the large solid wooden door and knocked. A moment passed before the door opened and Henri's face peeped out. His brow raised in shock then an enormous smile erupted over his cheeks and face. "Oh! Durand! Jehanne! Come, come in, come in!" He moved aside as he ushered us in, then turning his head he yelled inside, "Catherine! Jehanne and Durand are here."

Catherine appeared quickly, drying her hands on her apron. Upon seeing us, a smile broke out on her face. "Jehanne, Durand, you are most welcome! Please come in," she said, motioning us inside.

Uncle waved me on, so I walked in first, smiling, and Catherine hugged my shoulders in the doorway, and ushed me inside. "Come, Jehanne, we were thinking of you the whole winter!"

"We will get the bags," Henri said from behind.

Catherine and I nodded, and we walked down the dark hallway. It was warm, and only when we emerged through to the dining room and kitchen did the house brighten. The house had little natural light, and even some candles burned in the middle of the day.

"My girl, you caused quite the stir from the last time you were here! The whole town's been talking about you, even the Lord of Lorraine knows of you!" said Catherine, her excitement illuminating her eyes and her face.

I watched her back, puzzled, as she led me to the four-seated wooden table that sat in the centre of the room. The kitchen lay behind, and the hearth burned with a low fire. The room smelled of coal and wood. We sat down at the same time.

"The Lord of Lorraine?" I asked.

"Yes, my dear!"

At that moment, she looked over quickly to Uncle Durand and Henri who were coming in, carrying our bags. Catherine got up quickly and helped Uncle Durand. "Durand, thank you for bringing Jehanne. How is your wife?" said Catherine, while showing Uncle a seat next to me.

"She is doing very well," responded Uncle, leaning back into his creaky, wooden chair. He took off his cap and wiped his hand through his grey and thinning hair. "Have you heard much of the English in Burey-le-Petit?"

Henri began to answer. My attention wavered to our belongings that sat clumped on the chairs in front of the hearth. I began to notice different aromas that arose. I could smell bread and herbs from the kitchen, and I noticed the soft blankets that sprawled over the chairs, adding simple touches that made this space homey and comfortable. Little portraits of dried leaves and flowers hung on the walls.

I quietly stood up as conversation continued, and searched for my bag before I would forget. I fumbled through and searched its contents, recognising and fetching the discernible cotton bundle. I walked back and sat down at the table. Catherine was refilling the cups on the table with a large jug of water.

"What do you have there, Jehanne?" she said, side-looking me curiously as the water poured swiftly and elegantly into the humble wooden cups.

Durand and Henri's eyes both landed on me, and their conversation paused. "Catherine and Henri, I know our visit this time is unexpected, and I wanted to thank you for the hospitality you've shown us now and in our last visit. I would like to present a gift to show my thanks."

I unravelled the cotton wrap and revealed multiple blocks of different cheeses. Catherine smiled with gracious sweetness, and Henri's eyes were drawn in, looking at the gift inquisitively.

"My dear, Jehanne, this is too kind." Catherine swiftly left the jug on the table, and approached me, hugging me tightly. When she released me, her eyes were brimming with gratitude. "You are too kind. Thank you, my girl. But do not feel you need to give us anything for us helping you. We do this because it is asked of us, and we want peace in the kingdom, and you are our key! This is a lovely gift. We appreciate it so much, don't we, Henri?" said Catherine, enthusiastically.

Henri nodded deliberately several times. "Yes, Jehanne, it's lovely." He smiled and winked.

I chuckled, "It's the least I could do to show my gratitude."

Catherine went to the kitchen, returning shortly with a loaf of bread and a knife on a wooden board. After poking her nose in the fresh-made cheese, she said, "Mmm, these smell delicious! Come, let us try them." She lifted her eyebrows with approval. "I've heard these are particularly special."

We watched Catherine while she prepared a loaf of bread, a slab of cheese, and some nuts. Both Uncle and Henri eyed the cheeses hungrily.

Uncle Durand accepted heartedly and chewed slowly, appreciating the flavour. "Jehanne, your mother outdid herself!"

I smiled appreciatively, but the memories of a man flooded my mind, and Uncle, sensing my sensitivity, took over the course of the conversation.

He cleared his throat. "The markets you have during the day are so amusing. So many merchants with their goods!"

Henri nodded vigorously. "Oh yes! We often go once we have enough eggs from the chickens, for sale, you know. They run out so quickly from countless merchants who travel round these parts."

Uncle and I helped ourselves to generous servings of the butter and salted meats on the table. We hadn't eaten anything the whole morning. The moment of sadness passed quickly as conversation flowed with enthusiasm.

While we ate, Catherine prepared more slices of bread and cheese, while telling us about the events that occurred there last winter.

"Jehanne, everyone in town is talking about you and your mission. They kept asking us, 'Is she coming back, is she coming back?' They were disappointed when we simply told them the truth, that we did not know and it's not up to us."

"Here, have more, dears," she said to me and Uncle as she placed down a second plate with bread and cured meat. "You too, Henri, have some more. I find that you're too thin at the moment."

We accepted the second fat slice of bread and cheese with gusto.

"What are you going to do, dear? Are you here to pursue Lord Robert again?"

"Yes, but this time it will be different. This time I am not going back home," I said resolutely.

Catherine and Henri looked at each other, as if holding something. Then Catherine said to her husband, "Tell them, dear."

Henri placed his elbows on the table and leaned in. "I think we can help you, my dear. Since you went back home, we've been thinking about how to help if you were to come back." Henri smiled. "We thought if we get the town behind you, Lord Robert will have to listen. We can organise people at the town square tomorrow, so Lord Robert won't be able to dismiss you so readily."

"Can we do that?" I slowly asked, my tone uncertain.

They nodded, full of optimism. I looked over to Uncle Durand, we both exchanged looks of hope. "I need all the help I can get! You have no idea how helpful this is, thank you." Reaching over the table, I took Catherine's hands.

Catherine patted my hand gently, saying, "We believe you, and you know, the whole town believes you. We even found out on the last day that you were here that an elderly lady saw you surrounded by a light. She said the halo of light came from your right shoulder."

Catherine emphasised her point by tracing the outline of a halo over her head and shoulders with her hands. "She told everyone that the light must have come from God."

Hearing this, I nodded. "That light is Saint Marguerite. She is there to help me with Lord Robert. The light... The light is so beautiful. It's like staring into joy and peace, and happiness and love. The light the lady saw was real.

"That is how I see the angels when I am around people, when I'm not alone. The angels said they will not be visible to other people, but there are some exceptions for reasons unknown to me."

"I knew it! I knew it had to be real!" said Catherine vehemently with happiness.

"We can go and tell our friends that you are here and organise a crowd for tomorrow. What do you think, Jehanne?" said Henri, following his wife's enthusiasm.

"I would like that very much!" Feeling my confidence blossom, I smiled anticipatedly, sharing their excitement.

Early the next day, Catherine and I woke early and went to mass. The streets had people slowly making their way to the church, the chatter and liveliness subdued from the early hour. However, once we entered and seated ourselves inside, the church began quickly to fill up and murmurs and voices of the laypeople emanated and echoed off the high stone walls.

I noticed the lingering glances and curious looks of the villagers, their whispers confirming that the news of my presence was spreading in Vaucouleurs again.

"See what I told you about the villagers. You're very well-known, Jehanne," Catherine murmured to me in a hushed undertone. Even people sitting in the front rows turned and glanced over.

Once mass finished, the lay people shuffled their way out, but I didn't want to leave yet. Catherine began to move, but I stopped her.

"Catherine," I said suddenly.

Her eyes were tinged with concern as she looked at me.

"I would like to stay a little longer. May I meet you at the plaza later?" I asked.

"Of course, my dear. I will fetch Henri and Durand from the house and meet you in the plaza when you are finished." She smiled reassuringly at me and squeezed my hand.

After she stood up and left the pew, I shuffled aside as others who sat in our row made their way out. But once it was empty, I faced the front. Grateful for the solitude, I kneeled down and began to pray. I focussed on my breathing and recitation of prayer.

"Our Father, who is in Heaven, Hallowed be thy name..."

I couldn't say how long I stayed there, but all I can say is that I felt myself become so immersed in my prayer that my nerves began to wash away. I felt more grounded. Stronger. I opened my eyes, and slowly my eyes focussed on my surroundings. The wooden panels and stone walls came to view. The crucifix and the wooden statue of Mary sat silently as my only audience.

If the people of Vaucouleurs believe me, or even if they don't, I must do what I came here to do.

I made the cross signage as I left the pew. The church was empty, except for an older woman kneeling with her eyes closed in the last row. My eyes lingered on her small delicate frame; she wore a black shawl draped over her white, coarse hair. Her veiny, fragile hands were clasped together, and she kneeled undisturbed as I approached the open church doors.

At that moment, the morning sun shifted and poured onto her kneeling frame, illuminating her head with lovely sunlight. I just watched her as I exited the church, reflecting on Catherine's words of the elderly lady who saw the light on my shoulder.

The breeze welcomed me into the street, but I stopped short unexpectedly. A small crowd had gathered two steps away from the church steps. One by one, they fell silent as they spotted me. A man, apparently the leader, made his way to the front of the church where I stood.

I examined them closely as he came closer. All of them looked like humble villagers of Vaucouleurs; they donned simple clothes or were merchants with shoes and belts with buckles. Bracing for whatever they were to say, I stood solidly on the top steps of the church. I reminded myself to take a truthful and honest approach.

"Are you the lass who wants to talk to Lord Robert?" asked the man. The man had a heavy Vaucouleurs accent. His clothes were clean yet humble. He was certainly not a merchant but a well-to-do villager. He had a short reddish beard, with a scar on his chin and hazel eyes.

"Yes, I am," I simply responded.

"Are you coming from God?" I heard from the crowd.

"Are you going to see our Lord Robert?" was the voice of another.

"Are you going to see the King?" A woman said from the front. She had a clean cap over her curly ash-blond hair, and she held a small child in her arms. Her hazel eyes had a searching look.

I responded, "Yes." I began walking down to the stairs, towards them. "I'm here because the King of Heaven told me to come. But..." I grimaced. "Lord Robert is not listening to me, and it is urgent that I speak with him because I need to be in Chinon. I need to be with the King and help him."

By now, I was directly in front of the crowd. I could see their faces clearer and in more detail. The majority were middle aged and over. Other groups who had stayed behind and waited near the church began to join the crowd, making it bigger. They began to surround me, but I didn't feel overwhelmed or nervous.

One of the merchants of Vaucouleurs stepped forward from the crowd. He had a moustache and long, wavy brown hair that was tied back at the nape of his neck. "We'll help you, young lass. All the merchants will give you a horse and some money for the journey," he said.

Stunned, my face dropped.

An ovation erupted from the crowd around me. People were cheering and clapping. I could scarcely believe it. I was stunned. I looked again to the merchant, bewildered of my luck. I clasped my hands together at my chest. "Sir, thank you for your gracious offer. Your help is most appreciated."

I continued, "Lord Robert passes through the plaza at noon. If anyone would like to accompany me, to support me, I'll be very thankful. He will be more convinced if I have your support. This is a command from the King of Heaven, and it is of the utmost importance that I be by the King's side."

I could feel the gaze of the man with the scarred chin studying me.

"Are you the maid from the prophecy?" asked someone in the crowd.

The question took me aback. "I… I don't know anything about a prophecy. The only thing that I know is that the King needs help and I need to be by his side."

"We'll help you, Mademoiselle," the lady with her child said. Her eyes were worn and hardened. But looking at me, I could see a glimmer of faith.

"Yes, we will help you to get to the king," the man with a scar on his chin said decidedly. His eyes showed conviction.

I looked at him and the faces surrounding me, scarcely believing their support and undeniable faith. Catherine was right. During my absence in winter, the people of Vaucouleur had opened their hearts. Also, at that moment I remembered Archangel Michael's words.

It was necessary to go, so word of you would spread and people would know about you.

It all made sense now. The voice of the scarred man brought my attention back to the group.

"What is your name, young lady?" asked the man gently.

"Jehanne, Jehanne d'Arc."

By noon, I arrived at the town square with Catherine, Henri, and Uncle Durand. I had told them about the encounter outside the church, and they were exuberant and filled with determination. They were certain of our success.

The markets were normally crowded with faces of strangers, but this time I saw the familiar large crowd and recognised the scarred man, the mother with her child, as well as other discernible faces. I acknowledged them briefly, and with Uncle, Henri, and Catherine beside me, we waited until Lord Robert appeared.

We paced up and down the markets, pretending to look at the products and goods of the stalls. Only when I heard the hooves clicking on the stone pavement did I look around. There, Lord Robert Baudricourt slowly strode through the gates and the crowd. Flanked by the two same young lords, Lord Robert appeared surprised to witness such a dense crowd in the square.

I quickly broke from the crowd and advanced towards Lord Robert. I proclaimed, mustering my most confident voice, "My Lord! Listen to me. I am here by the command of the King of Heaven!"

Lord Robert stared straight ahead and passed me immutably. I yelled with confidence, "Do not turn a deaf ear to me, my Lord. This is not my whim, but this is a command of the King of Heaven!"

He continued on.

I felt the stare and attention of his younger companions who took notice of me and were looking back and talking amongst themselves. Yet my stare bore into the back of Lord Robert. My lips stiffened in one line, and I shook my head.

Lord Robert and his companions travelled through the crowd, unmoved and undeterred of their intended pathway.

Humiliation and disappointment crushed my spirit. The crowd around me began to flutter and resume its activity slowly. Yet approaching footsteps and a voice interrupted my gloomy defeat.

"Excuse me, mademoiselle." I looked up to the face of a smiling merchant. "Where are you from and why do you have to go see the King?"

Merchants I had seen in the stall not a few minutes ago were crowding me. Regaining myself, I made an effort to conceal my dejection, and replied, "This is a mandate from God. I have to see the King and help him unify the kingdom. I must leave for Chinon immediately. The King of Heaven commands it."

Uncle stood next to me while I was talking with the merchants. I could feel their faces glow with intrigue. Once the merchants left, Uncle urged me, "Come, Jehanne. Let's go home."

"Actually, Uncle, would it be alright if I went to church this afternoon?"

I felt his slight bewilderment, but he nevertheless agreed. "Yes, of course. I will tell Catherine and Henri. Come home before dark," he cautioned.

I smiled dryly. "I will, don't worry."

He patted my arm reassuringly and disappeared into the crowd.

By this time, the marketplace was beginning to empty. Some merchants were packing up their goods, loading wagons, and disassembling their stalls. Winter was still in our midst as snow began to fall, for the first time in a few days.

Calmly, I retraced my steps to the church. The clouds were descending, and the air was icy. I walked up the stairs and entered through the doors of the church. This time, all the pews were completely empty. I walked to the middle pew, the wood creaking under my weight as I kneeled, clasping my hands and closing my eyes.

I took a deep breath out, my shoulders slumped, and I hung my neck down.

"Hail Mary, full of Grace. The Lord be with thee..."

I dove into my prayers, submerging myself in the deep entrails of its repetition to save myself from the storm of emotions. This provided a small respite from the stream of anxious thoughts of the future and Lord Robert.

I heard movement and opened my eyes to find the local priest lighting the candles at the front.

It must be getting late.

I adjusted myself and stood up, studying the lines on the palms of my hands. My mind felt still and settled like a lake. I walked home slowly. Twilight stretched out on the sky like a myriad of white and different shades of blue. The snow had stopped, but my breath came out in white smoke.

Nobody said this was going to be easy, I thought to myself before I entered the Royer home.

The next day, I repeated this same routine. Catherine and I went to church in the morning, then I stayed behind. The church was empty after everyone left, and in my solitude, I folded my hands together and closed my eyes.

Like a painter, unfolding anxieties and disappointment onto a blank canvas, I prayed and prayed for a solution, for a breakthrough.

My hands fluttered, my eyes itched, I adjusted, I fidgeted.

I took a deep breath, standing up.

I need to calm myself, I thought to myself.

I continued praying.

"Hail Mary, full of Grace. The Lord is with thee. Blessed is this day amongst women." Focusing on the words, I internally reiterated this prayer, until I heard something. I heard a voice in my heart.

"Today, you will be heard."

I opened my eyes and blinked several times. It wasn't my voice. It wasn't a thought. It was *a voice.* It was not female or male but an inner knowing. I repeated the sentence to myself. "Today you will be heard."

I took a deep breath, my gaze fixed on the ceiling, and sighed in relief. *Today, Lord Robert will finally listen.* I smiled and made the cross signage. I decided I would keep the message from my heart in the privacy of my knowledge only.

I stepped out of the church doors, walking with firm and precise movements. Outside, the sun had risen over the houses, almost reaching the highest point of the sky. The snow from yesterday was visible in the cracks of the stone pavement, and had gathered in the nooks and corners of the houses.

The plaza came into view, and I could see crowds gathering and swarming, bigger than yesterday's audience. As I approached, I could see people turning and whispering to each other.

It seemed word had spread about me, I pondered.

Others smiled encouragingly and nodded in support. Entering the crowd, I caught a glimpse of Uncle Durand, Henri, and Catherine in the crowd.

"Oh, Jehanne!" Catherine walked to greet me, her voice strained as she whispered, "The people are here for you!"

I looked around curiously, but I had no time for them yet. Uncle Durand and Henri approached behind her. I kept my voice low but leaned in so they could all hear me. "I need you to all come with me."

They assented and we walked to the end of the market, so that we would be the last people at the end of the crowd. As we made our way to the end, I could hear many people shouting their well wishes and encouragement.

"We believe you!"

"Have courage, mademoiselle!"

"We pray for you!"

I turned, smiled, and nodded to the people and cheers erupted.

As we walked, I could see people beginning to follow us. I recognised the man with a scar on his chin, and the woman with her young child. They, with their families, accompanied us until we reached the end. Catching their glances, I saw their eyes brimming with strength and encouragement.

The chatter and bartering lessened as we waited at the edge of the group. I stared straight ahead. Absorbed in my own prayers, my hands twirled and played with the end of my auburn braid. Yet movement around me continued to shift. The group around us accumulated in numbers and grew into a crowd. Henri and Catherine looked around, impressed, but I stayed focused. I didn't need any distractions.

A biting cold wind blew, and it was refreshing as my cheeks were hot. Then, the slow pace of horse hooves clicking on the pavement brought me to the present. I closed my eyes and prayed. *Lord, please give the right words to call Lord Robert's attention.*

I heard the echo of horseshoes on the stone street getting closer. The crowd usually formed a pathway for horsemen, so the crowd dispersed into two long sections, with a cleared pathway for the horseman to pass through.

Opening my eyes, I saw Lord Robert on his steed, approaching the end of the crowd. And in a moment of impetuousness, I side-stepped out of the crowd into the cleared path, and I grabbed the reins of Lord

Robert's horse, forcing the animal to suddenly stop. Lord Robert's head sharply jerked toward me.

"What the…" He pulled the other side of the reins for the animal to steady itself. "You," he simply said, his eyes narrowed, his lips tightened into a line.

Not breaking eye contact, I looked back at him wilfully. I could see his skin was lined, but nevertheless he held an air of cold authority. His eyes were like dark balls of displeasure and frustration. "I told your uncle… Where is your uncle?"

"Here, my Lord," responded Uncle, stepping forward out of the crowd. Last year's faltering tone disappeared, renewed with a sense of confidence.

"There you are," said Lord Robert. He pointed a gloved finger at my uncle who was a step behind me. "I told *you* to take this girl to her father so that he could give her a good beating." Then looking back at me, while bending slightly forward, he harshly rasped, "So you stop inventing stories." Extending his arm, he roughly recovered the reins from my hands.

But I replied vehemently, "These are not stories, but a command from the King of Heaven! Why would I be here every day, seeking your help? To travel through English territory, exposing myself to danger? Instead of being at home next to my mother?"

At that moment one of the young companions inched his horse closer. "Hey, sweetheart."

I turned to the young man who had approached. He had a relaxed countenance and a youthful expression of someone accustomed to a good life; he wore rich clothes. "Why do you care if the English conquers the kingdom, eh? We will all become English anyway," he said, a playful smile hinting at his lips.

I looked at him closely. He was a young man in his early mid-twenties with light wavy brown hair and dressed as a noble. *A young noble. But I do not think Lord Robert's kin*, I thought to myself.

"No sir, that is not going to happen," I said with certainty. "But I must follow what is being asked of me by the King of Heaven! I have come to Vaucouleaurs to seek Lord Robert's help! To provide me with an escort to the city of Chinon, to the King. But he does not heed my words nor my presence. And yet it is imperative that I be by the King's side before Lent, even if I must walk to Chinon myself!"

The young man looked at Lord Robert questioningly, and looked down to me again. Lord Robert remained unstirred. His back was straight as an arrow, and he held his head high, avoiding my gaze and my words completely. The crowd was totally silent, not a drop heard.

I continued, "Sir, there is no one in this Kingdom, nor king or duke nor any other who can help the Kingdom except me. I would rather be next to my mother at home, because this is not my station in life, but I have been instructed to leave my life and help the King, to save the Kingdom! I do what I have to do because my Lord commands it," I finished.

The young gentleman was listening closely to my words. All playfulness had diminished from his face. After a moment's pause, he asked, "Who is your Lord?"

"God!" I replied with force.

Hearing my answer, his brow raised in shock. A staggering look crossed his face. "Are you saying God is commanding you to go to see the King?" he asked incredulously.

"Yes, my Lord. I must go because there is no one else who can help the king but me. I must do this by the command of the King of Heaven."

The young lord stared at me for a few moments. No one moved or stirred in the crowd. The lords were silent. Then after a moment of contemplation the young lord, in one swift agile movement, descended from his horse and walked towards me. He stopped right in front of me.

His face was serious, even solemn. Looking directly into my eyes, he said, "I promise with God as my witness that I, Jean de Metz, will take you to Chinon, to King Charles. When do you need to leave?" he asked, his clear blue eyes resting on my face.

Stunned, I stared at him incredulously. I was unable to move. My gaze was fixed on the young noble's, and it seemed as if the whole world stopped. I gave a bewildered laugh, and my face broke into gleeful. "Today is better than tomorrow, and tomorrow better than the day after!" My heart felt like leaping.

The crowd around us cheered and applauded in approval. I heard a few steps as the other rider, who'd also descended from his horse, approached me. He was a tall blond man, also young and in noble garments, and with a similar accent to Jean. He proclaimed, "And I, Bertrand de Poulengy, promise to bring you safely to the presence of the King."

The crowd doubled in its applause and ovations. Catherine, Henri, and Uncle Durand were beaming with pride and glee. I smiled widely and laughed, unable to contain my excitement.

Lord Robert shook his head in disapproval. He kicked his heels and the horse stirred and continued. His steed slowly walked through the sea of happy supporters. I whirled back to Jean.

"Would you like to travel in women's clothes or men's?" he asked.

Without thinking twice, I responded, "Men's clothes."

"Very well, I'll send you some clothes of my servants."

The woman who was with her child raised her voice for the lords to hear as well. "The young lass will also have the support and help of the people. Don't worry, my girl, we'll get you whatever you need. You will lack nothing."

I turned to the crowd, amazed and stupefied. "Thank you, thank you all so much!" I admired the kindness of the souls surrounding me.

Then I faced the two young lords standing in front of me.

"To Chinon?" Jean said. Bertrand looked back at me.

"To Chinon," I responded, beaming.

27

THE DUKE

Midwinter, 1429
Vaucouleurs, France

That afternoon, the Royers' front door stood languidly open. Although it stood hackneyed and forgotten, it ushered in the streaming visitors that arrived, casting the house into disarray and pell-mell. The Royers' home, usually orderly, was now effused with men's clothes, hoses, leggings, and tunics strewn across the chairs, and jumbled old boots of every size scattered across the floor.

Hurried footsteps echoed through the hall and walls, and muffled voices resonated through the floors. There was no need to close the large wooden door of the Royers that day.

Henri and Uncle Durand were out, running errands to find a horse suitable to travel, and Catherine played hostess, greeting and organising the women's donations of clothes. The curly, ash-blond woman from the plaza was among the first to bring her offering, and soon after a flock of women arrived in the Royers' living room, donating their clothing.

Amidst the conversational and enthusiastic voices of the women, a wide-eyed teenager appeared in the doorframe of the kitchen, holding a pile of neatly folded clothes in one hand, and a pair of recently oiled boots in his other. Catherine approached him in her friendly manner. "Lad, can I help you?"

The young lad's voice was respectful. "I've come to deliver these to the young maid. They're from Jean de Metz."

Catherine approached slowly, taking the clothes tentatively. "Thank you very much, young lad. You're very kind." As she placed them down on the chair, she added, "Help yourself to something lad, if you're hungry."

He shook his head. "Thank you, madame, but I have been asked to wait in case you need to report any message to my Lord."

Catherine nodded, starting to leaf through the tunics and leggings. Then the door frame was filled with Henri and Durand's tall and wide frames as they came through, suddenly making the once spacious room shrink smaller. They nodded to the boy as they passed, and the boy scurried out quickly.

Catherine asked, while looking at the different sizes of tunics, "Did you find a horse?"

"Well, yes. A merchant who saw Jehanne speak to Lord Robert this afternoon offered to give us one of his horses," Henri said, pleased.

Durand continued, "He also offered his equipment."

"Oh, how good! Well, I will let Jehanne know now." She went through the tunics and leggings on the chairs, adding them to the pile already in her hands. The pile now reached her chin and wobbled slightly as she carefully turned around to look at Henri and Durand again. "She's upstairs trying on some clothes. I'm going to give her some more to try on. I'll be back."

She carefully climbed the stairs, holding the staggering tower of clothes to one side.

A knock on the door caught my attention. I was in a large storage room that had wooden crates piled against the walls and a solid long trunk in the corner. A pair of rickety chairs were overlaid with leggings and tunics. In the middle of pulling up a pair of black hoses, I said loudly, "Catherine?"

"Yes dear, it's me," I heard from the other side.

I opened the door, first seeing the stack of folded clothing, then Catherine's light brown and grey hair, tied into a bun that hung limply at the nape of her neck.

"Here, my dear. Jean de Metz' page came just now with these clothes. See how they fit first."

I peered at them. They were non-chromatic and plain but of fine quality. I turned to her, letting her examine the tunic that fell to the tops of my thighs. "This tunic is slightly big. I think I will need a smaller one."

She scrutinised me, nodding in agreement. "Alright, dear. Let's be patient and find which ones fit you best."

Hearing more voices downstairs, Catherine grew alert. We were not sure if there were more newcomers arriving to give their clothes. "I'll be right back, dear." She hurried out, closing the door behind her and leaving me in my solitude.

I took off the tunic, my skin tingling from the chill air. I shivered as I looked through the folded clothes. I took out a pair of maroon breeches and was attempting to squirm into the leggings and its matching tunic when I heard a man's voice downstairs, distinguished amongst the other familiar voices.

After a few exchanges, the conversation ended. Urgent footsteps ascended the stairs, and there was a rapid knock on the door. I hesitated for a moment. I was mid-change and in no way decent, but after a second of thought I reasoned that Catherine would not send someone.

"Come in", I said loudly.

Catherine came in, her eyes singing with excitement. Her chest was rising up and down, showing the exhaustion from coming up the stairs so quickly. She closed the door behind her and made her way to me.

"Jehanne—" Her voice was high and shrill. She waved a letter in her hand. "—you have a message from the Duke of Lorraine! Charles II, The Duke! He has heard of your presence here and he wants to see you. A rider just came with the duke's request!"

"From the Duke? Are you sure?" I said incredulously.

I snapped the letter, flipped it over, and looked at it closely. I could see it had a red seal, but more importantly it had a crown stamped on it.

"Extraordinary..." I whispered in amazement. I could see writing on it, but to me it was just an intricate pattern of curved, fine lines. "I—I don't know how to read," I said, handing the letter back to Catherine, somewhat shyly.

"Oh, Jehanne. This is not a letter; this is safe conduct to enter the Duke's Chateau. The messenger said you need one of these to see the duke," replied Catherine.

I swallowed hard, looking at the letter intently. "A safe conduct?"

"Yes, probably every person who sees a Duke needs special permission. Jehanne, your name has reached the Duke, and he has invited you to see him. He is a powerful person in the Kingdom." Sensing my hesitation, she added encouragingly, "This is wonderful, my lass." Catherine searched for my delayed reaction.

"Yes..." I responded hesitantly. My eyebrows furrowed looking at the letter, then I glanced up at Catherine's expectant eyes. The King was my priority, I knew that, but I could not leave a Duke waiting. My mind was in fetters with what to do next.

I took a deep breath.

You can do this Jehanne, think, think...

A moment passed before the answer came. I turned abruptly to Catherine, who waited patiently. "Alright, Catherine. I need to send a message. I need to send a message to Lord Jean and Lord Bertrand."

"What is it, Jehanne? Do you not want to go?" Catherine asked.

"No. Well, it will mean that our journey to Chinon will be delayed," I said, disappointment creeping into my voice.

She glanced at the letter pensively and grimaced. "No matter. I cannot refuse an invitation from the Duke, so to Lorraine we will go," I said decidedly.

"Yes, use Lord Jean's page to send the message. He should still be waiting outside..." Catherine said.

"How far is the Duke of Lorraine's chateau?" I asked.

Catherine tilted her head, thinking for a moment. "About half a day on horseback."

Thinking only for a moment, I realised something. "I need a horse."

"A town's merchant and your uncle have already provided you with a horse, lass." Catherine reminded me with a smile. "Remember?"

"Yes, of course. I'll go tomorrow morning to Lorraine before day-break. I need to see if Lord Jean and Lord Bertrand will accompany me."

"Do you know how to ride a horse?"

"Yes, I rode a few times in Neufchâteau, and when I was helping my brothers."

"Good, it's a handy skill. It will come into good use now that you are going to travel half of the country to Chinon."

I chuckled, my expression lightening. My gaze travelled to the floor, looking at a few socks and leggings scattered around me. "Now about these clothes..." I looked down at my vestments.

Catherine commented, "Mm those leggings are still a little big. Try these on for better size." Catherine bent down and picked up a few from the neatly folded pile. She held them up to my hips, seeing if they would stretch.

Tossing one over her shoulder, she held up another, scrutinising and examining its width and length. She tossed this one over her other shoulder, and held up another and repeated the routine, clicking her tongue. "I think these two will fit you nicely. Put them on."

I turned and peered down. Although I always knew I'd need to wear boys' clothes, it nevertheless felt extremely odd—though appreciatively comfortable.

Catherine examined me from head to toe and nodded in approval. "Just... Here, let me." She reached over and bent down to adjust the length of the leggings, and the socks, pulling up and positioning them so the leggings would fold under the hoses neatly.

Rising, she straightened the tunic and stepped back. Catherine surveyed the outfit with a critical eye, pursed lips and her hand on her hips. "Not bad. You look like a young lad," said Catherine with a smile, but I could see in her eyes that something had occurred to her.

"Wait, there is something else you need." Turning, she went to a large trunk located in the corner of the room. Rummaging inside for a short time, she finally said, "I found it," then pulled out a long narrow piece of cloth. She passed it to me.

"What is this? I asked, holding it in my hands, confused.

"This is for your chest, to cover your breasts," she said, putting her hands in an upside-down L shape, and circling her torso. "You put it on around your torso to restrain and conceal your breasts. It will make it easier to ride, and perhaps more importantly, make you look like a boy."

"Of course…" I said, inspecting its length and extending it out. While I had never thought about it, it was good advice. "Let's try it now," I said while taking off the tunic and the shirt underneath. I wrapped the cloth around my chest and circled it a couple of times.

Reaching the end of the cloth, I tightly secured it under my armpit, tying it to the opposite end, which I had left free.

"Good, you got it the first time," said Catherine while looking at my work. "Does it feel too tight?"

"No, it feels good. A bit loose. I hope it does not end up around my hips," I said, laughing.

Catherine chuckled. "I hope not, but don't worry. You will have a lot of practice to get it right." Setting her eyes on my long braids, which fell down past my shoulders, Catherine added, "We need to do something with those braids. When you are on the road, try to arrange your hair up and hide it under your hat."

I lifted one braid over the crown of my head, and then the other.

"Here, sit for a moment." Catherine said, rummaging through the trunk and retrieving a miniature box.

The chair croaked as I sank into it. Catherine returned with pins between her teeth, protruding out of her awkwardly positioned mouth. "Let me see…" she said through her teeth and began to slide the pins carefully through my hair. After a few minutes, she appeared to be finished.

"Alright, not bad for the first time," she said, looking at her handi-work. "Alright, I'm going to check if any other visitors have arrived."

I nodded, and Catherine closed the door behind her. I sat feeling the slight tightness of the new hairstyle when I saw a flash of movement from my peripheral vision. Alert, I blinked, and, where Catherine was standing just a few moments prior, stood Saint Marguerite, as radiant and beautiful as ever.

I gave a small jolt of surprise. "Saint Marguerite!" I gasped.

Saint Marguerite was not deterred. "Jehanne, I have an important message. Listen carefully."

I nodded readily, accustomed to the angel's straightforward approach.

"A great defeat is going to befall the French army at the imminent bat-tle of Rouvray. Send a message with this news to Lord Robert. Also, now that you are going to begin your journey to Chinon, be confident that no danger will be present on the road. The King of Heaven has mandated this. And the two lords, Jean and Bertrand, will take care of you. They are here to fulfil their destiny with God."

Her look softened and she continued. "Jehanne, now you are a mes-senger of the King of Heaven. When you are in the presence of the Duke, stand and bow your head with respect in salutation. But remember while you are with the gentry, you are one of them. Stand with your head held high and think before you respond to their queries, always answering with the truth, and most importantly, if you cannot answer, tell them that you will consult in prayer. One of us will guide you."

Saint Marguerite's eyes turned earnest. "Remember, do not curtsy when you are in the presence of a Duke or a noble. Bow your head and put your hand over your heart, but remember you are a messenger of the King of Heaven. Do you understand?"

I nodded. It must be important if she was repeating her advice twice. "I will not curtsy. I'll bow my head with one hand on my heart in the pres-ence of the Duke and nobles, I understand," I said solemnly.

"Good," she said, approvingly. Then she added, "Be confident and at peace. The road to Chinon will be free of danger."

"Thank you," I said, nodding.

But she was already gone, and I was staring into an empty room once again. Looking down at my pair of hoses and leggings, I smiled and chuckled lightly escaped from my lips. *Curtsying in pants would be ridiculous*, I thought to myself amusedly.

It would not be too hard to comply with Saint Marguerite's advice as I had never worked with nobles or high-ranking individuals before. Their custom to curtsy was never embedded in me, because I worked among farmers and peasants. But I knew Saint Marguerite's offered her advice for a reason. I trusted in her superior wisdom.

Remembering her message, I briskly stood up. The odd sensation of leggings and hoses still made me feel like I was acting in some amusing play. Holding the letter, I opened the door and sped down the stairs. *Even moving is much easier*, I thought to myself incredulously.

Entering the kitchen, I asked hurriedly, "Catherine, have you seen my Uncle Durand?" The kitchen and fireplace were now empty except for Catherine, who was sorting through the strewn clothes. The others must have left.

"He was here a minute ago with Henri," Catherine said, sensing my urgency. "What is it, lass, has something happened?"

"I have received a message from Saint Marguerite." I walked into the hallway, and Catherine followed. Glancing back at her, as we walked, I said, "I need to tell Lord Jean about it and send a message to Lord Robert. Do you know if his page is still here?"

Reaching the front door, I grasped the iron knob, pulled, and found myself face to face with Jean de Metz. His hand was raised as if he were about to knock. He quickly masked the surprise on his face and replaced it with his usual respectful countenance.

My face lit up as I saw him. "I was about to call you, my Lord. I need to send a message to Lord Robert."

"What has happened?" asked Jean, his eyebrows furrowed slightly.

"Can you write?" I asked without answering his question. I led him inside, his tall figure taking up most of the space in the tight hallway.

"Yes, but what has happened?" Jean repeated.

I talked loudly over the echo of our footsteps bounding off the walls. "Saint Marguerite just told me there will be a great defeat in the imminent battle of Rouvray. I need to let Lord Robert know right away," I said with an increased sense of urgency.

"I see. Yes, I'll go and personally convey this message to Robert," said Jean, realising the gravity of the situation.

"There's something else. The Duke of Lorraine has invited me to his Chateau."

"The Duke?!" said Jean, his eyes fixed on me.

"Yes, I cannot refuse a duke. Therefore, our journey will need to be extended. Tomorrow, I plan to visit the Duke, then we will go to the King in Chinon as soon as we can. Do you agree with that, my Lord?"

Although pensive for a moment, he finally agreed. "Lorraine will be a little detour, yet it's closer to us than Chinon. Tomorrow we, Bertrand and I, will be ready," said Jean. "Anything else?" he pressed.

"No, that's it. And I prefer if we write a letter to Lord Robert."

He nodded, determined. "Let's write the Duke's letter."

Catherine, who had witnessed our entire exchange, was silent, but when we finished, she was already looking for some parchment and ink. She removed some of the clothes from the chair and brought a paper for Jean to write, then we began.

Jean sat and I stood in front, while Catherine leaned against the chair. Taking the ink and quill, and steadying his hand, Jean looked up at me. "What is your message?"

"Dear Lord Robert, I have just received a message from Saint Marguerite who has alerted me of a great defeat that will come upon us. The French will be defeated in the battle of Rouvray. I convey this news with much sadness. Jehanne d'Arc."

Quiet scribbling was heard as Jean wrote. The fire behind us crackled and sizzled.

"Is that all?" Jean said without looking up, finishing the last sentence.

"Yes."

"Can you sign?"

"Sign?" I asked, my tone uncertain.

"Write your name," Jean clarified, turning the paper and offering me the quill.

I cleared my throat, "Oh... yes, of course."

"Sign here," Jean said.

Kneeling down on the rough carpet, I took the quill. My fingers held it awkwardly. A few moments passed while I adjusted it, then I scribbled a line of writing at the bottom of the page. Jean did not comment on nor acknowledge my moment of insecurity.

"Alright, I'll take the letter to Robert tonight, and tomorrow I'll be here at dawn to accompany you to Lorraine," Jean said, allowing the parchment to dry before folding it up and tucking it into his doublet. Dusk was now arriving, and the house was ensconced in shadows.

"Thank you, Lord Jean, for helping me... and for believing in me," I said, as he stood up. The fire behind me danced on his face, illuminating his features. He had a wide face with a square jawline, and handsome, penetrating blue eyes with curly light brown ringlets that framed his face.

"Jehanne, I should say thank you for letting me help you. What is happening here is extraordinary. I am very humbled." He gave a short bow to me, sidestepped from the chair, and after acknowledging Catherine, disappeared through the hallway.

Catherine whistled and said, returning to the kitchen, "You will be safe in his company. God has sent you a good man!"

I smiled, the day's fatigue weighing me down. I sagged in the chair across from the fire and stared into its yellow and orange frames. "Yes, Saint Marguerite told me. She said God has sent two good men to take me to the King."

28

THE JOURNEY TO LORRAINE

Midwinter, 1429
Vaucouleurs, France

*T*he horse stirred lightly. I patted her down. Her long, straight, chestnut eyelashes moved under her alert eyes. "There, there my girl," I said, comforting her and patting her neck. I cooed softly, stroking the steed's neck, not rushing but enjoying our greeting.

Her hooves clicked the pavements as she shuffled. Her mahogany coat shone, and her muscles rippled as she moved. Good for first time riders, the merchant said.

I looked sideways to Uncle Durand, who was saddling his horse.

In front of the house, Catherine stood with her hands clasped, and Henri was beside her looking pensive. The fortress kept the air rigid and icy, but the air was also dense with the soft perfume of florals reminding us spring was not too far away.

That morning Catherine helped me get dressed into my clothes, making sure everything I did was done to perfection. As she helped pin my braids up, Catherine told me about the Lorraine region. "The capital city is Nancy. That's where the Duke's chateau is. The Duke of Lorraine is very old now, and he's been a good duke, although there have been rumours of his excessive number of mistresses..."

When she had finished, I laced my boots and stood up. My long black tunic reached to the tops of my thighs and was fastened with a weathered old belt that fell around the top of my hips. My leggings hugged my calves, and my boots squeaked and wobbled as I paced the upstairs room under Catherine's watchful gaze. "Don't forget this," she held up a small maroon cap.

"Of course," I said, sliding the cap over my tightly bound hair.

When we heard the horse hooves clicking in the street, we knew it would be Jean and Bertrand. Packing the Duke's letter into a satchel and pulling my cape over my shoulders, fastening it tightly, Catherine and I walked outside to greet them. Dressed in travellers clothes, they were accompanied by their servants, Francois and Louis.

Uncle and Henri arrived shortly after with two horses from the merchants' stables, and gently led them over to the house.

Once the chestnut steed was relaxed, I gently slipped my foot into the stirrup and gracefully pulled myself up over the saddle. Catherine and Henri moved to my side instantaneously. "Good luck, my dear, you are in good hands." She smiled her warm, comforting smile and squeezed my arm.

Henri said from her side, "We're behind you in Vaucouleurs, Jehanne. You needn't fear. You have our support."

"Thank you both so much, I would not be here without your help." They both nodded, and, satisfied with their farewell, backstepped to let the company pass. Jean and Bertrand looked at each other, and Bertrand nodded. Jean said aloud for all of us to hear, "Let us make our way to the gates and from there make headway." Then, to me, he said, "Are you ready?"

"Yes."

After looking back to Bertrand, Jean galloped ahead, his long cape rippling with each stride.

The dawn spring was chilly, and fog still clung to the horizon as we travelled through the green countryside. Swamps and dense forests passed by, and despite wearing warm clothes for the journey, my breath came out as puffs of white air, and the chill kept me shivering.

At first the chestnut mare was jittery and skittish, but as the dawn became day, the mare's anxiety receded. We stopped once to replenish our thirst, taking out our leather skin bottles, and to nibble on some dry bread and ham near a small swamp that was murky brown but with clusters of ice and snow still left on the bank. The day was full of grey bodies of dense clouds.

By the afternoon, we could see Nancy, the capital of Lorraine. Above the city were long sheets of rain, yet the distance and weather could not hide the city's size and grandeur. Inside, the narrow streets ran parallel to each other, separated by long rows of large grey and white buildings. The rain had made the road slippery and wet, but like any city, stalls were set up for business, and the city's merchants peered up with curious glances at our large party.

I kept my gaze forward, avoiding the eyes of the villagers. Bertrand and Jean did as well, as they impassively led us through Nancy. The only flicker of movement was the horses' tails swishing from side to side. An array of poor and well-dressed people busied themselves in the streets, rapidly coming and going, their faces serious no matter their status.

Nancy was larger than both Neufchâteau and Vaucouleurs, and we rode through the city for some time, until we reached the Duke's chateau.

"We're close," Jean said, turning his clear blue eyes on me, but I stared unimpressed.

Ahead of us, the street winded like a maze, but a few minutes later, in the distance, a white building appeared at the end of the street. Only when we approached did I realise it wasn't just one building; it expanded to multiple building complexes that were enclosed within the most elegant golden gate. I stared, struck.

The chateau rose high. Its wide and long panelled windows gave a sweet glimpse of the opulence and grandeur inside. Rapt, I stared at the most stunning building I had ever seen. Every panel, every corner, was splendid.

The pale sun shone onto the chateau, making it glow with affluence and highlighting the rich greenery of the elaborate gardens and grounds after the rain. Within the gardens were benches, sculpted bushes, and hedges hiding secret pebble pathways that weaved around the beautiful chateau like a precious necklace.

We walked beside the golden gate until we reached an archway with four guards standing in the entryway. "What business do you have here?" said one of the guards, a man in his mid-forties with pale skin that showed the blue and red veins on his neck, and a red beard peeking underneath his long mail headdress.

"I am Jean de Metz and this is Bertrand de Polengy. We have come to escort Jehanne d'Arc to the Duke as he requested."

The guard peered over to me, and then back at Jean. "You must have an admittance card."

Pulling it out, I edged my horse closer and gave it to him. He peered up at me, scrutiny written over his face. Opening the parchment and seeing the Duke's seal, he looked up to the entire company. "And who is everyone else?"

"Our servants, and Jehanne d'Arc's uncle."

The guard nodded and looked to his peers. "This is the Duke's seal, alright." He turned to the two guards behind him. "You two will escort the guests and report back once Vince has seen them."

The two guards behind him were younger but nodded obediently. The senior guard stepped aside. "Pass through. The guards will escort you to the courtyard and see to it that the servants escort you to the Duke."

"Thank you, sir." Jean tilted his head as his horse slowly advanced towards the end of the archway. As I slowly passed, the senior handed back the admittance, tilting his head to look me in the eyes.

I packed the letter swiftly in my bag. *Word has spread indeed.*

We made our way slowly through the long archway that opened to a large courtyard. The courtyard had statues of angels and saints against the walls, and a twin staircase that led to a pair of pearlescent white doors that stood firmly shut.

One of the guards went inside while the other waited and we dismounted. I looked up. The sky was the only remnant of familiarity from life outside the opulence of this chateau.

A woman dressed in servant clothes appeared next to the guard, and seeing our party, she descended the set of stairs from the double doors. "Are you Jehanne d'Arc?" she posed quietly but with authority in her voice.

"Yes," I responded.

"May I see your admittance letter?"

I brought out the letter again and handed it to her. Peering at it closely, she gave a curt nod. "You arrived with servants and pages. They will escort your horses to the stables. The rest of you will follow me," she said, her eyes resting on me.

I turned to Uncle. He smiled encouragingly but said nothing because the woman ascended the stairs swiftly, her dark skirt swishing as she turned inside the grand chateau. We followed quickly behind her, and once again I stared open-mouthed at the beauty and grandeur of the chateau.

It proved to be as impressive and opulent as its exterior. The roof was white, but the walls held the most exquisite wallpapers, with large paintings and tapestries that reached the floor, swallowing the whole room in the heroic and gallant artistic forms.

The rooms were large and filled with fine furniture with shiny wooden handles, bouquets of flowers in glistening vases, and curious golden trinkets and books adorning the shelves.

The woman's footsteps echoed ahead of us, following her through many corridors, and passing plenty of luxurious and beautiful rooms.

I must remain focused. I cannot let my curiosity distract me.

I concentrated on the woman's tiny feet, escaping from under her skirt with each stride.

Finally, we came to an arch-shaped door, well decorated and ornate with gold and white patterns. The woman stopped and knocked, and after a few moments of silence, quiet steps approached and the door creaked open, only so much as to peek out. The woman leant in and spoke quietly. I craned my neck to see who answered.

After a few exchanges, the door opened more widely, revealing a young servant girl. She had small brown eyes, and a button nose decorated with brown and red freckles. She appeared confused but wordlessly turned and disappeared into the room, leaving the door wide open. Her steps echoed, and it became clear the room was large. It took only a moment longer for my eyes to adjust.

The dimly lit room had a few candles flickering on the walls, giving it a ghostly and solemn atmosphere. My eyes caught the golden gleams of the small figurines on dark wooden furbished tables and lounges. The walls were also adorned with handsome lords and graceful ladies on tapestries and portraits, their presence the only remnant of the living until I saw the bed.

The curtains of the high windows were drawn, except for one that let light shine on the figure laying in the extravagant bed. The bed was made of sturdy dark wood and had four large metallic posts at each edge. A white translucent curtain surrounded it. The girl's dark figure pulled aside the curtain and there, breathing heavily, with gaunt and loose skin falling from his face was an old man who was in the clutches of illness.

She approached a slim man with fine, brown shoulder-length hair sitting next to the bed. He leant away from the bed, his feet crossed underneath the chair, so as to not disturb the ill figure in the bed.

She whispered to him hurriedly. He then, in turn, leant over carefully to the Duke. The Duke stirred, and quiet exchanges were made between the seated man and servant girl. It appeared the Duke was not quite ready, and the man, who appeared to be his physician, opened a belt full of instruments and sat in front of the duke, obscuring our vision.

Finally, the physician sat up and stood, wrapping a band around his hand. He motioned to the servant girl. The Duke began to weakly shuffle and lift himself to a seated position. He managed to get himself onto his elbows, then, seeing his difficulty with moving any further, his physician supported and lifted him carefully to lean against the bedpost, while the young girl accommodated the pillows behind the duke's back, supporting him in his new sitting position.

Meekly appearing in the doorframe, looking flushed, she opened the door a little wider. The Duke, now in a sitting position, turned his eyes in my direction. He weakly lifted his hand and bade me forward. The servant girl looked over at me expectedly and motioned me into the room.

My hands felt clammy. Dread rooted me to the spot, at the door. I had never been in the presence of a high nobleman before.

Even the lords of this great duchy suffer the inclemency of sickness and of old age... the poor man.

What did Archangel Michael say? We are all equal in the eyes of God, one creation for his glory. No matter our station in life, we are all the same.

He is suffering so much.

Sympathy for the old man touched my heart. Swallowing my nervousness, I walked bravely into the grand, dark room.

My footsteps echoed loudly. I could hear my own heartbeat racing in my ears. The room was warm and stuffy. But even in these uncomfortable feelings, I began to see the room in more detail, even noticing the seated gentlemen and ladies by the large window. They were as noiseless as the rest of the furniture, and I could feel their eyes bore into me as I slowly approached.

Reaching the bed, I bowed with my hand over my chest and looked upon the Duke's face. Up close, his face was pale and deeply lined with dark shadows under his eyes. His eyes were foggy with fatigue, but behind them I could sense a keen intelligence that was present in the Duke's youth.

"I've heard about you." His voice was low, and it sounded as if his throat was dry. Wispy white hair fell around his ears. "Jehanne, isn't it?"

I nodded. "Yes, my Lord."

"I heard you talk to angels. Can you cure me?" He looked at me as if I was his last hope in this world.

I felt a stone fall in the pit of my stomach.

What do you do when a Duke asks if you can heal him?

Breathing, I composed myself and I answered with the truth. "My dear Duke, I do not know anything about healing. I only know that I need to see the King…" I responded softly, then saw the defeated expression come over him. In that moment, I felt an urge to help him, so I said, "I—I can pray for your health, my Lord." I paused and then added, "If you wish so."

His eyes illuminated, and a faint smile appeared in his pale lips.

I knelt at his bed and gently clasped my hands together, closing my eyes. Preparing myself, I prayed to the light, to the angels I had become so acquainted with. After a moment, I heard Saint Catherine's voice and opened my eyes slightly. A soft light floated on my shoulder.

"The Duke needs to rectify his behaviour, and live a rightful life with good deeds and no excess."

I looked at the Duke. His eyes were closed. "My Duke."

He opened his eyes and stirred.

"My Lord, the light says you need to rectify your behaviour, live a rightful life, performing good deeds with no excess of any kind."

The Duke looked at me intently for a moment. Then he closed his eyes and he rested. I stood up, waiting for a response. After a long moment, the Duke's eyes opened again and rested on me for a moment longer. "Thank you, Jehanne."

"My Lord, may I ask for the company of your son on my journey to the King?"

"My girl, I cannot dispose of my son, but I'll give you four francs and a letter of safe passage while you travel through my lands." His eyes rose and fell with every word he spoke.

I bowed, smiling gratefully. I was thankful for any help he offered. I only needed the letter of safe passage, but the monetary gift was a bonus no matter how little. "Thank you, my Lord."

The Duke fell quiet. He lay his head back onto the bed post, his brow notched together, and he grimaced. "I feel the pain coming back, doctor," the Duke said, his eyes still closed in pain and his hands clutching the sheets of the bed.

"Yes, my Lord. I'll fetch the medicine." The man with shoulder length hair hurriedly walked to the corner of the room. His footsteps lightly kissed the polished wooden floor, as he returned with two glass bottles, glinting in the sunlight. The brown liquid inside swished and jumped freely in the translucent bottle.

The Duke opened his eyes and waved behind me. "See that this lady and the Lords are given rooms and nourishment. They are my guests."

I glanced behind us to see a servant with black and white uniform. He stood erect, hand on his belt, and eyes straight ahead. "Yes, my Lord," he said, nodding in a disciplined manner.

The Duke rested his tired eyes on me. "Thank you for coming so promptly after receiving my invitation. It is time now for me to receive my medicine. Please accept my hospitality and lodgings before you travel tomorrow to the King in Chinon."

"Thank you, my Lord, you are very kind." I smiled and bowed my head with my hand over my chest.

The Duke nodded tiredly, though his eyes remained closed and he leant his head back on the bedrest. The physician began to prepare his medicine, his hands darting around the Duke, working urgently but precisely.

"Follow me, please," I heard a voice say.

A tall man, with long brown hair tied at his neck stood tall with his hands folded in front of him. His white gloves shone brightly in the dark room, and he turned and wedged himself between Jean de Metz, Bertrand, and Uncle in the hallway.

He led us through the long, ornate halls of the chateau. We walked in silence, only the footman's polished black shoes brushing against the immaculate floor.

Slowing down, he stopped before another set of white double doors, painted with intricate golden shapes. He opened them both at the same time, like a fan, and the dining hall's splendour opened to us like a sun-rise bursting through a landscape. Unlike the Duke's bedroom, this room was bright, as to one side a series of tall windows were open, but nevertheless the short wintery day saw the sun descending behind the chateau.

The room was lined with extravagant candle holders on one side, and to the other side beautiful portraits of elegant nobles. In the centre was a long dining table, and at the end, opposite the table, was a tapestry hanging on the wall depicting a herd of elegant horses on a hill.

"Please wait here, my lords and lady. Your meal will be brought in shortly." Bowing, the servant left the room.

"Please sit, Jehanne, Durand," said Jean De Metz, strolling in comfortably with Bertrand, their capes floating gently behind them.

Uncle and I approached the dining table hesitantly, both of us staring at the luxurious spread. Tall candles sat in the centre, but the most eye-catching was the dining pieces. Large, white and cream coloured plates sat with an array of golden and silver cutlery. Jean and Bertrand positioned themselves at the other side of the table, leaving the head of the table vacant. Uncle and I approached the other side, and we gingerly sat opposite Jean and Bertrand.

"The Duke seemed not well at all," commented Bertrand, while taking his cape off his shoulders and putting it on the chair next to him.

"No, he apparently was suffering some pains. The man next to him seemed to be his physician," I said, eyeing the fine and detailed cutlery in front of me.

"What did he want from you?" asked Jean, his elbows resting on the table.

"Well, he wanted for me to cure him. He asked me if I could mend his illness… but I said I did not know anything about healing."

"Hmm, not the answer he wanted to hear, I presume," said Jean.

"No, but I offered to pray for him. I also asked for his son to accompany us, but he said he could not dispose of his son. Instead he gave me four francs and a letter of safe-conduct to travel his lands." I reached into my pocket, showing the coins to Uncle then dropping the coins onto the table gently.

Jean looked down at the coins, then he looked at Bertrand wryly with a trace of disbelief in his eyes. Bertrand met his eyes for only a moment, looking uncomfortable, and only smiled awkwardly back at me.

Jean collected himself. "The Duke's free passage will help us travel through his lands with no worry."

We all looked at the meagre collection of coins on the table and the Dauphin's minted profile shone underneath the candlelight. My lips made a thin line and I shrugged, my stomach growling with hunger.

***

The servants came in one by one, their chins held high, and their black and white uniforms pressed and polished to perfection. They moved in a way that was impersonal and instinctive. They all carried a bowl filled with water and positioned themselves beside each of us.

Jean and Bertrand rolled up their sleeves, exposing their thick and calloused hands. The servants bent over, and the lords washed their hands with ease. Bertrand's freckled arm, and Jean's veiny and dark arm, were dripping when they lifted them out of the bowls, but they were significantly cleaner than before.

I glanced at my own as I folded my sleeves up to my elbows. The servant man next to me stared straight ahead as I dipped my hands inside the watery depths of the bowl. The liquid was pleasantly warm, and I scrubbed and rubbed my hands, steadily making the water murkier from the dirt and dust of the travel.

As I was beginning to lift them, the man said, "Madame, there is a towel in my arm. Please use it." He stared unblinkingly overhead. Grabbing the folded white towel on his right arm, I dried my hands. The men then swiftly left the room, the water in the bowls still swishing.

They returned shortly after holding fine, large platters with bowls of vegetable soup. The soups were placed in front of us, served in the same cream and white bowls. I looked at the fine knives, forks, and spoons with their gold metal handles. It was the first time in my humble life I had ever seen such fine dining and was exposed to the noble dining etiquette. I felt strange, confused.

"Jehanne." I heard a whisper.

Jean was looking at me. He grabbed the big spoon at his right side and without any shred of arrogance, he smiled and said, "The big spoon is for the soup."

Looking down, I held up the big spoon to Jean.

"Yes, that one," said Jean, satisfied.

Uncle followed my example as he was as lost as me in the art of fine dining. With Bertrand and Jean as our guides in etiquette that afternoon, Uncle and I enjoyed our first dining experience in the house of the Duke. Soon, the soup disappeared, and the next course of roasted meats, pastries, and vegetables was served.

Jean and Bertrand showed a large knife, and we hungrily ate while conversation continued. "Jehanne, we were impressed by your riding skills. Does your father own horses?" asked Bertrand.

"Oh, no. Well, my father would pay to borrow the horses of our local Lord for a few days. But I knew how to ride from when we lived in Neufchâteau. I worked in an inn and needed to handle and ride horses for the clients."

"You worked in an inn?" asked Bertrand, lifting his eyebrows.

"Well done. Did it take you long to learn?" asked Jean as he took a glass just filled with wine by the servants.

"Yes and no. Not very long, I think. A day or two. The innkeeper, Madam Margerie, taught me." I smiled, remembering the innkeeper and her toughness.

"Is your father a worker of your local Lord?" Jean said after he took a sip.

"Oh no, Papa owns his own land and animals. He grows wheat and oats, and cures meat and sells them, sometimes to my uncle in his shop in Neufchâteau or to local merchants."

"Your father is an independent farmer," said Jean, an easy expression on his face.

"Does your brother know about your mission?" asked Bertrand, serving himself a little more of the pastries and meat.

"My brother Pierre knows. He is coming soon, when we get to Chinon."

"Why not now? Is he busy or sick?" asked Jean, curious.

"Oh no, he is in good health. It is my father, you see. In order for me to go to Vaucouleurs, I had to summon my uncle, so my father would not interfere. He does not know about my plans, and it would be difficult to convince him. So, the angels advised me to ask for help from my uncle and aunt who live in Burey-le-Petit."

Both pairs of eyes landed on Uncle Durand, but at that moment several servants inundated the room with dessert. They cleared away our used plates, glasses, and cutlery, and left a small flat plate filled with dried fruits and nuts with glasses of light red sherry in smaller glasses.

Uncle Durand waited for the servants to go and then continued. "Aye, my niece is right. She sent a message to me and my wife to collect her from home, but a week before, my wife and I had dreams where the Archangel Michael appeared before us. In those dreams he said we should help Jehanne because she had a mission, a mission from God to unify the kingdom under one King."

"Really sir, you had a dream with an angel?" asked Jean, amazed. His gaze travelled from me to my uncle.

"Yes, my Lord, I did. My wife as well. We both had dreams with Archangel Michael," said Uncle, smiling through his glass of wine.

"This is extraordinary!" said Jean, taking his glass up in the air. "I propose a toast."

All eyes were on him, and we all took our glasses, holding them up.

"I toast for a safe journey and successful arrival to Chinon." His eyes travelled amongst the company and landed lastly on me.

I smiled at Uncle. Our cheeks were red, and our eyes were glassy from the sumptuous meal.

Bertrand smiled, and, full of gusto, said, "Cheers!" He brought his glass into the centre, and we all joined him.

"Cheers!" Our glasses clinked and the wine flicked, and we drank to Jean's toast. The sweet acidity ran down our throats.

After our meal, we were shown our lodgings for the night. We were guided onto the second floor, on the eastern wing of the chateau, and given separate rooms. Before the servant went away, I asked him quietly, "Excuse me, can you show me where I can find the chateau's chapel?"

"Yes madam, would you like to go now?" The servant was younger than the others, and I could see some kindness in his eyes.

"Yes, I would, if that is alright."

"Of course, madam. Follow me."

I nodded to Uncle who was watching our interaction, and I disappeared around the corner through the maze of the chateau's long halls.

The chapel was small yet ornate and decorated like the rest of the chateau. In fact, it resembled more of a room than a church. A statue of the Virgin Mary holding Jesus stood in the centre. Few candles that stood next to the walls were lit despite their abundance, casting a dim light across the room.

Small portraits of Christ and saints decorated the walls, and on the opposite wall were the familiar tall windows, their curtains pulled back, yet dusk was slowly fading, and the black sky was inching closer to the horizon. The Virgin Mary's statue sat next to a white marble altar; an old book sat between two high candles.

The door closed behind me, echoing loudly in the vastly empty room. I knelt in front of the altar, clasping my hands and bowing my head in reverence. Nothing moved, but the candles flickered, as I submerged myself in meditative prayer.

Dear Lord…

Please protect us as we travel to Chinon tomorrow. Please guide us and help us perform our duties well.

My heart poured into my pleas.

Please protect my mother and father at this time. Please protect my brothers in their travels to Chinon.

When I felt my prayers fall and reach their conclusive ends, my heart heard a voice.

This time Robert de Baudricourt will receive you. He has received the news of the battle of Rouvray.

⚜

The following morning came quickly.

Knock, knock, knock.

The deep knock on the door persisted, until I sluggishly made my way to the door. I squinted as I opened it slightly to a girl of about fourteen years peering up at me. She appeared to be a servant girl with a white apron underneath a long dark blue tunic.

"Mademoiselle, the Duke requires your presence," she said in a soft, juvenile voice.

At that moment, any disorientation I had was whisked away. I nodded. "Yes, thank you. I'll be ready soon. Please wait."

Closing the door, I hastily dragged out the chamber pot and relieved myself. Beside the bed was a tall dressing table with a bowl of water and a high pile of clothes. Shivering slightly, I stood in front of the pristine water, splashing my face quickly. Using a soft cloth, I scrubbed underneath my armpits and feet.

And with small and quick movements, I rubbed my teeth clean with a smaller clean white cloth. Finding my clothes, I quickly attired myself. Only as I was lacing up my boots did I hear the knock again.

Knock, knock.

The door opened slightly, and my head shot up. "Excuse Mademoiselle, do you need any help?"

I could see the girl's head poking through, and her timid voice muffled from behind the door.

"I am almost ready," I said, tying the other boots and sitting on the most comfortable bed I had ever slept. I grabbed my cloak and draped it over my shoulders. "Please, lead me to the Duke."

We walked through the chateau, servants passing impassively, and the chateau as quiet and still as a tomb.

Soon we arrived at the familiar hallway outside the Duke's chambers. The door was open, and the curtains were drawn fully and open, inviting the morning light to hug every curve and alight all the decor in its golden brilliance. Even birds could be heard singing outside. The Duke was sitting up in his bed, with a tray filled with fruits and a hot steaming soup.

The girl stopped at the door and gestured for me to step through. Stopping at the end of his bed, I bowed my head, hand on my chest as a gesture of respect.

"My Lord," I said.

"Jehanne, after you prayed for me, I felt much better." His smile touched my heart. "Thank you, mademoiselle." And he motioned for me to come closer.

I stepped quietly closer to the unwell noble. Though his body was still sunken and weak, he seemed revitalised.

"My dear Duke. It is God who has listened, and God knows what we need to get better," I said humbly.

Looking at me, the Duke became more sombre. He spoke slowly. "It is not easy. I try, but sometimes it is very difficult. In these dark and difficult times, to lead a rightful life is precarious. I try to follow the Christian way in my daily interaction with the lords and gentry, but I don't know if I could leave my lady friend. She has been a good companion in my last years, mitigating to some degree the pain I suffer. I hope the good Lord understands."

I looked down, unsure of how to proceed.

Who was I to pass judgement, when I knew the compassionate and peaceful love of the light, of God?

"I am sure the King of Heaven understands, my Lord," I said reflectively.

The Duke turned to his bedside table. "Here is a letter to Charles. If you are going to travel to my lands, you will have no problem," said the Duke.

Taking the letter and bowing, I said, "Thank you, my Lord."

Suddenly a voice disrupted our conversation. "Excuse me, my Lord, the companions of Mademoiselle are waiting in the patio."

A servant with a blank expression and a high chin stood closely behind me.

"I am sorry. I have held you back from your mission. Go, mademoiselle. Godspeed," said the Duke with a sincere smile.

"Thank you, my Lord." I bowed again and followed the servant through the many rooms to the patio. I held the letter in my hand, and we soon arrived at the patio where Bertrand, Jean, and Uncle were waiting for me, mounted on their horses.

Just as I arrived, another servant brought my horse along. Greeting her gently and patting her, I bestrode the horse, careful to not crumple the letter. Once atop, I held up the letter for Jean, Bertrand, and Uncle to see it.

"Our safe passage."

They all nodded, and I tucked the precious envelope into my clothes.

29

TO CHINON

"See, I am sending an angel ahead of you to guard you along the way to bring you the place I have prepared."

– Exodus 23:20

Midwinter, 1429
Nancy, France

*T*he city of Nancy and the Duke's chateau were slowly fading into the green horizon, dissolving over the hills and fields of the country. The air was chilly. It whipped past us as we rode, the horses galloping heavily through the dirt crossed roads.

A strange feeling left me, looking back at the city and the Duke's chateau. We had stopped over the crown of a hill, for a break to replenish our dry throats. The city of Nancy was like a series of small dots that interrupted the smooth line of the horizon. I knew my destiny would take me far from these lands.

The gates of Vaucouleurs were closed by the time we arrived.

The sun was almost set, the sky velvet blue, and the stars painted the dark backdrop in silver dots. We could see torches being lit around the gate of Vaucouleurs, and guards stationing themselves around the outskirts of the city.

One guard approached, with two flanking him, holding torches. "Who goes there?" he asked as we shifted from a gallop to a halt at the gates.

Ten or more guards were spread around the walls. As we halted, I could see few grasp the hilts of their swords. Others grew very still, losing their friendliness and masking their own fear. Their eyes, hidden behind their helmets, followed our every movement.

Jean, who led the party, raised his voice. "I am Jean de Metz and this is Bertrand de Poulangy. We travel with this young maiden and her uncle."

The guards walked over to Jean, who was still mounted on his horse, and held up their torches. Bending his neck slightly, the lead guard squinted at the lord's face. A visible change occurred in his expression, then his eyes and mouth relaxed, and his hands held onto his hips instead of the hilt of his sword in his scabbard.

"Begging your pardon, m'lord. Can't be too careful these days, especially when—" He faltered.

Jean waited, puzzled.

"—well, you'll find out soon." The guard continued, "I won't disturb you any longer, sire. Open the gates. It's Jean de Metz and Bertrand de Poulangy!" he yelled behind him.

A flurry of guards moved about as the heavy gates began to creak and groan open. Their torches flickered beside us as we entered the dark city.

My legs were aching, and my sides were cramping from riding all day. Uncle peered over at me, making sure I was alright. I nodded, but closing my eyes I felt fatigue weigh my body down. I slouched as the horse walked through.

Through the silent streets we made our way, the horses heavily breathing and snickering. We reached the Royers' home in minutes. Jean descended first and addressed his page to let the Royers know of' our arrival.

None of us spoke as we dismounted. The combination of our aching muscles and exhaustion from riding all afternoon left us muted. Soon Henri and Catherine's voices floated out into the dusk air. Their front door opened and flooded the grey and blue night with halos of lights from the candles they held. They were wearing thick coats, for the night had a clenching chill.

"Oh Jehanne, Durand, you look tired as death. Come inside at once!" Catherine's voice was almost pleading.

"Dear, you should tell her..." Henri said.

"What is it?" I asked, wincing as sharp pain shot up my legs from landing on the soles of my feet.

She grimaced. "Dear, you have just arrived and you must rest. But you have a note from Lord Robert. He has requested to see you." From her long apron, she pulled out an envelope from her pocket.

My shoulders fell and I hung my head back, staring at the sky. Now silver dots decorated the black sky in plenitude, filling my eyes with millions of silver jewels that hung so simply above me. A bark-like laugh escaped my throat, and my hands cupped my eyes.

"At last."

"At last, he listened, eh?" Durand said.

I felt thick, rough hands pat my shoulders gruffly. Uncle Durand. His face revealed pure joy.

Limp from exhaustion and relief, I shrugged. "Finally! Tomorrow, I will see him. It is too late now," I said, shaking my head.

Hearing this interaction, Jean de Metz appeared next to me. "Tomorrow, I shall accompany you."

"As will I," Bertrand said, without lacking conviction.

"Your support is appreciated," I said, looking at them both.

"We too shall retire. It's been a long journey and we and our servants need the rest before we journey to Chinon," Jean said.

Despite their worn-out expressions and their fine clothes, faded from the dust and dirt of the road, they still appeared in good spirits.

"We will meet you here before you go to see Lord Robert tomorrow. Good night," said Bertrand, and with that they tipped their hats in salute.

Catherine curtsied, pleased to have met such gentlemanly nobles, and Henri and Uncle Durand inclined their heads deeply. With my hand over my heart, I bowed, eyes growing wearier as we watched them go. The night slowly enveloped them until their figures disappeared and the streets grew silent.

The dawn was frosty, and mist clung to the streets of Vaucouleurs in thick white tendrils. The Royers were already awake, preparing my clothes and readying themselves. I soon emerged with a new set of fresh boys' clothes: a dark maroon tunic, with black breeches and white hoses. This time I tied my hair in two braids and let them fall in front of my shoulders.

Soon Jean and Bertrand appeared at the door, and Uncle stood by me as we prepared to embark to see Lord Robert. The streets were asleep, and the dewy crisp morning refreshed our lungs.

Sir Robert's home sat atop the highest point of the hill of the fortress. After seeing the Duke's palace, this was by far no fair comparison in luxury. It was a large complex to be sure, but it was similar to a large two-storey house. Its walls were a simple cream-coloured stone, and it had smaller narrow windows than the Duke's castle.

Opening up before us was a large courtyard made of faded stone with some trees on both sides of the house. A small flight of stairs led to polished, dark double doors that were resolutely closed. Guards were posited at the doors like statues, and others stood around the courtyard, eyeing us with curiosity.

Unsaddling, Jean approached the guards first. "Please let Lord Robert know Jehanne has come as he's requested."

The guard simply nodded and turned to go inside. Jean looked at me and nodded, a glint of solidarity in his eyes.

Lord Robert's home was made from polished dark oak, and although his position of Lord of Vaucouleur was noble, his home appeared spartan and dark. Yet as we passed through, glints of finery began to sprout like flowers, and rich portraits hung frozen, illuminating the dark house.

Waiting in a spacious hall, Jean, Bertrand, and I stood with our backs against the long wall. Uncle was content to stay outside with the horses. The servants noiselessly travelled around us like ants, and it wasn't until the large door at the end of the hall opened that a servant emerged, dressed in a simple white tunic over black breeches. He bowed before saying, "Lord Robert awaits."

Jean, being closest, went in first, then Bertrand, followed by me. The room we entered was large, echoing the style found throughout the rest of the house. The windows were open, yet the light seemed to be drowned out by the dark walls and furniture. And even more so by the sitting figure behind the magnificent wooden desk.

Lord Robert's lips were tightened into a razor thin line, his forehead scrunched up with several lines of skin that creased above his brow. He watched us with his chin raised into the air, yet his eyes were red and worn with dark lines underneath as if he hadn't slept. The room was still, despite four soldiers standing in a line against the windows, impassive as statues. Lord Robert watched us carefully and waited until we were standing directly in front of him.

"Your message," he addressed me, and uttered each word as if it cost him dearly, "turned out to be true. There was a great loss of men in the battle of Rouvray. A great defeat, two thousand French deaths and the loss of many lords."

Everyone grew very still. The sheer numbers silenced me.

All those soldiers, all those men who died…

The defeat hung in the air as moments passed and we faltered under its sorrow. The stillness of the room became heavier. Both Jean and Bertrand grew very rigid; Jean's face tightened, and he cast his head down in solemnity, and Bertrand's knuckles were white from clenching his fists. Lord Robert stared at his desk, his face gaunt-like.

We stood like this, feeling as if time had frozen like a lake in winter. I stared at the desk.

All those lives lost.

"Well, Jehanne. I will give you the escort you want to Chinon."

My eyes darted up to Lord Robert, without moving my head.

He stood up and motioned to the soldiers. "Come."

They moved so they also stood beside us in a line, facing Lord Robert.

The noble then addressed them. "You will escort this young maiden. You will swear by me and by your king that you will protect and lead her safely to Chinon."

The soldiers unsheathed their swords and held their pommels against their chests. "We will sire," they said in unison.

Looking satisfied, Lord Robert reached into a drawer in his desk, taking out a sealed letter. "Jean."

Jean stood up straight, determination now shielding his shock from not moments ago.

"This is a sealed letter for the king. You will present this to the King when you arrive, announcing Jehanne."

Jean nodded, but Lord Robert didn't look finished. On his desk was a sword sheathed in a scabbard that was attached to a belt. "This is a dangerous journey. You will need this." He lifted the belt for me to take.

I grasped it carefully. "Thank you, Lord Robert."

"And I will repay the money for your horse, Jehanne."

"Thank you, my Lord. My uncle will appreciate that," I said, admiring the leatherwork on the belt and scabbard.

He sat back down again, slumping his shoulders and casting his eyes down in deep contemplation. "This can't get any worse…" he said, not particularly to anyone. With a sigh, he continued. "This is it. What else do we have to lose?"

"Good luck on your journey, Jehanne," he said instead. "Let what is meant to be come to pass."

He sat back down again, slumping his shoulders and casting his eyes

Jean and Bertrand wore pensive expressions as we left Lord Robert's room. Escorted by the servant through the dark hallway and out the front doors, I sensed a shift in their mannerisms. Their steps were invigorated with fresh purpose, and the sorrow of the defeat was cast behind their minds like trees shedding their leaves in autumn.

The horses were standing to the side with Uncle nearby sitting on a crate. Thin sheets of translucent clouds covered the sky like a sheared curtain, masking the sun's glow and making it look like a giant orb. A cool wind ruffled the branches of the trees in Lord Robert's open courtyard.

"Let us make our way to the markets," Jean said, climbing onto his horse. His eyes bore his similar good-natured self, yet I could see they were bright with a new resolve.

As we saddled our horses, I briefed Uncle on the fine details of the meeting. When I finished recounting, Uncle said, "You were right, Jehanne."

His tone was filled with grief for the defeat, but I also sensed a tinge of pride. For his faith in me was just that—faith. And seeing that everything that was foretold by the angels was coming true, the foundation of his faith was strengthening.

"Uncle, why did you not come in with me?" I asked, looking sideways to him.

He kept his gaze forward as he answered. "Well, Jehanne, Lord Robert requested *your* presence. And I suppose, at the beginning, I knew I needed to stay with you, to protect you, to support you. But I don't think you've noticed that you are more than capable of doing things by yourself now. You've visited the Duke of Lorraine and challenged Lord Robert of Vaucouleurs, on multiple occasions."

He chuckled. "I'm quite proud of you and believe you are more than capable. I'm sure your mama and papa will be very proud too."

I smiled. I felt a flicker of truth in his words. I had changed, and though my life back in Domrémy was part of me, I knew I was meant to be part of something more.

Once arriving at the edge of the markets, Jean and Bertrand turned their steeds side-on and Jean addressed us. "On the morrow, we will leave for Chinon at dawn. It is a ten-day trip and we need supplies. Bertrand and I have agreed to go into town today and purchase dry meat, bread, fruit, nuts, and cheeses for our journey. We will saddle these goods onto the servant's horses tomorrow."

"Jehanne," Bertrand said looking at me. "Like we did to travel to Lorraine, prepare yourself. Get your clothes ready, your horse rested, and your saddle re-oiled and tightened." He glanced up at my hair and braids. "If you want to look more like a lad, I say cut your hair shorter."

My hands instinctively went to the ends of my braids, and I nodded.

"Durand, will you be travelling with us?" Jean inquired.

"No, my Lord. I came to help Jehanne with her work here in Vaucouleurs. But the rest of the way... She's more than ready for her mission."

Jean and Bertrand both nodded, content with that answer.

<hr />

Uncle and I trotted leisurely back to the Royers' home. The streets were alive, and people walked around our horses as we talked quietly. Holding the sheathed sword in my lap, I looked at it approvingly. My hand traced over the carvings, and I even unsheathed the sword a little to glance at the silvery steel underneath.

"What is it, Jehanne?" Uncle said as we were approaching the Royers' home.

"I was just remembering what Pierre said about real swords."

I dismounted and looked around the empty neighbourhood for any passersby. I unsheathed the sword fully. The blade caught in the sun and brilliantly shone with white. Uncle and I watched it, mesmerised by its glow.

"He was right. They're not as heavy as the wooden ones," I said, manoeuvring it under the light.

"You will see him soon, and you can tell him yourself," Uncle said, leading his horse away.

"There are many things yet to accomplish before I do," I said, sheathing my sword back into the scabbard.

"What do you think, Jehanne?" Catherine said from behind me. She held a pair of scissors in her hand.

I looked into the old hand mirror, then glanced down. There on the floor were the long, strewn lengths of my auburn hair. A tinge of regret and sadness pierced my heart. My hands ran around the naked side of my neck. My hair sat just below my ears in strange tufts. Never having had it this short before, I felt like I didn't even know myself.

"Much shorter?" she asked, tilting her head to see around my shoulder.

"I think it's a good length. Thank you, Catherine," I said, attempting a smile and touching my hair again. A whiff of cold air bit the bare skin on my neck.

I will pass like a lad with no problem. The hair, the clothes, it will all add to my camouflage.

Catherine bent over, picking up the locks. "Such beautiful hair, the colour of red wine," she said, straightening up and holding them tenderly, as they dangled down like limp ribbons.

As she scooped extra tendrils of hair from the floor, her tone brightened. "I'll keep them in my trunk as a souvenir, a remembrance, if that is alright with you, Jehanne?"

Looking at the lifeless braids in her hands, I shrugged. "Yes, keep them, Catherine. Who knows, perhaps it will come into use someday," I said, playing with the end of my hair around my ears. "Besides, it will grow again in no time."

I turned to her, facing her with my short hair. She beamed down at me and kissed my forehead. "It's very becoming and suits you very well. I'm going to find a cloth for your braids. No doubt your mother would like them." Catherine then left the room, saying something about wasting and beautiful hair.

Alone, looking at the mirror, I saw all vestige of the young Jehanne disappear. Touching the sword that lay on my bed, only Jehanne the soldier was before me.

This is my last day as a child of peasant parents, for tomorrow I am Jehanne d'Arc, a messenger from the King of Heaven.

⚝

Dawn was filled with grey clouds that basked us in silver shadow. Thunder rumbled in the distance. I clasped my coat over my shoulders, the long coat rippling around me. My cropped hair was tied to the back. I fastened my cap, pushing it down snugly, and tugged at a few tendrils of hair.

This is it.

I made my way out of the house, stepping into the street. Uncle was leading my horse to the front, his mouse brown coat covering his round shoulders as he hunched over against the cold.

Henri drew close to the saddle and attached my small bag, which held my clothes and belongings. Catherine stood to the side, her posture straight and her hands clasped together in her lap. Her thumbs fidgeted, and she had a perturbed look on her face.

Henry and Uncle paced around the horse, adjusting a strap here, giving it a last brush there. They looked up as I approached, admiring my new men's clothes. My thick dark blue tunic smelled new and fresh, the black breeches hung limply over my legs, and navy hoses stretched up to my knees. Holding my belt and sword in my hand, I was ready.

We all knew the moment had come. It was time to say farewell.

Uncle and Henri smiled despite appearing despondent, but Catherine couldn't, and her lips quivered; she turned away to hide her face. Henri made his way to her and wrapped one of his thick arms around her.

"Well, Jehanne," Uncle said, as he walked over to me. "It looks like today you leave to be the heroine I know you to be. It's been an honour, mademoiselle."

Taking my hand, he bowed, but I chuckled, and we embraced for the last time. Uncle Durand's tears left my right cheek soaked, but I didn't mind. "Thank you for all your help, Uncle, and tell Aunt Jehanne I'm so grateful for both of your help and support. Take care of yourselves. And Lord Robert will reimburse you the money for the horse," I said before I could forget.

We separated, and he cupped my hands in his own. His voice came out clear and strong despite his reddened and tear-filled hazel eyes.

"Do not worry yourself, lass. Make sure to take care of yourself. Be brave and strong." He squeezed my hands slightly, "This journey will test you, but hold in your heart this truth. God will not abandon you." His words gave me the last ounce of strength I needed, and we hugged one final time.

Henri and Catherine, who heard Uncle Durand's farewell, stood respectfully still until Durand and I parted. They—especially Catherine—seemed touched by Uncle Durand's encouraging words. Henri stepped forward with his arms raised, embracing me with his bearlike hug.

"Thank you for all your help, Henri," I said into the side of his head.

"It was our duty. We are thankful to be part of your mission. Your uncle is right, Jehanne," Released from our embrace, he held my hands, squeezing them. "You've shown us your strength and courage. We can only support you along the way."

I smiled, emotion tingling in my eyes, and nodded. Catherine, who was smiling sweetly, held out her long slender arms, and we locked in embrace without any words. Her body trembled slightly against mine as she sniffed. We stood locked in embrace for a minute. When we parted, her hands were on my shoulders, and she stared at the floor.

I waited, not rushing her in her delicate state.

She finally looked up, her eyes concerned, almost pleading. "My dear, my dear... this task... it's enemy territory! What if you encounter any soldiers?!"

She said it true and well. Unconscious or not, everyone knew this was dangerous. This task was asking me to go into English territory, to put myself in harm's way. How could one not be afraid of an attack or an ambush?

Henri tried to hush her, but Catherine couldn't contain herself. "How are you going to do it, Jehanne? The roads are full of English soldiers... The stories... Everyone knows the cruelty of the English soldiers, what they do..." Her voice broke and her eyes refilled again.

In the quiet dawn, Catherine softly snivelled, and Henri shifted again to comfort her for the poor thing was out of sorts. Yet I'm not sure whether it was the early hour, or perhaps Uncle was right and I had changed over the last few weeks, but I looked at Catherine unfazed and benignant. Even placid.

My voice even sounded peculiar. It was gentle, yet a strength emanated from it. "There are soldiers on the road, I know," I said, looking not only at Catherine but at Henri and Uncle. "But I'm not afraid. The path will be clear of English troops, for Saint Marguerite said it will be so. I will reach the King, unsullied and unscathed. I was born to do this. This is my destiny. I will be safe."

They stared, struck by my words, my conviction. At that moment, the sun burst through the dark clouds, alighting the streets with a yellow glow and warming our faces. Although the dawn was chilly, the rays were a welcome sight. I hugged Catherine reassuringly a second time, and like a cool cloth on a burn, her trepidations were lifted.

We heard Jean, Bertrand, and their servants approach on their horses. I smiled and nodded to them. But before I could saddle my horse, out of the corner of my eye I saw a flicker of movement. That flicker turned into a flurry, as a small crowd emerged from the dark corner and into the sunlit road of the Royers' street.

I stared, speechless.

The people of Vaucouleurs were walking behind Jean and Bertrand's company. A few faces I recognised from the group at the church, and there were others who supported me with Lord Robert in the market. A mixture of young and old, men and women and children came. Their faces were determined and hopeful.

Catherine and Henri were stupefied, seeing the size of the crowd, which had slowed to a halt. Jean and Bertrand, who were now within earshot, lumbered over on their horses.

"Looks like you have a farewell party, Jehanne," Jean said, with a side-smile.

I let out an incredulous chuckle. Knowing I shouldn't linger, I fastened the belt over my hips. The sword in the scabbard on my side dangled into place. Readying myself, I bestrode my chestnut mare.

Uncle then checked all the belts were fastened and checked the length of the stirrup and reins.

"Did they come with you?" I asked Jean.

"No, they must have found out we were leaving at this hour," Jean said.

When Uncle appeared satisfied, I glanced down at him. "Everything ready?"

"All good to go," he said, patting the horse and looking up at me.

"Very well. Henri and Catherine, I cannot thank you enough. Trust. All will be well. Goodbye and take good care. And Uncle," I said, grasping his hand, "thank you again for your help. I wish you well. Farewell."

We clasped our hands, both knowing we would never see each other again.

Unsure of what to do next, I slowly trotted my mare forward. The crowd was silent, yet I could see hope in their eyes. The man I recognised, with a scar on his chin, was at the front. Behind him, a woman stood close to him holding a young boy who slept on her shoulder peacefully. The man glanced back to her and to their son, then down to his feet. Standing by his side, stood a six-year-old girl; she stared straight at me with her big blue eyes.

As I approached slowly, the man spoke. "Mademoiselle, Jehanne, if I may, you speak of angels and of God. You speak of your mission to seek out the King. You have even challenged Lord Robert. You've shown us your piety, strength, and determination.

"You have shown us your mission is true. Your words inspire hope where there is none. You've given us something to fight for, mademoiselle. The kingdom is being torn with war and violence, and the Lord knows we need this more than ever now."

I steadily looked at him as he continued. "Everyone here believes in your plight. We have come here to show our support for you and your company."

"I thank you." I inclined my head, but then raised my voice for everyone to hear. "I thank all of you for your support, for your help. I would not be here without your support. I'm grateful beyond words." I dipped my head with my hand over my heart, and the crowd cheered and clapped.

I smiled back at the man, his wife, and their little son and daughter. Turning back to look at Jean and Bertrand, I motioned for them to lead, and they trotted over to the front. The crowd split to let us pass.

As we walked through the city, I couldn't believe my eyes. Clusters of families emerged from their homes, even from their high windows and wished us well.

"Good luck, Jehanne!"

"We believe you, Jehanne!"

"Get them English, Jehanne!"

I beamed and nodded to the people as they cheered and clapped, all the way through Vaucouleurs, until we arrived at the gates where Lord Robert's soldiers sat on their steeds, waiting for us. As the crowd followed us, the dawn air was filled with chatter and vivacity. The frosty morning air brightened our cheeks and, once the gates opened, I could see the early morning mist rolling over the hills of the country.

We waved one final goodbye, and I darted my eyes swiftly over the sea of heads. My head whipped back as I saw a glimpse of the familiar profiles of Uncle Durand and Catherine, but Jean's voice brought my attention back.

"Jehanne, are you ready?" he said, raising his voice to be heard over the crowd.

"Yes. Yes, I'm ready." I spurred my horse on, following Bertrand and Jean, as they began to slowly trot our way out of the city gates and into the wilderness.

The countryside looked unfamiliar in the early hours of the morning, as long stretches of grey clouds covered the still lightening sky. The grass was wet, and the dirt road was muddy with small puddles of water. Yet, the sunrise from the east broke through a gap of clouds again, shining brilliantly onto the country.

Millions of bright blades of grass shone, contrasting deeply with the dark bodies of clouds in the distance. As we descended the hill of Vaucouleurs, the crowd's cheering faces quickly disappeared behind us, and I felt thick droplets of rain. Thunder reverberated from the heavens, and breathing in deeply, I enjoyed the musky smell of the dawn shower.

Jean and Bertrand led our small party down the road. I rode behind Bertrand, with Francois, Louis, and Lord Robert's three guards at the rear.

The countryside began to surround us as we travelled onward, and I felt an invisible strength coming from my heart, wrapping around my whole body, and at that moment a renewed feeling of purpose filled my mind with the determination and the urgency of a bearer of important news.

I know my role. I know I have a mission that will change the course of this war.

I rode confidently, even earnestly, eager to fulfill my destiny that was written by the invisible hand of God before I was born.

It begins.

ABOUT THE AUTHOR:

*A*lexia Saint Claire lives in NSW, Australia, with her family. While writing and studying old languages fill her days, she usually finds inspiration on her walks, travels, and podcasts.

Milton Keynes UK
Ingram Content Group UK Ltd.
UKHW030950260824
447446UK00001B/166

9 781922 913975